PART ONE

THE COURTSHIP

How beautiful you are, my darling! Oh, how beautiful!

Song of Songs 4:1

GILBERT MORRIS

LIONS OF JUDAH

NO WOMAN SO FAIR

BETHANYHOUSE

MINNEAPOLIS, MINNESOTA

No Woman So Fair
Copyright © 2003
Gilbert Morris

Cover design by Lookout Design Group, Inc.

Published by Bethany House Publishers
11400 Hampshire Avenue South
Bloomington, Minnesota 55438
www.bethanyhouse.com

Bethany House Publishers is a Division of
Baker Book House Company, Grand Rapids, Michigan.

Printed in the United States of America

Library of Congress Cataloging-in-Publication Data

Morris, Gilbert.
    No woman so fair / by Gilbert Morris.
       p.   cm. — (Lions of Judah ; bk. 2)
    ISBN 0-7642-2682-7 (pbk.)
    I. Abraham (Biblical patriarch)—Fiction. 2. Sarah (Biblical matriarch)—Fiction. 3. Women in
the Bible—Fiction. 4. Childlessness—Fiction. I. Title. II. Series: Morris, Gilbert. Lions of Judah ;
v 2.
    PS3563.O8742N6   2003
    813'.54—dc21
                             2003001433

To Dr. Ruth Mills

I always vowed that I would never have a lady doctor, nor a Yankee doctor—now I have *both* in you, my great and glorious physician!

How good it is to have a warm, charming, witty, and compassionate doctor and friend to take care of me! I count you, dear Ruth Mills, as one of the blessings that God has put into my life.

GILBERT MORRIS spent ten years as a pastor before becoming Professor of English at Ouachita Baptist University in Arkansas and earning a Ph.D. at the University of Arkansas. During the summers of 1984 and 1985, he did postgraduate work at the University of London. A prolific writer, he has had over 25 scholarly articles and 200 poems published in various periodicals, and over the past years he has had more than 175 books published. His family includes three grown children, and he and his wife live in Alabama.

CHAPTER

I

The hot desert wind swirled dust devils across the parched earth, whipping up the sparse vegetation that had managed to sprout after the meager rains of spring. Two sluggish, muddy rivers—the Tigris and Euphrates—divided and carved out a large Y in this featureless plain. Few trees offered any relief for man or beast from the shimmering heat. Birds darted over the marshes where the rivers overran their banks, and tiny ripples in the shallows marked schools of fish feeding on insects. Bordering the rivers to the north and south, fields of grain spread across the desolate flat land. Occasional date palms offered fruit and shade for travelers coming from outlying farms into the city of Ur of the Chaldees, on the Euphrates River.

As the sun began to set in the west, a solitary vulture circled languidly over the busy metropolis, where fortified walls formed an elongated triangle that lay in the flatland near the confluence of the two rivers. The high wall surrounding the city was broken only by a few gates. Within that wall, in a broad, open section of the city, lay a sprawling temple complex, with a mud-brick ziggurat—dedicated to the moon god Nanna and his wife Ningal—rising eighty feet in three-step terraces.

The vulture tilted to his left and made a sweeping curve, searching for an evening meal. He studied the crowded mass of houses and bazaars surrounding the temple and the broad canal that circumscribed the city, connecting it with the larger of the two rivers leading to the big sea beyond. Another waterway cut through the heart of the city, along which path the vulture now soared until reaching the large harbor at the southern tip. The bird circled above the boats that sat quietly at anchor in the dead calm of evening. Having not spotted any carrion on the city streets, the vulture moved on, sailing effortlessly over the farmland that spread outward in every direction. There he would more likely find food.

A short, fat man, whose expensive robe barely covered his midsection, stopped along the streets of Ur to glance upward at the setting sun. A glittering stone on his pudgy finger caught the last rays. Eliphaz hesitated, tempted to return to the safety of his home. He was a timid fellow who knew that being out as darkness was gathering was inviting trouble. Nonetheless, he urged himself on, muttering under his breath, and scurried down the narrow, twisting streets. He knew them well, having spent all of his forty years within the city walls. He rarely stepped outside the gates into the open land, preferring the close comfort of the crowded houses, bazaars, and shops. The security of being around people was necessary for Eliphaz. He loved nothing better than the festival days when the farmers brought their produce and the city swarmed like a giant anthill.

Rounding a corner, Eliphaz halted at the sight of a large yellow dog emerging stiff-legged from the gathering shadows, his lips pulled back from his teeth. Eliphaz clasped the box he was bearing to his chest and backed up against the nearest wall. "Get away!" he shouted in as rough a tone as he could muster. The animal continued forward, his eyes glittering.

Two street urchins, no more than ten or twelve, were scuffling in the dust. Seeing Eliphaz shrinking against the wall, the boys grinned and pointed.

"Look at him! He's afraid of an old dog," one of them said, laughing.

"Give us the box, and we'll make the dog leave you alone," the other said. When Eliphaz did not answer, both boys approached him and demanded, "What's in the box?"

Eliphaz stared at the dog, then at the boys, whose sticks were raised threateningly. He reached into the purse that hung around his neck, pulled out a sack, and stuttered, "H-here, you can have these dates."

The smaller of the two boys darted forward and snatched the sack. "Come on, Nopaz." The boys turned and ran, whistling to the dog, who stiffly trotted away after them.

Heaving a sigh of relief, Eliphaz hurried on down the street. Humiliated by the scene, he purposed that the next time he ventured out at dusk, he would bring one of his slaves with a weapon.

By the time Eliphaz reached the house he was seeking, the sun was disappearing below the top of the city wall. Eliphaz entered the courtyard of the large house, which was set back from the street. Even in the growing darkness, he could see the lush greenery of the plants in decorated clay pots. He called out, "Hello!" and immediately a man emerged from one of the inner gates. He was a wiry fellow, below average height, who grinned and bobbed his head as he approached the visitor. "You are late tonight, sir."

"Yes, I am, Hazil."

Hazil reached out his hands. "Can I carry your box, sir?"

"No, I'll take it in. Am I late?"

"The meal hasn't started yet, but they have been expecting you."

"I'll go right on in," Eliphaz muttered, hastening into the house. Hazil turned, his hand on his hip, studying the man as he disappeared. Then he laughed softly and entered the house again himself, walking down a long corridor toward the cooking area. An oven half buried in the earth was sending up tendrils of smoke, which swirled about the dried onions and vegetables hanging from the ceiling. On one side of the room a woman was slicing vegetables with a knife, her back to Hazil. A mischievous grin tugged at Hazil's thin lips as he silently tiptoed toward her. He threw his arms around her full figure, laughing when she shrieked. No sooner had she turned than he planted a kiss on her mouth, shutting off her objections, then stepped back and plucked a piece of roasted meat from a dish on the table.

"You stop that! That's for the master—and keep your slimy hands off of me!"

The woman wore a tunic supported by a single strap over one shoulder. Although she was no longer in the flush of youth, her thin face was still attractive. Her lips drew down in a frown as she said, "You keep your hands off of everything in this kitchen—including me!"

"Oh, come on, don't be angry, Mahita."

"You're a scoundrel, Hazil!"

Hazil reached up and plucked a grape from a cluster hanging from a beam in the ceiling. He chewed it, then reached for another before answering. With grape juice running over his chin, he grinned. "I'll be by your room tonight for a visit."

"You come near my room and I'll gut you like a fish!"

Hazil only laughed, pulling her toward him and whispering in her ear, "It'll be a treat for both of us." This time Mahita barely resisted as he kissed her on the cheek, then sat down and helped himself to the meat on the table.

Mahita laughed softly and feigned annoyance. "What if you found Taphir in the room? He'd slit your skinny throat."

"He's not the man I am."

"He's twice as big."

"Twice as big doesn't mean twice as good." Hazil winked and chewed thoughtfully on the meat. "This is good. What is it?"

"Goat. If the master comes in and catches you eating his food, he'll stripe your back."

"He's too busy to worry over things like that. After all, his future son-in-law is here."

"He's come, then?"

"Yes—he just went inside. You think Hanna will have this one?"

Mahita began grinding corn in a hollowed-out stone, expertly crushing the kernels to powder with a smaller smooth stone. Without hesitation she nodded. "She's got to have a man . . . at least she thinks so."

"Well, she's tried hard enough to catch this one. He's not much of a man, though."

"He's rich." Mahita nodded. "That's what counts."

"There's more to a man than money."

"Don't you wish that were true! But she'll have him—you can be sure."

As Mahita moved about, efficiently preparing the meal, Hazil followed her, sampling the supper and speaking of family matters. These two were well aware of the innermost secrets of the house of Garai, as were all the servants. Their master and his family labored under the delusion that the servants were all deaf. Either that, or they had grown so accustomed to the servants' presence that they simply forgot to speak quietly or in private. Even if they had tried to maintain some secrecy, the houses of Ur provided precious little privacy. There were no doors to close, only openings between each room, which were occasionally covered with blankets or animal skins, but most of the time Garai and his wife, Rufi, lived in full view of servants and visitors alike.

Mahita looked around and gave a sigh of satisfaction. Picking up a clay jar, she poured some wine into a clay goblet and offered it to Hazil. She then poured herself some and sat down with another sigh.

"So Hanna's going to get a man at last," Hazil said, sipping his wine. "I never could figure her out. She's not bad looking—she's even pretty in a way. She should have been married two or three years ago."

"Why, Hazil, I thought you were sharper than that!" Mahita sipped her wine, tilting her head back to savor the coolness of it, then grinned at the man across the table from her. "It's Sarai, of course."

"What does she have to do with it?"

"The men come here and all they see is Sarai. Hanna's not exactly plain, but alongside Sarai, she's like a desert toad!"

"But she comes with a good dowry—that must be worth something to a man."

"That's what Garai's hoping for, of course—to find a man who wants money more than a beautiful wife."

Hazil reached over and pinched Mahita's cheek. "Now, if you had a dowry, I'd marry you myself."

"You'll never marry anybody. You're not the marrying kind."

"Don't be too sure about that." Sipping his wine slowly, Hazil's eyes narrowed. "But Sarai is even a bigger puzzle to me. She's as good-looking as a woman comes, and Garai's offered a bounty as big as a camel to go with her. And yet she still awaits a marriage offer."

"Even a big dowry's not enough to entice a man to take her."

"Why ever not? What about old Rashim? He was taken with her, wasn't he?"

"Yes, until she opened her mouth! She got rid of him fast enough." Mahita laughed shortly. "It's her tongue that scares the men off."

"Yes, she's got a tongue, all right," Hazil said ruefully. "She's used it on me often enough."

"That's right. She's run off every suitor who's ever come."

A call came from inside, and the two got up. Hazil wrapped his arms around Mahita, kissing her soundly. "Don't go to sleep early. You'll miss a real treat if you do."

"Leave me be. Supper's late. You know how Garai will yell."

Hazil laughed and winked at her, whispering, "I'll see you later."

Zulda pulled the bone comb down through the jet black hair of her mistress. In her opinion, Sarai's best feature was her hair, blacker than night itself, long and soft and glossy. It was a pleasure to comb it, and now Zulda said, "You want me to tie your hair up?"

"No, leave it down, Zulda."

Zulda made two or three more passes through her mistress's hair with the comb, then shook it out.

Sarai moved over toward the stone tub, slipped out of her robe, and stepped in. With a sigh of pleasure, she slid down into the water. "Don't let my hair get wet, Zulda. Maybe you'd better tie it up after all."

"Yes, mistress."

Zulda secured the hair up with copper pins and began to scrub her mistress's back with a soft cloth. Sarai hummed to herself, enjoying the coolness of the water, and finally she got up and allowed Zulda to dry her off. Zulda rubbed a soft, sweet-smelling oil into her body, all the time chattering away. At times Zulda's constant talk grew tiresome, but Sarai was fond of the little servant girl, whose life was devoted to pleasing her mistress.

"... and so your sister's going to marry Eliphaz, and you'll be the only daughter left in the house. Your brother will spoil you."

"She hasn't married him yet," Sarai murmured. She began to rub herself down with a soft cloth, then stepped into the undergarments Zulda held for her. Her gown was pure white and, in the fashion of the aristocracy, was suspended by one strap over her right shoulder. She waited until Zulda fastened a belt studded with stones around her waist, then slipped into her sandals.

"You aren't going to marry Abiahaz?"

"No!" Sarai said shortly.

"But he's been coming around here for a year. You never said you wouldn't have him."

Sarai loosened her hair and let it fall down her back, staring into the polished bronze mirror on the wall. "It was amusing to watch him come sniffing around."

The blurry image staring back from the mirror revealed a tall, proud woman, with a prominent nose, high cheekbones that accented the hollows of her cheeks, and black eyes with strange green flecks in them. Her skin was as smooth as a baby's, the envy of every woman in the land. Sarai's family was originally from the city of Uruk, many miles upriver. Being from the privileged class, and having been successful in business, they owned homes both in Ur and in the smaller, but also impressive, city of Uruk. The entire household would travel upriver with Garai and stay in their other house whenever he had business to attend to.

Zulda went on with her questions as she once again combed out her mistress's hair. "What will your brother say?"

"I've already told him."

"Well, what *did* he say, then?"

"He screamed like a wild donkey—as he always does."

Zulda finished off Sarai's hair by inserting two decorative jeweled combs. "But you've *got* to get married, mistress."

"I do? Why?" Sarai's well-shaped lips parted. Her enormous eyes, almond shaped and deep set, now sparkled with amusement. She loved to tease Zulda, for the girl was easily fooled. "Why do I have to get married?" she asked again in her deep voice.

"Why... what else is there for a woman to do?"

Sitting down at a dressing table filled with cosmetics, Sarai put the tip of her finger into a small jar carved out of semiprecious stone. She pressed the contents of it to her cheek and began spreading it on. "What else is there for a woman to do? Why, nothing much. When I find a man I can love, I'll marry him."

Zulda stared at Sarai with astonishment. "But fathers choose husbands for girls! And since your father is gone, your brother will choose your husband."

"I'll pick my own husband."

Zulda took in a short breath. She was shocked but intrigued. "Nobody but you would say that, mistress."

"I'll do it, though."

"What kind of a man will you pick?"

Sarai paused from putting on the cosmetics and thought for a moment. "He won't be old like that... that old Malater my brother wanted me to marry! Why, he was so old he would have died on the marriage bed."

Zulda was accustomed to Sarai's half-ribald statements, and she merely giggled. "What will your husband be like?"

"Oh, he'll have to be young and good-looking."

"Is that all?"

"No, he's got to be intelligent too," Sarai insisted. Her eyes flashed with indignation. "Most men can only talk about business. The man I marry must have a broad knowledge of life... and most of all, he must know that women are equal to men."

"Mistress, you mustn't say that!"

Laughing, Sarai reached out and caressed the maid's cheek. "I do shock you, don't I?"

"There's no man like that in the world."

"Then I'll buy a young slave. I'll train him up to be my husband. He'll do everything I tell him to do. If you see a good-looking, strong young fellow for sale, let me know about it." Sarai laughed and rose, moving swiftly and gracefully toward the doorway.

As Zulda watched Sarai disappear, she shook her head and murmured, "I don't know what's going to become of you, mistress."

———

The family was gathered in the dining room with Garai, the head of the house, who paced about impatiently. He was a small man with sharp, light brown eyes and well-kept brown hair. His wife, Rufi, watched him moving back and forth nervously. She was a pretty woman, a few years younger than her husband, and she kept glancing at the door, waiting for Sarai to enter.

Zaroni, the mother of Garai and Sarai, stood calmly next to her daughter-in-law. She was a small woman with greenish eyes, and traces of her youthful beauty still remained. Turning to Garai, she said, "Don't be impatient, son. Sarai will be here soon."

"She's *always* late. She'll be late for her own funeral!" Garai muttered.

Hanna, Sarai's sister, stood next to Eliphaz. She was a pretty young woman, but her attractiveness was eclipsed by Sarai's beauty. She stayed very close to Eliphaz, as if he were apt to run away, and now she smiled at him flatteringly. "I had them fix your favorite foods for supper."

"It's always a pleasure to dine here," Eliphaz said, nodding enthusiastically.

At that moment Sarai entered and cooed innocently, "Oh, am I late?"

"You're always late," Garai growled.

"I'm so sorry, brother, but I'm here now, so we can eat."

"You look very nice," Zaroni said.

"Thank you, Mother." An impish look touched Sarai's eyes, and Zaroni knew at once that her daughter was up to some outrage. She watched as Sarai walked over to Eliphaz, smiled warmly, and said, "How well you look, my dear Eliphaz. That's a new robe, isn't it?"

"W-well . . . as a matter of fact, it is," he stuttered, flushing at Sarai's intent gaze and proximity.

"It suits you splendidly." Sarai reached out and fingered the robe, feeling its texture with an admiring glance. She then touched his cheek lightly and leaned against him. "You'll have to tell me all about your trip to Akadd."

Hanna turned pale, and the others saw her fury as she grabbed Eliphaz's arm. "Come along!" she snapped. "It's time to eat!"

Sarai smiled blandly as her mother came to her side and whispered, "Why do you torment your sister so?" She was not angry, however, but simply shook her head in a mild reproof.

"Because it amuses me, Mother. Come along. Let's eat."

Two young servant girls served the meal, while Mahita oversaw them with a sharp eye. They carried in flat metal plates filled with wild roast duck, goat, boiled eggs, leeks, and cucumbers, and poured wine from metal flagons.

Midway through the meal, Garai remarked, "I understand that the decision's been made about where to put the new canal."

"Yes, it has," Eliphaz said, nodding eagerly. "It's taken a long time, but the city council decided it just this afternoon."

"Where will it be?"

"Across the northern sector of the city."

"That's foolish," Sarai spoke up. "It should go where the old road was. There'll be enough incline there to carry the flow."

Garai threw his head back and glared at his sister. "You don't know anything about it, woman!"

"I know that the council's made a total wreck out of it," Sarai answered with a sweet smile.

Hanna snapped, "Women have no place arguing with men!"

Sarai turned to glare at her sister but said nothing.

Her mother watched the exchange, well aware that this would not be the end of the matter. *Sarai will find some way to get even with Hanna for that comment,* Zaroni thought. *She always does.*

After the meal Sarai smiled slightly and went directly to Eliphaz, taking him by the arm and pulling at him gently. "Come along, I must show you my garden . . . and you must tell me about your trip."

Eliphaz stared at her, unable to speak. Her beauty was enough to stop most men in their tracks, and he allowed himself to be led out of the dining room. As the two disappeared, Hanna threw herself into a chair and began to cry.

Her mother went right to her, putting her arm around her older daughter. "Don't let her see you crying, Hanna. She's just doing this to torment you."

"No, she'll take him away from me!"

"No, she won't. She doesn't really want him," Zaroni said quietly. "She does this only to stir you up. Just laugh at her, Hanna."

Garai's temper exploded at this and he blustered, "She's driven away every man who has come to court her, and now she's trying to drive Hanna's man away!"

Zaroni shook her head. "It will be all right. The more you oppose her, the more she will resist. Haven't you two learned that yet?"

"It has got to stop!" Garai blurted out. "She will have to marry now!"

Zaroni stared at her son. "Who have you picked out this time?"

"Elam."

"Elam who owns the vineyards outside of town?"

"That's the one." Garai grinned and rubbed his hands together. "He's one of the richest men in Ur."

"He's also old and fat and has three wives," Zaroni said sardonically. "She'll never marry him."

"She'll marry him or I'll beat her!" Garai shouted. "I've had enough of her proud ways!"

"You shouldn't torment your sister like that, Sarai."

Sarai had known when her mother entered her bedroom that she was in for a lecture. She shrugged her shoulders and ran her hand over her glossy black hair. "I know it, but I couldn't help it."

"I think I'd better tell you before you hear it from your brother."

Sarai stared at her mother. "What is it now?"

"Garai's making a match for you."

"Who is it this time?"

"Elam."

"I won't marry that old man. He's already got two wives. Or is it three?"

"It's three, but it doesn't matter."

"I won't do it, Mother. You may as well tell him and let him have his screaming fit."

"Sarai, you have strange notions about marriage." Zaroni came closer and put her arm around her daughter's shoulders. "We have to settle for what we can get. You want the ideal, but the ideal doesn't exist. Not in this world."

"In the next world, then? That's when I'm supposed to have a husband that I want?"

"No, that's not what I mean. You've got to see things as they are."

Sarai loved her mother, but now there was a hard look in her dark eyes as she said between clenched teeth, "I'll marry the man I choose, Mother, and that's all there is to it. You may tell my brother I said so!"

CHAPTER

2

The bleating of the sheep and the sight of the young kids butting each other pleased Terah. He stood on a slight mound looking over the herds of goats and flocks of sheep that spread out in every direction. He always felt a glow of satisfaction when his eyes fell on his possessions. In his mind he could see these animals transformed into houses, expensive furnishings, jewelry, and other signs of wealth. He was a burly man, tall and deep in the chest, with sharp brown eyes, curly gray hair that had been black in his youth, and a beard to match. Some individuals' looks matched their personality, and so was the case with Terah. He was burly both inside and out, aggressive and bold at all times, a man who had to have his own way.

Picking his way through the animals, Terah stopped from time to time to lean down and pull the wool on one of the sheep, testing it. His mind was working ahead, considering ways to increase the size of the family holdings. Though he was old now, he was still the strong, vital presence he had been ever since taking over the family's business from his own father. His forehead wrinkled in a frown as he thought of that time when his father, Nahor, had left the family. The thought still rankled him, but he consoled himself at the thought of how he had stepped into his father's place. Since the day Nahor had disappeared on his fruitless quest, Terah had been the unquestioned leader of the family.

A shout brought Terah out of his deep thought, and he turned to see his middle son, who bore the same name as Terah's father, winding his way through the flocks. Nahor was built like Terah—tall, broad shouldered, with a deep chest and sinewy limbs. His face was coated with the dust raised by the animals. Coming to stand before his father, he looked around and smiled, his teeth white against his suntanned complexion. "They look good, don't they?"

"We're going to have more increase than last year, aren't we, son?"

"Oh yes. We're going to have to hire more help. Maybe buy some more slaves. That's cheaper than hiring the work done. Those freed men are always walking off and leaving when we need them the most."

Terah scanned the horizon and frowned. "Where's Abram?"

A scowl twisted Nahor's lips, and he shook his head as he exclaimed bitterly, "Gone to worship—back to that blasted temple!"

"The temple? But he was there yesterday!"

"And he'll be there tomorrow. Father, you've *got* to do something about Abram. He's got his head in the clouds and is no help at all with the animals."

Terah licked his lips and paused, a dark cloud gathering across his features. He stared at Nahor for a moment, then asked, "Did you tell him what I said?"

"I told him you'd left orders for him to stay here, but he insisted he had to go to the temple and would be back early tomorrow morning."

The two men looked at each other, puzzled by Abram's idiosyncrasies. He had always been different from Nahor and from the oldest son, Haran. Given to constant introspection, Abram had often disappeared out on the hills, even as a youth, and whenever he returned, he had always said, "I was just out thinking."

Terah gnawed on his lip nervously. "At thirty the man should have settled down and had a family."

"He never shows any interest in that sort of thing," Nahor scoffed.

"Why can't he be like you, or like your brother?" Terah asked.

"Or like you," Nahor said, grinning. "That's what you'd really like. You know, sometimes I think he's not right in the head."

"Don't say that!" Terah retorted.

"But I'm right about it. He's like Grandfather. I remember him fairly well. He was always talking about the gods, wasn't he?"

"Yes, he was. And I made offerings, pleading that Abram wouldn't be like him!"

"Well, you'd better make another offering, because he sure doesn't show any sign of coming out of it. You've got to do something about him."

"All right, I will." Terah's jaw set firmly, and he nodded emphatically.

"What will you do, Father?"

"I'm going to tell him right out that he's spending too much time in the temple, and he's got to settle down and act like a man."

"You ought to make him get married."

Terah laughed shortly. "It's a shame when a man has to *make* his son get married. I didn't have that problem with you and Haran."

Nahor laughed loudly. "No, you didn't. But Abram's different from us. I think he's lost his mind over religion, but if we all work together, maybe we can make something out of him yet."

For Abram, leaving the crowded streets of Ur and coming into the magnificent temple area was like entering another world. The streets swarmed with the sounds of barking dogs and braying donkeys as they pulled their burdens, of people talking and shouting, of children screaming as they played their games—a world of busy activity. But now as Abram mounted the steps and entered the temple complex, the raucous noises faded and the smells and sights of the bustling city passed away for him. The huge temple area sprawled out over acres of ground, much of it in a level courtyard paved with stone hauled, at considerable expense, from the distant quarries of Akkad. To his left were two flat-roofed buildings that housed the numerous priests who served the gods of Ur; a third building was devoted to the multiple activities of the temple, including the lucrative temple prostitution business.

Dominating everything, however, was the huge ziggurat that rose high into the air. It was the highest structure Abram had ever seen, and he always felt a sense of awe as he approached it. He paused for a moment, looking up at the huge steps and remembering what he had been taught—that this ziggurat was relatively new. It had been built upon older temples, which time had eroded, and the remains of which had gradually grown upward in a mound. The steps had been added, and now the sunbaked bricks of the structure glistened as they caught the rays of the sun.

Abram stopped beside the god of water, Enki. He bowed low before the shrine and then dropped down to his knees. He prayed fervently to the stone god, which stood six feet high with wings spread as if they were arms. On top of the god's head was a sharp-peaked hat, and he was clothed in a garment made from the stalks of rye that filled the fields around the city. Because the Chaldees lived in fear of both prolonged drought and severe floods, Enki was one of the more important deities, often glorified in sculpture and sacred verse. Abram opened his eyes and read the inscription on the base supporting the idol: *When I draw near unto the yellowing fields, grain piles are heaped at my command.* Abram prayed aloud, "Oh, most powerful Enki, send no floods to wipe our fields away, and yet send rain so that the crops may grow." He continued to pray for some time, and his voice rose unconsciously as he worshiped this stone god of Ur, in the manner that he had been taught by his parents.

Finally he rose and made his way past other gods, each occupying their own shrines. The temple contained no fewer than three thousand deities; almost every element—including rain, sun, and wind—was represented by its own god. The gods, however, were not considered equal. The most powerful was An, ruler of the heavens. Often considered his wife, and queen of the universe, was the fertility goddess, Ishtar. It was to this idol that Abram now made his way.

When he entered the interior of the ziggurat, he was impressed, as always, by the magnificence of it. Artists had covered the walls with paintings, and sculptors had adorned the inside with many statues. Most of the men depicted in the wall murals had long, curling beards and long hair parted in the middle. They were bare chested and wore skirts drawn in severely at the waist. The women on the frescoes wore their hair in braids coiled around their heads. Abram passed by many of these sacred paintings, pausing from time to time to offer a brief prayer.

When he arrived at the goddess Ishtar, he prostrated himself before the statue, which was made in the form of a beautiful woman wearing a clinging robe, with eyes wide and staring. Abram began praying vehemently.

Two men approached, one wearing the garments of a high order of the priesthood. His name was Rahaz, the high priest of the temple. No more than medium height, he was vastly overweight. Even at the age of sixty there were no lines in his face, which was as smooth as marble. He was completely bald, and his skin glowed with the oil he had anointed himself with. Though not attractive, he had an authority about him. He stopped, as did the priest by his side—a tall, thin man with a name as short as he was tall, Huz.

"Master," Huz said, "he's here again."

"Yes, I see him." Rahaz was gazing steadfastly at the prostrate Abram. He listened as the young man cried out loudly to the goddess and examined the worshiper as if he were a rare insect. Indeed, Rahaz had come to consider most of the populace who dwelt in Ur and the farms roundabout as nothing more than insects. Earlier in his life he had known human compassion, but he had lost that virtue along the way as he had become more and more entrenched in the despicable life of the temple priesthood. The generous offerings given to the temple granaries had made religion powerful and per-suasive, a power that mostly benefited the priests and their temples. For the people who faithfully brought their oblations, the religion of Ur offered no hope of freedom from their servile existence. According to the generally accepted story of creation, the gods had fashioned people out of clay for the sole purpose of using them as slaves. Anyone who failed to appease these deities with offerings would be subject to catastrophes, such as floods or pestilences or raids by neighboring tribes. Such calamities frequently did occur, and Rahaz was always happy when they did. It meant that the people would bring even more offerings to increase the wealth of his kind.

Huz shook his head. "He stayed here through most of the night yesterday."

"Yes, I saw him."

"I wish," Huz said thoughtfully, "that everyone in our city were as devout as Abram."

Rahaz, however, did not smile. "He's not content with worshiping our gods. Three thousand gods are not enough for him."

Huz was shocked. He had never heard of such a thing. Most people complained that there were too many gods. "I can't believe that, sire!" he exclaimed. "What's the matter with him?"

"He wants more."

"More of what, master?"

"Fanatics never know what they want." Rahaz bit off his words. "He wants what he can't have. A god all his own, I suspect. His grandfather was exactly like him. Nahor—he was before your time."

"I thought Nahor was one of Abram's brothers."

"Yes, Abram has a brother with the same name as their grandfather. But it is Abram who is more like the grandfather. Always asking questions. Demanding answers. He's got the same hunger inside."

"Hunger for what?"

"Hunger for the gods, of course."

"But isn't that a good thing, master?"

"It ought to be, but it causes trouble for us. What we want are people who will bring their offerings, worship one of the gods—whichever one pleases them—and keep their mouths shut."

Huz was shocked. "I don't understand, sire."

"No, you wouldn't."

Abram had heard none of this conversation as he worshiped before the goddess Ishtar. But now as he rose and turned to leave, he saw the two priests. He smiled and rushed over to them. "Master, it's good to see you. Do you have time to answer some questions? I have several."

"Greetings, Abram. I suppose I can spare a moment." He nodded to Huz, who scurried off at the unspoken command. Rahaz turned to Abram and thought carefully. The family of Terah was wealthy and powerful and needed to be appeased. "Come along," he said. "It's good to see you in the temple again, but I must warn you, I don't have a great deal of time."

Rahaz led Abram through a maze of corridors until he finally stopped and waved toward a seat in a pleasant room filled with comfortable furnishings. The room was located on one of the outer walls of the ziggurat, and an open window allowed in sunlight and air. A female slave, one of the temple prostitutes, entered the room at once and smiled brilliantly at Abram, who averted his eyes uneasily at her brazen stare. Rahaz jumped in briskly. "Bring us some wine, girl." Lowering his heavy body into a chair, he turned to Abram as she left and asked, "Will you have something to eat?"

"No, thank you, master. But I do have some questions. I've been thinking about a lot of things while out tending my sheep."

"I'll wager you have." Rahaz's lips curled in an indulgent smile. "What is your question?"

"I've been wondering. When a man commits a wrong, does it matter which one of the gods he confesses it to?"

It was a question most dwellers of Ur would never think to ask. Rahaz cleared his throat and replied, "The important thing is to bring an offering and make your confession. If you feel no assurance from confessing to one of the gods, then perhaps you've found the wrong god. Go to another. If necessary, come to me, and I'll give you instruction."

Abram studied the face of the fat priest. The answer did not satisfy him, but he left that one and went on. "How do the gods know when a man has done wrong? The gods are here in the temple, but I'm out in the field alone. If I wrong my brother, the gods would not know it, would they?"

Inwardly Rahaz struggled for an answer to the young man's question. He studied him carefully, noting that he was taller than most men, with a strong, athletic figure. Abram was quite handsome, he decided, with deep-set brown eyes. He had a wide mouth that was tough yet could show tenderness. His prominent nose and high cheekbones gave him a noble look. He wore an ill-trimmed short beard, and when he spoke he often waved his hands in sweeping gestures.

Finally Rahaz heaved himself out of his chair and said, "There is much about the gods that we cannot know, young Abram. Our job is simply to make our sacrifices and offerings so that we might hope to find favor with them. I must go now. We will have another one of these talks later."

Abram jumped up and followed the priest to the door. "But, master, I have not yet asked the most important question. I want to know what happens to a man when he dies—and another thing. Do any of the gods ever speak to you?"

Rahaz turned and glared at the young man. "Speak to me? What do you mean?"

"I mean you and I can speak to each other, but do Enki or Nanna ever speak to you as I am doing now?"

"Why, of course not!" Rahaz's corpulent face twisted in a scowl at the rash question. "Why would the gods want to speak to a man? Look, my son, I must caution you. These questions are fruitless. They're not going to profit you. Your father has come to see me more than once. He thinks you ought to marry and settle down. You must learn to live in the real world. You trouble yourself needlessly with these questions about the gods."

Abram stared at the priest, his face troubled. "But aren't we supposed to think about them?"

"Let me do the thinking for you, my son. You go along now. Leave your offering. On your next visit, bring payment for a meeting with one of our temple prostitutes, who can lead you into a closer spiritual encounter with Ishtar. Perhaps then the goddess might be more willing to grant you a fertile wife. For now, say your prayers, and let the other priests and me worry over how best to please the gods."

Abram nodded and sighed. "Yes, master, as you say." But in his heart, Abram knew he would not obey Rahaz's instruction to meet with a temple prostitute. For reasons he could not fully explain to himself or to anyone else, Abram found this aspect of temple worship most distasteful and would have nothing to do with it. Yet he felt drawn to this sacred place that was set apart for worship. His visits, however, never left him satisfied. Rather, they raised more questions every time he came.

Rahaz stood aside to allow the tall young man to leave the room, then shook his head, grumbling, "He is indeed a troublemaker, that one. He must think he's better than other men, but we can change that. I'll have a talk with his father. Terah needs to sit down hard on Abram, or he'll turn out just like his grandfather Nahor!"

———

Metura took one look at Terah's expression and knew at once that her husband was troubled. He had never been skillful at concealing his feelings. She watched as their slave girl set his food before him and then asked with concern, "Is something bothering you, dear?"

Terah stared at his wife. A small woman in frail health, she had borne him three fine sons and was totally obedient to his will. He had wished at times that he might have married a stronger woman to have more sons, but in most respects he was pleased with her as a wife. "I'm worried about Abram," he told her.

"Why, what's wrong with him?" Metura asked uneasily. Of her three sons, Abram was the most like her. He had her gentleness, an attribute one did not see in Nahor or Haran, and like her, he also enjoyed solitude and was a dreamer of sorts. "What's wrong with him? He's not sick, I hope."

"Only sick in the head," Terah snapped. He picked up a portion of meat, ripped it apart with his fingers, and began stuffing it into his mouth. He chewed hurriedly, bolting his food like a hungry animal. "He left the flocks to go to the temple again. That's all he's interested in."

"Well, I'm glad he's religious."

"There's such a thing as being *too* religious," Terah grunted. He picked up a cup, drained the last of the wine, and rapped the table impatiently until the slave girl came and refilled it. He drank again and slammed the cup down with unnecessary force. "He's got to grow up, Metura."

He would have said more, but at that moment Abram entered the room. He had just washed, and his face glowed as he greeted his parents. "Good morning, Father." He came over and kissed Metura. "Good morning, Mother. You're looking well today."

As Abram took his place and accepted the food that the slave girl brought, Terah studied his son. He could see traces of Metura in Abram's features—not that he was in the least feminine. Still, there was a tenderness about his eyes and mouth that men should not have. Terah certainly did not have it, nor did Abram's brothers. He considered tenderness a valuable virtue for women but not worth anything in the character of a man. As Abram ate his meal, Terah thought about his youngest son. *He's got to learn. He can't go on for the rest of his life praying in temples. A man's got to be a man.* Aloud he said, "I'm going to talk to you, son, as straight as I know how."

Abram looked up with surprise. "Why, yes, Father. What is it?" He knew what was coming, for he had heard it before, but he let nothing show in his face.

"You left the flocks yesterday to go to the temple, and the day before that."

"Yes, I did, Father. And I'm going back today."

Terah leaned forward and put his hands flat on the table. "Son, I've tried to talk to you before about this, but evidently you've got a hearing problem."

"I'm sorry, Father."

"Look, I'm not saying anything against religion. Why, I've got religion myself. I make my offerings when it's convenient, but I don't go running to the temple every day. There is no need for that. You're losing your balance over this, son. You've got to put religion in its proper place. There's nothing wrong with washing your face occasionally, but if you start washing it every day, or five times a day, people will think you've lost your mind. Too much washing is worse than none at all. And too much religion is worse than none at all."

"I'm not sure I agree with that, Father. With all due respect, of course."

"What don't you agree with me about? The washing?"

"Oh, you're probably right about that, but not about religion. It seems to me that religion is the most important thing there is."

"More important than making a living? Son, I'm surprised at you!" To hear such words was heresy to Terah. He had not realized his son had sunk to such depths. "A man's first business is to make a living. To marry and have children. A family is what's important, son. We keep religion in its place. We pay enough in offerings so that we can ward off plagues and droughts and floods, but you can't go around praying nonstop."

"I don't think that's what I do, Father."

"You go almost every day to that temple! And you're driving the priest crazy with your questions. Why can't you just be normal like the rest of us?" Terah's tone had taken on a strange pleading quality.

Metura stared at him, for she was more accustomed to his lashing out than begging his children to reason with him. *Why, he's afraid of Abram,* she thought with a shock. *His own child!* It was an insight that had never occurred to her before, and she could not understand it.

Terah was surprised at himself too. He was accustomed to speaking, then having his word obeyed, but something about his youngest son intimidated him, though he had never before allowed it to show. The same thing had been true of his father, Nahor. He remembered well his father's eyes—how they appeared to burn at times, clear down into Terah's heart. The old man had seemed to know what Terah was thinking, and this had frightened him. He now saw some of this in Abram and covered up his feelings by insisting, "You've got to get over this, son. You know what happened to my own father, Nahor. Why, he went crazy over religion."

"I barely remember him, Father. I was just a child when I last saw him, but I do remember his kindness."

"Oh, he was kind, all right." Terah nodded. "I'm not saying anything against him. Up until he got mixed up with the temple and the priests, he was as good a man as you ever saw. Took care of his family. Took care of his business. But then he started hearing voices."

Instantly Abram stared at his father. "You never told me that before!" he exclaimed. "What kind of voices?"

Realizing he had made a mistake, Terah threw up his hands and said, "Who knows? They were all in his head."

"But what did he say?" Abram insisted. "I must know."

When Terah clamped his lips tight and turned away, Metura interjected quietly, "He said he heard a god whispering to him. He spoke to me about it often before he left."

Abram turned to his mother, his face animated. "What god did he hear?"

"I never quite understood that." Metura shrugged her shoulders. "But he was a good man. One of the best I've ever known."

Terah shook his head furiously. "He was good only until he went crazy!"

"But what did he do?" Abram asked anxiously.

"The same thing you've been doing. He went around asking the priests questions that no man needs to pry into. And the local gods weren't good enough for him. Oh no. Of course we've got several thousand gods, but he had to have his own!" Terah's mouth twisted with bitterness at the painful memory. He ran his hand through his thick hair and pulled at it in despair. "You know what he wanted? I can hardly believe I'm telling you this."

"What was it he wanted, Father?"

"He wanted this god of his to talk to him face-to-face. Now, you can't get any crazier than that!"

Abram sat rigid. He recalled his question to the high priest—*Do any of the gods ever speak to you?*—and how Rahaz had denied such a thing. And now to learn that his own grandfather had heard the voice of a god. He started to ask another question, but Terah got up and paced the floor angrily. "Finally he went completely mad," he said. "He started making trips."

"Trips to where?" Abram asked.

"To the cities around here. He went to the temples of all the gods looking for the one who had spoken to him—or so he said. The trips kept getting longer, and he kept staying away, until finally he stayed for months. And then"—Terah's face twisted in shame at the memory—"he went away, and he never came back. A fine father he was!" Bitterness glittered in Terah's eyes, and he stared at Abram with accusation in his manner. "And you're getting to be just like him."

Abram sat quietly listening as Terah paced back and forth, spewing bitter diatribes against his father, Nahor. After venting his anger, Terah faced his son and declared, "I'll have no more of this craziness, Abram. I've made a plan for you."

"A plan? What sort of plan?" Abram asked with apprehension. He was not particularly happy about his present life, but he knew that his father was capable of launching him into a life he would like even less. More than once Terah had suggested that Abram help his brother Haran with his business in the city of Ur. Abram hated business, much preferring to be out with the flocks, but he understood that his father wanted him in town where he could be more easily controlled.

"I'll have no more of your craziness," Terah repeated. "You're going to get married and have a family. You're going to settle down like your brothers and live a normal life."

"Well, I will one day, of course, Father." Abram hoped to appease his father with such a promise, but Terah was well beyond that.

"Not one day. Now! And I've got the woman picked out." Then Terah hesitated, seeming unsure of himself. "She . . . she's a relative."

"A relative?" Abram asked. "What sort of relative?"

"Oh, that's not important. Her family owns homes in Ur and Uruk. We've been doing business with her brother, Garai. It'll be a good thing for both families, this marriage." He cheered up at the thought. "We can expand our trading venture. Garai owns many boats, and we'll send them up and down the river trading."

"But what about the woman?" Metura asked nervously. "What sort of woman is she?"

"Her name is Sarai," Terah said. "She'll bring a fine dowry."

Abram was appalled. He had not expected this! "But that does not answer Mother's question. I must know too—what kind of a woman is she?"

"The kind who'll be a good wife." Terah nodded vigorously. "Of course, she'll need a firm hand—like all women."

Metura shot her husband a troubled glance as he walked over and put his hand on Abram's shoulder. "Look, I'll build you a fine house. You'll have many children. It'll be a good thing. You've always liked children, haven't you?"

"Of course I love children, but—"

"Well, a wife and half a dozen children will keep you from running to the temple every day." Terah squeezed Abram's shoulder and said, "Listen to me, son. It's time for you to settle down."

Metura came over also and put her hand on Abram's other shoulder. He looked up to see the anxiety in her eyes and it grieved him. Her words, however, seemed to belie her worries. "Please, son, listen to your father. It would be wonderful to see you marry and have children. Won't you do it?"

Abram felt trapped, but he did not want to displease his mother. As she continued to urge him, he finally agreed. "All right. I'll go meet her at least."

Terah expelled a big breath and said excitedly, "Good! You can leave this week. I have spoken to them already, and they told me you can meet them in Uruk. You'll have to take lots of gifts." Then he added, grinning, "We'll get them all back and more with this woman's dowry!"

CHAPTER

3

The captain of the small craft that made its way upriver toward Uruk was a brusque individual named Sargon. He had welcomed Abram on board at Ur, and between cursing the crew of four, who busied themselves with the oars or adjusting the triangular sail, he spoke constantly to his single passenger. "Can't remember a time when I wasn't on the river," Sargon said. He took a series of swallows from a jug he kept handy, and Abram watched as his Adam's apple bobbed up and down. The master of the boat was crude, his speech studded with profanity. But he had traveled up the big river farther than any man Abram had ever met and was full of stories, most of which would not bear repeating in mixed company.

"I been up and down this river all my life, and let me tell you"—Sargon winked lasciviously—"the women of Babylon are the *best!* Now, I been all the way up to Mari, and all the way down past Ur to the big water. I been up the other river too, but there ain't nothin' there in the way of good-lookin' women. But you take Babylon, now. Why, they got women you wouldn't believe! Some of them black as night and some as pale as milk."

The captain smacked his lips and gave details of the orgies he had participated in, obviously enjoying the sound of his own voice. From time to time he would cast his eye ahead, but there was really nothing to see. The river curved slightly, making no large sweeping turns, and the brown water looked almost thick with the silt that came down from distances so far Abram could not imagine it. Some called this "the land of the two rivers," but the area to the north was unknown territory to Abram. In fact he wasn't very familiar with any of the upriver places, such as Babylon. Intrigued, Abram leaned back and listened as Sargon continued to speak.

He had been troubled with a vague discomfort ever since his father had announced this expedition to meet his prospective bride. He knew he should have been excited at such a thing, yet he was not. His hunger to delve more deeply into spiritual matters consumed him, and he could not force himself to become interested in finding a wife. There were certainly enough women in Ur, had he been so inclined. Many of them had shown an interest in him, but he had not responded to their obvious suggestions. He remembered the words of his mother just before he left. *"Son, you must find a good woman and have children. It would please me and your father greatly, for I know you're lonely."* She had put her arms around him and held him, saying, *"You can't be alone in this life. Everyone needs somebody to cling to, to hold to, to know that they're there. I've made an offering to the chief of the gods, An, that you'll find the woman who can make you happy and give you many sons."*

As the boat forged its way steadily through the brown stream, Abram pulled his mind away from his mother's admonitions. He glanced around at the boat, which was made of papyrus reeds bound together. There were few trees in this world to provide timber for boats. Any lumber had to be hauled from long distances and was used only for expensive furniture.

Abram let his eyes rest on the banks as they slid slowly by. All the houses were built from baked bricks and had flat roofs. Many of them, he saw, had gardens planted on the roofs, mostly in pots. A few people were tending to their roof gardens, and occasionally one of them would lift a hand to wave to the passing boat. From time to time Abram would wave back. He noticed a young woman walking along the riverbank with a child tied on her back. She waved too, and he saw the whiteness of her teeth and wondered, *Is she happy? Does she have a good husband? Will the child she's carrying grow up or will he die of some sickness? Does she seek after the gods?*

Such thoughts were not uncommon for Abram. He was a man whose inner life was, in many respects, more powerful than his outer life. He had learned all that could be learned about taking care of sheep. He was far more able in this respect than his brothers or his father. They saw the sheep and goats merely as a way to make money and get ahead, but Abram had a real feeling for the flocks and herds, and the sight of a crippled animal made his heart ache with compassion. He had never seen this quality in his brothers, and he wondered at times if he was a fool to act this way.

As the time passed, Abram dozed off but was awakened by Sargon's rough voice. The man was intensely curious and pried into Abram's life. Abram finally let slip that he was going to visit the family of Garai in Uruk.

"Rich family," Sargon grunted. He had smallish eyes, so deep brown they were almost black, and they never stopped darting here and there—sometimes taking in the banks, going to the river road ahead, and now they came to rest on his passenger. "You going to do business with him?"

"Well, actually I'm going because my father's trying to work out a match between his sister and me."

Sargon broke into laughter. He scratched his woolly head, which he kept uncovered, soaking up the sun, and his eyes sparkled. "I know a little bit about those girls. Of course, everybody in Uruk does."

Abram's interest was captured. "What about them?" he asked curiously.

"Well, one of them is good-looking and one of them is plain. Which one are you going after?"

Abram said, "I believe her name is Sarai."

"Oh ho! You're in for it, then, boy!"

"What do you mean by that?"

"I mean that woman's got a tongue like a snake! She's already run off half a dozen men who came to her brother. She'll bring a fine dowry, but she's got a temper like you never heard of. Take my advice—try to get the other one, Hanna. I hear she's got a man that wants to marry her, but you can beat him out. She ain't much to look at, but she'd never give a man a hard time. Not like that Sarai!"

———————

As the boat nudged in toward the quay and the hands leaped out to secure it, Abram turned to Captain Sargon and took some coins out of his purse. "It was a good trip, Captain."

Sargon took the coins, and his eyes were sharp as they rested on Abram's face. "You mind what I tell you, young fellow. Stay away from that woman Sarai. She'll make a man's life miserable. Might as well marry a wild boar as that one!"

Abram smiled. "I'll keep it in mind." The sound of music floated out from the city, and he turned to see many people milling about, most of them dressed in their finery. "What's going on?"

"Oh, it's the Festival of Ishtar." Sargon winked and nudged Abram with his elbow. "Plenty of fun at these Ishtar festivals. Them girls they keep in the temple, they're pretty well used, but if you get yourself a fresh one, they ain't bad." Abram knew that the temple of Uruk was dedicated to the worship of Ishtar and that prostitution was a central part of the worship here. Abram was appalled to realize he had arrived at the time of such a festival and resolved to avoid the degrading festivities.

Ignoring the captain's suggestions, Abram repeated, "It was a good trip, sir. Thank you."

"I'll be heading back downriver in a week. Leave word with the harbormaster if you wish to return to Ur with me." The captain hesitated, then laughed. "If you decide to bring that woman with you, you'd better put her on a chain. I wouldn't want her loose on my boat."

Abram smiled briefly as Sargon turned and went his way, laughing roughly at his joke. After hearing the captain's comments, even if exaggerated, Abram now had even less inclination to seriously consider this woman Sarai as a wife. He would have to carry through with the visit out of duty, but he would make some excuse not to marry her. Digging through his travel bag, he pulled out a scrap of papyrus with the directions he had been given to the home of Garai. He turned and made his way through the town, finding that it was a much smaller place than Ur. The streets were full of the sounds of music and singing by rowdy crowds, who were clearly drunk with wine. He saw more than one man lying senseless in the street.

As he followed his directions he went past a small shrine of Ishtar in which the goddess was depicted with a skirt decorated with swimming fish amid flowing lines of the river. He almost stopped to pray, but the sight of two temple prostitutes heading his direction caused him to keep going. His stomach turned in confusion, wondering now if indeed it was even right to worship a goddess that demanded such degrading acts as he could see going on around him. He began heading down the street, but one of the prostitutes, a small bright-eyed woman with a painted face and wearing a gauzy gown over her full figure, caught up to him and asked, "Have you come to worship?" Then taking hold of Abram boldly, she said, "Come with me. I will help you."

"N-no, thank you," he stuttered. "I'm looking for the house of Garai."

"You can go there later. Come on. It's time to worship now."

She began to pull off her gown right there in the street, and Abram panicked at the thought of giving himself to such "worship." He shook his head vigorously and dropped his travel bag to stop her from disrobing fully. "Do you know where Garai lives?"

The woman glared at Abram in disgust, frowned, and shrugged. "Down that street until you come to the main thoroughfare. Turn right, and go that way. Ask anyone. He's a rich man."

Abram thanked her, and she turned with a burst of shrill laughter and grabbed another man, who seized her willingly.

Abram followed the woman's directions, and the crowds increased in number. He asked a group of people who appeared to be somewhat sober, and they indicated that Garai's house lay ahead. He finally came to a crowded bridge over a canal. He looked both ways and saw that the canal traversed the city in the same way as the one in Ur. The water level was quite low, the main channel no more than ten feet wide. On either side of the channel lay foul-smelling black mud. Waste matter and garbage had been thrown into it, and the stench made Abram wrinkle his nose. He started over the bridge, having to turn sideways to pass through the crowd, but just as he reached the middle, he remembered that he had dropped his travel bag back in the street by the shrine when the prostitute had grabbed him. Alarmed that he had likely lost the gifts he had brought for the family of Garai, along with his money and clothes, he turned back and broke into a run.

Near the end of the crowded bridge, he bumped into a woman. There were no railings, and he had time only to catch a glimpse of her beautiful but stunned face as she tumbled over the side. He made a wild grab for her but missed, and to his horror he saw her turn a somersault and land facedown in the stinking mud. Gales of laughter went up, and Abram looked about wildly. Feeling like a clumsy idiot, he knelt down and tried to reach the woman, but it was too far. He saw that she was struggling to get up, and when she rolled over, he could not make out her features, for the black muck covered her completely.

Abram jumped down and sank up to his knees in the mud. Reaching down, he took the woman's arm and pulled her upright. "I'm so sorry. . . ."

The woman was wiping the mud from her eyes and trying to speak, but mud had gotten in her mouth.

Abram said, "Here, let me help you." He put his arm around her waist and picked her up. She was rather light and was no burden, but it was difficult to pull his feet out of the sucking mud. He struggled to the solid bank, where he put her down and pulled off his neckerchief. "Let me clean off—"

He had no time to say more, for a young woman had come racing up to them. "Mistress! Mistress, are you all right?"

"Look at me! This mud stinks and it's all over me!"

"Come, we'll take you home," the servant girl said.

The mud-covered woman glared at Abram, fury in her eyes. She reached out and struck him on the chest with her fist. "You clumsy dolt!" she cried.

"That's right! Give him a few!" a hulking onlooker cried out from the bridge. Abram looked up to see that the bridge was lined with laughing people. The woman saw it too, and she turned and fled, leaving Abram standing there.

Abram had never felt so stupid and clumsy in his life. He endured the jeers of the crowd as he made his way up the bank and back to the street. His legs were black with mud up to the knees, but he paid them no heed.

He was soon lost in the crowd and found his way back to the shrine. His travel bag was still there, and he sighed with relief and picked it up. He was ready to go when one of the priests of Ishtar approached him and said, "You're a stranger here, are you not?"

"Yes, sir, I am."

"You appear to have gotten into some sort of difficulty." The priest, a thin man with kindly eyes, waved at his feet. "Come inside, and I will see that you get cleaned up."

"That would be most kind," Abram mumbled. He followed the priest, and all he could think of was what a fool he had made of himself. He did not want to stay in the temple precinct, but he could not go to the house of Garai like this and was grateful for the priest's offer. He would wash, change, and be on his way at once.

———————

Garai held a writing stick with its wedge-shaped tip and made indentations in a small holder of damp mud he held in his hand. He had become an expert at the new art of writing, an invention that priests used to keep records of which worshipers had made their annual contributions of barley to the temple granary. Traders had also found the record-keeping method invaluable for listing what was sent on their ships, and city administrators needed records of land surveys and civic activities. Businessmen like Garai had quickly found uses for the new system as well. The writing sticks could easily make marks in the damp clay, which would then harden into permanent records. At first the temple scribes had etched pictures of people and animals, but this had become so time consuming that a system of symbols had developed, such as Garai used now. He made a series of marks in a horizontal row going from left to right, and his hand moved quickly as he recorded his business activities.

As he worked, Garai wondered, not for the first time, if the new materials being developed, such as papyrus, might be more practical for storing large amounts of information. Papyrus reeds could be pressed flat and dried in the sun into thin sheets that would take marks from a small reed filled with a dark liquid. It seemed to Garai that they would take up far less space, but no one had yet figured out how to keep the dark marks from fading. So for this and other reasons, this method had not yet caught on for business purposes, and the cumbersome system of keeping thousands of clay tablets was still the most efficient way of preserving records.

"Sir, you have a visitor."

Garai looked up at Hazil with annoyance. "I'm working. Who is it?"

"He says his name is Abram. Shall I send him away?"

"No!" Garai said quickly. "I've been expecting him. I'll take care of this."

"Yes, sir."

Garai put the clay tablet down, washed his hands quickly, and moved out of the small storeroom into the corridor and toward the courtyard. He found a tall man waiting there, apparently in his thirties, wearing the simple dress of a shepherd. "Abram," he said. "Greetings. My name is Garai."

"My father sends his greetings, sir."

"Come in. You must wash, and I'm sure you must be hungry. When did you arrive?"

"Yesterday."

"Why didn't you come at once?"

Abram had wound up staying the night in the priest's private quarters at the temple, where the priest had insisted on having his garment washed and dried before he left. But Abram did not want to get into the story of why he was delayed. He simply said, "I got here rather late in the afternoon, and I thought it might be best to wait until today."

"Well, I'm glad to see you in any case. Come along, and we'll give you some refreshment."

Abram submitted to Garai's wishes, and soon he was sitting down drinking a thin, sour-tasting wine while the other man talked. "Your father and I have worked out all of the details—about the marriage, I mean. But now you must let me show you around."

Abram nodded at once. "I'd be glad to see your city."

"I'll take you down to the river first to see our fleet of boats. I'm sure you'll be interested in that," Garai said. "And I'll have the cook make a special dinner for when we return, and you can meet the family." He beamed and said, "And, of course, you'll meet your bride-to-be. I'm sure you're anxious for that."

"Of course, sir," Abram said, inwardly wondering how he was going to get out of marrying the woman Captain Sargon had warned him about. Garai seemed to assume that the marriage deal was already done.

Abram mulled this over as he accompanied Garai to the waterfront and spent the afternoon looking over the family's considerable assets. Garai was very proud of his fleet and spoke expansively of the advantages that would accrue to Abram's family when the two joined forces.

"My family has been mostly into herds and flocks," Abram said. "I know nothing about the boating trade." He hoped Garai would not find Terah's marriage offer so enticing when he learned of Abram's business ineptness.

"Oh, there's no reason why you can't keep that up, but the big fortune is to be made in trading. We'll send ships up the river and down. We'll charge freight for some," Garai went on excitedly. He grew animated as he spoke of the profits to be made, and for the rest of the afternoon he entertained the prospective bridegroom royally.

Finally he said, "Well, we'll talk more of this later, but now it's time to go home. I'm anxious for you to meet the rest of my family—especially Sarai!"

"Another suitor," Zulda said, helping Sarai dress. Her nimble fingers quickly fastened the abundant black hair of her mistress with ivory pins. "Aren't you excited?"

"No, I am not. He's probably so old he's toothless and has legs like sticks."

Sarai was in a bad mood. It had taken a great deal of effort to remove the stinking mud from the river the day before. She had insisted that Zulda give her three baths, and when she was satisfied, she was anointed with sweet-smelling oil yesterday and again today. In her imagination she could still smell the stench of the mud that had coated her from head to foot. It had been almost impossible to get out of her hair, and she had almost vomited because some of it had gotten into her mouth.

She had slept poorly that night, going over and over in her mind the humiliation of the mishap on the bridge. She imagined that many who had seen her plight were aware of who she was and were laughing at her all over the city.

Knowing her mistress well, Zulda flitted around, making adjustments to the silky dress Sarai had put on. "But it's so exciting that this may be the husband you'll have."

"I feel like a prize sheep that my brother's auctioning off," Sarai grunted. "He might as well say, 'How much am I bid for this woman?' Slaves are sold the same way."

"But maybe this will be the one you want."

"All Garai is interested in is how much money his family has," Sarai sniffed. She stood up, looked down at herself, then drew her lips into a tight line. "Well, this will be a brief courtship, I can tell you that." She moved toward the door, determination in every line of her body.

———

Abram had brought only one formal robe, and he wore it now as he waited in the room where the family gathered for their meals. It was a fine room, large and airy, with the tables made of wood such as he had never seen. It was polished smooth and had a dark glow to it. He commented on it, and Garai nodded with pride. "I don't know where that lumber came from. I've never seen anything like it. I only know I paid a pretty price for it!"

"It is indeed beautiful—worth the price you paid, I'm sure."

Abram looked around the room, which was lit with lamps burning with a sweet-smelling oil. He had met Garai's mother, Zaroni, and his sister, Hanna, who was very curious. She had asked many questions, and Abram had answered them politely. He was surprised at her attractiveness. She was a small woman, dark-complected, and not at all unattractive as Captain Sargon had insisted. He found her even pretty, though her mouth was small and her eyes somehow seemed too close together. But she certainly was not the homely woman the captain had described. Hanna had informed him that she was engaged to be married and had gushed, "If you and my sister get married, it would be very nice. We'd probably be having children at the same time."

Abram had flushed, embarrassed that she should speak of such things when he had no intention of going through with the marriage plans.

Zaroni had smiled at her older daughter's carelessness and smoothed it over. She now sat beside Abram questioning him gently, and Abram found himself liking her very much. When she asked about his family, he gave her a quick overview of them, and she smiled, saying, "It sounds like you have a fine family."

"I have," Abram said quickly. "Of course, I'm one of the lesser members."

"Lesser in what way?"

"Pretty much every way," Abram admitted. He smiled lamely and shook his head. "I'm not enough of a businessman to please my father and brothers."

Garai, who had been listening, exclaimed at once, "Well, we can change all that, Abram! If you marry Sarai, you and I will be in business together. I can teach you all there is to know about trading up the river."

Abram tried not to let his face show his dismay at this comment. He merely smiled as if in agreement and listened as Garai went on talking about the business.

"Sarai is always late," Hanna said petulantly.

"Maybe I'd better send for her again," Garai said. "You know how women are, Abram."

Abram had no chance to reply, for at that moment a woman in a flowing, silky gown entered the room. Abram stood up and his eyes flew open. He had only caught a glimpse of the face of the woman he had shoved off the bridge, but he knew he would never forget it—and there she stood before him.

As for Sarai, she stared at Abram, shocked beyond belief. She had not forgotten the face of the man who had been so clumsy, and now she took a deep breath, anger racing through her. "What are *you* doing here?" she demanded.

Abram could not speak. Garai and the others stared at Sarai without understanding. "What's wrong, Sarai?" Zaroni said.

"This is the man that shoved me off into the mud!"

Abram could feel his whole face and neck turning red as everyone in the room stared at him. "Yes, I'm afraid I am that man," Abram said meekly. "I'm so sorry."

"Sorry!" Sarai cried. Her eyes were flashing, her fists doubled up. "I won't have this man in my sight. He's nothing but a country bumpkin! Get him out of the house, Garai!" She whirled and ran out of the room.

A dead silence followed, and Abram realized with some relief that his embarrassment might well be his salvation. He waited for Garai to dismiss him so that he could make his apologies and return to his home immediately.

Garai, however, smiled apologetically and cleared his throat. "My sister is a little excitable at times."

"That's right," Zaroni put in quickly. "Let me talk to her, Abram. She gets over things quickly."

Abram managed a smile, but it came hard. "I'm not sure that you should even try. I don't blame her. It was an awful thing."

Zaroni was greatly pleased by the young man's humility. She put her hand on his arm and said, "Try to be patient, Abram. She has a good heart."

She turned and left the room, and Garai said quickly, "Sit down, Abram. You must eat."

But Abram had lost his appetite. He wanted nothing more than to be out of this house and back in the fields with his flocks in Ur. He sat down heavily, hoping that this woman would refuse to forgive him and he would have his wish.

CHAPTER

4

Although Abram wanted to leave the house of Garai immediately and return to Ur, it quickly became obvious that his host wanted him to stay for the entire two weeks his parents had arranged for the visit. For almost a week he remained a nervous and uncomfortable guest. He saw Sarai several times but only briefly, for she avoided him whenever possible. She refused to eat meals with the family as long as Abram was there.

As a result of Sarai's avoidance, Abram became very well acquainted with Zaroni, Sarai's mother. Garai was constantly busy with his trading ventures, and Hanna was equally occupied with Eliphaz, who seemed a weak man to Abram, but he said nothing of it to the others.

Zaroni had made it her business to make Abram feel as comfortable as possible, knowing that he was deeply embarrassed by the accident on the bridge and Sarai's refusal to forgive him for it. He showed much humility and understanding over Sarai's rejection of him, and as the days passed, Zaroni found herself liking him more and more.

Zaroni loved flowers and was surprised to learn that Abram knew more about them than most men. He even helped her with some transplanting. Late one afternoon the two of them were working together over a particularly fine specimen he had found outside the city on an early walk that morning and had brought to her as a gift. Zaroni had been very pleased, and now the two talked of flowers as they reset it in a decorative pot. "Not many men love flowers as you do, Abram."

"I've always loved flowers. I suppose it's because I'm out in the fields all the time. My mother loves them too. I think you'd like her. You two are much alike."

"Really? That pleases me very much. Perhaps we'll be able to arrange a visit soon." She turned to face Abram and saw his embarrassment at her suggestion. Now she drew the young man out by saying, "Tell me more about what you do when you're home."

"Oh, nothing really exciting." Abram smiled faintly. "My brother, Nahor, is a shepherd and so am I. We stay with our flocks most of the time."

"What about your other brother? Haran is his name?"

"Yes. He manages the family's business in Ur. He works in town most of the time."

"And your father. What does he like to do?"

"He likes business." Abram shrugged. He said no more for a time and then finally admitted, "They think I'm too religious."

"Oh?" Zaroni looked startled. "Is that such a bad thing? I would think it good."

"They don't think so. They say I'm like my grandfather. His name was Nahor, the same as my brother."

"And he was very interested in the gods?"

"Well . . . not so much the gods. He was interested in one particular God. From what I understand, he thought there was only one God—an all-powerful God."

"You mean An, ruler of the heavens?"

Abram bit his lower lip, then shook his head. "I don't think so. I don't think he put his trust in any of the gods of Sumer."

"I don't understand that."

"Neither did the family," Abram explained, "but my grandfather didn't believe that any of the gods were very powerful. He was convinced that there was only one God who was supremely powerful . . . and he struggled to find Him." Abram shrugged his shoulders and said, "I guess I'm like him, or so my family says."

"But you've told me that you pray to quite a few of the gods."

"Yes . . . but I think these stone gods have ears of stone. I don't think they hear my prayers. And there are so many of them! Gods for the sun, the moon, the rain, the animals, the plants. Even tools! My brother has a stone idol he prays to each morning for the staff he uses to tend the sheep. Imagine! How can anyone know which gods to pray to—and what it will take to placate them?"

Zaroni had never really thought about their religion in this way. Nor had she ever met anyone who had questioned it as this young man was daring to do. Not knowing how to answer him, she sat quietly waiting for him to continue.

Abram watched Zaroni's questioning face and, for a fleeting moment, thought how attractive she was. Like her daughter Sarai, he realized. He had found himself thinking more and more about Sarai. Her harsh attitude toward Abram had not diminished her beauty in his mind. In truth, he had never seen a woman so beautiful in all of his life. But now he put her aside in his mind and said to Zaroni, "I think for most people, religion is a dreadfully miserable affair."

"You surprise me, Abram."

"Why? It's true, isn't it? People fear all these deities who hover over us, supposedly ready to punish us for displeasing them. If we don't bring the proper offering, we'll get a flood or maybe a drought. That's what has made religion so powerful—fear."

"But, Abram, don't you think we *should* fear the gods?"

"Something inside me tells me we should love the gods. . . . But how can we"—Abram shrugged his shoulders—"when they bring nothing but troubles."

The more Abram talked, the more Zaroni admired him. He was utterly honest and humble, not like the other suitors who had called on Sarai. Feeling more comfortable with this man than any previous suitor, she said gently, "I know Sarai is upset with you right now, but I hope you won't give up."

Abram shot her a glance. "She'll never forgive me."

"Oh, yes she will. I've told you before she has a fiery temper, and she's spoiled to the bone. But deep under all that, she has a good heart."

"If she has a heart like you, then she certainly does." Abram smiled. "But I'm sure she would never consider me as a possible husband."

———

"He's nothing but a clumsy oaf!" Sarai cried to her mother later in her room.

After Zaroni's conversation with Abram, she had gone to Sarai's bedroom to try to talk to her about him. She passed along her impressions that the young man had a gentle heart and was basically good, but Sarai merely tossed her head and denied it.

"He's very intelligent," Zaroni insisted, "and one of the kindest men I've ever met. Not like most young men, who are very selfish."

"He shoved me off the bridge into the mud!"

Zaroni's temper flared, unusual for her. "You're acting like a fool, girl! He accidentally bumped into you, and you hate him for it. I thought you had better sense."

Sarai stared at her mother open-eyed, amazed at her uncharacteristic outburst of anger. "Why, Mother, I've never seen you so upset."

"I've never seen you make such a fool out of yourself! You go around crying and whimpering and complaining because you can't find a husband who's young and strong and yet kind to women. And when one comes along, because of one incident, you shut him out. Don't you see how foolish you are?"

Sarai dropped her head, and her face flushed at her mother's cutting words. She finally lifted her eyes and whispered, "I'm sorry, Mother."

"That's my girl." Zaroni smiled and embraced her daughter. "He's very shy. You'll have to show him that you have no ill feelings. Will you do that?"

"I . . . I'll try, Mother. Really I will!"

———————

Abram was shocked when Sarai stepped into the dining room later that evening after the meal had already started. He stood up at once and was surprised when she managed a small smile.

"Hello. Am I late?" she asked meekly.

"Not at all," Zaroni replied. "Here, sit down. This is fresh mutton, and you know how good it is when Mahita cooks it."

Abram said little, but there was a break in the tension. He could not help admiring Sarai's smooth, pearly skin. She had the most beautiful complexion he had ever seen on any woman, and her eyes! They were enormous and beautifully shaped, and when she occasionally lifted them, he saw that the anger and bitterness in them had given way to a gentleness he had not seen before. *She's so beautiful*, he thought. When she suddenly asked him if he were enjoying his visit to Uruk, he said quickly, "Oh yes."

Abram was so inexperienced with women, he did not know how to take the matter any further and finished his meal in awkward silence.

When the men rose to take a walk around the courtyard and talk business, Zaroni pulled Sarai aside and told her, "You'll have to be more outgoing, Sarai. He's painfully shy."

"Why should he be shy? He's thirty years old. He should have had some experience with women."

"From what he tells me, I don't think he has. But for that very reason, he is more likely to be a faithful husband to you, Sarai. Be kind to him. I know he admires you. I can see it in his eyes."

Sarai was well aware that Abram admired her, for she could gauge the admiration of young men. But she was not sure how to mend the breach between them as a result of her unkindness. The whole next day she thought about it. She had actually gotten over her anger by now, but she still found Abram to be a strange young man. Although he had a good smile and sometimes spoke with feeling about things, she was disturbed that he was so tongue-tied around her. *Why doesn't he say something?* she often wondered. *Why doesn't he even try to take my hand or express his feelings for me? That is what most men would do who come around looking for a wife.*

For the next several days, Abram spent much time out with Garai studying the business, although Sarai sensed he did not particularly care for it. More than once he brought in flowers from the fields for Sarai, which pleased her, but it was not enough. She told her mother, "He'll have to do more than bring flowers if he's going to win a bride!"

———————

At the marketplace one morning Sarai moved slowly past the stalls, accompanied by her maid. Zulda carried a basket for the fruit Sarai selected from the vendors. She ignored their shrill cries of "Buy here, lady! Buy here!"—choosing whatever pleased her the most. She enjoyed her visits to the market, which gave her a good excuse to get out of the house.

As she looked over the produce she found herself thinking more and more of Abram and wondering how long he would stay. *He might as well go home if he's not going to make any effort to win me,* she thought. She was disappointed at his reluctance to woo her, for as her mother had said, the young man did have much to commend him. Perhaps of most importance, he was not old. Sarai had a horror of being given to an old man. And he was not crude, as many of the men had been who had offered themselves. *If he would only speak up and show a little more interest in me,* she said to herself, realizing by her own inner comment that her pride was hurt. She was accustomed to being courted in a more aggressive manner, and for the first time in her life, it occurred to her, *Maybe he doesn't think I'm attractive.* The thought startled her, and as she moved down the line of stalls, she became preoccupied with it.

She was brought out of her thoughts by the sound of screaming. Glancing ahead, she saw a large, burly man beating a young woman no more than fourteen or fifteen with a cane. The girl wore the dress of a slave, and the stick left stripes on her bare shoulders. She cowered on the ground, covering her head with her arms and trying to protect herself, crying piteously as the blows descended.

Sarai was not an especially cruel young woman, but she had grown up in a society that showed little pity toward the unprotected. Slaves could be beaten at the whim of their master, and this was not the first time Sarai had seen a slave beaten. True, the girl was younger than most, and the man was striking harder, so she felt a brief moment of compassion. But she knew there was nothing to be done. The slave was the absolute property of the owner, and no one could interfere.

But suddenly a form appeared coming down the street, and Sarai was surprised to see that it was Abram. She was further surprised when he stepped between the burly man and the girl and heard him say, "Sir, she's young and a valuable slave, I'm sure. Please don't beat her anymore."

The strongly built slave owner flushed red in the face and cursed Abram, yelling, "Get out of the way! It's none of your business!"

Abram was fully as tall as the slave owner, though not nearly as thick in body. Sarai could see the anger in Abram's eyes, yet he was struggling to keep his composure. With his voice even and controlled, he said, "I hate to see anyone mistreated, even a slave."

The big man laughed coarsely and shouted in a drunken rage, "You want to see someone mistreated, then I'll mistreat you!" He cursed again and raised the stick toward Abram, but Abram's hand shot out and grasped the man's wrist. Sarai expected to see the big man pull away, which indeed he attempted to do. But surprise washed across his face as he was obviously unable to release himself from Abram's grasp. And then his surprise changed to shock as Abram apparently kept increasing the pressure. Finally the stick dropped from the man's hand, and he cried out hoarsely, "Let me go! You're crushing my bones!"

At once Abram released the man's wrist. He reached down and picked up the stick, broke it in two, and said, "I usually don't interfere in matters that are none of my business, but I don't like to see a helpless person hurt."

"It *is* none of your business, and you can't stop me! I'll do what I please with her!" He rubbed his wrist and backed off a step. "You're a strong man— I can see that—but you won't always be around." He glanced at the girl, who had turned her face upward, tears running down her cheeks.

Sarai watched closely and saw that something was working in Abram's mind. His eyes were fixed on the burly slave owner, but some thought was taking possession of him. She was surprised when he said, "I'll buy her from you. How much?"

"Buy her!" The man stared at Abram with shock. "All right," he said quickly. When he named an extravagant price, Abram reached into the pouch he carried slung around his shoulder and pulled out a small pottery jar. "How about this instead?"

Sarai watched as the man took the jar and pulled out the stopper. "Why, this is purple dye," he said. Then a crafty look came into his eye. "The girl for the dye?"

"Done," Abram said.

Laughing roughly, the man said, "You're not much of a trader. This dye is worth a dozen of her kind."

Abram ignored the man's gloating over the deal as he raised the jar to the gathered crowd and laughed at Abram's stupidity.

"Come," Abram said simply. "We'll have this recorded."

Sarai watched Abram reach down to help the girl to her feet and heard him say gently, "Come along, girl. No one will hurt you now." The girl wiped the tears from her face and followed the two men quickly to a scribe sitting at a table, where the transaction was recorded. She stayed very close to Abram the whole time while the business matter was completed, then followed him down the street.

Sarai ordered her maid to take the basket of fruit home; then she followed Abram and the slave girl from a discreet distance, carefully staying out of sight.

As for Abram, he did not know what had possessed him. He had always hated to see any helpless thing hurt, even an animal that was beaten or mistreated. After they had gone some distance from the crowded marketplace, Abram found a shady spot under a palm tree to sit down and let the girl rest. He saw she was trembling as she sat by his feet, and he asked kindly, "What's your name, child?"

"Layona."

"Don't be afraid," he said. He put his hand out to touch her head, and she flinched. "No one's going to harm you." Then, after they had caught their breath, he stood and helped her up again, saying, "Come along."

Sarai, watching and listening from a close hiding spot, sneaked back into the street, merging once again in the crowd, where she could watch Abram's tall figure as he led the girl along. She saw him bend down more than once and speak to her, and she saw the gratitude on the slave girl's face.

Sarai had said nothing to anyone about what had happened, but she was aware that Abram had asked her mother to take care of the girl until he could locate a new owner for her.

At the evening meal Abram was quiet, as usual, while Garai talked ceaselessly. The slave girl, looking quite frightened, came in bearing a large bowl of fruit, but as the meal continued, she seemed to relax. She had been washed and was wearing a clean garment and her hair was tied back. She was a pretty girl, despite the scars on her face and body from the frequent mistreatment by her former owner, and Sarai wondered what it would be like to be a slave. She herself had never suffered badly, and now, for the first time in her life, she wondered what it would be like to be forced to do every depraved thing a man could think of and to be beaten for no reason. Her heart flooded with compassion, and she looked toward Abram, who was smiling at the girl. Again she wondered what kind of a man would do such a thing.

After the meal Abram and Garai went to the courtyard to talk of business, and Sarai went to Abram's guest quarters, where she found the girl alone.

With a frightened look on her face, the girl said timidly, "Master Abram's gone, lady."

"Yes, I know," Sarai replied. "You're new here, aren't you?"

"Yes, I belong to Master Abram."

"Well, he's a good man. I think you will like being in his service." She began to question the girl gently and found out, after some difficulty, that she had had an even harder life than Sarai had imagined. The girl's family had died of a plague, and she had been passed around to various relatives, the last of whom had sold her into slavery. The burly man had mistreated her frightfully, although she would not give specifics.

"And what will you do now, Layona?"

The girl looked at her and smiled. "I belong to Abram. I will do as he says."

"That's a good girl." Sarai smiled, then returned to the living quarters until she saw Garai come inside and head for his bedroom. She went out to the courtyard, where she found Abram alone, enjoying the cool night air. He nodded to her respectfully as she approached and asked, "Have you had a good day, Abram?"

"Why, yes, I have. Very good."

Sarai hesitated. "I was there on the street. I saw what happened between you and the man, the one you bought Layona from."

Abram looked surprised. "I didn't see you."

"No, you were concerned about the girl. I don't think many men would have done what you did."

He dropped his head, embarrassed. "I . . . I don't like to see anyone mistreated."

Sarai suddenly found herself liking this man a great deal. "Come inside.

Mahita's made a special brew. It's very good."

"All right," Abram said, surprised at the invitation, the first he had had from Sarai. He followed her inside and waited in the living area while she went into the kitchen. She quickly returned, carrying a gourd with two reeds sticking out of the top.

"We'll share this," she said, sitting down and indicating for him to sit beside her.

It was a form of sharing Abram had never seen before, but he sipped the brew through the reed straw, conscious of the sweet anointing perfume Sarai had on. "It's very good," he said quickly.

"Mahita knows how to make the best things. She's a fine cook. She makes this concoction from grape juice and some other ingredients. I'm going to get her to show me how to do it."

"I'd like to know myself. My mother likes recipes like this."

Sarai began to question Abram about his family, and for the first time he spoke freely with her. She noticed he said little about himself, his father, or his brothers, but it was clear that he loved his mother deeply.

"You and your mother are very close, aren't you?"

"Yes, I think we are," Abram said, looking down, embarrassed. "My brothers say I'm too much like her."

"Well, I think she sounds like a wonderful woman."

"She's the finest woman I ever met."

"I suppose you want a wife who will be like her."

Abram looked up quickly and saw that Sarai was watching him with a smile. He smiled back. "I'm not sure I could ever find one as kind and generous as she is."

His candor pleased Sarai. She had heard so much flattery from suitors that it sickened her, and now here was a young man who refused to say that she might be even better than his mother. "Well, what does she look like?" Sarai asked.

"Oh, she's about as high as my heart."

"What a nice thing to say!"

"I mean she's small. She has nice brown eyes—very warm—but unfortunately she's not in the best of health," Abram said, and a concerned expression crossed his face. "I worry about her sometimes."

Sarai continued to draw the young man out, and as he relaxed in her presence, she found he had a wit that lay beneath the surface. He told her about several misadventures he had had with the flocks that made her laugh.

Finally he turned to her and said, "I'm sorry about knocking you into the mud. I felt terrible about that. . . . I still do."

Sarai discovered that all of her ill will was gone. "Please don't speak of it anymore, Abram. It was an accident. I was a fool to take it personally." She laughed suddenly. "My mother told me so. So I have a good mother too."

"Yes, you do. I like her very much."

Suddenly Sarai had a thought. "I'm going outside the city tomorrow to visit my mother's sister, my aunt Bernia. Would you like to go?"

Abram noticed her enigmatic smile and wondered what she had in mind. "Why . . . yes, I'd like it very much—if I wouldn't be in the way."

"Oh, you won't be. We'll leave early in the morning and spend the whole day and a night there."

Sarai's aunt Bernia was much older than her sister Zaroni. Her hair had turned to silver, but her eyes were bright and alert. She looked up when she met Abram and said, "My, what a tall, fine fellow you are! Come and sit down. You must tell me all about yourself."

Abram quickly discovered that the old woman meant exactly that. She had an inquisitive mind, and Sarai sat to one side laughing at him, saying once, "She'll want to know everything about you. I warned you that she was like this."

"Of course I want to know everything," Bernia said. "Like why aren't you married?"

The blunt question took the wind out of Abram's sails, and he could only stammer, "Why . . . why, I'm not sure."

"Don't you like women?"

Abram suddenly found he liked the old woman, despite her quick, penetrating questions. "I like sensible ones."

"Don't they have to be pretty?"

Abram hesitated then, keeping his eyes on her face, and said, "For me, better a plain woman with sense than a pretty face with nothing in the mind."

"Well, a man who tells the truth," Bernia said, laughing. She looked over at Sarai and said, "And you're the current hope, are you, Sarai?"

"Hope, Aunt? What do you mean?"

"Well, Garai's tried to marry you off to every rich man he can find. Are you rich, Abram?"

Sarai was humiliated. "Don't talk like that, Aunt!"

"Why not? I suppose that's why you came, isn't it, Abram, with Sarai in mind for a wife?"

Abram could not look at Sarai. He dropped his head and said, "My father and your sister's son have discussed it."

"Never mind them. What about you?"

Abram felt his face flush at the twinkle in Bernia's eye and at her laughter as she went on, "Well, friend Abram, let me tell you. She has a sharp tongue, this girl, but she's beautiful, isn't she?"

"Y-yes, she is," Abram stammered.

Sarai was very pleased. It was the first time he had said anything about her beauty, but now she wanted to rescue him from her aunt's interrogation. "Don't pester him, Aunt."

"I will if I want to." She put her old hand over Abram's and said, "She's a good girl underneath all that sharpness." Then she turned and smiled, her eyes sparkling. "I like this one, Sarai. He'll do. He'll make you a good husband."

"I'm sorry if my aunt embarrassed you," Sarai said later that evening.

"She did a little," Abram said, "but it's all right. I like her very much."

The two were standing in Bernia's garden in the cool of the evening. They had had a good supper prepared by Bernia's servant, and the old woman had gone to bed. Abram turned to Sarai and said, "She reminds me of my mother."

Sarai gazed into his eyes. The sweet fragrance of the flowering plants was heavy on the air, yet he could smell the perfume Sarai wore, and he was very conscious of her beauty. She was wearing a simple outfit made of soft cloth dyed a light blue, and earrings that sparkled when she turned her head.

"I've thought about the slave girl you bought. What will you do with her?"

Abram flashed a smile. "I have a confession to make."

"A confession? What is it?" Sarai was intrigued and saw laughter in his eyes. "What is it?" she urged. "Come on, confess."

"I had brought you a gift from Ur, but I used it to buy the girl."

"Why, I'm surprised at you, Abram."

"It was a terrible thing to do."

"No, it wasn't at all."

"What I'd like to do is give the girl to you as a gift. She's a sweet little thing, I think, and I believe she'd be useful to you."

"Maybe I'd mistreat her."

"No, I wouldn't offer her to you if I thought that."

"I don't know why you'd think that after the way I treated you. I was awful."

"Well, it was awful of me to shove you in that mud."

"Let's forget that." Sarai reached up and touched Abram on the chest. "I was angry at first, but I'm not now."

Abram wrapped his hand around hers and said, "There's one thing I need to tell you about myself, Sarai."

"What is it, Abram?"

"I'm not like other men." He shook his head sadly. "My father and my brothers tell me that often enough." He looked deeply into her eyes and said quietly, "There's something in me that cries out to know the true God—the God who is above all the gods of Sumer."

"My mother has told me how religious you are."

"I'd like to tell you what it is that's within me if you don't mind."

"Come. Sit down and tell me."

The two sat on a stone bench, and Sarai listened as he spoke of his hunger to know an almighty and all-powerful God. She did not fully understand it. She herself made offerings to the many Sumerian gods, but she had never even imagined that there could be a God that was more powerful than all these gods put together. She found herself intrigued by the idea that there might just be one God alone.

Abram admitted to her that he had never before fully shared this idea with anyone, afraid that he would be thought crazy. But deep in his heart he had a yearning to learn the truth, and a growing conviction that the religion they had all been taught from childhood was totally false. Even while he had been here visiting in Uruk, he had become convinced that this unseen God was speaking to him—not in an audible voice, but clearly in his heart and mind while he was out in the fields on his early-morning walks.

When she said nothing for a long while, he asked, "Do you think I'm crazy?"

Sarai saw that here was a man like no other she had ever known. He had a gentle spirit, and she knew he respected women, because of his love for his mother and his quick defense of an innocent slave girl. It was the very quality she had been looking for in a man, and now she had found it.

"No, Abram, I don't think you're crazy at all." Yet one thing about him troubled her. Even in these close moments, he made little move to touch her. True, he had taken her hand, but then he had dropped it again as they sat together on the bench and kept a respectful distance between them as they talked. This puzzled Sarai greatly, for men always wanted to touch her. She had always been beautiful and expected men to be overcome by her beauty. He had only commented about her beauty once, to her aunt earlier that day, and he certainly had made no advances to her. Having spent so much time fending off unwanted caresses from men, she was troubled by this. *Why doesn't he even try to kiss me?* She leaned over against him slightly and knew that for most men this would have been an invitation, but Abram did not respond. For one brief moment she was hurt, but then she thought craftily, *I can make him want me. He's a man, after all!*

———————

After their return to Uruk, Abram explained to his new slave his intention to give her as a gift to Sarai. Layona was pleased with the arrangement, for she thought she could not find a better situation than to be a servant to this well-off family.

As Sarai taught her to serve alongside her personal maid, Zulda, Layona become quite fond of Sarai. She was anxious to please, which caused some jealousy on the part of Zulda. But Sarai ignored Zulda's annoyance and gave much attention to Layona.

"Are you going out today, mistress?" the girl asked.

"Yes, I am, Layona."

"May I go with you?"

"Not this time. I'm going to a betrothal celebration with Abram—for one of my friends who is getting married."

"You'll be the prettiest one there, mistress," Layona said, and she turned worshipful eyes upon Sarai.

Sarai reached out and touched her cheek. "I thank you, Layona. That's a nice thing to say. I'll tell you all about it tomorrow."

Leaving her bedroom, she went to find Abram waiting for her near the front entrance. "I don't know if I ought to go," he said shyly. "I won't know anybody there."

Sarai smiled but said firmly, "You've got to go. You promised me."

"All right. If you say so."

The two made their way out of the house and walked the short distance to Heri's house. Sarai introduced Abram to Heri and her prospective husband, Gorzi, an ugly fellow—*Not unlike a wild boar*, Sarai thought, wondering how her friend could marry such a man. *If Abram refuses to ask me to marry him, I'm going to wind up with someone like this bloated fellow or, worse, with some old man who looks like a corpse.*

Abram felt out of place at the celebration, where huge flagons of wine were consumed and dancing girls provided lewd entertainment. Abram was relieved when Sarai finally said, "I'd like to go home."

"All right. We can leave now."

As they left the house and the sound of the merriment faded, they walked along the dark city street in silence. Sarai saw Abram glance at a shrine they passed and she asked, "Do you think it does any good to pray, Abram?"

He was silent for a time as they walked slowly down the street, then said, "I have come to believe that this stone goddess cannot hear our prayers. I know somewhere there's a true God who is not made of stone and who *does* hear us . . . and I'm going to find Him no matter how long it takes."

When they reached the house, Sarai said, "Let's not go in right away. It's too early."

He followed her into the garden, where they talked on into the night, Abram keeping his usual safe distance from her. Finally Sarai turned her uplifted face to his. "Don't you like me at all, Abram?"

And then Abram, the son of Terah, put his hands on her shoulders and said what was on his heart. "Sarai, you're the most beautiful woman I've ever seen. I think you're the most beautiful woman in the world."

Sarai had heard many compliments from men, but never before had she felt a man speak to her with such simple honesty. She saw a light in his eyes that he had kept hidden from her, then felt his arms go around her. His kiss made her knees go weak as he drew her close. She had always had power over men, yet for the first time she felt helpless in a man's embrace. Her heart was lifted to a height she had never before experienced, and deep inside she knew this was the one man she could love for the rest of her life.

Abram lifted his lips from hers and watched her beautifully fashioned face in the moonlight, then put his hand on her cheek and whispered, "I love you, Sarai."

"I didn't think you even liked me," Sarai whispered. "I've got such a terrible temper, and I behaved awfully."

"I think I loved you from the first time I saw you."

She laughed suddenly and put her hand over his as he held it on her cheek. "When I was all covered with mud?"

"Yes, even then."

Sarai waited for his proposal of marriage, but he was silent. "What's wrong?" she asked quietly.

"I don't think I'd make a good husband."

"What do you mean? Of course you would."

"People say I worry too much about religion. My family's afraid I'll wind up like my crazy grandfather."

"Don't worry about what other people think. I think you're good, Abram, and you're honest."

"Would you have me, then, as your husband? I know you could do better."

She reached up and kissed him again, then leaned back, a sparkle in her eye. "You know, I've often threatened to buy a handsome slave and make him into the kind of husband I want, but now I won't have to do that. I can just make you into what I want."

"I believe you could." He ran his hand over her black hair, sweet smelling and soft. "I'll always love you, Sarai."

"Even when I'm old and skinny with gray hair?"

"Even then."

She smiled, feeling full and complete in his embrace. Finally she drew back and laughed joyously. "Let's go tell everyone, and let me handle the dowry, Abram. I'll gouge Garai until he squeals!"

PART TWO

THE MARRIAGE

[Abram] said unto Sarai his wife, Behold now, I know that
thou art a fair woman to look upon.

Genesis 12:11 KJV

CHAPTER

5

Abram had yielded to Sarai's plea to have the wedding at her home. He had not found it hard to persuade his parents and brothers to attend the wedding. They gladly traveled to Uruk and were staying in the guest quarters at Garai's home.

"This will be a good time to settle some business matters." Terah nodded with a satisfied expression as he and Metura dressed for the ceremony.

"No, it will not," Metura said firmly. "It's the time to celebrate the joy of our son in finding a good wife."

Terah stared at Metura, who very rarely stood against him, but something in her eyes, a certain glint to which he was unaccustomed, warned him that this was no time to argue.

"Well, you're right, of course, wife. And he is getting a good girl. A little sharp with her tongue, but—"

"She'll change for the better, I'm sure. Abram is very much in love with her. I've never seen him so happy."

Terah nodded. "I think you're right. It's a good thing all the way around. I'm looking forward to getting some grandchildren out of this."

The two of them donned their finest robes and made their way out of the guest quarters to the front of the house, where a large and noisy crowd had gathered in the street and the courtyard. It seemed Garai knew almost everyone in Uruk. The hired musicians played lustily on harps and other stringed instruments, while drummers beat out the rhythm on handheld drums. The air was thick with the smell of strong drink, which had been flowing for two days now.

"These people know how to have a wedding," Terah said, grinning. He put his arm around Metura and drew her close. "I remember our own wedding." He gave her a squeeze and said, "You were the prettiest thing I ever saw."

Metura was stunned, for her husband was not a man to pay a compliment. Tears came to her eyes, and she looked up and said, "That's a nice thing for you to say, Terah."

Terah saw the tears and mumbled, "Well, no sense in making a big thing about it. I've always thought you were a beautiful woman. I guess I'll have to tell you that more often."

Metura was overcome, but she blinked away the tears and looked around at the dancing team that was performing in the courtyard. "This is going to cost Garai a fortune," she murmured.

"Well, he's got the money. He's one of the richest men in the land. I can't think of a better alliance for Abram to make for the family."

At that moment a crash sounded, and both Terah and Metura whirled to see a couple, obviously drunk, pulling themselves up from the ground. They had joined the dancers and then careened into a table covered with platters of food and jugs of drink. The woman was simpering and giggling, and the man was so drunk he could hardly get to his feet.

"We'd better have this wedding pretty soon," Terah growled, "or everybody will be too drunk to know what's happening."

Matura looked across the courtyard and saw Abram surrounded by a group that included Garai and several other men of the city. "He looks a little uncomfortable, doesn't he?" Metura whispered.

"Every man, I suppose, feels a little afraid when he takes a wife."

As a matter of fact, Abram was not so nervous about taking a wife as he was about the business plans Garai was making for him.

"There's no reason why we can't go up the other river," one of the guests said, a tall man with penetrating black eyes. "There are cities up that one as well as this one."

"Exactly what I say," Garai agreed, nodding enthusiastically. "And we've got a young man here who's willing to back us. Isn't that right, Abram?"

Abram hesitated, then smiled faintly. "I'm planning on mostly taking care of our flocks and herds, while Nahor and Haran take care of business matters with my father."

Garai slapped the tall young man on the back. He was grinning broadly and had been imbibing freely of the wine. "It's all right," he said. "We will make a businessman out of you yet. You'll do us all proud, Abram."

Abram said nothing at that point, but a few minutes later he pulled Garai off to one side. "Really, I'm serious, Garai. I think it will be much better if

Nahor and Haran attend to the trading business. I'm better with sheep and goats than I am with matters like that."

Garai blinked owlishly. "Well, it's not what I had planned, but we'll see how it goes. Whatever happens, we're all going to make a lot of money. Why, there's no—" He broke off, for he saw his mother motioning to him. "I think it's time for the ceremony to begin. We'd better get down to the temple." He grinned and slapped Abram on the back heartily. "You're getting a good girl, Abram. And she's getting a good man."

Abram moved over to accompany his parents, and the entire crowd, those who were not too drunk to walk, made their way down to the temple of Ishtar.

The ceremony that followed was complicated, with the high priest of Ishtar in charge. Abram actually paid little attention to the goings-on until Sarai was escorted in, led by her brother and followed closely by her mother. Garai brought her up to him, and Sarai smiled, reached out, and took Abram's hand.

"You're beautiful, Sarai, as always," Abram whispered.

Indeed she was beautiful. She wore a snow-white gown, and her black hair cascaded down her back in curly locks. She wore a little makeup but scarcely needed any. Her skin was like glowing alabaster, and her large expressive eyes were filled with mystery as she looked toward Abram. Her lips were red and turned up at the corners as she smiled. "Thank you, Abram."

They had no time to say more, for the ceremony was continuing. Abram paid little attention to the formalities of the wedding ritual. During his stay in Uruk, he had lost what little confidence he'd once had in the powers of Ishtar or any other idol. And though he had ceased to pray to them, he no longer feared their displeasure. Rather he felt a deep inner peace as he looked at his beautiful bride, a confidence that he was indeed being blessed by a God who was greater than any lifeless stone god in this temple. He could not keep his eyes off Sarai, and he knew with pride that no one else could either. Every eye was fixed on her, for she was the fairest woman of all the land. Of that Abram was sure.

Finally the two heard a shout go up, and Sarai turned to him. "I belong to you now, Abram," she whispered with tears in her eyes.

"Don't cry. I belong to you too. We'll have each other as long as we live."

She smiled and took his kiss. Then they turned to receive the congratulations of the crowd, and Abram felt a strength in his heart as he thought, *At least I've done one right thing.*

"I think you're wise to go away with Abram, just the two of you." Zaroni had come into Sarai's room and was helping her pack her clothes. The two maids had done most of the work, so Zaroni came and put her arm around her daughter. "You looked absolutely beautiful at the ceremony."

"Thank you, Mother." Sarai hesitated, then said, "Mother, tell me how to be a good wife."

"You waited a long time to ask that." Zaroni smiled gently.

"I don't know anything. I've heard stories, of course, about what happens with a man and a woman, but I won't know what to do. I'm afraid I'll be a disappointment to Abram."

"You won't be that, because you have a gentle husband, and that's more important than anything else. Some have looked down on Abram because he's not outgoing, but there's a kindness in him. I saw it the first time I met him, and that's what is important in a husband."

"I know. I see it in him too. But what do I do?"

"You love him, and love will find a way. But I want to caution you, Sarai."

"About what, Mother?"

Zaroni had thought this over carefully, and now she said quietly, "Abram is not an ordinary man. He's different."

"Different in what way? I know you're right, but I haven't been able to put my finger on it."

"I think he's a better man than average. But people don't always understand quietness and goodness and gentleness. We live in a world where men get ahead by clawing their way up—and women too, for that matter. But Abram isn't like that. He's thoughtful and introspective. I imagine he could be a poet if he put his mind to it. The thing is, he's going to be misunderstood, and you must always be supportive, Sarai. Always. Even when you don't understand him yourself."

Sarai listened to her mother's wise words, and finally, when Zaroni kissed her, Sarai promised, "No matter what, I'll always be on Abram's side."

The boat swayed gently in the water, straining against its moorings. The unusual craft belonged to Garai, and he had insisted the couple use it for their honeymoon. It consisted of one large guest cabin with four oarsmen in front of it, four behind, and one man to steer. It could skim across water faster than any craft Abram had ever seen, and it had been his delight to stand on deck with Sarai after they had left Uruk and headed upriver. They were going to Babylon and planned to take as much time as necessary.

The crew had docked the boat at a small town as the sun was setting and had gone ashore to find food and shelter for the night. They could sleep belowdecks in an emergency, but the space was cramped and the men preferred to sleep out in the open air. Abram and Sarai had retired to their cabin for the evening and had just dined on the food Zaroni had prepared for them. They sipped the last of the good wine that sparkled in their cups.

"This is a fine boat," Abram said. "Garai must have spent a fortune on it."

"He did," Sarai said. "I've made several trips in it. He let me help decorate it."

The cabin was not wide, no more than seven or eight feet, but it was fully twelve feet long. A bed at the stern end took up part of the room. There were two fine leather chairs covered with animal skins, and on the floor lay a luxurious carpet. A built-in cabinet was well stocked with food and drink, and two windows on each side admitted light and air.

Abram leaned over to look out the window, having to bend slightly, for the ceiling was low. "It's getting dark. I suppose we should turn in for the night. The crew will be back at daybreak."

"Yes . . . I suppose so," Sarai said nervously. She had told the truth to her mother that she had no idea how it was between men and women on the wedding night. Thoughts flitted through her mind—stories she had heard some of the servants tell as they laughed and joked among themselves—and she found herself afraid. This was unusual, for she was not a woman easily frightened.

Abram turned and studied her face. She was sitting on the edge of the bed, and he came over and sat down beside her. He put his arm around her and sat silently for a while. They heard the gentle ripple of waves against the side of the craft as other boats maneuvered into the dock for the night.

He turned her toward him and kissed her gently on the cheek and then on the lips. Suddenly Sarai grabbed him and said, "I don't know anything, Abram."

"You know you love me, don't you?"

"Oh yes, I know that!"

"And I know I love you. And I think that's all we need to know."

Sarai stroked his cheek and said, "I'm too sharp at times, Abram. I know that. Just beat me if I ever get that way again."

Abram laughed softly deep down in his chest. "I doubt if that will ever happen. But I'm worried about something."

"What is it?"

"You've always lived in town, and I've made an agreement with my brothers that I will take care of the flocks, for the most part, while Nahor and Haran attend to business in Ur. We'll have to live in a tent outside of town."

"I think that's a good arrangement. It's what you like."

"I know, but it won't be as comfortable as you're accustomed to. And it'll be lonely."

"You'll be home nights, won't you?"

"Days too, at times."

She stroked his cheek, feeling the smoothness of his beard, and said, "My mother says I'm to always be on your side, no matter what happens, and I will be. I promise, dear."

"And I'm always on your side. That's the way it should be with a man and wife. We may fight in private, but if anybody wants to get to you, they'll have to climb over me."

"And I feel the same."

The two sat quietly holding each other, and then Abram began to stroke her neck, sending chills down her back. She hardly realized she had lost her fear as she enjoyed his caresses. He made love to her with a gentleness that she had expected. But what was a surprise was finding out how passionately she returned his kisses, clinging fiercely to him with a desire he had awakened in her for the first time as they consummated their marriage.

Later, as they lay quietly in each other's arms and he stroked her shoulder, she whispered, "I'll always love you, Abram."

He propped himself on one elbow and looked at her beautiful face in the moonlight coming in through the window. His eyes danced teasingly as he asked, "And what will you do when I run off with another woman?"

Sarai laughed and grabbed his hair with both hands. "I'll never let you do that," she said, smiling. "I think I know how to keep you home."

"I think you do," he said, and then he kissed her with a passion that surprised them both.

CHAPTER

6

Gehazi had been the chief herdsman for Terah's family as long as Abram could remember. He was a short man, as lean as a desert lion. The sun had cooked his skin until it looked like burnished leather. His age was impossible to tell—it could be guessed at anywhere between forty and seventy. He and Abram now stood on a rise, inspecting the sheep that stretched out of sight before them.

"The increase has been amazing, Gehazi."

"Yes, it has, master. I've never seen a year like it," Gehazi replied in his husky voice, which was no more than a half whisper. He had spent more time with sheep and goats than he had with humans—indeed, felt more at home with them than with people. Scanning the flocks, his deep-set eyes were narrowed and wrinkled at the corners from years of enduring the blistering Sumerian sun. He nodded with satisfaction and turned to face Abram. "You've done well, master. How long is it? Five years since you took over from Nahor?"

"That's right."

"Well, you're a better man than he is."

"I wouldn't say that," Abram objected.

Gehazi had a special affection for Abram, having known him since he was an infant. "You'll have to make a good offering to Ishtar for this increase," he said.

Abram shook his head. "I'm going to give *you* the bonus, not Ishtar."

Gehazi blinked in surprise. There was a quality about his master that sometimes awed him but at other times troubled him, as it did now. "Don't do that, master."

"Why not?"

"You wouldn't want to get the gods upset."

"Gehazi, do you really think that a piece of stone in a temple twenty miles away has anything to do with the increase of our herds?"

"It's not wise to question the gods. Who knows what they might do?" Gehazi muttered huskily. "And I'll tell you what. She's a female god, and that makes it even worse."

Abram laughed aloud. "What do you mean it makes it worse?"

"Well, you know how women are."

"No. How are they? You tell me. You've had half a dozen wives."

"They get notions, that's what! They like to get us men in trouble."

Abram laid his hand on Gehazi's muscular shoulder and said, "You're the one who deserves the bonus. Don't worry about Ishtar."

"I don't like it, master. You're just asking for trouble."

Abram shook his head to signify that the conversation was over. "I'd like to move the flock tomorrow over to that grass by the river. It's better this year than I've ever seen it."

"I'll take care of it, master." Then Gehazi scratched his head and asked, "What about your brothers? I never see them anymore."

"Oh, they've become so busy with their business and trading in town that they don't care about coming out to see smelly goats and sheep."

"They'd better care," Gehazi said grimly. "This is what's real, not all that trading. A man can go broke and lose everything."

"Men can go broke raising sheep too."

"Not us," Gehazi said firmly. He had few fixed ideas, but one of them was very solid: town was bad and the world of nature was good.

"I'll send some of the other shepherds over to help you move the flock," Abram said. He turned and left Gehazi, feeling good about the increase in the flock. But as he made his way toward his and Sarai's tent, he began to think about how he had prospered. Even before he had married, he'd begun to doubt the power of the idols that kept their place in the temple. He knew with certainty now that a greater, unseen God heard his prayers. He said little of this to anyone other than Sarai, and he prayed more now than he had as a younger man. But it troubled him that he still did not know the name of the God to whom he prayed.

Threading his way through the flocks, he came to their large tent. It was bleached white to reflect the rays of the sun, and when he stooped to go in through the door flap, he smelled the fragrance of the incense that Sarai almost always burned. A sudden thought came to him. *I've been married for five years, and I've prospered. But Sarai isn't happy.*

He was more in love with her now than ever, and when he saw her lying facedown on their sleeping mat, he sat down beside her and put his hand on her shoulder. "What's wrong, Sarai?"

Sarai was wearing a light blue dress. She had bathed recently, for even in the desert Abram had made a tub for her out of animal skins set on a frame. He had assigned one of the shepherds the task of bringing river water and filling the tub up each day so that she could submerge herself in the coolness of the water. He knew she loved this daily ritual, but he also knew it was not enough to soothe her aching heart.

Pulling her up gently, Abram asked, "What's wrong, Sarai? I hate to find you like this."

Her enormous black eyes glistened with tears as she told him bluntly, "I'm not a good wife."

"Not a good wife? Why, you're the best wife in the whole world." He put his arms around her and stroked her jet black hair. She laid her cheek against his chest and let the tears flow. "Of course you're a good wife," he insisted, rubbing her back.

"But I've given you no son," she cried. "Not in five years."

"There's plenty of time for that. We're young. We'll have a dozen sons. You wait and see." He knew how her barrenness troubled her. She wanted desperately to have a child, and Abram had often wondered why they had not. They were very much in love, and by all the normal ways of the world, they should have had at least one child by now, and probably more. But no child had come. Sarai remained despondent, though not once had Abram let her see that he was disappointed. He knew that she often cried when he was not there, but now, even in his presence, she could not hide her sadness.

"Look, Sarai, I've made up my mind. We're going to spend some time in town."

Sarai brightened up. She had learned to live in the desert with her only companions the shepherds and the few other women who followed their husbands' flocks. They were not that far from town, and they went in from time to time for supplies and to visit their families. And yet she spent most days alone in their tent waiting for Abram to come home, after doing the few chores she had for just the two of them. She had found the loneliness overwhelming, and now she dashed the tears from her eyes. "Really?"

"Yes. We've had a good year, so we're going in, and we're going to buy you a whole new set of clothes, some jewelry, and a beautiful ring, and we're going to see your mother and your family again. Maybe we'll take a second honeymoon on that boat. Would you like that?"

"Oh yes!" Sarai threw her arms around him, and Abram patted her shoulder. At least for a time this would take Sarai's thoughts from her barrenness.

———————

The fact that Gehazi was completely and utterly dependable permitted Abram to leave the flock for an extended time. He took Sarai to her home in Ur, where they were royally greeted as always. Her mother, especially, was delighted that they could stay for a while, and they spent two weeks there being entertained. After that they went upriver on the same boat they had used for their honeymoon. This time they went even farther than Babylon, and when they returned, the boat was loaded with gifts for everyone. Babylon had a thriving market, and Sarai had spent days there picking out the most delightful gifts she could find.

When they returned, they stayed at Terah's house in a large room built especially for them. They were comfortable, and yet there was a sadness in being with Abram's family. Milcah, the wife of Nahor, had given him three sons, and Dehazi, the wife of Haran, had borne him a son, whom they called Lot. Sarai loved babies, and she spent every minute of her day helping to care for the two infants and playing with the older nephews. She tried to keep her sadness from Abram, but he was aware of it all the same.

After staying a month at Terah's house, Abram's father approached him, and Abram knew almost instantly that Terah was troubled. The older man insisted that they sit down, and he asked a servant to bring wine. For a time they talked of the flocks and herds and of the family trading ventures. It was the kind of talk Abram expected from Terah, for his father was primarily a man of business. His father acted nervous, however, and Abram kept waiting for him to bring up what he really wanted to talk about. Finally Terah cleared his throat and got to the point. "Son, I spoke with the high priest yesterday. He's been asking about you."

"Oh? What about, Father?"

"I think . . ." Terah faltered and lifted his cup. He drained it and said, "Well, he told me you haven't made an offering to Ishtar in a long time."

"Well, that's true enough."

Terah stared at his son, waiting for an explanation. Abram gathered his thoughts, then asked bluntly, "Father, do you really think Ishtar has any power?"

Terah's jaw dropped. "What are you talking about?"

"I mean just that. Do you really think that a block of stone has any feelings? That Ishtar knows anything?"

"It's dangerous to talk like that, son! The goddess might hear you."

"Father, Ishtar is made out of stone. Her ears are stone. How can stone ears hear anything?"

Terah was stunned by what Abram was saying. He himself was a solid individual who thought of little beyond the profit he could turn in a day. He liked his comfort, and he was fond of his family, but like all other dwellers of Sumer, he was deathly afraid of offending the gods. He lived in a world that was filled with catastrophe. Droughts burned up the crops, and floods wiped out whole communities. Sickness could come without warning, ravaging populations. Wild beasts could tear a man to bits. Terah had seen all these things happen, and although he had no deep feelings about religion, he was faithful to make offerings. With his voice lowered, he said urgently, "I hope you don't say things like this to anybody else."

"Only to Sarai."

"That's good." Terah breathed a sigh of relief.

"But think about it, Father," Abram protested. "Some man made Ishtar. A worker in stone took a chisel and a block of senseless rock and made a statue. And then after he made it, he bowed down to it—the very thing he himself made." Abram leaned forward and said, "Father, I'm desperate to find the God who made *me*, and it certainly wasn't Ishtar."

Terah was shocked to the very depth of his being. He had once been upset with Abram for paying too much attention to the gods, and now he was upset because he was paying none at all! He also knew that Rahaz, the high priest, was a powerful man in the community. He had ways of getting at people who did not bring their offerings to the temple. He had grown wealthy on such offerings, and for some time Terah tried to persuade Abram to at least make some outward gesture of appeasing Ishtar and the high priest.

He finally ended by saying, "A man needs to keep on good terms with the gods, son."

Abram saw that it was useless to argue with Terah. His father's thoughts were as shallow as those of most other people in Ur, and Abram wondered sadly if anybody except himself would ever believe in the true God. He listened as his father continued to urge him, and finally he put up his hand wearily. "All right. It means nothing to me. I'll take an offering by tomorrow."

"That's a good son!" Terah exclaimed with delight. He clapped Abram on the shoulder and heaved a sigh of relief. "That takes a load off my mind."

Abram kept his promise to Terah and made a token visit to the temple.

The high priest beamed to see him, exclaiming, "Well, I'm so happy to see you, my son!"

"I brought an extra offering since I've missed a few," Abram said. He saw a light in the eyes of the priest, eyes that were almost encased in fat.

"I'm sure Ishtar will bless you," Rahaz said, his words as oily as his skin.

Abram went through the charade of worship, then turned to leave, glad that it was over. When he reached his father's house, it was late afternoon, and he sat outside watching the sun go down. The outer court was quiet now, and the servants were busy inside preparing the evening meal. He could hear their voices faintly. He took his seat on a bench, leaned his head back against the wall, and for a time simply meditated on his life. It was a habit he had of letting all else fade away, and eventually he had discovered he could become completely unconscious of his material surroundings. He found himself praying silently, *Help me, O God that I do not know. I do not know your name, but I know that everything I see around me did not make itself. Nor did blocks of stone make anything. I believe that you made it all. Please hear my prayer and show yourself to me.*

Suddenly a shadow fell across his face, and Abram opened his eyes, startled to see an old man standing in front of him. He jumped to his feet and bowed, for the man appeared to be very old and rather weak. "Can I help you, sir?" Abram asked gently.

The old man had been tall once, as tall as Abram himself. Now time and difficulties had brought a stoop to his frame. Age lines crisscrossed his face, and he had few teeth, but his dark eyes were bright and alert. He leaned on his staff and coughed several times with a deep racking sound that alarmed Abram.

"Come in and let me give you something to eat," Abram offered, "and perhaps you need a place to stay tonight."

The old man straightened up, controlled his coughing, and stared at Abram. "What's your name?" the old man demanded. His voice was shocking, for it had the strength of a much younger man.

"Why, my name is Abram. This is my father's house. His name is Terah." The old man smiled slightly, and Abram could not fathom what it was about the ancient fellow that troubled him. "Come in," he repeated. "We're always glad to welcome a traveler."

The old man did not move, however, but stood silently for so long that Abram began to wonder if he was in his proper mind. He seemed to be alert, but he also appeared to be listening to something Abram himself could not hear.

"You don't remember me, do you?" the old man finally said.

"No, sir, I don't think I do. Have we met?"

The smile grew more pronounced. "Yes, we have met many times. The last time I saw you, you were very young, and I took you fishing down at the river. You caught a turtle and it frightened you. But we ate him for supper that night."

A faint memory began to stir in Abram, and then suddenly he straightened up and gasped with surprise. "Grandfather?"

"Yes, I'm your grandfather. Old Nahor come home to die."

Abram could not believe his ears, but he had to believe his eyes. The memories were faint, and the family had long ago decided that Nahor had died on one of his journeys. But as Abram stood before him, something in the wise old eyes convinced him, and he stepped forward and put his arms around the old man. "I remember you well!" he cried. "You used to tell me wonderful stories!"

When Abram went to fetch his father, Terah did not want to believe that Nahor was out in the courtyard, and he was reluctant to follow Abram. But follow he did, and when Terah saw Nahor for himself, he was stupefied. He spoke to the old man cautiously, trying to convince himself that this was an impostor.

The old man's mind, however, was sharp, and he saw Terah's plight at once. "You think I've come home to take over as head of the family, don't you?" Nahor said.

This was exactly what Terah had been thinking, but he blustered, "Why, certainly not, Father!"

Abram was standing beside his grandfather. He almost laughed when he saw how easily the old man read his son.

Terah's face could conceal nothing, and now he stammered unconvincingly, "Why... why, I'm happy to see you!"

"Well, you needn't worry that I'll usurp your place," Nahor assured him. "I've just come home to die."

Terah blinked with shock. "Why, that's no way to talk!"

Nahor smiled and shook his head slightly. "All I need is a bed to lie on and some bread once in a while."

"We can do better than that, Father," Terah said. "Come inside. I'll send for my sons. We'll have a celebration."

Terah scurried off, and Nahor turned to his grandson. "He hasn't changed much."

"Really?"

"No, he's as easy to read as a child." Nahor stepped closer and peered into Abram's face. "You're not like him. You're more like me."

Abram grinned broadly. "That's what everyone says."

"Do they, now?" Nahor's dark eyes danced with amusement. "We'll have to have some talks, you and I."

"I'll look forward to that, Grandfather."

Nahor's return to Ur made little change in the household. He received the greetings of the family as if he had been only gone a week. For the most part he resisted the urge to tell about his travels, and for several days did little but sleep and eat. Sarai saw to it that he received nourishing food. She was fascinated by the old man and made sure that he got the best of care.

Terah still remained unconvinced that his father had no intentions of taking back his place as the head of the house.

"You haven't been listening to him, Father," Abram told him.

"What do you mean, son?"

"He's not interested in this world."

Terah stared at Abram. "Which world, then?"

"The one that exists beyond death."

Terah shook his head doubtfully. "He's not still looking for that one God, is he?"

For a moment Abram did not answer. Then he said so softly that Terah almost missed it, "I believe he's found Him."

"The river hasn't changed," Nahor said. He was sitting down with his feet in the waters that swept by, and Abram sat cross-legged beside him. The two had formed the habit of coming down to the river in the cool of the evening after the sun had set. At first, Nahor had waited for Abram to pepper him with questions but soon discovered that the young man knew how to be silent. It was a quality Nahor admired, and he found a great deal of pleasure in simply sitting beside this tall young grandson of his.

The western horizon still glowed red, but the desert air was cooling quickly now. From time to time Nahor reached down, cupped his hand, captured the water, and poured it over his head, washing the sandy grit from his hair. Finally he turned to Abram and said, "Well, the others think the crazy man has returned. What do *you* think?"

Abram had discovered that Nahor had a quick sense of humor, and he answered lightly, "I think I'm as crazy as you, Grandfather."

Nahor laughed with delight. "You're like me, all right. I can see it in you."

"Are we both crazy, then?" Abram asked, more serious now.

Nahor gazed deeply into the younger man's eyes. "Any man who gives up this world to find God will be called crazy."

A chill ran down Abram's back as he digested this thought.

Nahor watched Abram's serious countenance, pleased that the young man did not dismiss his words. *He's a thinker. He doesn't talk a great deal, but he doesn't forget much either. He's like me, all right.*

Finally Abram said, "My family has told me that you left us to find God. Did you find Him, Grandfather?"

Nahor stared down at the waters at his feet, then lifted his eyes to the broad stream that flowed eastward, carrying the rich silt down to the big sea. Then he began to speak as he had not done since his return. He spoke of his journeys to impossible places, and his voice grew tense as he told of the sufferings that he'd endured on his travels.

"I almost gave up more than once, grandson," he said, his voice little more than a whisper. "In every town I came to I went to the temples, and I prayed to whatever god was there. You wouldn't believe, grandson, how many crazy idols I've prayed to—and all of them were worthless."

Abram was absolutely silent, straining his ears to hear every word. He was fascinated by this old man, blood of his blood and bone of his bone, and he knew that there was a mystic bond between the two of them, such as he had never felt with any other human being.

Finally the old man fell silent, staring up at the rising moon. Taking a deep breath, he turned to Abram and said, "And then—I found Him! I was in the desert, at the end of my rope, tired of searching. I had found out that there were almost as many gods as there are men, Abram. For years I had sought for truth among these gods, but I found nothing. I was so tired, I was sick of myself." He suddenly lifted his hands and, with exultation in his voice, exclaimed, "But there in the desert the one who whispered to me so many years ago came to me!"

"You saw Him?" Abram whispered urgently. "Did He tell you His name?"

"He has many names, and yes, He spoke to me, grandson. He actually *spoke* to me! I heard His voice. It wasn't just something in my head or in my heart. I think if you had been there, you would have heard it too. I saw a light that glowed like nothing on this earth, and then He spoke to me. He said, 'Nahor, you have sought me faithfully, and I desire to be your friend.' "

"Did He tell you His name?" Abram repeated breathlessly. "I long to know His name, Grandfather."

"I asked the same question . . . and He told me to call Him the Eternal One."

Abram gripped his grandfather's arm and demanded, "What did He look like?"

Nahor shook his head and answered sternly, "He is not a *man*, Abram! He doesn't look like anything. God is not a man like us. He made us."

The old man talked until his voice grew weary, and finally Abram said, "I want to hear Him too."

"I see that you have a great hunger to know Him, my son, but only those who seek Him with all their heart will find Him."

"Then I will seek Him with all my heart," Abram said solemnly. "I will seek Him if it takes my entire life."

Nahor smiled with pleasure. He reached out to take the young man's hand and felt the strength of it. Then he said, "And you *will* find Him, Abram. It may cost you everything—but it will be worth it!"

CHAPTER
7

Abram was spending more and more time with his grandfather. The two had become inseparable, and it disturbed Terah so much he finally complained to Haran one day as they watched Abram and Nahor from the portico across the courtyard.

"Those two bother me," Terah muttered.

"Why is that, Father?"

"You know very well why. You've heard me tell often enough how my father lost his mind over religion."

Haran looked out to where Abram and his grandfather were sitting in the shade of a potted palm in the late afternoon. The old man was moving his arms about in expansive gestures as Abram listened.

"I don't think there's any danger of that," Haran said. "Abram has settled down now that he's married. He's got more sense than to go off and lose his mind over religion. As a matter of fact, you had to force him to make an offering to Ishtar, didn't you?"

"Yes, but my father's always had this wild idea that there's only *one* God. I'm afraid Abram is being taken in by such dangerous thoughts."

Haran's eyes opened wide. "*One* God? I can't believe it. Why, everybody knows there are thousands of gods."

"Everybody except my own father," Terah grumbled bitterly. "Look at them. I wish he hadn't come home."

Haran stared at his father and shook his head. "I think it'll be all right. Abram's a little strange, but he's got a good head on his shoulders."

"He's got a head that's being packed full of all kinds of nonsense! I wish I could do something about it, but he won't listen to me. Why don't you try to talk to him, Haran?"

"I will if you want me to, but I doubt it will do any good."

From the courtyard, Nahor was aware that he and Abram were being watched. He smiled and said to Abram, "Your father is worried about you. He thinks I'm going to poison you with my ideas." The thought amused him, and he laughed deep in his chest. "He was always a worrier—always worrying about the wrong things!"

Nahor nodded across the courtyard at Terah and Haran, and the two men, embarrassed at having been spotted, turned quickly to go back inside. Abram watched his father and brother leave, then turned his eyes back to Nahor and said, "Tell me about our family, Grandfather. I know practically nothing."

"Our family? Well, I've been meaning to talk to you about that. Terah doesn't seem to take much pride in the family, but I do." He settled himself on the stone bench and locked his fingers together, his eyes growing dreamy, it seemed to Abram. "My own father's name was Serug. I left his home many years ago, when I was young and impetuous—and not interested in learning the wisdom he had to pass on. I will tell you more of him—when the time is right—but you should know of those who came before. My grandfather's name was Reu, and Reu's father was Peleg. Peleg's father was Eber. His father was Shelah, and Shelah's father was Arphaxad. I could tell you stories about all of these men, and I will if I live long enough, but Arphaxad's father was a very unusual man. His name was Shem."

"Shem? I think I've heard of him."

"Well, you should have. He was one of Noah's sons. You *have* heard of him, haven't you?"

"No, not a great deal."

"I ought to beat that son of mine! You'd think he'd have enough pride in his family to pass along the stories of the great men."

Nahor looked up and watched as a line of birds flitted their way across the sky toward the river. After they disappeared from sight, he said, "After the world was created, men sinned and grew very bad, until the Eternal One was wearied by the iniquity of men. He chose to destroy the whole world by a flood, but He had His eye on one man, a righteous and just man whose name was Noah. . . ."

Nahor spoke for a long time, describing the history of the flood and how God had saved Noah and his wife, his three sons, and their wives. Then he turned to Abram and said, "Noah had three sons—Shem, Ham, and Japheth. It would take too long to go into the history of Ham and Japheth and their descendants. But I will tell you of Shem, for it is through his line that the

Eternal One has chosen to bring a great gift to the world."

"What gift?" Abram whispered, his eyes fixed on his grandfather.

"I'm not exactly sure, but the Eternal One has told me that out of our family will come One who will redeem the whole earth and bring peace and righteousness."

"When will that happen?"

"I cannot say. The Eternal One has not told me." Nahor put his hand on Abram's knee. "But you come from proud stock, grandson. You are a chosen one, a son of the Eternal One. We may never see the promise fulfilled, but we can be sure that one day from our blood will come a redeemer."

Abram sat listening as his grandfather spoke of his family, that which had been and that which was to come. The shadows grew long as the sun descended in the western sky, and still the two of them talked on—the older one speaking of the greatness of the God he had found, and the younger one aching with the desire to meet this Eternal One. Abram finally whispered, "I can't believe that out of all the people on earth, the Eternal One has chosen our family."

"He is the great and almighty One. The One who always was. The One who created all that you see—the stars, the moon, the sun, the rivers. He made the mountains, and He made the plains. But His joy is not in these things. His joy, my son, is in man. Even though man has gone far away from what the Eternal One intended, He has told me that He will not destroy the earth again—at least not by water—but He will redeem men. Even our own family does not recognize that through them lies the whole hope of the world."

Nahor suddenly pulled at the leather thong around his neck. Abram had noticed it and watched curiously as the old man opened a pouch with a drawstring. He removed a round object and, for a moment, held it in the palm of his hand so that Abram could not see it.

"Look, grandson. . . ."

Abram looked at the object that Nahor handed to him. It was a round medallion made of gold, and Abram saw that it was engraved with the image of a lion. The beast was very lifelike. He had one paw uplifted in victory, but it was the eyes that caught Abram's attention. They were made of brilliant gemstones such as he had never seen. Even in the fading light they glittered like the stars overhead. He stared at it in silence, then whispered, "It's beautiful, Grandfather! Where did you get it?"

"That which you hold in your hand is older than anything you've ever touched," Nahor said quietly. "It once belonged to Seth, the son of Adam, the first man. Seth gave it to his son, and it's been passed down for many generations. Noah received it and gave it to his son Shem. Each man who receives it has the obligation of keeping himself close to the Eternal One— and of passing the medallion on to the next one God chooses."

"What does it mean, Grandfather?"

"I don't know, Abram. I don't think any man who has carried it knows the full significance of it. But it means *something* special—I know that much. I believe the lion has something to do with the redeemer who will come, though I'm not sure what. Look at the back of the medallion."

Abram reversed the disk. "A lamb."

"Yes, and that has meaning too—but no man knows what it is. One day it will be clear to the bearer of the lion."

"Who will you give it to?"

"I will give it to whomever the Eternal One tells me. It's not my choice, Abram, but God himself will show me the man who is to bear this medallion, and I will place it on his neck before I die!" He then took the medallion, replaced it in the leather pouch, and slipped it under his robe. "And I think that will not be too long, grandson!"

Months passed, and Abram returned to his flocks with Sarai, but he also took his grandfather with them. He was aware that Terah was relieved to have his father out of his home, although he made a formal protest that the desert was no place for an old man. "He needs to be here where we can care for him and give him comfort."

When Nahor heard this he snorted, "Comfort! I'm not interested in comfort. You can have the town. It was made by men. I want to go out and live in that part of the world God made, with the open spaces stretching before me and the sky above me."

As Abram and Nahor tended the flocks together and talked often of eternal things, Abram absorbed more and more of the spirit that was in his grandfather. And the desire to know God, the Eternal One, the true God, grew in him so much it was painful.

Sarai watched all this with a careful eye. She had learned to love Abram's grandfather, for she found Nahor had some of the same qualities she admired in her husband. The old man was at times sharp with his words, but he also had a gentleness about him that Sarai found endearing, and she cared for him tenderly, seeing after his comfort.

"Do you think he will live much longer, Abram?" she asked one day when the two of them had drawn aside. Abram had spent all morning listening to Nahor teach him more of the lessons and insights he had learned over a lifetime.

"I hope so. I have so much more to learn from him. There's no one like him, Sarai."

"I agree, he is unusual." She sometimes listened as Nahor spoke about the one true God he claimed to have met, and she wanted to know more herself. Now as she and Abram walked together, looking over the flocks that grazed in the distance, she asked, "What do you make of all that Grandfather says about this one God he professes to know?"

"I think it's all true," Abram said simply. He reached down and took her hand, a habit he had which pleased her very much. Having no child, Sarai reveled in his shows of affection.

Smiling up at him, she said, "If this God is anything like you, my dear husband, I want to believe in Him too. But I can't help wondering how everyone in the world can be so wrong. We've all been taught that there are thousands of gods. Where did such an idea come from if it's not at all true?"

"I can't answer that, but I know in my heart that this God that my grandfather has met is the One I've been seeking for all these years."

"But why doesn't He speak to you? You've been such a good man, and you've been searching for so long."

"I don't think our time is the same as His time. He's called the Eternal One, Grandfather says. We live for a few years and then we're gone. Just think what His name means—the Eternal One—He has always been, and He always will be! Isn't that exciting?"

Sarai smiled at her husband. She remembered that she had promised to support him in every way, and now she said, "You'll find Him. I know you will."

"And you'll find Him too, Sarai. I know that one day—" He broke off and lifted his gaze. Shading his eyes, he peered off in the distance. "Someone's coming in a hurry. Look at the dust they're raising."

The two stood waiting for the figure on a donkey to approach, and then Abram said, "Why, that's Hillel. There must be something wrong at home."

The two of them waited until Terah's trusted servant brought the donkey to a halt in front of them. Hillel's face was fixed with a strange expression.

"What's wrong, Hillel? Is someone sick?"

"It's your brother Haran," Hillel said. He hesitated, licked his lips, and then went on. "He's been hurt. Your father wants you to come at once."

"How bad is he?" Abram demanded.

Hillel dropped his eyes and shook his head. "Very bad, I'm afraid," he muttered. "A wall fell on him and crushed him. He was examining the new building he and your father are working on."

"Sarai, stay here and take care of Grandfather," Abram ordered. "I'll be back as soon as I can."

Sarai watched as Abram mounted his own donkey, and he and Hillel disappeared toward the city. She turned and started for the tent to give Nahor the bad news, and when she told the old man, his face grew sad. "I hope he lives. Haran is a good man. He's become too interested in business, but there's still time for him to change. He's young."

As soon as Abram went into the bedroom where Haran was lying, he knew immediately that his brother could not live. Haran's wife, Dehazi, knelt on one side of his bed, while the other members of the family stood around the walls of the room. Abram went at once to kneel beside the bed. He took Haran's still hand and whispered, "How are you, brother?" He thought at first that Haran was already dead, but then he saw the faint rise and fall of the chest. Haran's face was battered and scarred, his chest black and blue. There was, however, a flicker of life, and the eyes opened. "I came as soon as I could," Abram whispered.

Haran tried to speak, but his voice was so faint Abram had to lean forward. He caught the words, "Please... look after Lot, Abram. Dehazi cannot raise a son all alone."

Abram at once squeezed his brother's hand. "I will. I'll be a second father to him. You have my promise on it, my dear brother."

Haran nodded slightly and then closed his eyes. He said nothing more, and Abram got to his feet. He turned to his parents and saw his mother's tear-stained face. He went to her and put his arms around her, and she fell against him, her body shaking as she wept.

"He can't live," Terah whispered, sadness in his eyes. He had always been very close to his Haran, and now great sorrow etched the old man's face. He looked drawn and wan and shook his head. "There's nothing we can do."

Indeed, there was nothing to do, and despite the many prayers and special offerings made to the gods, Haran died the next day. He struggled for life, but his body had been crushed beyond any healing that man or stone god could offer.

Abram went back to get his grandfather and Sarai and bring them to the funeral. After Haran was laid to rest, Abram said to Sarai, "We'll stay in town awhile and comfort my parents and Dehazi as best we can."

"That's the right thing to do," Sarai agreed.

"I made a promise to my brother to look after Lot, to be a father to him."

"That is good, my husband," Sarai said. "And I will be only too glad to help Dehazi with her baby in any way I can. As the boy grows he can visit us whenever he likes," Sarai went on. "You can teach him the things of the desert."

"Yes, he'll be like a son to us." He squeezed Sarai then, and she smiled up at him.

"It'll be all right," she assured him.

The death of Haran affected Abram strongly. He was silent, for the most part, but thought of his brother often. They had not been as close as he would have liked, and now Abram regretted he had not spent more time with his brother.

He told his grandfather of his feelings and then asked, "Do you think I will ever see him again? What happens to us when we die?"

Nahor had grown visibly weaker during the past weeks. He ate practically nothing now, except that which Sarai forced upon him, and he stayed flat on his back most of the time. Abram was sitting by him where he could see his face. Nahor had lost so much weight that Abram thought it impossible for him to live much longer. That gave Abram all the more reason to listen to him and ask questions. "I've wondered about what happens after we die. What do you think, Grandfather?"

"I've heard all kinds of notions in my travels," Nahor whispered. His lips scarcely moved, and his eyes were dull, not sharp as they once were. "I believe that men live in another life after this one."

"Have you ever asked the Eternal One?"

"He has told me very little about the life to come." Nahor drifted off to sleep then, and Abram sat with him for a long time. Finally he got up heavily and went back out to the flocks, leaving the care of his grandfather to Sarai.

He had not been gone long when Sarai came running to him. "It's your grandfather. I think he's dying."

Abram broke into a run and reached the tent before Sarai. He rushed inside and fell on his knees. "Grandfather!" he cried and saw that the old man's eyes were open. "Don't die," he pleaded. "I have so much yet to learn."

Nahor spoke then in a weak voice. "Take the pouch from off my neck."

The leather pouch that Nahor always wore had slipped to one side. Abram slipped it off his head and held it. "What shall I do with it?"

"Open it, my son."

Abram opened the pouch and removed the round disk. He remembered Nahor showing it to him several months earlier, but now he studied it again. He held it up before his eyes and admired the beautifully executed carving of a lion. Turning it over, he studied the peaceful lamb.

"I remember this, Grandfather." He looked down to see that his grandfather's eyes were clear and that he was smiling.

"That is, I think, the most precious object in the world," Nahor said. "Remember how I told you it has been passed down through our family from Adam himself?"

"Yes, I remember."

"It is only given to the one that the Eternal One chooses. It is not always passed from father to son, but it is always kept in our family. After the Eternal One showed himself to me in the wilderness, he told me to return to the home of my father. In our time together my father taught me much about the One I had sought for so long. . . . If only I had not left my father's home as a boy. . . things would have been so different. I would not have had to search so long and hard to know the Eternal One. But life is what it is. . . ."

Nahor's words faded. His eyes closed, and Abram feared he would not speak again. But after a moment the old man smiled and began again. "During one of our discussions my father passed the medallion to me—his message was clear. He told me that the Eternal One had told him to give it to me, and he charged me to wait until I heard from God before I gave it to anyone else." Nahor placed his trembling hand on Abram's arm. "God spoke to me last night, my dear grandson—the Eternal One, the One who is the God of all love, appeared to me. And He instructed me to give this to *you*."

Abram felt his hands trembling. "But I'm not worthy," he said.

"No man is worthy. The Eternal One alone is worthy."

"What does it mean?"

"It means the Eternal One is working out His purpose. Somehow you have a great work to do for Him. He has not told me what it is, but He will speak to you. After I'm gone, wait for Him and He will come. Keep yourself free from the bonds of earthly concerns. Your father and your brother think only of this world, but you must think of another one, a world where the Eternal One is king. Think of the redeemer who is coming, the one who will be of our blood."

Nahor reached up with a frail hand, took Abram's hand, and whispered,

"Kiss me, my son. I go to my beloved, the Eternal One."

With tears flowing down his face, Abram leaned forward and kissed his grandfather on the cheek. The old man embraced him strongly for a moment, almost with the strength of a young man, and then Abram felt the old arms relax.

Abram saw that Nahor had ceased to breathe. He had almost imperceptibly slipped out of his body, a body that now lay withered and still. Abram closed the old man's eyes, arranged the arms, and pushed back the hair. Then he turned to Sarai, who had entered the tent. "Did you hear?" he asked her.

Sarai's eyes were large. "Yes, I heard."

Abram rose, and Sarai came to stand beside him. They looked down at the old man and did not speak. Somehow they knew their lives would change, and Sarai felt a sudden fear. She clung to her husband, wondering what time would bring.

For two months after the funeral of his grandfather, Abram went about his work in a perfunctory way. He could not get away from the last words his grandfather had spoken, and many times he would reach up and touch the pouch that he now wore around his neck. Often he would take out the medallion and stare at it, wondering what the lion and the lamb meant. He knew that Sarai was worried about him, for although he tried to be cheerful, his mind and heart and soul were constantly reaching out to the Eternal One, desperately seeking His presence. He fasted and prayed almost continuously, so much so that he lost weight.

He went out very early one morning, long before the sun was up, intending to look for several sheep that had wandered away. He had left Sarai sleeping, and now he traipsed across the rocky earth in the chill air of the predawn hours. He picked his way through the scrub brush by the light of the moon, thinking not so much of the missing animals as of the Eternal One. He finally found the wayward sheep and sat down near them as they were feeding. He sat there for a long time, just thinking and remembering and wondering what was to come.

Gradually he became aware that he was not alone. He looked up, expecting to see one of his shepherds coming for the sheep, but he saw no one. Still he had an uncanny feeling that he was not alone. And then immediately in front of him he saw what appeared to be a light. At first he thought it was simply the glare of the sunrise, but then he realized that was impossible because the sun had not yet risen.

The light continued to grow, and fear seized him when he realized he was in the presence of the Eternal One, the God of his grandfather Nahor. He fell on his knees and put his forehead on the ground, conscious that the light was growing. It expanded more and more until, even with his eyes closed, he could sense the brightness of it. And then the voice spoke:

"Abram, you have been faithful to seek my face. I have chosen you, and you will serve me in a way that will bring glory to my name."

Abram rose and tried to open his eyes, but the light was unbearable to look at. He felt as if he were being washed in it, not only outwardly but also inwardly. The light seemed to flow down through his entire body, and tears began to roll down his face. He could not speak a word, but he listened as the voice continued:

"I will make you into a great nation and I will bless you. I will make your name great, and you will be a blessing. I will bless those who bless you, and whoever curses you I will curse. And all peoples on earth will be blessed through you."

Then Abram cried out, "O strong and eternal God, how can I be father of a great nation? I don't even have *one* son."

There was silence for a moment and then the voice came again, and as Abram listened, comfort and joy flowed through him. Both the voice and the light were powerful, life-giving.

God said, *"Obey my voice. My promise is sure, and my word is sure. I have chosen you, and you will be my servant."*

Abram never knew how long he knelt there with his head bowed to the earth. Time did not seem to matter. The light continued to flow through him until finally he was aware that it was fading. Quickly he lifted himself and looked around. The light and the voice were gone.

Shakily, on weakened legs, Abram got to his feet. He turned and stumbled away, crying aloud, "O Eternal God, I will never again pray to any god except you! And I will believe you. Even though I have no son, I will believe your promise."

He stumbled blindly back toward his tent to tell Sarai. He did not understand how or why, but somehow God, the Eternal One, the One who never changes, had chosen him. An inexplicable joy filled Abram of Ur of the Chaldees, for he knew that now, at last, he had found the true God!

CHAPTER

8

For some reason Abram had never considered the problem of getting old—but the truth occurred to him late one afternoon while he was hunting with his nephew Lot. Perhaps he had never thought about it because his people all lived to an advanced age. Even one hundred was still considered quite young. Abram's grandfather had told him that before the flood it was not unusual for people to live over five hundred years.

Abram had always been an extremely strong and healthy man. He was not large, but he was quick and agile, with muscles like those of a leopard—lean rather than bulky. He had never been sick a day in his life and had given no thought before to passing out of youth into middle age. Not until late one afternoon when he was with Lot, now fifteen years old, and he discovered he was not the man he had been at his marriage twenty years earlier.

Since the death of Lot's father, Haran, Abram and Sarai had practically adopted the boy as their own son. Abram felt a great affection for the lad, who had grown strong and powerful. Lot's mother had become so depressed after the death of her husband that she needed much help in raising her son. Her mother-in-law and Sarai both helped with the infant, and as the child grew, Abram had taken the boy out of the city to grow up among the sheep and goats. Dehazi's family arranged for her to marry an uncle, a man with two other wives and many children. It pained her greatly to part with her son, but she agreed that Lot would be better off with his loving uncle and aunt, who still had no children of their own, than becoming part of such a large family, where he would have to work in town to help support them. Lot had been a joy to Abram and Sarai and had grown large for his age and proficient with the bow and sling.

Abram and Lot had left on their hunt at noon and had been unsuccessful until they finally came upon a hart at a small watering hole. They had crept to a hiding place downwind from the animal, and at a signal from Abram, both had loosed their arrows. Abram saw with chagrin that his own arrow missed by a fraction, but Lot's arrow caught the hart in the body. The wound was not instantly fatal, however, and the animal bounded off.

"He's getting away!" Lot cried. "Come on, Uncle!"

The two plunged after the wounded animal, and for a time Abram, with his longer legs, stayed in the lead. But the animal, apparently not as seriously wounded as they had thought, ran a good race. They were following him by the blood marks that he left, and after fifteen minutes of strenuous running, Abram felt his side aching and his breath coming in gasps. He was forced to slow his pace, and as he did so his young nephew shot by him.

Lot cried, "Come on, Uncle, he's getting away!" and ran even faster. Abram was stung by the lad's challenge and forced himself forward as rapidly as he could move his legs. After another few minutes, however, he knew he could not keep up and had to slow down to a walk. He put his hand over his aching side and saw Lot's black hair in the distance. The boy was jumping up and down, waving his bow and shouting, "Come on, I've got him, Uncle Abram!"

Abram walked along painfully, dodging the scrub bushes that contained knifelike thorns, and, for the first time in his life, he became aware of his own mortality.

There was a time, not long ago, when that boy could not have outrun me. He's only fifteen years old, and yet I can't keep up with him. I'm getting old. I can't do the things I once could. For some reason these thoughts shot through him like a shouted warning. He had known, of course, as a matter of theory, that he would grow older and one day would die as all men do, but this was the first sound of that distant trumpet. *You're getting old, Abram.* He knew he was still much stronger than other men his age, but it half angered him that his body refused to obey his will. Abram was not a proud man—at least not consciously so—but this failure stung him.

Lot greeted him, laughing and shouting, "Look, I got him, Uncle! He slowed down, and I ran forward and wrestled him down and cut his throat." He held the scarlet-stained bronze knife high, and the boy's face was filled with exultation.

"Well, let's dress him out and take him back," Abram said wearily.

"But wasn't it exciting, Uncle?"

"We should have hit him in the heart so he wouldn't have run us half to death," Abram said grumpily. He saw the boy's face fall and knew he had hurt his feelings. Lot was a sensitive young man in almost every way, and Abram at once felt compunction. He went forward and tapped Lot on the shoulders. "You did fine, son. I missed him altogether. You've gotten to be a better hunter than your teacher."

"Oh no, it was just fun, Uncle," Lot said quickly.

As Abram helped the boy dress the hart, he felt a sense of gratitude. Lot had become a handsome lad, with glossy black hair, rich and thick, and noble features. His nose was small for one of his race, and his cheekbones were high and almost delicate. His mouth was sensitive and often turned upward in a smile, and he had a rich golden tan from the suns of fifteen summers.

I may not have a son, but this boy is like a son to me, Abram thought. *If it doesn't please the Eternal One to give me children, at least I'll have this one. He will be a son to me.*

They took only minutes to dress out the deer, and dividing the bloody load, they started back toward the camp. As they moved along through the scrub and scant grass of the desert, Abram listened with half of his mind as Lot chatted on about the hunt and other things that interested him. Abram's attention was turned toward the time that Nahor, his grandfather, had died. Unconsciously he reached up and touched the pouch that he wore constantly around his neck. He could feel the hard form of the medallion inside the soft leather and had the sudden urge to take it out and look at it. He had little need to do so, however, for he had fixed the image firmly in his memory after years of staring at it. He still had no idea what the lion signified, nor the lamb on the reverse side, but he could remember clearly, as if they were spoken the previous day, the words of Nahor telling him that the Eternal One had chosen him to carry the medallion and to pass it along when his time was done.

A gathering of tents loomed up before them. The camp in which Abram and Sarai lived had grown to include the families of the shepherds and herdsmen that worked for Abram. The colored tents were woven of wool and dyed blue and red and green, while others were blinding white. This was Abram's home, and as always, it gave him a feeling of joy and satisfaction. True enough, he had a moving home, not like his father's house, which was built of sunbaked bricks. No, Abram's life was that of a nomad. One day he might be in the south, in the dry country, and the next week they might move to find fresh grasses and feed for the flocks. As always, there was an ongoing search for water, so the tents had to be light and easily transported. But no matter where the tents were set up, they were home because Abram's life centered on Sarai, who was, after all these years, still the love of his heart.

As they moved into the encampment, Abram reached down and stroked one of the dogs he had domesticated. It was in his mind to breed them and teach them to herd sheep. This was a heretical idea to most herdsmen, for dogs had never been used for such a purpose. Wild dogs were the natural enemies of the flocks. But Abram had found this particular dog when he was no more than a puppy, apparently abandoned by his mother. He was a strange color—almost blue—with shaggy, coarse hair and was large, with a broad forehead and intelligent deep brown eyes. He was a powerful animal but had become a companion to Abram as he tended his flocks. Abram had named him Nimrod. He remembered how his grandfather, in reciting the ancestry of his people, had named Nimrod as a mighty hunter before the Lord, and since the dog proved to be an excellent hunter, often running down wild hare and other small game and bringing them to Abram's feet, the name seemed suitable. He bent over and said, "Nimrod, good dog." The dog whined and, as was his habit, opened his mighty jaws and closed them on Abram's wrist. He held the man there for a moment and then released him.

"You like that dog, don't you, Uncle Abram?" Lot asked brightly. "So do I. I wish I had one like him."

"You have to train them, boy. They're wild by nature. You have to get one when it's just a pup. I fed this one by hand until I was like his mother. You can't just take a half-grown wild dog out of the desert. He'll turn on you every time."

It was the sort of instruction Abram gave Lot constantly. There were schools in town for the boys who lived there, but Lot seemed to care little for them, although Abram had offered him the choice of going. Now he looked with approval at the boy, for Lot was a handsome, bright lad. In Abram's mind he was the best-looking and quickest of all the boys in Ur.

A thought flashed through his mind as he moved toward his own tent, where Sarai was standing to greet him. *I've been waiting all these years for the Eternal One to appear to me again, but He's been absolutely silent. I wonder if I've offended Him in some way so that He will not speak to me.* This thought often troubled him. After that first appearance, he had expected the Eternal One to appear regularly, but there had been nothing but silence since. One good thing had come of it, though. Abram had learned for certain that he was praying to the right God. Even though he had not heard from Him for many years, Abram was confident that one day, when it was time, the Eternal One would come to him again.

"So, you've brought supper." Sarai moved forward and lifted her face for Abram's kiss. Their affection was strong and deep, stronger than it had been when they were young. The early flames of their youthful passion had subsided now to a steady, warm glow, but for each of them, the other filled the world in which they moved.

"I shot it, Aunt Sarai," Lot said proudly.

"Good for you!" Sarai exclaimed. She reached over and kissed the boy and hugged him. "You're getting to be a great hunter."

Abram thought of how the boy had outrun him, and his pride rose up, but he fought the urge to defend himself, praising the boy instead. "He did indeed make the kill... *and* he outran his old uncle here to bring the beast down!"

"Well, you will get the best part of the meat, son," Sarai said proudly. "Here, let me get started on this." She called loudly, "Layona, come and help me."

Layona came forward at once, and as Abram glanced at her, he could see little sign of the frightened, skinny girl he had purchased twenty years ago. She was a mature woman now and had been a faithful servant to Sarai's household all these years. She had not always lived in the desert with Abram and Sarai, but in recent years she had agreed to join them there. She was really more like one of the family than a slave, and she smiled at Lot and winked, saying, "I hear that you killed this beast yourself."

"I did, Layona, and Aunt Sarai says I get the best part of it!"

"Well, you come along, and I'll let you pick it out."

Abram began to follow them, but as the two moved away, he felt Sarai grab his arm. "You come with me," she ordered. "You're filthy. You need to wash and lie down and rest."

"Why, you treat me like an old man!" he griped.

"I don't think you're an old man," Sarai said and smiled knowingly up at him. "You've proved that to me often enough."

Abram laughed and reached out to embrace her. "I'll prove it again tonight, my love!" He kissed her and marveled again at her beauty. She was, to him, even more beautiful now than when he had first seen her. Her figure was still that of a young woman, and even the desert sun had not been able to destroy her complexion. True, she was not as pale as she had been when he had first seen her. But her complexion was now even more attractive— golden, tinged with the sun, but as smooth and clear as alabaster. Her outdoor life had given her a fresh, hearty coloring, and Abram felt a pride as he looked at her. He was aware that every man who saw her was taken by her beauty, but there was no jealousy in him, for he knew that her love was only for him.

After he had washed up, the two sat down in front of their tent, the largest one in the camp. He looked out over the work that was going on, noting that one woman was churning cream in a device he himself had invented. It consisted of a tripod of saplings on which was suspended a long stick. At one end of the stick was tied a goatskin bag filled with the cream. A small woman was rocking the stick back and forth, her mind elsewhere as her arm moved rhythmically. She would keep this up, Abram knew, until the butter was rich and creamy, and then it would be removed from the goatskin bag.

He looked over to his left and saw a woman on her knees in front of a flat stone that was slightly hollowed out in the middle. Holding a smaller stone in her hand, she was grinding meal for the daily flatbread. After the grain was cracked, it was further refined into flour with a mortar and pestle. After this it was moistened, shaped into flat loaves, and then baked on hot stones. The bread was the mainstay of the nomadic diet, for it was light and easily carried to the next campsite.

"It's nice here," Sarai murmured, looking about them. "The flowers are beautiful this year."

It was the sort of thing Sarai would notice, and indeed the flowers were striking. Many of them were yellow, but there were delicate purple and blue ones, and here and there among them a crimson flower dotted the landscape. The lowing of the cattle made a soft music, and the bleating of the goats became an antiphony to their song. It was music to Abram's ears because these were his riches—these cattle with their calves, goats with kids, and the pure white sheep that dotted the landscape with their lambs frolicking in the late-afternoon sunshine. The harsh, abrasive cry of the Damascus donkeys that were used almost universally for beasts of burden punctuated the softer cries of the cattle, and Abram found even this sound pleasing.

After a time Layona announced that the meal was ready. The family ate in the open—the meat of the hart flavorful and tender on the inside and crisp on the outside, washed down with goat's milk, and afterward butter and honey smeared on flatbread to satisfy the sweet tooth.

While Lot ate with the appetite and exuberance of youth, he looked over to see Abram tenderly touching Sarai on the cheek. She responded by leaning over and kissing him.

"I don't know any other old people that kiss each other like you do. Why is that?" Lot asked curiously. "Most old people fuss a lot and argue. Some of them even hit each other—like old Hamaz hits his wife, Lamer. Why don't you two ever do that?"

"Because we love each other," Sarai said quickly.

"Don't those other people love each other?"

"Not as much as we do, son," Abram said. He had gotten into the habit of calling Lot "son," which gave him a feeling of pride, as if he himself had produced the boy. "But mostly it is because your aunt here is the sweetest, most beautiful woman in all the world. Any man who wouldn't want to kiss her needs to be buried."

Lot thought this was funny and laughed. "When I get married I'm going to marry someone as pretty as you, Aunt Sarai."

"Oh, I hope much prettier!" Sarai smiled at him. "I want the very best wife for you. But that'll be a long time yet."

The meal was almost finished when a rider came in. He slipped off of his donkey and came forward quickly. It was one of his father's servants, and Abram got to his feet. "Hello, Bamud."

"Sir, your father sent me to get you. He's not well."

"Is it serious, Bamud?"

"I can't say, sir." Bamud was a stocky, muscular young man with shaggy hair and an unkempt look. "He just asked you to come and visit him."

"You'll have to go," Sarai said at once.

"We'll all go. It's time we had a holiday in town."

Lot let out a shrill yelping cry and said, "I get to go too, Uncle?"

"Of course you do. Maybe there'll be a festival, and at least we can buy you some of the sweets you like so much."

Lot left at once to get ready, and Sarai said, "I'm worried about your father. He hasn't been well for the past year."

"He's getting quite old," Abram said. "We'd better get ready quickly. It'll be late when we get there."

"I don't know what's wrong with me," Terah grumbled. He was half lying down, propped up in a bed with pillows. He held his stomach and grimaced. "I feel like I've swallowed a thorn bush. My stomach is killing me."

"Maybe you're eating the wrong things."

"No maybe about it. I know I am. A man hates to admit he's not as strong as he once was."

Abram nodded. "I know what you mean. Lot and I were hunting this morning and wounded a hart. We took out after it running as hard as we could, and I gave out. That boy just shot by me like I was standing still. Made me feel old for the first time in my life."

"You're not old," Terah growled. "You're in the prime of life."

"I don't know. I'm fifty now!"

"I'd like to be your age again," Terah said. "Metura wants me to do nothing but drink milk and eat baby's food. A man likes good, strong drink and fresh meat with garlic. I can't even taste the stuff she feeds me! You know, son, things don't taste as good. Why, I can remember when I was your age I'd go out and pull an onion out of the ground, wipe the dirt off of it, and eat it like a piece of fruit. It was strong and good, but now I've lost my taste. I'm getting old."

"You're good for a lot of years yet, Father."

Terah hesitated, then answered cautiously, "I've been making offerings to more of the gods. Surely one of them will be able to help me. The trouble is there's so many of them! Why can't there be just one god in charge of stomachs? Then a man could go and make his offering and get well."

Abram did not answer at once. He knew that there were gods for almost every excuse, even a god in charge of keeping rats from the house. And none of them were any help. He did not want to say this, however, for his father looked poorly.

Terah suddenly turned to him. "What about this mysterious God of yours? The one you call the Eternal One—like my father did. If He's all-powerful, He ought to be able to cure one man's stomach, shouldn't He? Do you think He can make me well?"

Abram hesitated. "I don't know Him too well, Father."

"Don't know Him too well! Why, you've been running around for years talking about Him."

"Well, that may be so, but He's not an easy God to know."

Terah stared at him and grumbled. "Hmmph. Then maybe He's not worth knowing! I'll just have to keep on sending offerings to the temple until I get lucky and hit on a god who will help me."

Abram sat quietly thinking over what his father had said. He knew that the Eternal One had power to heal, but Abram did not know yet whether God would choose to listen when people asked Him for things. As for offerings, he had never once thought of offering anything to Him. The Eternal One seemed above all that. Abram was jolted out of his mental wanderings when his father said, "Aren't you listening to me?"

"Why, I guess I was still thinking about your stomach problem."

"I was saying that what really worries me is the business—it's going into the ground. Nahor works hard at it, but we're not making any headway."

"What about the trading business with Garai and those people in the north?"

Terah shook his head glumly. "Nothing is going right. What have I done that the gods are punishing me like this?"

Abram tried to comfort his father, but as he sat beside him, he was still wondering, *Why is God not speaking to me? Why don't I sense Him near me all the time? Perhaps if I knew Him better, I could ask Him, and He would heal my father.* It was a question he had often wrestled with but even now found no answer to.

Days later, Terah was up and about, feeling no effects from his ailment. He insisted that he had finally made an offering to the right god—but he grumbled that he couldn't figure out which one had answered his pleas. In his heart, Abram knew the stone gods had no power, but he wished with all his heart that he could know the Eternal One well enough to make requests of Him.

———————

Sarai was having a wonderful time visiting Nahor and Milcah and their children. Milcah had given birth to a baby girl only three weeks earlier, and Sarai was cuddling her, touching her cheeks and laughing when the child laughed. "She is beautiful, Milcah, absolutely beautiful!"

"You're so good with babies, Sarai. It's a shame you don't have children of your own." Milcah had spoken quickly, but seeing Sarai's face fall, she said, "Oh, I'm sorry, Sarai. I know it's a grief to you."

"Yes, it is. I feel like I'm failing Abram."

"Has he said anything to you?"

"No, he's never reproached me once. I know he loves me, but I know also that he would love to have a son."

"Well, you have Lot. He's become like a son to you."

"That's true, but still I'd give anything to have one like this." Sarai cuddled the girl in her left arm, smoothed the silky hair down, and looked deep into the guileless eyes of the child. "She's such a sweet baby."

"Well, she is now, but what will she be when she grows up?"

"Let's hope she'll always be sweet like she is now."

Milcah shook her head sadly. "People don't stay sweet. They turn out to be adults."

"Adults can still be good. Look at my husband. He's the best man I know."

Milcah laughed. "You're like a young bride, Sarai." Then changing the subject, she asked, "Did you bring Lot to town with you?"

"Oh yes. He likes to visit his friends here. Speaking of good boys, Lot certainly is one."

Milcah started to say something regarding the goodness of young boys but refrained. She was very fond of Sarai and knew that the woman had enough to bear without her adding to it. Silently she thought, *Lot may be a good boy, but he's a boy, and he'll become a man. And I never knew a man that didn't get into trouble sooner or later.*

———————

Milcah's thoughts were prophetic, for Lot, at that very moment, was being taunted by several of his friends. He liked them all, and they obviously liked him, but they were city boys, and he was from the country. They teased him constantly about this, and finally one of them said, "What about girls out there in the desert? I'm sure those shepherds must have daughters." The speaker was a tall, spindly boy named Luz. He was the ringleader of the group and now winked at his followers. "Those country girls ought to be pretty sweet."

The others joined in teasing Lot, and finally Luz said, "Come on, Lot, tell us about those girls. Are they pretty sweet?"

"I don't know any girls. N-not the way you mean," Lot stammered.

Luz winked again at the others. "Well, that's easily enough remedied. You're as old as I am. You should have had half a dozen girls by this time."

Lot could not answer. Indeed his body had been changing, and when one lissome young woman, the daughter of one of his uncle's herdsmen, had smiled at him, he had felt strange things happening inside him. He had been embarrassed by it, although he knew from hearing men talk that this was the way it was. Now he felt somehow ashamed in front of Luz and the others that he knew nothing about girls.

Luz said, "I think it's about time Lot here found out what women are like." A loud chorus echoed this, and Luz leered at Lot. "Do you have any money?"

"Yes, I've got some."

"Then I think we'd better go to the temple and make an offering to Ishtar."

Lot clearly understood his meaning. When men gave offerings to Ishtar, it was to visit the temple prostitutes. He had heard his uncle Abram speak of this in a disparaging manner, but still he was fifteen years old and curious. He was also anxious to appear to be a man in front of his friends. "All right. I'm ready," he said defiantly.

A yelp of assent went up, and the small band made its way to the temple.

Luz whispered, "There's one right there. Go tell her you want to make an offering."

Lot's heart was beating fast, and he walked up to the woman, who was no taller than he was. She turned to him and smiled, and he saw that her gown was very revealing and for a moment he could not speak a word.

"Well, what a fine man you are," the woman said. She had full lips, and her face was painted, especially her eyes, which were large and lustrous. She leaned against him and said, "Have you come to make an offering to the goddess Ishtar?"

"Y-yes, I have."

The woman laughed and put her arm around him. "You come with me, and we'll make your offering. Then we'll see what happens."

Lot felt hot then cold, but as the woman led him away, he heard his friends calling, challenging him, and he knew there was no turning back.

PART THREE

THE CALLING

The Lord had said to Abram, "Leave your country, your people and your father's household and go to the land I will show you. I will make you into a great nation. . . ."

Genesis 12:1–2

CHAPTER

9

The blazing sun sent its blistering beams down over the land, causing shimmering heat waves to rise over the irrigation canal that lay just west of Ur of the Chaldees. Sarai sat on a low stone wall, holding a baby close to her breast. A beatific expression was on her face as she rocked the child slowly, cradling the precious treasure. She loved children of all ages, but especially helpless newborns. A longing reflected itself in her eyes, which her sister-in-law Milcah, who was standing a few feet away, recognized. *She wants a baby worse than any woman I ever saw. Why the gods have made her barren, I can't imagine. She and Abram are good people and would make wonderful parents.*

Milcah had thought this many times before, but being a practical woman, she knew the gods were fickle and often brought evil things to good people while at the same time lifting those who were downright evil to positions of prominence and wealth. Looking up at Sarai, she smiled. "You're going to spoil Bethuel."

"Well, he's such a sweet child. He deserves a little spoiling." Sarai held the baby up. His pudgy body squirmed, and he smiled toothlessly at Sarai. "Isn't he the handsomest baby that ever lived! Yes, you are," Sarai crooned.

"He's not so sweet at times." Milcah shook her head firmly and her lips pursed. "Sometimes he can be aggravating. He's strong willed."

"Like Nahor, I suppose."

"Just like him."

The two women continued their conversation. From time to time Sarai looked around at the outskirts of the city where they sat, and where Nahor and Milcah made their home. Sarai had come for a visit on her own while Abram and Lot were away hunting.

The outer fringes of Ur were composed primarily of square houses built of sun-dried brick, scattered over the landscape in no particular pattern, some of them at right angles to the others. From where she sat Sarai could see the irrigation canal. The river overflowed once a year, if the gods were kind, and the workers had built ditches to bring water to the arid ground. Water was life in this place, and each year prayers were sent up to different gods to bring the precious fluid into the land. After the growing season was over, men and women alike would get out and repair the canals, which were their lifeline.

Overhead some birds were circling, and Sarai watched them idly. She was an observant woman, and now she turned her eyes out over the distance, studying the man who was plowing with a large ox. She had heard Abram's grandfather tell about the early days, when life was so hard that men and even women were used instead of beasts to plow the land. She felt a sudden gladness that things were better now.

A boy of about ten years of age appeared, walking from the canal holding a string of small fish. His brown hair had a reddish tinge in the bright sunlight, and his eyes were dark and lustrous. Sarai's eyes followed him, as they always followed children, until he walked past a collection of small round reed huts, where the cattle were kept. There was little good grazing land left this close to Ur, so the cattle were kept in huts and carefully fed the grain that was stored from the harvest.

"Where has Abram gone this time?"

Sarai started at Milcah's question, for she was caught up in her surroundings and in the pleasure of holding the baby. "He and Lot have gone off together hunting. I think they were going to try to bring in some birds and look for new forage."

"Those two are so close. Abram is very fond of Lot, isn't he?"

"So am I, Milcah. He's a fine boy." A brief smiled lifted the corners of her mouth. She was forty-five years old now but still had the creamy skin and good looks of a woman of twenty. "Yes, we love Lot as if he were our own son."

"Does it worry you, Sarai, that Abram is so unsettled?"

"Unsettled? Why, he's the steadiest man I know!"

Milcah's lips tightened. "Well, I suppose he is about most things, and I know he's a good husband. But I'm not the only one who wonders about his seeking after a God nobody has ever heard of."

Sarai did not answer. She had long since given up trying to explain to anyone Abram's preoccupation with the Eternal One. She herself had never had an encounter with the God whom Abram served, but she knew he was a man of truth, and there was nothing in her husband's life any stronger than his belief that the Eternal One was the one true God. She had often seen him sitting and staring at the medallion he always wore. He seldom spoke of it, and she had long ago ceased to ask him questions about it. But she knew that he believed it came straight down from his ancestor Seth and that somehow it marked him as being a special servant of the God in whom he believed so fiercely.

The two women were silent for a time, submerged in observing the life of the townspeople about them. It was a busy time of day, and old and young had come out to enjoy the afternoon. Milcah's face was thoughtful. She cleared her throat and then tentatively expressed what she'd been thinking. "Sarai, I've been wondering about something."

"Wondering about what?"

"Well, I know that you want a child more than you want anything else." Milcah saw a pain flare in Sarai's eyes and hurried on. "I'm just wondering if you and Abram shouldn't offer sacrifices to some of the gods of Ur."

"Which ones?" Sarai asked sarcastically. She might not have seen with her own eyes or heard with her own ears the God that Abram spoke of, but she had little faith in the thousands of stone idols that were so precious to the inhabitants of Ur. Families even had their own special gods, and Sarai had, for a long time, observed that little came of the offerings given to them.

She did not like to speak of her lack of bringing a son into the world, but Milcah loved Sarai and spoke of it forthrightly. "Time is running out for you and Abram to have children. I do wish that Abram would offer sacrifices to the gods before it's too late."

Again Sarai gave her sister-in-law a strange look. "Which god would you suggest?"

Milcah shrugged her shoulders. "It doesn't matter. Start in and try one, and if that doesn't work, try another one. Sooner or later you're bound to find the right one. Why, you know my cousin Denae. She didn't have any children for four years, and then she took an offering to Ishtar, and now she's got three. Why don't you try Ishtar?"

"Abram would never do that."

Sarai rose, anxious to get away, and Milcah said quickly, "Well, Lot is almost a son to you."

Sarai handed the baby to Milcah, saying sadly, "It's not the same thing, Milcah."

Milcah shook her head sadly as Sarai ran back toward the house. "Those two are stubborn," she muttered to herself. "I can see no harm in asking the gods for help."

The river made a pleasant sibilant murmur as it purled at the feet of Abram and Lot. They were standing in a grove of reeds that rose over their heads, peering out at the river as it spread itself before them. The water was brown, warm as stew and almost as thick. The bank was slick, and Abram peered through the reeds carefully. The sinking sun made slatted bars of alternate light and shade across his bronzed skin, and he shut his eyes against the glare of it. Although he was fifty-five now, he was still strong and hearty, and the sun had tanned his skin to a golden glow. He was wearing a simple garment that met at one shoulder and hung down to his knees. His arms were corded with muscle, and he hefted the spear in his hand and glanced over at Lot, who stood beside him.

"We're going to have to do better than this, boy."

Lot was twenty now, fully grown and much slimmer than Abram. He was a fine runner, although not physically as strong as some of the other young men. He had handsome features, and Abram had noted that young women, both in town and among the sheepherders' families, found him pleasing indeed, and Lot returned their admiration.

"There they come. Look!" Lot whispered.

The two men swung their heads to gaze toward a flock of white birds that were approaching.

"We'll get them as soon as they land, son. You take the closest one. I'll take one a little farther away."

"Yes. I'll bet I get one." Lot's eyes glowed, and Abram felt pleasure in just being with the young man. Lot had become an integral part of his life over the years, taking away at least some of the pain he felt at having no son of his own. This nephew of his had managed to work his way into Abram's heart.

The birds came in, and as soon as they settled, Abram whispered, "Now!" and with all of his strength, he flung the spear. It made a whistling sound, but he saw that he had overthrown the bird.

Lot's spear, however, caught his prey squarely with a solid *thunk*, and the bird fell into the river and floated there. Lot began to laugh. "I told you you'd miss, Uncle. I'm going to have to give you throwing lessons."

Abram reached around and picked Lot up. He was still a powerful man, and now holding his nephew pinioned, he said fiercely, "I'll teach you to make fun of your elders. I'll throw you to the crocodiles!" He moved out from the reeds and stood on the riverbank, ignoring Lot's futile attempt to get away.

Finally, reaching out, he set Lot down until his feet sank in the mud up to his knees. "Now, go out and get that bird. I want it for my dinner."

As soon as Lot was free, he reached forward and grabbed Abram's ankle. Throwing himself backward, he said, "We'll both get him. Come on!"

Abram was caught off balance. He wheeled his arms in an attempt to catch himself, but it was too late. "Why, you young—" He could say no more, for he fell full-length in the mud. At once he reached up and grabbed Lot, dragging him down with him, and for the next few minutes he proceeded to smear the thick river mud all over Lot.

Lot did his best to do the same to his uncle, and the two men wallowed in the thick, juicy mud.

"Now," Abram panted, winded from the exertion, "go get that bird."

"I will, but you'll have to split him with me for dinner."

Lot floundered out into the slow-moving stream until he reached the bird. He brought it back, and the two men cleaned themselves off as well as they could and then climbed out on the bank.

"You're making a fool out of your old uncle, boy."

"Why, you're more fun than any of my friends," Lot said. He reached up and patted Abram's arm, looking at him with obvious affection.

For one moment Abram could not speak. His throat was tight, and he felt a surge of thanksgiving. As he often did, he offered up a quick prayer. *O Eternal One, thank you for this boy! He has indeed become a son to me.* Aloud he said roughly, "Well, well, come along. Sarai will pull every hair out of our heads if we don't get home soon."

The two men started back toward home. As they walked briskly along under the hot sun, Lot began to chatter about the young woman he was presently smitten with. "She's the only girl for me. I've made up my mind to win her," Lot said exuberantly.

"Seems I've heard this before," Abram said, smiling. "What about that other girl? The one from the village of Laniel?"

"Her? She'll be fatter than a hippopotamus by the time she's thirty. No, I've got a new system for finding a woman now."

"I'd be pleased to hear it," Abram said dryly.

"Well, you have to look at her mother. If you find one with a pretty mother, then you'll have a woman who'll never be fat and ugly."

Abram laughed aloud. He was always vastly amused by his nephew's schemes. "What if she's a poor girl?" he asked.

Lot chewed his lip thoughtfully, swinging the bird by its legs as he walked. Now he reached down and plucked out a handful of the white feathers and tossed them into the sky. As they fluttered downward, he said, "There's bound to be a rich woman whose family has a lot of money and whose mother is good-looking as well. I'll tell you what. When I find one whose mother is as pretty as Aunt Sarai, that's the one I'll have."

Abram was pleased at the young man's fondness for Sarai. She was indeed a second mother to him. Lot's own mother had died not long after she had remarried, which had made the boy even more dependent upon Abram and Sarai. Lot continued to talk about girls, and finally he remarked, "Well, you know a man can't take the first woman he falls in love with."

Abram was quiet for a moment, then said with a peculiar inflection, "I did."

Lot suddenly turned. "That's right, you did. Saved you a lot of trouble, but I suppose the gods must have helped you. Did you pray for the gods to find you just the right wife?"

"Back in those days I prayed to a lot of gods."

"Which ones?"

"All I could find. I was looking for the true one."

Lot considered this for a while. "Most people," Lot said cautiously, "think that all of the gods are true gods."

"I can hardly remember a time when I believed that. When I was even younger than you, I began to think that there was just one God. I don't know why I thought that, but it came to me clearly." Abram continued to speak of his search for God and how he had found Him in the desert that day long ago. Finally he said, "I'll hear from Him again someday."

"Do you really think so, Uncle?"

"Yes. I can't believe that such a God would only appear to me once and never again. There is such a longing in my heart to know Him more. I can't believe that He would not want to satisfy that longing."

"What do you mean by that?"

"Well, you get thirsty, don't you, Lot?"

"Yes, of course."

"Suppose there was no such thing as water. Water was made to quench your thirst. Food was made to satisfy your hunger. Rest was made to meet your need for sleep, and somehow I know that this longing I have is the same thing. I believe that the Eternal One, whom I have met, longs to satisfy the deepest need of every man."

Lot admired his uncle more than any other man he knew, and for a time he questioned him about the God he prayed to. "Uncle, can I ask you a question? A personal one."

"You can ask me," Abram smiled, "but I won't promise to answer."

"Well," Lot said hesitantly, "did you ever... ever..."

"Did I ever what?"

"Did you ever go to one of the temple prostitutes?" Lot blurted.

Abram shot a quick glance at Lot, who was deliberately looking away. He saw that the boy's face was flushed and said quickly, "No, I never did, Lot. Those women aren't good for a man."

"Most of my friends have gone," Lot said defensively.

Abram almost said, *And have you gone too?* but he managed to choke back the question. He knew what a temptation it was for young men when women were readily available, and he knew also that temple prostitutes were considered a form of worship. The whole idea disgusted him, and he said, "I think a man ought to do better than that."

Lot did not answer, and finally he turned to his uncle with a warm smile. "I think so too."

The two walked briskly along the road with Abram speaking of the Eternal One. He desperately wanted Lot to find God, and he saw the young man was soaking all of it in.

Finally Lot interrupted him to say, "There's Gehazi."

The men waited until Abram's chief herdsman came forward at a trot. Gehazi did everything fast. He walked fast. He ate fast. He even slept fast, it appeared. He stopped before them, a sunburned individual, scarcely larger than an adolescent boy but wise in the way of flocks, knowing more about animals than any man Abram had ever seen. "About time you two came back," he grumbled.

"We found some good grazing ground over to the north," Abram said. "When this grass is gone, we ought to move some of the flocks over there."

"I knew about that already," Gehazi said, shrugging his shoulders. He looked down at the bird in Lot's hand. "Did you bring that bird for me?"

"No, it's my uncle's dinner."

"You get only one?"

"*I* got one. My uncle here, he couldn't hit a ziggurat from ten paces away!"

Abram laughed. "I think you're right about that. You're better at hunting birds than I ever was."

Lot laughed and wandered off to speak to another one of the herdsmen.

Abram said, "How's the boy working out?"

"He's bright and good with the animals. He's a little lazy, though. You should've taken a stick to him when he was growing up."

"Perhaps I should have," Abram said, smiling.

Gehazi sighed, his eyes fixed on Abram's face. "You would never have done it, not you. Spoiled the boy rotten, I'd say."

Abram nodded. "I guess I did, Gehazi. I love him so much—I just never can say no to him."

———————

Sarai rose to meet Abram, taking his hands and kissing him. "I've missed you," she said.

"I've missed you too."

"Did you find more grazing ground?"

"Yes, and we'll be moving some of the flock there. I talked to Gehazi about Lot. He says he's a good herdsman. Just a little lazy."

Layona came out to meet him and said, "I fixed you a good supper, master."

"Well, that's good. We only got one bird."

"I'll fix it for you just the way you like."

"You always do." Abram smiled at the woman fondly.

Sarai watched this brief scene cautiously. Layona had become a most helpful servant and an excellent cook. She was still an attractive woman, even though she too was getting on in years. Sarai had expected that long ago some young man would have taken her for his bride. Several had made offers for her, but Layona had begged each time to be allowed to remain with the family. It was common practice for men to take on female servants as concubines who would bear them sons, and Sarai often wondered, as she did now, if Abram had ever considered doing so with Layona. But then she dismissed the thought. She wasn't being fair to him. Abram had never expressed anything toward Layona other than simple affection.

Now Sarai waited until Layona brought out the meal—mutton soaked in sour cream along with wheat cakes dipped in oil.

"What have you been doing while we were gone?" Abram asked his wife.

"Oh, nothing really. I've been visiting with Milcah and the baby."

Abram was very sensitive to his wife's sadness over being childless herself. Quickly he said, "We need to go into town to stay for a time, Sarai. To have an extended visit with the family—and buy you some new things." He reached over and touched her cheek. "A pretty wife like you deserves pretty things."

Sarai reached up and covered his hand with hers. "That would be fine," she said quietly.

Abram's parents now lived in one of the finer homes in Ur. Though the trading business was faltering, its earlier success had provided a fine house. It had two large stories, built of mud bricks around an open courtyard. There were lavatories and drains, but no baths. The upstairs housed the bedrooms, all of which looked down on the open courtyard, and the area around the courtyard on the ground floor had rooms for cooking, washing, and spinning, and bedrooms for the servants.

As Abram and Sarai entered the house, they were greeted by Abram's parents, Terah and Metura. "About time you came to stay for a while!" Terah said. "You've neglected your mother and me badly."

"I'm sorry, Father," Abram said. "You're right. We'll have to try to see you more often."

Metura came over, and Abram bent over and kissed her. She patted his cheek and said, "You look thin, son. I'm going to fatten you up a little bit."

Abram was very fond of his mother. He embraced her and said, "That's good. And you'll get to pamper me all you want to. This woman here never pays me any mind."

Metura looked at Sarai, who was smiling. "I believe you've taken up lying in your old age, son. Come along, Sarai. Let's see what we can scare up for these two hungry men."

As the two women prepared the meal, Abram accompanied his father up on the roof. The shadows were growing long now, and a breeze was coming over the rooftop. Terah had been listening to Abram's report of the flocks, and he expressed his gladness that the herding business was going well.

"I wish things were going as well for me."

Abram glanced at his father with surprise. "The business still isn't going well?"

Terah had purchased several boats lately for his trading business, sending them upriver past Uruk to the distant villages along the route to Babylon. People there seldom got into the larger cities, and Terah had done well with the trading in the past.

"It's not as easy as it used to be. There are other traders now. Some of them are pretty sharp fellows." He turned suddenly and said, "I want Lot to stay with us and learn the business."

Abram shook his head firmly. "I don't think we could do that. Sarai and I need him, and he hasn't learned the herding business well enough yet."

Terah was a man who did not like to be crossed, and he argued for a time, but in the end he saw that Abram was determined. He stared out over the city, then said, "You know, I have thought about leaving here and settling farther north."

"I thought you'd be here forever," Abram said in surprise.

"A man needs a change every once in a while. You ought to change too, Abram."

Abram did not answer but said instead, "Mother wouldn't like moving."

"No. Women like things to stay the same."

"She hasn't seemed too well lately."

"She'll be all right," Terah said brusquely. "But I'm pretty sure we're going to move."

Abram said nothing of this to Sarai. The two stayed in town for a month. Sarai bought many things in the markets and enjoyed their stay, but Abram, as always, tired of the town quickly. When they went back home, he fell at once into the life of a herdsman. He thought about his father and wondered what would come of his intention to move.

———————

The sun had barely risen as Abram walked along the rocky way. He had a staff in his hand and was seeking a yearling that Gehazi said had wandered off. Such things often happened, and Abram was always concerned about every animal in his herd. This one was a particularly fine one, and his eyes moved to and fro as he strolled along looking for it. The morning breeze was brisk, but already the land was beginning to heat up.

Abram searched for several hours and then decided that a wild beast must have gotten the lamb. He sat down on a rock and pulled out his water bottle and took a few swallows. As he corked the top, he felt something strange about the landscape. He looked around and saw nothing different, but then he heard a voice behind him.

"Abram?"

Instantly Abram fell down on his face. He had the sensation of a tremendous pressure, and somehow the light was different. It was purer than sunlight, clear and pale and strong. There was no doubt in his mind who was speaking to him.

"Yes, O Eternal One?" he whispered.

The voice spoke clearly and sonorously. *"Leave your country, your people and your father's household and go to the land I will show you. I will make you into a great nation and I will bless you. I will make your name great, and you will be a blessing. I will* bless those who bless you, and whoever curses you I will curse, and all peoples on earth will be blessed through you."

Abram's heart was full, so full he could not speak. For a long time after the voice had ceased, he stayed on his face, his forehead pressing into the earth. Finally he lifted his head and saw that the light had faded. Getting to his feet, he stood still for a moment, his head bowed, and then he nodded slightly. "Yes, O maker of all things—I will obey your voice."

He turned, and as he made his way homeward, he knew that something had changed inside his very being. He remembered his grandfather saying once, *"Sometimes a man bends over to pick up a small thing—and when he straightens up, his whole world has changed."*

"Yes, Grandfather, I went looking for a small thing, and now my whole world has changed!"

CHAPTER

10

Abram looked toward Sarai, who was sitting across from him in the tent. The two of them had just had a good meal, and now the darkness had fallen so that the lamps cast a flickering shadow on Sarai's face. He thought again what a beautiful woman she was. *She's more beautiful to me now than the first day I saw her.* He saw also that her face had matured, and he knew that her failure to bear a child had left an emptiness in her that nothing he could ever give her or do for her would fulfill. Now he hesitated to tell her his news, for he was certain she would be disturbed.

"Sarai, we're going to have to leave this place."

Sarai looked up quickly. "You mean move the flocks farther north as you were talking about?"

"No. I mean we're going to leave Ur."

"Leave Ur? Why would we do that?"

Abram dropped his head, and Sarai gave him her full attention. She knew her husband well, and now she said quietly, "What is it, Abram? Is something wrong?"

"The Eternal One appeared to me again and told me that we must leave this place."

Sarai was stunned. Both of their families lived in Ur, and she had many friends there. She loved to visit with her in-laws and her parents.

"How far will we travel?"

"I don't know," Abram said quietly. "The Eternal One only told me that we were to leave."

Sarai could not think for a moment. Confusion kept her silent, and finally she asked, "When will we have to go?"

"I think very soon." Abram rose and came over to sit beside Sarai. He put his arm around her and said huskily, "I know this is hard for you, but it's the right thing to do."

A few days later Sarai heard a strange sound as she was leaving her tent. She stopped to listen, then moved around to the back of the tent. It was early in the morning, and she was surprised to see Layona bent over vomiting. Sarai stood for a moment staring, and then when the servant straightened up, Sarai saw that the woman was pale, her lips drawn together in a pucker.

"What's the matter, Layona?"

"Nothing," Layona said, but her face betrayed her answer.

Layona was a strong woman and never got sick. There was only one explanation for this illness. Sarai felt cold as she asked, "You're going to have a baby, aren't you?"

Layona dropped her eyes and could not answer. Finally she nodded, her whole body a posture of misery.

Sarai stood absolutely still, and her mind worked quickly. It was not at all unusual for servant women to become pregnant, even those who were not married. No one really thought about such things a great deal, but Sarai was struggling with a thought that intruded on her mind. It seemed to push its way in, and she felt the beginnings of doubt and anger.

"Who's the man?" she asked harshly. She waited, but Layona merely shook her head.

"Did you hear me? Who's the father of your baby?"

Layona was a meek woman and always obedient, but though Sarai continued to question her, she steadfastly refused to answer.

It could be Abram! The thought would not leave Sarai's mind. She was well acquainted with the fact that many men in Ur and many of those who herded the cattle thought little of forcing themselves on their female slaves. When a child was born it was simply one more hand to help with the work, an extra slave at no extra cost.

Sarai stared at the girl, then demanded, "You'll have to tell me sooner or later!" Her voice was sharp, and she turned to leave, determined to ask Abram. But suddenly she stopped.

What if he says it's his baby? Sarai found this possibility alarming. Her lack of a child had marked her deeper than she knew, and she decided not to go to Abram. Instead she went back into her tent, sat down, and remained silent, her thoughts writhing within her breast. Tears filled her eyes, and when they ran down her cheeks, she shook her head. "I'll never ask him—and he'll never tell me!"

———————

Abram approached his father's house with trepidation. He had put off telling his family as long as he possibly could about his plans to leave Ur. He knew his father had no confidence at all in the existence of the Eternal One. Terah had as much religion as the average dweller in Ur—which was little enough. He went through the formality of making an offering to some of the gods, just enough to keep on the good side of them—not to mention pleasing the priests, who had ways of forcing a man's hand.

Abram entered the house and was glad that his mother was not in the room. It would be hard enough to deal with Terah without Metura's tears.

"Well, what are you doing here?" Terah asked. He was sitting at a table with some clay tablets before him, studying his transaction. He was genuinely surprised at seeing Abram, for his son usually spaced his visits far apart. "Something wrong? Someone sick?"

"No one's sick," Abram said. He came to sit down opposite his father, saying, "I've got to talk to you."

"Something must be wrong. What is it?"

"I don't know that you'd call it wrong," Abram said, "but I've come to tell you that Sarai and I will be leaving."

A blank look washed across Terah's face. It was as if Abram had announced that he was going to reach up and touch the moon.

"Leaving!" He immediately jumped to the obvious conclusion. "You've run out of pasture? You going to move the flocks farther away from Ur?"

Abram hesitated. There was no easy way to say this. "I know you won't believe this, but the Eternal One appeared to me."

At once Terah's face hardened. He put his hands flat on the table and seemed to push against it. "You're still on that business, are you? You'd be better off to leave that alone."

Knowing that it was useless to argue with his father, Abram said simply, "The Eternal One has told me that I have to leave."

"Well, I suppose you can move up close to Uruk."

"No, I think it's more than that. I believe I'll be going away from this whole part of the world."

Terah stared at his son. "You're going to tear your whole life up and leave the only family you have because you've dreamed up some God, and he's told you to do it?"

"You spoke of leaving yourself——you talked of looking for better business opportunities to the north. You said that change is good."

"Bah! That was just foolish talk. Your mother would not want to leave, and business is picking up. You cannot leave—it will break your mother's heart."

Abram saw how useless this discussion was. He sat listening as Terah spoke harshly, then finally he said, "You can tell Mother or I will. I think we'll be leaving very soon." He got up and left the room, ignoring Terah's mutterings.

Terah sat at the table, stunned by what he had heard. He could not concentrate on his business, and finally he got up and went to the bedroom, where his wife was lying down. She sat up as he came in, and he said abruptly, "Abram was just here."

"Abram? Was something wrong?"

"Yes, something's wrong. That son of ours has lost his mind." He went on to explain Abram's intention and ended by exploding, "He's gone crazy! Lost his mind."

Metura could not speak for a moment. She was not well at all, but her whole life was in Ur. She had married here, had her children here, and had lost one of them. Now her favorite was going to leave.

"We must do something, Terah."

"*Do* something! I don't know what you expect me to do."

Metura got off the bed, came over, and put her hand on his arm. Her voice was pleading. A thought had come to her instantly, and now she whispered softly, "Terah, couldn't we go with him?"

Terah suddenly turned to face her. "Would you be willing to leave here?"

"I can't bear to lose him."

"He always was your favorite," Terah grunted. He stood there for a moment and then said, "You know, I've been thinking of leaving here myself and trying to find a more profitable place for business. We've talked about it."

"Then let's go with him."

"We don't know where we'd be going. Business might be even worse."

"We could sell out everything and just go with him. You could go into business in another city when he settles. I can't bear to lose him!" she pleaded.

———

In all truth Terah's business was in worse shape than he had admitted to his wife or to his sons. It was not that he was a bad businessman, but the competition for business was so fierce that it had become much harder than when he had first decided to become a trader.

One of the first things he did was go to his son Nahor and explain the situation. Nahor listened, but when his father finished, he snorted and shook his head fiercely. "You're getting to be as bad as Abram! My mother's not well, and you're talking about taking her out to who knows where!"

"Nahor, I'm at my wit's end. I might as well tell you the worst. When I sell out, I'll just about be even with the debts that I owe. We've got to go, and I want you to go with us."

"Absolutely not!" Nahor said. "I'm not getting rich, but I'm making a living, and I think you'd be crazy to go with Abram!"

Terah felt his age. He was caught in a bind that he could not get out of, but he said finally in a defeated tone, "I've got to go. Your mother and I will hate to leave you, but perhaps we won't go far."

Nahor shook his head. "You're going to go out to someplace you don't even know and all because some god that Abram's made up is telling him. You'll be sorry, Father. You'll be very sorry!"

As soon as Terah appeared at the camp, Abram knew something had changed. It had been two weeks since he had told his father that he must leave, and since that time Terah had been strangely silent. Abram knew that his father was not silent by nature, and now as he went to greet him, bowing in respect, he said, "Father, I'm glad to see you."

Terah scarcely spoke but followed Abram into his tent. Sarai was there, and she at once began pouring him a drink of water from a pottery pitcher and asking about Metura.

Terah drank thirstily, then saw that the two were sitting silently. "I've been thinking about what you said about leaving, Abram," he said. He cleared his throat and nodded. "I've decided that you're right."

Abram smiled at his father, surprised. "I'm so glad that you can see it in that light. It's something I have to do."

As though Abram had not spoken, Terah said, "And your mother has talked to me about this." He looked up, sadness in his weary face. "She can't bear to be separated from you, Abram. So I've agreed. I'll sell the business, and she and I will come with you."

Sarai immediately uttered a glad cry. "That's wonderful, isn't it, Abram!"

Abram tried not to show his feelings. As soon as his father had spoken of his plan, an alarm had gone off. The Eternal One had clearly said, *"Leave your father's household.*" But now how was he to do that? He cleared his throat and said, "Are you sure that's the wise thing to do? I mean... Mother's not in good health, and she's used to the comforts of a house. It's quite different living in tents."

"We'll take care of her, you and I," Terah said quickly. He knew Abram's intense love for his mother and said, "You wouldn't leave her behind, would you, not when she's begging to go?"

And then Abram knew he had no choice. He tried to pray. *O Eternal One, my parents cannot live long, and perhaps you meant the rest of my family. It must please you for a man to take care of his parents.* Desperately the thoughts raced through his mind but brought him no comfort.

Finally Abram smiled and reached out and embraced his father. "Of course, Father. It'll be good to have you and Mother with us."

CHAPTER

11

Despite Sarai's initial apprehension of what lay ahead for her and Abram, she had found the first few weeks of their journey exciting. Seeing new places fascinated her, and this was the first time she would be traveling north of Babylon. But as the weeks turned into months, her enthusiasm waned. The pace was slow, since they had to travel on land and the large group of travelers and animals could go no faster than the smallest lambs. They made their way tediously northward along the grazing grounds near the Euphrates River.

The sun burned fiercely, and Sarai adjusted her head covering, protecting her face from its damaging heat and the stinging sand swirling in the wind. She heard a cry and glanced up to see Lot running by. He was chasing a young woman named Meri, the daughter of one of Abram's herders. Sarai frowned. Her nephew was a good worker when he wanted to be, but there was a laxness in him that she saw as a weakness. He was a fine-looking young man and could have had his pick among the young women of Ur, but he had preferred the life of a bachelor and had gained a questionable reputation where women were concerned. Sarai narrowed her eyes and thought for a moment, *I ought to stop him. Meri's a foolish girl. She doesn't need to get mixed up with Lot.*

Sarai kept in front of the animals and the choking dust they raised. She thought often of her family back in Ur and Uruk, wondering how they were doing and missing them now as she realized more and more that she likely would never see them again. As the days of travel wore on, she also found herself worrying about her mother-in-law, whose health was suffering from the rigors of the trip. She had initially wanted Abram's parents to come along, but now she wondered about the wisdom of having subjected them to the hardships of travel. It was a demanding trip for a healthy person, and for a sick woman like Metura it was even harder. Sometimes they would stay several days at one site to rest the animals, and at such times she was glad to spend time watching after Metura.

Sarai turned suddenly and caught a glimpse of Layona, now large with child. Even as Sarai watched, she saw Abram, who had come in from the outlying flocks, stop and speak to the servant. Sarai's eyes narrowed as she saw the younger woman lift her eyes to Abram, and she could not miss the light that was in them. Just the sight of it sent a pang of jealousy through Sarai, and she muttered aloud, "He's more concerned for her than he is for me!"

Whirling around, she stalked away so that she would not have to endure the sight. The very thought that Abram had fathered a child with another woman was intolerable to her. Ever since she had married, she had longed for a child to present to her husband more than anything else in the world. Now the thought that Layona's child might belong to him angered and humiliated her.

Even as she hastened to get away from the sight, she recalled a conversation she had heard days before. Lot had been talking with Meri, and they had not known that Sarai was within hearing distance. Meri had spoken of Layona, saying, "I wonder who the father of her child is."

And Lot's answer had cut into Sarai like a knife. "Why, it's my uncle's, of course."

"Your uncle Abram! What makes you think that?"

"Well, all you have to do is watch her when Abram's around. She never takes her eyes off him."

"That's so," Meri had said, nodding. "I wonder if he will claim the child."

"I doubt it," Lot had said carelessly. "But she's always loved him. Anybody can see that."

Now as Sarai moved along, the thought became intolerable. *I'll find out who the father is. I'll make her tell me!*

For several days after Sarai resolved to question Layona, she found herself being short with Abram, and he, of course, noticed it. He said little, only asking her if she was not feeling well, and she had answered curtly, "I'm very well." He had left her then, but she was aware that he was watching her curiously and with some concern.

Her opportunity came one evening after the flocks were grazing and the evening meal was being prepared. Sarai found herself working on a pot of thick porridge prepared with sesame oil, which Abram loved. They had stopped early to bake barley cakes, milk the goats, and fill their earthenware pots with river water. Abram and Lot had gathered together the herdsmen who were not on guard against wild animals and predators of the two-legged kind, and Sarai saw that she was alone with Layona. Moving closer, she studied the woman for a moment. Layona was a slim woman, but the child she bore now filled her shapeless smock, which hung loosely from throat to hem and displayed her bare feet. Her black hair had a slight curl to it, and two braids curling at the ends hung across her cheeks and down upon her breast. She had stopped for a moment to gaze out toward the desert, one hand toying with one of the braids. She had a sweet face, and Sarai had always loved the woman—until now.

"Layona?"

"Yes, my mistress."

"I have to ask you something."

Layona's fear at the question was obvious in her eyes and in the tremor that shook her breast. She said nothing, standing defenseless before Sarai.

Finally Sarai said, "Layona, you must tell me who the father of your child is."

Layona swallowed hard and met Sarai's eyes fleetingly but then looked downward and remained silent.

Sarai took Layona's silence as a confirmation of her suspicions, and her voice grew sterner. "Speak up, Layona! I insist that you tell me!"

The slave woman continued to stare at the ground, and in the silence Sarai heard the voices of the men and the lowing of the cattle. From far away she heard happy children's voices as they participated in a game. After waiting several moments for Layona's response, Sarai's face hardened and her lips drew into a straight line. "You've always loved my husband!" She waited for Layona to deny or to confirm this, but Layona did not lift her head. "It was him, wasn't it?" Sarai demanded.

Layona suddenly lifted her eyes, and Sarai saw the misery in them. Layona was a small woman, strong and well shaped, but despite her years, she still seemed almost childlike to Sarai.

"No," Layona whispered finally.

"Then who is it?"

Still Layona said nothing.

Sarai grew angry and, moving forward, yelled, "Tell me the truth!" To the surprise of both of them, Sarai slapped Layona, something she had never done before. "Tell me!" she cried fiercely. "You're lying! It's Abram, isn't it?"

"No, it is not."

Sarai stared at the servant and saw that she would get nothing out of her. She said bitterly, "You managed to trap him! I hope you're happy, but he'll never claim your baby, I'll tell you that right now!" She whirled and walked away, her back stiff. She felt somehow that she had lost something in the encounter, and the scene had so disturbed her that she could not join in the meal. She went instead to her tent and lay down. She found her hands were trembling, and she had to struggle to keep the tears from running down her cheeks. As she had grown older she had become a placid, even-tempered woman as a rule, but the idea of another woman giving birth to a child by Abram shook her to her very foundations.

Anger swept over her after a time, and she thought bitter thoughts about the slave. *I'll make Abram sell her! No, she's mine. He gave her to me. I'll sell her myself to the first traveling band we meet.* She let these thoughts run through her mind and savored them, but deep down she knew she would never do a thing like that. Finally she heard Abram come into the tent. He stood over her, then knelt down over her. "Are you not well, Sarai?"

Abram's voice was tender as always, and Sarai blinked her eyes to keep back the tears.

"I'm just a little tired, husband."

"You didn't eat anything," Abram said with concern. "I'll go fetch you something."

"I'm not hungry."

"You must eat. You lie there, and I'll get it for you."

Sarai reached up and caught his hand. "No. Just sit here beside me for a while."

Abram sat down and put both of his hands around hers. The size and strength of them gave her comfort, and she looked up and saw his warm eyes gazing at her with concern.

"I'm a trouble to you," she whispered.

"How could you be that?" Abram reached over and ran his hand over her hair. He whispered, "I couldn't ever let anything happen to you. What would I do without you, Sarai?"

"Do you really feel that way, husband?"

"There is no woman so fair," Abram said. "Not just outwardly, but in your heart and your spirit. That's what I love even more than your beauty."

The tears did come then. She could not hide them but suddenly sat up and put her arms around him. She lay against his chest, holding him tightly.

Abram, surprised by this, continued to stroke her hair. "You'll feel better after a time," he said.

"Yes, husband, I will."

_____

"Son, we're going to have to stop and give your mother a chance to get better," Terah said to Abram after several more weeks of travel. They had left the Euphrates River now to follow northward along a tributary—the Balikh River. Traders along this well-traveled caravan route had told them that in that direction lay several settlements, where they hoped to replenish their supplies and perhaps rest for a time.

Abram and his father were moving along at the head of the procession. Behind them came the beasts of burden loaded with the household equipment, and Abram caught a quick glimpse of Layona as she trudged along beside a heavily burdened donkey. She occupied his attention for a moment, and a worried frown pinched his brow. For months now he had watched her swell with the child that was to come, and although he was no judge of such things, he could tell that Layona was not doing well at all.

"Did you hear what I said?" Terah's voice was sharp, and he waited until Abram turned around to face him. "You don't pay any attention to me most of the time, son."

"Oh, I heard you. I was just thinking about what to do."

"Well, I can tell you what to do," Terah snapped, pointing up ahead. "There's a good-sized town up there—one of the ones those traders told us about. Our scouts just told me that they've spotted it on the horizon. We're going to have to wait there until your mother recovers before we can go any farther." Irritation tinged his voice, and his eyes were hard as he stared at his tall son. "I think sometimes you care more about these sheep and goats and cattle than you care about your mother!"

"That's not true, sir," Abram said defensively. He loved his mother, and he was aware that Terah knew it, but the patriarch had gotten snappy over the months of travel. They had been on the road for six months now, having stopped twice for extended periods of time because of his mother's health. Abram had never complained of this, which his father well knew, but Terah was unhappy.

"We should never have left Ur," Terah grumbled, his lips drawn together into a tight line, dissatisfaction reflecting in his eyes. "We'll probably all die out here in this desert."

Abram had to keep a close rein on the words that rose to his lips. For a moment he felt a raw bitterness toward his father. He wanted to say, *It was your idea to come along! Nobody invited you!* Almost from the time they had left Ur, Terah had started complaining about the hardness of the way and more than once had urged Abram to turn back. Now Abram kept silent, despite his anger. He trudged along, listening as Terah griped, and tried to figure out his own feelings.

Something is wrong with all this. The Eternal One told me to leave my country, but he also told me to leave my father's household. I know that somehow the Eternal One has a mission for me, although I have no idea what it is. But whatever it is, He intends for me to do it alone, not with the rest of my family. Maybe I ought to insist that Father and Mother stay in this place or turn around and go back to Ur if that's what they want.

As they drew near the town, Abram tried to sort out his thoughts and Terah continued his complaints. When they reached the outskirts of it, Terah said, "Well, this looks like a place we could stay until your mother is stronger."

Abram slowly turned to his father and said grudgingly, "All right, Father, we'll wait here until Mother is better, but then I'm moving on."

Having won the victory, Terah smiled. "Well, that's more like it. Now, let's see what kind of a place this is."

As they made their way toward the town center, the inhabitants watched them curiously. Living along a well-traveled trade route, they were accustomed to travelers who often stopped for long periods to trade and rest before heading west to Carchemish or east to Nineveh. These people were, as far as Abram could see, very much like those he had left in Ur. They came to the temple area, where a ziggurat, much like those in Ur and Uruk, rose above the rest of the city. They stopped in front of an official-looking building with tall columns, and a man, evidently one of the city leaders, came out to greet them. He was short and broad, encased in fat, and his eyes were sly as he advanced. "Greetings, travelers. Have you come far?"

Terah stopped and bowed. "We come from Ur," he said.

"My, that's quite a ways south of here. You've come a long way. My name is Oliphaz, and I welcome you to our city."

The three men studied each other, and it was Abram who said, "We would like to stay for a time, sir. We will keep our herds and flocks well away from the town so they will not disturb you."

"You are most welcome to stay as long as you like," Oliphaz said. "Perhaps we can do some trading. My people are fine workers in metal. Also they make clever pots with clay from the riverbed."

"What is the name of your town?" Terah asked as he cast his eyes around, studying the homes and small shops.

"This is Haran."

Instantly Terah turned to face him. "Haran," he whispered.

"Why, yes," Oliphaz said. "You've heard of it?"

"No, but that was the name of my son who died."

"I'm sorry to hear it. Was his passing recent?"

"No, a long time ago." Terah stood there pensively staring at the buildings around him and appeared not to listen.

Abram continued the conversation, making arrangements with Oliphaz to come in and do some trading after they found a good place to let the herds graze. Finally, when the arrangements were made, Abram said, "My mother has been ill for some time. We would like to keep her in town for a while if we could rent a place."

"I have just the place you need," Oliphaz said quickly. "And I would trade it to you for some of your fine cattle or sheep."

The two men discussed the barter terms, and when both were agreed, Oliphaz said, "I will go see that it's made ready. You may bring your mother in anytime."

"Well, that's fortunate," Abram said, turning to his father. He would have said more, but he stopped at the strange expression on Terah's face. "What's wrong, Father?"

"Haran! The name of this place is Haran."

"Yes, it's quite a coincidence, isn't it?"

"Coincidence!" Terah snorted. "It's not a coincidence—it's a sign, boy. It's a sign!"

"A sign of what?" Abram asked.

"Why, that this is the place where we're to stay."

"Well, we've agreed on that, but I don't think it's a sign. It's just a coincidence."

But Terah would have it no other way. He grew excited and hurried back to tell Metura what had happened. He turned around and shouted over his shoulder, "It's a sign, Abram! The gods have provided this place for us. You'll see."

Abram did not respond but shook his head imperceptibly. He knew that his father was tired of traveling and would welcome any excuse to settle down permanently, but deep in his heart Abram knew that Haran was not the place to which the Eternal One was leading him. He prayed as he stood there. "O Eternal One, I fear I have not obeyed you in bringing my parents, but please help my mother to get well so that we can continue our journey." The prayer seemed feeble and weak to him, but he knew no other way to pray. Wearily he turned and went back to inform Sarai of the change in plans.

Everyone seemed happy to settle down at Haran. They were all tired of the hard travel they had endured, and Haran was indeed a good place, very much like Ur, only smaller. The house that Oliphaz leased to Terah was not as nice as the one they had left behind in Ur, but it was comfortable. And as soon as they were settled in, Terah set out for the temple to pay homage to the special god of the city and pray for his wife's recovery. He found out that Nanna, the moon god, was held in high esteem by the dwellers in Haran. He quickly hunted up the high priest of the cult and made a generous offering. The high priest, a fat, oily man with smallish eyes, took the gifts and assured Terah, "Your wife will be fine, sir. Have no fears."

Terah did not wait long after this, only a few days, to confront Abram. "You see," he cried, his eyes shining. "Your mother is better already."

"And you think the moon god had something to do with it."

"What else could it be?" Terah demanded. He was happy and had already made friends in Haran. He had found that he and Oliphaz had a great many things in common, and Abram had heard him talking about starting a trading venture based in Haran and sending craft downriver to the Euphrates. Terah was more excited about this prospect than his son had ever seen him, and Abram felt it necessary to warn him, "Father, don't get too involved here. We'll be moving on before long."

"Not until your mother is well," Terah insisted. "I've done my part. I've left my home, and we've come all this way with you. It would be cruel to drag your mother on a tiresome journey to nowhere."

Abram argued long and finally said with exasperation, "Perhaps you may want to stay here, but I must press on."

Terah grew incensed. "After all we've done, you would leave us! You're her favorite. You always have been. Would you leave her here to die?"

The words cut into Abram, and he could not answer. He sat beside his mother for long periods during the days that followed. He could see that she was still ill, although she had improved some. She clung to him, and his heart cried out at the choice that lay before him. Just the very thought of leaving her here to die and never seeing her again vexed and pained his heart.

He talked to Sarai about this, and she said, "I don't see how you could leave your mother, Abram. She may not live long. How would you feel if you left her alone, knowing she loved you more than anyone else?"

"But what about the Eternal One's command?"

Sarai said nothing, and his heart was heavy as he turned away. *I should never have allowed my parents to come!*

———

Sarai was weary of the journey too, and to her Haran suddenly looked like a very restful place. The long months of travel and worry over her mother-in-law and the upcoming birth of Layona's baby had taken their toll on her, and she tried to soothe Abram, thinking, *If he just stays here awhile and settles down, maybe he'll forget about this journey he's on.* This left her feeling disloyal, for she knew how much the Eternal One meant to her husband. At times she was resentful of Abram's experience with this unseen God, thinking, *Why doesn't He ever speak to me?* But the Eternal One had not spoken to anyone other than Abram, as far as she knew, and she said no more about it. She knew Abram was engaged in a tremendous struggle, but deep in her heart she had no desire for going on to whatever lay ahead of them in the trackless desert.

———

"What's wrong, Sarai?"

Sarai was hurrying toward her tent when Abram stopped her. He had come in from keeping the herd and was covered with a fine dust.

"It's Layona. The child is coming."

Abram blinked with surprise. "Why, it's too early!"

"It's coming anyway," Sarai snapped.

Abram saw the strain in Sarai's face. There was some constraint between the two about this subject. He had found out by picking up on the gossip that many among his workers felt the child was his. He had waited for Sarai to ask him about it, but she never had. Now he stood there helplessly, as a man will at such times. He glanced over toward the city of Haran and thought of going there to find a midwife. When Sarai came out of the tent again, he asked her about this, but she said, "I doubt there is time, but you can try."

Glad to have something to do, Abram went at once into Haran. He looked up Oliphaz, told him the problem, and Oliphaz said, "Why, yes, we have many fine midwives here. I'll choose the very finest."

"Thank you, my friend—and I think you'd better hurry."

Oliphaz did hurry, bringing Abram an older woman with white hair and sharp black eyes. Abram promised her a rich fee and then hurried her back to the camp. When he saw Sarai exiting the tent, he asked anxiously, "Has the child come?"

"No," Sarai said, shaking her head sadly, "not yet, but I don't think Layona will live."

An expression crossed Abram's face that Sarai could not read. She knew he was very fond of Layona, and she wondered at the pain she saw reflected in his eyes. "Who is this?" Sarai asked, nodding toward the old woman.

"This is the midwife."

"You'd better come and see if you can do anything," Sarai said sharply. The two women disappeared into the tent, and Abram stood outside helplessly. He bent down to get a drink of water from a clay jug on the ground and sat down with his legs crossed. Thoughts ran through his mind, and from time to time he jumped at the cries of pain issuing from the tent. It disturbed him so much, he got up and walked away out of hearing range.

"Come quickly," Sarai called out to him many hours later. She had come to find Abram standing on the outskirts of the camp gazing out at the flocks.

"Is the child here?" he asked.

"Yes. It's a boy." Sarai's voice cracked with brittleness, and she stared at Abram, waiting for him to speak.

"How is Layona?"

"Not good. She wants to see you."

Abram stared at Sarai and saw that she was worn out by the long ordeal. Everyone in camp was nervous, aware of the difficulty of the birth and anxious for Layona's life.

"Come quickly. She's going fast," Sarai urged.

Abram followed Sarai through the camp until they came to their tent. He stooped and went inside and saw the old midwife standing there wearily, her face tense. She gave Abram a sad look, then shook her head and left the tent.

Abram went at once to Layona, who lay still and gaunt on the sleeping mat. Her face was paler than any face he had ever seen, the long and painful ordeal having drained the life out of her. He reached out and put his hand on her forehead, aware that Sarai was watching from the door of the tent.

"Is it well with you, Layona?"

Layona did not answer. Fear gripped Abram, and he wondered if she was still alive.

"You have a fine son, Layona," Abram said tenderly.

Layona's eyes opened slowly. Gazing up at Abram, she whispered, "I have a son?"

"Yes, a fine boy."

"I'm dying, master."

"No, no, you will be fine."

"No." The single word was all she had the strength for, and again Abram was seized with fear.

Abram turned to see Sarai watching, her face tense. Turning back to Layona, he touched the child that she held to her breast. "A fine boy," he whispered.

Layona was dying—there was no question about it. She lay there for so long that both Abram and Sarai thought for a moment that she had already died, but he could still see her chest rising and falling gently. She stirred and in a burst of strength pulled the child closer to her lips and kissed his forehead. Then she looked up at Abram and said, "Will you take care of him?"

Abram said quickly, "Yes, of course I will."

"Will you take care of him . . . as your own son?"

"Yes, Layona, I will."

When Sarai heard these words, she stiffened as if she had been struck by a harsh blow. But it was an inward blow, and she did not move. She watched as Abram picked up the child and held him in his arms. Then he reached down and touched Layona's face once more, closing her eyes. He rose and stood before Sarai. Sorrow was written on his countenance, and he held the child tenderly. "She's gone, Sarai." Hesitantly, he said, "We must care for the boy."

Sarai reached for the child. "One of the slave women has a baby. She can nurse him. Give him to me."

Abram extended the infant and watched as Sarai took him.

"Will you name him?" Sarai whispered as she gathered the baby to her. It was a poignant moment. Sarai could not tell what was taking place within her own spirit. She held the child tenderly, but the tenderness she felt was tinged with bitterness. This was not her son but another woman's. And from Layona's last request, she still did not know if the boy was Abram's. She looked at Abram and asked again, "Will you name him, Abram?"

Abram hesitated, then said, "I would like to call him Eliezer."

"None of your kin are named that."

"I know, but I like the name. It means 'God has helped me.' Poor little fellow. He will need God's help!"

Sarai stared at Abram's face again before turning and saying, "I'll take him to the wet nurse." She left the tent, and as she walked across the ground, conscious of the slight weight of the child and of the feelings that mingled in her breast, she wondered how she would ever reconcile her love for Abram with this new development.

———————

Sarai's fears proved groundless. She grew very fond of the baby, and except for nursing him personally, she took care of him constantly. As the days passed and the child grew stronger, she searched his face every day for some sign of resemblance to Abram, but it was impossible to tell. Abram himself took great interest in the child, and more than once she almost demanded of him if he was Eliezer's father, but somehow she could not bring herself to do this.

Despite Sarai's uncertain feelings about Layona and Abram, the child proved to be a great comfort to both her and her husband in the loss of their beloved servant, who had been with them almost their entire married life. Except for her recent jealousy, Sarai had loved Layona, and she grieved over her loss, even in the midst of her confused feelings.

Abram loved the child as he loved all babies and always had. One day Sarai asked him, "Will we stay here for a long time, Abram?"

Abram was holding Eliezer on his lap, gazing at him fondly. He looked up and for a moment did not speak. It was as though he were weighing something in the balance. Sarai could not know that he was trying to settle in his mind whether it would be in the will of the Eternal One for him to go on and leave his parents here. He had struggled hard over this and had reached a decision.

"We'll stay here until my mother is well."

Sarai was content. She had no desire to leave Haran, and she was taken up now with the care of the child. Her love of babies overcame her doubts and fears, and she looked ahead to a time of peace and quiet and of raising the son that was not her own.

CHAPTER

12

A spirit of festivity filled the city of Haran with the jubilant sounds of singers and musicians in every street. The city was like an anthill swarming with men, women, and young people of every age. The air was filled with the scent of the harvest, especially the sharp, aromatic smell of grapes, which always pleased Abram.

Leaning back against the wall of his parents' house, he thought, *This is the tenth harvest I have watched in this place. It's hard to believe that Sarai and I left Ur ten years ago.*

The thought brought a frown to his face, disturbing the evenness of his features. He was sixty-five years old now, but he still felt like a young man. His limbs were strong, his face was relatively unlined, and if his wife were to be believed, he was more handsome than when she had taken him for her husband.

Ten years!

Despite the festivities surrounding him, Abram felt grief at the thought. He had waited for the Eternal One to speak to him, but there had been nothing all this time. The divine silence was profound, echoing in his heart more than the sound of singing that was coming from a group treading grapes.

Something rubbed against his bare calf, and he leaned down to see a strangely colored cat touching him tentatively with a paw. Leaning over, he picked up the loudly purring animal. Stroking the fur, he turned his attention to the crowd around him. Everywhere was shouting, and processions were coming in and out bringing harvest offerings to the city. The grapes had been plucked with singing, and now young men and young women were laughing and shouting, treading them with their naked feet into the stone winepress.

Their legs were purple to the thighs, and a sweet juice flowed through a trough into the vat.

The seven-day feast would begin as soon as the wine was racked. There would be sacrifices of cattle and sheep, also of corn and oil, followed by much feasting and drinking. Abram's eyes narrowed as they brought the idol from his temple. Six strong young men, priests in training, carried Nanna, the moon god, on a platform, lifting it by two long poles. Musicians playing drums and cymbals lead the procession as the neophyte priests bore Nanna around to bless the city. He would then be carried out to the fields and the vineyards to give his blessing there.

Abram was unhappy as he stared at the idol, disgust rising in him when he watched people crowding forward to kneel down and kiss the idol as it passed.

"Kissing a block of stone and singing songs to it," Abram muttered. "People should have better sense!" His eyes narrowed as he saw that Lot was in the way of the idol, waiting until it passed. Then he too reached out and kissed the stone block, raising his hand in worship.

"You ought to have more sense, Lot. That's a fool thing to do," Abram grumbled. Leaning back against the wall, Abram thought of the possessions that had come to him throughout the ten years he had tarried at Haran. He had thousands of sheep now, not just hundreds, and thousands of cattle too. He had numerous household servants and more shepherds and drovers than he could count to tend all the animals. He lifted his eyes to the hills beyond the city and could see his tents in the distance. He wished he were there now. Haran was a fine city, and his father, Terah, had prospered in business here. But it held no charm for Abram. A persistent restlessness possessed him, urging him to move on from here. Shoving himself away from the wall, he began to walk among the crowds. He was greeted by name time and again and returned the greetings. It distressed him that he had become so settled in this place that no one thought of him any longer as a visitor but rather as a permanent member of the community.

He made his way to the winepress and caught sight of Eliezer, leading a group of youngsters around the outside of it. An involuntary smile came to Abram's lips. The baby that he had held only moments after his birth was now approaching ten years and was as fine a boy as Abram had ever seen in his life. The children he led were shouting and, from time to time, snatched at the grapes piled high waiting to be pressed. Purple juice ran down Eliezer's face, and Abram could not restrain the surge of pride that ran through him.

He watched a young woman, who was bringing a huge cluster of grapes to be pressed, step up on the rim of the stone press with her arms full. She was about to throw the grapes down when Eliezer suddenly darted forward and gave her a tremendous shove. The young woman uttered a piercing scream and threw the grapes high in the air. Her arms cartwheeled as she tried to keep her balance, but it was too late. She fell full-length into the mixture of juice and crushed grapes, and a great shout of laughter went up from everyone.

Despite himself, Abram laughed aloud. He knew that there was a naughty streak in Eliezer, but he could never bring himself to worry about it.

Suddenly Sarai appeared, grabbing Eliezer by the arm and shaking him. Abram moved forward to hear her accusing him.

"What do you think you're doing, shoving Lina into the vat? You might have hurt her."

"No, she's all right," Eliezer said quickly. He looked up to see Abram watching with a half smile on his face. "Did you see her fall, sir?"

"Yes, I did. You're a naughty boy."

"But it was funny, wasn't it?"

Sarai waited for Abram to say a word of chastisement to the boy, but Abram merely said, "You'd better be careful. You might find yourself in there too." He quickly moved forward, snatched the boy up, and held him out over the grapes.

Abram could hear the others crying, "Throw him in! He deserves it!"

Eliezer screamed and yelled, grabbing helplessly at Abram's robe. "How would you like to be stomped like these grapes here?" Abram said.

"Don't do it, sir—don't do it!"

Abram then laughed and pulled the boy back. He gave him a hug and said, "Go along, now. And don't shove anybody else into the winepress." He watched as Eliezer darted away, followed by his friends. Then he turned to find Sarai staring at him.

"You ought to be ashamed," she snapped.

"Why should I be ashamed?" He came forward and put his arm around her in an embrace.

"Let me go!" she said. "You ought to take a stick to that boy."

"He was just having a bit of fun. Look, Lina's all right." He pointed toward the young woman, who was up and laughing now, wiping the grape juice from her hair and face. She joined the rest of the grape treaders, and Abram said, "See? She's fine."

"You spoil that boy terribly."

Ignoring her words, Abram kept his arms around her and pulled her closer. "You know, you're a fine-looking woman. The best-looking woman in Haran—or anywhere else for that matter."

Sarai tried to keep a frown on her face and shoved at him uselessly. She was proud of Abram's looks, even at the age of sixty-five. His face was strong, and although he was not as handsome as some men, there was a leanness and a strength in him that made her feel secure. She was pleased at his attention and finally broke into a laugh. "What are you going to do—throw me in there too?"

"No. Come along. Let's just walk around for a while."

The two walked among the celebrants, and the time passed quickly. They stopped to eat some of the succulent melons a vendor was selling, and with the juice running down her chin, Sarai said, "It's a good time of year, isn't it?"

A shadow crossed Abram's face, but he smiled. "Yes, it is," he said. "Harvest time is always good."

Sarai had noticed his reaction, however, and she took his arm and turned him to face her. "You're worried about your mother, aren't you?"

"I never thought she'd live this long," he said, "but she's really sick this time."

Sarai almost asked what they would do if Abram's mother died. He had talked to her before many times about leaving Haran, but the thought of his parents, who needed him desperately, had always held him back.

The two walked over to the edge of the festivities and sat down in the shade of one of the houses. They watched for some time in silence, and finally Sarai asked an unexpected question. "Do you ever still think about the Eternal One, Abram?"

Abram looked up, startled, then dropped his head and stared at his hands. Finally his voice came out in almost a whisper. "He's forgotten me, I think, Sarai, and I can't blame Him."

Sarai put her arm around him, feeling the strength of his body. "You don't worship any of the gods in Haran."

"No, and I never will."

"You still love the Eternal One."

"Yes, I do. But I think . . . I think the Eternal One gives a man a chance, and if he fails to carry out His will . . . why, God finds another man."

"How did you fail the Eternal One?"

"I didn't obey Him." Abram turned and faced her, saying in a quiet but intense voice, "He is the God above all gods, and I disobeyed Him, Sarai."

Sarai saw the pain in her husband's eyes and on his face. She reached for his hand and he took hers, holding it in both of his. As always, the strength of his hands made her feel secure, but she was aware that Abram was an unhappy man. "You haven't failed Him."

"Yes, I have. He told me to leave my country and my father's house."

"You did leave. We left Ur ten years ago."

"I left Ur—but not my kindred."

"Surely the Eternal One knows you have a duty to your parents."

"I don't know, Sarai. I've thought about it in every possible way, but one thing is clear—He hasn't spoken to me since we left Ur."

Sarai knew then what she must do. She squeezed his hand and tightened her grip. "When your parents die," she said quietly, "you can go."

"No, I'm afraid not. I'll be too old. The Eternal One will find another man." He fingered the medallion and said, "He hasn't even told me who I should give this to."

"You could give it to Lot."

"Lot? No, he's too frivolous. It has to be someone that the Eternal One puts on my heart. But I don't think He will ever speak to me again."

––––––––––

Abram's mother died quietly in her sleep a week after the harvest festival. Abram hurried to town, but when he got there it was too late. He sat beside the body of his mother, grieving over her. He had loved her dearly, and now she was gone.

Terah was distraught. He had loved his wife as much as he loved anything on earth, and now he was afraid. Abram could see it in his eyes but said nothing to him until after the funeral. Terah stood before him then, his hands unsteady. "I know what you're going to do now, Abram. You're going to leave me, aren't you?"

"Why do you say that, Father?"

"Because you've always intended to. You didn't want your mother and me to come with you in the first place."

Abram said quietly, "You shouldn't talk like that."

"But you are going to leave, aren't you?"

If the question had been asked five years ago, Abram would have said yes. But he was now totally convinced that the Eternal One, who had been silent to him for ten long years, had put him aside. *Somewhere*, he thought, *God is speaking to another man. He'll not speak to me again.* He looked down at his father and saw how he had aged. He was an old man now, weak, and had been almost as sick as his wife. *He can't live long*, Abram thought, *and besides, what else is there for me to do but take care of him?*

"Don't worry, Father. I wouldn't know where to go. The Eternal One will never speak to me again."

———————

Later that day Sarai saw that Abram was troubled. "I saw you talking to your father," she said. "What did you say to him?"

"He was afraid that we were going to start out on our journey again."

"Well, are we?" Sarai's voice was sharper than she intended.

Abram looked at her and sadness welled up in him. "No," he said heavily. "My father can't live long. You can see it in him. Death is a shadow that's over him. I'll stay until he dies, but even then where would we go?"

Sarai knew that something had changed in her husband, and she came to stand beside him. She loved him with all of her heart, and now she said quietly, "Whatever you do will be right."

The two stood there, and Sarai knew that her words had meant little to Abram. His thoughts were in the past, and she knew he was thinking about the time that the Eternal One had appeared and given him a glorious promise.

Now a gloom settled over him, and he shook his head. "I do not think He will ever speak to me again."

He turned and left Sarai, who stood looking after him, a sadness in her own heart. She had never seen Abram's God herself, but now she prayed to him. "O Eternal One, do not forsake my husband. He loves you dearly!"

PART FOUR

THE PHARAOH

When Abram came to Egypt, the Egyptians saw that she was a very beautiful woman. And when Pharaoh's officials saw her, they praised her to Pharaoh, and she was taken into his palace.

Genesis 12:14–15

CHAPTER
13

Abram sat in his home in a long, narrow room between pillars that supported the roof, looking out over the darkening sky to the fields in the distance. It was a pleasant and airy haven from the heat of the day. Turning his head, he looked out past another pillar into the quadrangle of the inner court, hung with colored awnings and with a wooden gallery running around it. The silence of the afternoon was broken by the hum of the servants' voices, and from far off a wild donkey brayed raucously.

Evening was coming quickly, and now a maidservant fetched fire from the hearth and lit the three earthenware lamps that stood upon tripods. Abram watched her listlessly and could sense the aroma of fresh bread baking. To his right stood a great earthenware jar filled with goat's milk. Two large wooden chests occupied the outer wall of the room, and two dark brown dogs slept soundly in a patch of sunlight that flooded the outer court.

Knowing that the evening meal would soon be served, Abram got up and left the house. He had purchased the home from Oliphaz since his mother's death. His father had become almost helpless and it was necessary for Abram to stay close to him. Ten more years had passed in Haran, and he now spent much of his time here at his home in the city, dividing his attention between his father's needs and those of the herds that proliferated out in the pasturelands close to the river. Now he made his way through the city, needing a break from his father almost as much as he needed air. He passed by the houses on the outskirts of the city, nodding or speaking to those he knew, until he finally reached the edge of the city.

He paused beside a large wall of unmortared blocks of stone on which was perched a statue of the god Nanna. Abram observed the remains of offerings that had been left—food and flowers—and he watched three mangy dogs fighting over the scraps of food.

"That's about the only good that'll come from those offerings," he muttered. Then he turned and made his way to the well that lay on the outer side of the city. When he got there he paused and, feeling thirsty, leaned over and stared into the water. Even in the fading light he could see his reflection in the still water below. He stared at it, noting how white his hair had become in the last ten years. He saw his dark skin, bronzed from a lifetime of exposure to the sun, and the ever-deepening wrinkles around the corners of his eyes. He noted that his neck was not as strong and muscular now as it had once been, and he could foresee the day when it would be scrawny and thin and weak.

"What are you looking at, master?"

Abram whirled around, startled, and saw that Eliezer was standing behind him. "Oh, nothing," he said quickly, shaking his head at the tall young man.

Eliezer, not fooled, came over and looked down into the well. "Admiring yourself in the water, eh?" he said, smiling.

Abram bent over again next to Eliezer and studied the two reflections. "Who is that old man in there, Eliezer?"

"Why, it's you."

"That's not me! That old man is seventy-five years old, my son." Abram looked at the reflection in the water again, then picked up a pebble that lay on the wall surrounding the well. He tossed it in and watched the stone break the water's smooth surface, turning his image and Eliezer's into rippling waves of concentric circles. He muttered to himself again, "Who is that old man? Where is the young man who could run like a deer and never grow tired? Where is that young fellow who could lift more than anyone in the city of Ur? Where is he?"

Eliezer was staring at Abram. He had a worshipful attitude toward this man, who had always been like a father to him. He smiled quickly and reached out to touch Abram's arm. "Why, you look like a man of forty, and my mistress, Sarai—why, she looks like a young woman!"

Abram turned quickly and smiled. "You're right about her at least. She may be sixty-five years old, but she's more beautiful to me than any woman on earth."

Eliezer nodded quickly. "That is so true, master. But it's true of you too. You're still tall and strong, and if you would enter into the games that the young men sometimes engage in, why, you'd put them to shame."

Abram shook his head, but his eyes lit up with humor. "You must want something, Eliezer, talking like that." He regarded the twenty-year-old man, who was tall and slender with a muscular build. He could win most of the races among the young men of Haran, and in the feats of strength, he held his own. He was a handsome man too, with lustrous black hair and dark eyes.

The young Eliezer was aware that his master was staring at him and stood patiently. It was something he had done all of his life. Sarai had told him many times how Abram had saved his mother from the bondage of slavery at the hands of a cruel master, and he had found great delight in serving this man.

"Did you just come in from the flocks, Eliezer?"

"Yes. I went out to check the animals over in the north pasture. There were seventeen new lambs, and every one of them looks healthy."

Abram beamed. "Did you give them names?" he teased. "You know every animal in the herd, I do believe."

Eliezer returned Abram's smile. "No, not really, but the flocks have never looked so good, master."

Eliezer knew every sheep, goat, cow, and bull in the flocks and herds. He always knew when it was time to change pastures, and there was no one like him for treating sick animals. Even in his youth, no one had thought it strange when Abram had named him his personal steward. No one had ever thought of him as a slave, and there were those who were convinced he was Abram's son, though Eliezer never presumed such a thing himself. He was totally devoted to Abram and Sarai, and the first thought in his mind was always, *What would be good for my master and mistress?*

"I suppose we'd better go back. It's time to eat," Abram said.

The two men started back home, and Abram noticed, with some pride, that Eliezer had reached his own height now. The two of them were the tallest men in Haran and always attracted attention as they walked together through the streets.

Eliezer continued to speak of the flocks, but then he changed the subject. "My mistress has told me so many times about how you saved my mother."

"That's right. I was courting Sarai at the time—and not doing a very good job of it."

"I can't believe that," Eliezer protested. "She must have loved you at once."

"I hate to disillusion you, but she didn't. Our romance had a rough beginning. I pushed her off a bridge into the mud, and she hated me for it, or seemed to."

Eliezer wanted to hear all about it. He loved to hear Abram tell stories of his youth. When Abram stopped speaking the young man said, "And you saved my mother, master. I can never be grateful enough to you for that."

Abram was quiet for a moment. They were approaching the house now, and he stopped and turned to the young man. "Your mother was a fine woman, Eliezer."

"I wish she would have lived so that I could have known her."

"So do I. You would have loved her."

"But you and Mistress Sarai have been like a father and mother to me."

Abram lifted his eyes and peered into the young man's face, looking for some key of meaning in the words he had just spoken. Abram had been aware for years that many considered Eliezer his own son. He knew that Sarai had those thoughts too, although she had kept them to herself. Now he was wondering if Eliezer was referring to this possibility, yet he saw nothing in his gaze but a firmness and an openness. "I hope so, Eliezer. I couldn't have asked for a finer man to have for a son." His voice grew husky, and he cleared his throat. "Come along. Let's go in to the meal."

The meal that they finally sat down to, along with Sarai, was filling. The mutton was cooked exactly right in sheep's milk, just as Abram liked it, and was flavored with coriander and garlic, mint, and mustard. They ate flatbread dipped in olive oil, and the wine was heady and refreshing.

"If you keep feeding me like this, wife, I'm going to grow as fat as old Oliphaz."

Sarai sniffed. "You never gain a pound! You walk it all off, and you too, Eliezer."

Eliezer swallowed a mouthful of the sour wine and grinned. He made a handsome sight, his skin bronze and his eyes and hair as dark as night. "I'm not afraid of growing fat, but you are the best cook in the world, mistress."

They were concluding their meal with a compote of plums and raisins served in copper bowls when Sarai turned serious. "Your father's not doing well, husband."

Abram put down his goblet and stood to his feet, an anxious look on his face. "I'm worried about him," he admitted. "Perhaps I'd better go see him."

After Abram left the room, Eliezer said quickly, "Is he very sick, mistress?"

"Yes. He's not going to live much longer, Eliezer." Sarai looked up and shook her head. "I don't understand how he's lived this long."

Abram stepped inside the darkened room lit by a single lamp. A male servant sat beside his father, and when Abram nodded, the servant immediately rose and left the room. Sitting down beside Terah, Abram put his hand on the thin, withered shoulder and said, "Is it well with you, my father?"

Terah's face shadowed death so clearly that Abram was shocked. He had not seen his father for three days, and when he had left him last, the old man had been sitting up and taking nourishment. Now it seemed the life that was in him was so faint it was hard to believe he could exist. He had been ill for several years now, going steadily down, and Abram had been faithful to procure the best care for his father. Now, however, he knew for a certainty and with a dull shock that death was imminent.

"My son . . ." Terah struggled to get out those two words, and just the effort of it seemed to exhaust him. His eyes fluttered, and his lips moved faintly. He had lost his teeth ten years earlier and was able to take only that which had been turned into a mushy liquid. His lips were drawn in now, and his face seemed to have collapsed. His hands lay on his breast, and they twitched feebly, so Abram put his hand over his father's and said, "My father, I trust you are resting easy."

The voice seemed to arouse Terah. He opened his eyes fully then. They appeared enormous because the face was so shrunken. Abram leaned forward to catch the whisper that came from the withered lips.

"Abram . . . what's going to . . . become of me . . . ?"

"Become of you? Why, I'll take care of you, Father."

"No, I mean . . . after death."

Abram could not speak for a moment. He could almost smell the fear in the old man, and he thought quickly how his father had grown more fearful of death as the years had mounted up. Terah had made offerings to every god he could think of in these past years, but the fear had only increased and now flickered in his eyes. He lifted his hand, and Abram took it. The bones felt like the bones of a bird, so tiny and fragile, and Abram could think of no answer. He saw his father looking at him, straining to lift his head and waiting for an answer—and then suddenly the moment passed.

Abram was shocked, for he saw his father give one sudden expulsion of air along with a tiny cough, and then he lay totally still.

"Father!" Abram whispered. "Father, can you hear me?"

But Terah could hear nothing nor ever would hear anything again in this world.

Abram sat there with his hands on his father's in the stillness of the room. There was a grim finality in the lines of his father's face. Abram could only sit and stare at him.

Finally he reached out, touched his father's forehead, bowed over the old man, and kissed his cheek. Then he got up and left the room. When he returned to the living area, both Sarai and Eliezer turned. Sarai started to speak but with one look at his face, she rose up, saying, "What is it, husband?"

"My father is dead."

Abram's voice sounded flat in his own ears, and he was aware that both Sarai and Eliezer were speaking to him, but his mind was fragmented. He was thinking of their words and of the still, dead face of the one who had given him life, but somehow he knew that something different had come into his own life at the moment his father died.

Abram went through the funeral ceremonies in a daze, saying hardly a word. His silence had been so pronounced that Sarai was troubled about him, but she could think of no comfort to give. For two weeks after the funeral, he disappeared into the hills alone.

Sarai knew that Abram had always done this during times of crisis, yet it troubled her.

For Abram, the death of his father was like a door that had opened. A numbness had come over him, yet a tiny spark glowed inside, and he knew that something vital had changed in his life.

The sun was almost over the low-lying hills far away to the west as he sat beside the river. He had been there for hours simply watching the water birds and an occasional fish breaking the surface. The fishermen were all gone now, and a strong silence lay over the land. He could smell the river with its moistness and strong odors of mud and decaying vegetation.

He had been praying almost continually since his father had died, and now as he sat there, he prayed again. "O Eternal One, maker of all things, hear my voice."

Abram perhaps expected no reply. After all, it had been decades since he had heard the voice of the Eternal One.

But then the voice came, and instantly the memories came flooding back. He remembered the voice! Abram fell down on his face, conscious that he was in the presence of the great Eternal One. He quaked and could not speak again, nor did he dare lift his face, for fear filled him.

"Do not be afraid, Abram, for you will see the promise I have made fulfilled. Leave now and go to the land I will show you. I have told you that I will make you into a great nation, and I will bless you and make your name great, and you will be a blessing. I will bless those who bless you, and whoever curses you I will curse, and all peoples on earth will be blessed through you."

As the voice of God spoke to Abram, he continued to kneel before the Lord. He never knew how long he stayed there, but afterward he could not forget the voice, and there was a new determination on his face when finally the voice fell silent and Abram became aware of the night sounds around him.

Startled, he stood to his feet and saw that the moon was high in the sky. His knees felt weak and his legs unsteady, and he breathed shortly. He could not speak, and tears were running down his cheeks. He stood for a long time unable to move, and then he straightened up, wiped his face on his robe, and started back toward Haran.

He spoke to no one, and when he came into the house he found Sarai waiting for him.

"Where have you been?" she said at once. "I've been worried."

Abram took Sarai by the hands, and when she looked up, she was startled. Her husband had looked tired and worn for so long—for years, she realized—but now his eyes were glowing and it seemed there was a fire somewhere deep inside him that could not be contained. His grip was so strong that he hurt her hands, but she could not speak, so shocked was she at his appearance.

"Sarai," Abram said, "the Eternal One has spoken to me again." Words tumbled out of Abram's mouth, and he told her what God had commanded him to do. "It's the same as he told me back in Ur. I was wrong to take my father and mother along. I know that, but it's not too late. He still has a work for me to do. Sarai, the Eternal One has not forgotten us."

"But where will we go?" she asked.

Abram seemed to have regained his youth. He picked Sarai up, swung her around, and then put her down and laughed. "The Eternal One will lead our way. We will go where He commands. Oh, Sarai, He has not forgotten me! The Eternal One still loves me!"

Sarai could not feel the same joy that she saw in Abram's face. She had made friends and a life in Haran. At this late age, she had given up on ever having her own children, but they had Eliezer. One day soon he would marry and give her grandchildren. But she saw the light in Abram's eyes and knew that this dream must go. She put her hands on his chest and then spoke softly. "All right, my husband, I will go with you—wherever the Eternal One leads you."

CHAPTER

14

Sarai held Meri's child high in the air and smiled as the girl screamed with delight. "You're a sweet one!" Sarai crooned. "The best baby I've ever seen."

Meri, Lot's wife, sat in the shade, resting from the midday heat. She could not, however, escape the incessant wind, which blew the sand in her eyes and covered her hair and skin with a fine film of dust. She shook her head and scowled. "I don't see how you have the energy to pick her up, Sarai." Meri nodded her head toward her other three daughters, who were playing in the sparse shade of a scraggly tree. "I don't know how they have the energy either. This trip is killing me."

With the baby resting on her hip, Sarai turned to face Meri, who had taken off her sandals to massage her feet. She resisted the retort that came quickly to mind: *If I could have had babies like you, I would never have complained about the heat or the dust.* Of Meri's four daughters, the older two were almost ready for marriage, while the younger two had come along much later. One was still a toddler, the other just crawling. Sarai had fought her own feelings of jealousy each time Meri had produced a baby, having never stopped grieving over her own childlessness. By now she should have had many grandchildren and great-grandchildren.

"Let me bathe Susea," Sarai offered as she headed toward the riverbed, where only a small trickle sufficed to water the flocks.

Meri made no protest, always willing to let Sarai take care of her children. She was a selfish woman, constantly complaining about her situation and giving her husband no end of grief. She had thrown a furious tantrum when Lot told her they were leaving Haran. She had settled into the comfort of city life there and had made many friends. Her children were well cared for by servants—and by Sarai—and she herself spent her days letting her maid-servant wait on her hand and foot.

While Meri watched from the shade of the tree, Sarai knelt down by the stream with the baby on her knees. She captured a handful of the muddy water and splashed it over the girl's face, then set her down by the trickle and let her dabble her feet in the water. On the other bank, Abram and Lot were bringing a few sheep at a time for water. It took all day to water the entire flock, and the next day the struggle would start over. *Oh, to live in a place again where there is plenty of water,* Sarai thought longingly. *Back in Haran we never had to worry.*

Sarai was not given to finding fault, but ever since they had left Haran, the journey had been a struggle as they ventured into desert lands far from the safety of nearby rivers. Early on in their journey from Haran, they had traveled back down the Balikh River to the Euphrates, connecting once more with that great river they had known in Ur. But then they had turned westward, leaving the safety of the river to wander trackless deserts of sand and rock with few signs of life.

Sarai was startled out of her thoughts by a voice. "Good afternoon, mistress. Giving the little one a bath?"

She looked up to see Eliezer, who had come from the other direction downstream, where he too was watering the sheep. Dust covered his face, and his black hair was now gray with it. He smiled at her with cracked lips, then lay down by the water to drink his fill.

"It's like drinking mud, isn't it?" Sarai sighed. "I miss the big river."

"We'll find another one in a few days," Eliezer said, standing. "That's what I hear from the travelers we met coming from Egypt."

Abram, Eliezer, and Lot had chosen to follow an ancient trade route that led into Canaan. Ordinarily, there were plenty of watering holes and streams, but recent years of drought in this already arid land had changed all that. They were reminded of the danger each time they passed by the skeletons of sheep and cattle, felled by thirst, then picked clean by desert scavengers.

Squatting down by the water's edge, Eliezer touched the cheek of the little girl, who grinned up at him. "What a pretty child," he remarked, returning her smile.

"Yes, she is." Sarai beamed, as though Susea were her own baby.

"I've been worried about the youngsters," Eliezer said, sitting down next to Sarai and looking around. "This is hard on all of us, but it is especially difficult for the oldest and youngest."

"How much longer will it be before we get to a better trail?"

"I hope not more than three or four days." Eliezer frowned. "We've already lost too many animals."

"I think you've done a wonderful job," Sarai said, smiling at him. She reached out to brush a lock of black hair from his forehead. "You look so tired. You need to rest more."

"I'll rest when we get to Canaan."

"Do you think this new land will have better grazing than we had in Haran?"

"I believe so, and what's more, it will belong to you and Abram."

Sarai flashed a penetrating look at the young man. "You've been talking to Abram. He talks like that land is his already, but there are people there, aren't there? Surely they won't let us just march in and claim it for ourselves."

"They can defend it all they want to, but it doesn't really belong to them. The Eternal One has promised the master that it will be his land, and yours too. It will be ours—for our people."

Sarai searched the young man's face and marveled at his optimism. He had such confidence in her husband—and such unshakable faith in Abram's God, whom Eliezer himself had never seen or heard. So convinced he was of their divine leading that he never complained, no matter how bad things got. She had seen him so tired after keeping the herds that he simply slumped down on his blanket to sleep, without even the strength to eat. But never once had he complained. "I'll be glad when we get there," Sarai said, rising to her feet. "I'd better go see about helping with the evening meal."

"There are plenty of servants for that, mistress. Sit down."

Sarai was happy to comply, for she too was weary. She sat down again, put Susea on the ground, and listened to Eliezer talk about matters of interest to him. He was altogether consumed with his service to Abram and Sarai. She felt a sense of pride mixed with love as she looked at him. *If we'd had a son, I'd want him to be exactly like Eliezer*, she thought. She listened as he continued to speak and finally asked him, "Have you ever thought about yourself?"

"About myself? What do you mean, mistress?"

"I mean having your own wife and family. I think you'd be a wonderful father. You love children so much." She smiled and tugged his black hair again. "I've seen several of the young women watching you."

Eliezer frowned. "I don't have time for that. It's all I can do to serve you and the master."

"But you must have a life of your own."

Eliezer laughed. "I've got all I can handle taking care of these smelly cattle and sheep." He leaned over, tousled Susea's hair, then stood once again and bowed toward Sarai. "I think I'll just take one more look before supper." He turned and walked away, and Sarai watched him go. He was a tall man, as tall as Abram, though not as strongly built. She saw him stop to speak to several of the servants and observed how quickly they responded. She also saw that the most attractive of the female servants, a tall, dark-haired young woman, pulled at his sleeve and then walked beside him. "All the young women are in love with him," Sarai murmured to herself, "but he doesn't seem interested. Eventually he'll have to be, though. He's got to have a life of his own."

A valley lay sharply defined between two steep hills that arose on either side of it. Eliezer studied the valley carefully as he made his way forward, accompanied by the most trustworthy of the herdsmen, a short, squatty man with a bristly beard. His name was Gar, and now he came up to walk beside Eliezer. "The land's been looking better," he grunted. He had a low-pitched growl of a voice, and his dark eyes moved constantly. "We need to find water and quick, or we're going to lose more animals."

"I know, Gar, and I think through this pass, if what the traders said was right, we'll find it."

The journey had been hard, and they had lost animals, but not as many as they might have, for Eliezer had spent weary hours looking for tiny pockets of water. Now, however, he could tell that the land was falling, and from the description he had gotten, he was sure that they would connect with a river just beyond the pass. Licking his lips, he realized he was dried out, and holding up the small bottle suspended by a leather thong, he let the precious water flow into his mouth. "Have a drink," he said to Gar.

"I've got my own. You'd better save it for yourself."

The two men continued to advance, and from time to time they both would look back to where they could see the other herdsmen, led by Abram and Lot, bringing the cattle and the sheep slowly on. The day was bright, as always, and the sun heated the rocks to an unbearable temperature.

Gar took another look back and saw Sarai riding on a donkey. "I can't get over how fine looking the mistress is," he grunted.

From any other man Eliezer might have thought this an unsuitable remark, but he knew Gar meant nothing by it. The little herdsman had a wife as homely as he was, but he was completely devoted to her.

"Yes, she is fine looking," Eliezer agreed.

"I can't believe she's barely over sixty-five years old," Gar chattered on. "Why, she could pass for thirty."

"You're right about that—and Abram, why, he's over seventy-five now, but none of us younger fellows can keep up with him."

Gar nodded agreement. "He can walk the legs off of most of us, and he's still strong too. It's a shame he and the mistress never had children. They would have been fine parents."

"It's strange," Eliezer remarked, "how they haven't aged as much as anyone would expect."

"Well, you know the stories that the master tells about the old ones in ancient times—how they lived many hundreds of years."

"You love those stories, don't you, Gar?"

"Yes, I do. I wish I had lived in those days. Think what it would be like to live for nearly a thousand years!"

"That would be all right if a man stayed young in body, but I wouldn't want to live to be that old and be helpless."

"Well, the master's not helpless."

"No, he certainly is not. He puts us younger men to shame!"

Eliezer quickened his pace, and Gar, with his short, stubby legs, had to walk rapidly to keep up with him. They approached the crest of the hill, and Eliezer said, "When we cross this we'll be able to see the valley that the traders told us about. The river should be down there."

The two hurried, but they had not gone more than fifteen or twenty paces when suddenly a small group of men appeared. They apparently had been concealing themselves behind the rocks that rose on either side of the narrow pass.

Eliezer felt a chill around his heart and thought, *They look like bandits.* He let none of this show on his face but studied the leader who came forward. The man was fairly tall and very broad. He wore coarse-looking leather clothing, and as he approached, Eliezer could smell the stench—a raw, rough smell that matched the man's appearance.

"Hello, strangers. My name is Bedoni."

"I am Eliezer, chief steward of Abram."

"Abram? What kind of name is that?" Bedoni said, grinning. His muscles were thick and bunchy. A long sword dangled from his belt, and he carried a wicked-looking staff in his hand. His companions were similarly armed with knives, swords, and sharply pointed staffs.

"My master's called a Hebrew," Eliezer replied calmly.

"Hebrew? Never heard of it." Bedoni turned around and laughed as he studied his men. "I think we can handle a Hebrew or two."

A scornful laugh went up, and it was obvious that the crew was ready for trouble. They began to form a semicircle around Eliezer and Gar.

"We're headed for Canaan," Eliezer said, still keeping his voice calm and his eyes on the leader as the other men surrounded them.

"A long way to Canaan." Bedoni laughed again. He grinned boldly, showing yellow teeth. "We take a toll from everyone that comes through the pass and then a toll for the water down below."

"This land belongs to no one," Eliezer protested, for he saw the conversation was headed toward robbery. He and Gar were armed only with shepherd's crooks and short knives in their belts. They were only two against the five that stood before them, all rough men clearly accustomed to using weapons.

"We don't argue about that. We'll let you off easy this time with a dozen sheep and a dozen of your cows for making your way through the pass, and that many more for watering them down below."

Eliezer shook his head firmly. He knew that when word got out that they were an easy mark, there would be no end to the so-called keepers of the pass. "I might give you one sheep and one cow, just as a token—but that's all."

Bedoni stepped forward and lifted his pointed staff. The grin disappeared, and he snarled, "Boy, it's better to have something than nothing." He quickly lifted his staff in a threatening gesture. "We'll take what we want!"

Gar stepped forward and shouted, "You'll take nothing!" Pulling his knife from his belt, he snarled, "Get out of our way!"

As a single unit the bandits moved in, while Bedoni raised his staff and brought it down swiftly at Eliezer's head. Eliezer parried it, surprised at the strength of the blow. On the rebound, he swung his staff and struck Bedoni on the shoulder, staggering the man.

"Get them!" Bedoni yelled, and in the ensuing scramble, Eliezer and Gar fought for their lives. Both of them were tough, strong men, but the odds against them were too great. If the bandits had come at them singly, the herdsmen might have done better, but their attackers ganged up on them. In the confusion, Eliezer managed to knock down one man but then felt a fiery pain along his side as another bandit struck him. He lashed out in that direction, driving back the bandit, who held a bloody knife.

Bedoni urged the men to finish the job, and Eliezer and Gar fell backward toward a wider space in the pass, still fighting as they frantically searched for a means of escape. Eliezer heard a shout behind him and took a quick glance back. With a surge of gladness, he saw Abram, Lot, and more than a dozen of the herdsmen rushing forward. He saw the light of battle in Abram's eyes as he threw himself into the fray.

The surprise attack drove the bandits backward, and it was Abram who delivered a crushing blow of his staff to the head of Bedoni, who fell heavily. His legs twitched momentarily before he lay absolutely still.

The fall of their leader was all that was needed to send the other four running for their lives.

Abram called out to his men who were chasing them, "Let them go!" He turned and knelt down beside the bandit leader, then looked up with sad eyes. "He's dead."

"Rather his life than Eliezer's," Gar grumbled. "He's bleeding like a stuck pig."

At that Abram commanded his men to get rid of the body, then threw himself down beside Eliezer, who had fallen back against a rock. "Let me see," Abram insisted, concern in his eyes.

"I don't think it's bad," Eliezer mumbled, but he could barely speak as he held his side and gasped for breath.

"It's a deep cut." Abram at once began binding it up with his outer tunic. "This'll hold until we can get you to a better place."

"I think the river's right over this rise through the pass," Eliezer whispered. He tried to say more, but the weakness overcame him. He took one last look at Abram, then closed his eyes.

———

The next thing Eliezer knew was a coolness on his side, and he opened his eyes to see a woman bending over him. He tried to move, and she put her hand on his chest, saying, "Lie still."

Memory came swirling back then, and Eliezer looked around. He saw that he was lying in a tent, but the sides were drawn up, and he could see a river flowing close beside them. The sheep and cattle were drinking, and the grass was green, making a good meal for the first time in a long while for the herds. He turned his eyes back to the woman and whispered, "Beoni, what's happened to me?"

Beoni was a tall slave girl, no more than eighteen. She had dark hair with a reddish tinge and peculiar green eyes. She was well formed and had a golden cast to her skin. "You were hurt in the fight."

"Yes, I remember." Eliezer tried to sit up, but again Beoni put her hand on his chest and held him down. "You lie right there until I change this bandage."

Looking down at his side, Eliezer watched as she removed the cloth. His side had been sewn together. He had patched enough sheep and goats to recognize the stitching, and he shook his head. "That was a pretty close call for me."

"You nearly died," Beoni said, nodding. Her eyes grew gentle then. "We've all been worried about you."

"How long have I been here? I don't remember anything."

"Just a day. It was painful putting the stitches in, so Sarai gave you some strong drink to kill the pain."

"Ahh, yes, I am beginning to remember. It tasted awful!"

Beoni laughed. "You must be thirsty. Here . . ." She reached for a tumbler, filled it with water from a leather bottle, and helped him sit up. Her arm was around him for support, and he was comforted by her soft form pressing against him. He guzzled the water and said thankfully, "That's the best drink I ever had in my life."

"You'd better lie down again."

"No, I want to sit up."

Despite her protests, he pulled himself to a sitting position. He swayed dizzily, and she knelt beside him and held him, her arm behind him.

"It looks like a good place," Eliezer said, looking out toward the river.

"It is. There's lots of grass, and everyone had a bath in the river."

Eliezer turned to her and saw her glowing skin. "That must have been a relief to wash off all that dust."

"Sarai and I gave you a bath last night."

Eliezer's eyes flew open. "Both of you?"

"Yes." Beoni gave him a shy smile.

"Nobody's given me a bath since I was a baby."

"Well, you needed it."

At that moment Sarai and Abram entered the tent and knelt down on either side of him. Beoni moved back to allow Sarai to take her place. "So, you've decided to live," Abram said with relief in his voice.

"I think so, but it's a good thing you came when you did."

"We'll be more careful from now on. We'll first send out a group of scouts who are well armed."

"You think there are more like that bunch?"

"Yes. There are always men like that."

"How do you feel?" Sarai said softly, stroking his cheek. "I was so worried about you, Eliezer."

"Why, I'm all right. Who sewed up my side?"

"I did it myself," Abram said, grinning. "I'm a better seamstress than my wife."

"I couldn't stand to do it," Sarai admitted.

"You had a pretty good nurse," Abram went on. "Even gave you a bath, I understand." He winked at Beoni, who turned her head away, her cheeks flushing pink.

"I've just been finding that out," Eliezer said, grinning at the young woman. "I think I'll let her spoil me for a day or two."

"At least that long," Abram said. "We've got to stay here a week and let the herds fatten up and soak up as much water as they can."

"Are we really in Canaan?" Sarai asked.

"We really are, and we're here to stay."

Eliezer moved about stiffly, but his wound was healing well. They had stayed even longer than a week beside the river, where the grass was so plentiful. Abram had a new light in his eyes and a new spring in his step, and at night he would tell those who gathered around him stories he had heard from his grandfather about the old days, even about the first man, Adam, and his wife, Eve. He felt compelled to plant these stories firmly in the minds of his hearers and to help them memorize, as he had, the names of his ancestors all the way back to Noah.

Abram and Sarai noticed that the young woman Beoni seemed quite smitten with Eliezer, but now that he was getting better, he paid little attention to her. They discussed this during one of their walks together along the river.

"When I was his age I wouldn't let a good-looking woman like that get away," Abram griped.

"Don't give me that," Sarai scoffed. "You didn't know any more about women at Eliezer's age than he does."

Abram wrinkled his brow at Sarai. Like most men, he didn't like to be reminded of his past inexperience in that area, and in his own mind he had revised his own personal history to be more to his liking. His wife occasionally enjoyed reminding him of the truth, but not wanting to embarrass her husband just now, she changed the subject.

"What peoples have lived in Canaan? I know almost nothing about this place."

Abram shrugged. "Neither do I. I've tried to pick up what I can—which is little enough."

"If the Eternal One says you will own it all, I think we should know as much as possible."

"Do you believe that . . . that all this will belong to us?"

"If God says so, then yes, I do."

Abram stopped and turned to face Sarai. "You have such great faith."

"I believe what you tell me, Abram."

"You're a good wife!" Abram suddenly leaned forward and kissed her. "And better looking than ever!"

"Never mind that." Sarai pulled away in feigned protest. "What's that thing over there, that little hill?"

"It was built by people who lived here long ago. I think they're ancient tombs."

"I wonder about people like that," Sarai murmured. "They were once as full of life as we are, but now they've gone back to the earth."

"I think they're still alive." Abram had thought long on this matter, and now he said simply, "I don't think we're here just for this life. I believe one day I'll see Noah and Adam." He smiled at her, then shrugged his broad shoulders. "I can't prove it, but I don't think that the Eternal One made us just to let us disappear forever."

Abram waved his arm at the lush landscape before them. "All sorts of people have lived in this place, Sarai. I can see why they would want to come here—to conquer this land. Why, before the time of Noah and the great flood this land must have been filled with farmers and shepherds like us!"

Sarai cast her eyes over the hills and sighed. "It's a good land, husband."

"Yes, but it needs more water. Except for the land along the rivers, everything is dry." The thought troubled Abram, and he shook his head. "Everything is in the hands of our God. He hasn't brought us to this place for nothing."

The two continued their walk along the river, from time to time casting their eyes south and wondering what lay ahead of them.

CHAPTER

15

"So that's Damascus," Abram murmured. He stood at the front of the caravan on a hill overlooking the city, with Sarai on his right hand and Eliezer on his left. "I hear it's quite a place."

Eliezer nodded in agreement and replied, "Damascus donkeys are the best in the world. I think we need to buy some and start breeding them."

Sarai laughed and put her hand on the young man's arm. "You are the strangest young man I've ever seen!"

"Strange? What's strange about me?"

"Thinking about donkeys!"

"Well, what should I be thinking about, mistress?" Eliezer smiled. "That's my business, to look after the livestock of the master."

"A young man like you should be thinking about having some fun. Some dancing and music. Even a little wine."

"That's right," Abram agreed, nodding. "You're getting to be an old man." He looked at his young steward with obvious affection. "We'll bed down the herds out here where there's plenty of grass and water. Then we're going into Damascus! And all of us are going to have a good time."

"I think we deserve it," Sarai said. "It's been a hard journey." Their stay in Canaan had not lasted very long. The drought that was affecting the entire region had dried up the rivers and parched the grazing lands of Canaan. Therefore, they had headed northeast toward Damascus, where traders had told them there was still water and green grass.

Now Sarai looked down on the bustling city from their observation point and said, "I've heard so much about Damascus."

Eliezer grinned at her. "Have you heard that it's called the 'City of Wild Asses'? Not a very romantic name, is it, mistress?"

"You made that up!"

"I did not!"

"He's right, Sarai," Abram said, smiling. "I've often heard it called that."

"I would refuse to live in a place with an awful name like that!" Sarai sputtered.

"You won't have to live here for long," Abram said. "Just until the rains come again to Canaan. It's a good place to rest awhile."

———

Damascus was an active place—a city where caravans bound west and south for Canaan and Egypt were outfitted. Situated on a fertile plain, the city was a welcome relief after the dried-out plains that Abram's party had been enduring. The city was surrounded by flowering fields, rushing streams, and beautifully tended farms. It was also an exciting center of trade, where one could pick up news from almost anyplace.

As Abram, Sarai, and Eliezer threaded their way through the city, Sarai took in the large open squares and the dark, narrow streets. She eyed the crowds of people, who reflected a variety of races, representing dozens of tribes and nations. The streets were packed, and she found herself jostled by the crowd, dazed by the babble of languages that rose on the air.

"Look, those are Egyptians," Abram whispered, nodding toward a group of dark-skinned people.

"They look haughty," Sarai commented. "I don't think I'd like to live with them."

"They *are* proud." Abram nodded. "After all, they rule most of the world."

Sarai watched a group of bearded Armenian caravaneers bargaining with Phoenician traders for dyes and spices, and Hittite merchants calling out the virtue of their wares.

"I've never seen so many donkeys," Eliezer said. "There must be a thousand of them."

Abram had also noted the beasts, which were heavy shouldered and colored a dark brown. "They're sturdy-looking creatures," he commented. "I agree with you, Eliezer. We should buy some and begin breeding them."

The day passed quickly as Abram became absorbed with watching various caravans being assembled. One of the caravans included over three hundred donkeys, which amazed the three of them. Abram noted the care with which the caravan leaders planned their routes to ensure fresh water from rivers and jealously guarded wells.

Abram found more and more to interest him as they continued on their tour of the city. Finally he said to the others, "We'll have to be careful here. We're foreigners and strangers to these people. We don't want to make the wrong impression."

Sarai glanced up at Abram thoughtfully. "What do you mean?"

"It means that we have to watch how we speak and what we do, so as not to offend these people."

"I don't think you have to worry about that, master," Eliezer said quickly. "Our men are well behaved."

"But we are strangers here nonetheless, and you know how people can be toward newcomers," Abram said. "The city dwellers here are used to seeing a variety of people, but just the same, I think we must be careful and not let the men get into any trouble."

"What about the women?" Eliezer winked at him. "One woman can cause more trouble than any ten men."

Sarai knew his teasing was aimed at her. She sniffed and said, "I don't think I agree with that! You just take care of the men. I'll take care of the women."

Sarai and Abram wandered slowly through the famous Damascus bazaar, listening to the vendors hawking their wares. The stench of the skinned carcasses of sheep and goats hung thick in the air but was sweetened by the fragrant aromas of spices and incense.

"What about this? It would make a nice-looking garment for you, Sarai."

Abram had stopped at a vendor of textiles and now held up a piece of delicate purple cloth toward her face.

Sarai touched it, feeling the fine weave, and exclaimed, "Why, it would take three of these to cover a woman up!"

The vendor, a wiry man with razor-sharp features and a dark complexion, laughed. "The Egyptians don't worry about that. This is fine Egyptian cloth. It's what the finest ladies in Egypt wear, even the wives of the Pharaoh."

"But you can almost see through it!" Sarai protested.

"That's what Egyptian ladies like."

"Well, I wouldn't be caught wearing this! It would be like going naked."

"Some of them do that too." The vendor winked at Abram.

"I think you ought to buy it and make yourself a beautiful garment," Abram urged.

"I couldn't wear it. It's too immodest."

"You could wear it just for me—or under your other clothes."

Sarai protested, but it was a beautiful piece of cloth, so she allowed Abram to buy it for her. Tucking it under her arm, she muttered, "I don't think those Egyptian women can be much if they wear clothes like this."

They continued on down the street and finally Abram touched her arm. "Look, there's Eliezer."

Sarai looked over to where their steward was walking down the street alone, and she shook her head. "He never seems to care anything about himself. Look at him. Why, he could find a woman anytime he wanted to. He's so fine looking."

"I don't think he needs to find one among these people."

Sarai looked up at Abram. "What do you mean?"

"Most of them worship Baal or Astarte."

"You're right; he doesn't need one of those!"

"That's all he'll find here. Astarte worship is very strong in these parts. I'll be happy if our men don't get involved with that."

Eliezer was disgusted when he passed by yet another of the small temples that were found all over Damascus. He had wandered all day long and seen many of them, feeling nothing but distaste for them. To him the worship of Astarte was an abomination, involving temple prostitutes. The use of these women attracted men who had no more interest in religion than a stone. He had seen the lust that pervaded the temple worship and shook his head. More than one of the priestesses, as the harlots were called, had attempted to draw him in.

As he scanned the crowd he was startled to see Gar being guided into one of the temples by a short woman with a painted face, who looked up into his eyes, laughing at him.

"Gar!" Eliezer shouted and went to him at once.

Gar turned around, and his face reddened. "Oh, hello, Eliezer."

"Where do you think you're going?"

"He's going with me, and you can go too." The prostitute smiled brazenly at him. "I'll get one of my sisters for you."

"Never mind!" Eliezer snapped. "Come on, Gar. This sort of thing's not for you."

Gar pulled free from the woman, whose eyes suddenly turned hard. She flashed the two a disgusted look, cursed, and then turned to catch at the robe of a man who was passing by.

"I wasn't really going with her," Gar said weakly, his face filled with shame.

"Yes, you were. But you won't now, even if I have to tie you down out with the sheep and goats."

Gar dropped his head. "Some of the others went," he muttered.

"I'm sure they did! They'll probably pay a price for it too," Eliezer said dryly. "You've got a good wife. Now, stay away from things like that."

———

Abram was walking alongside the river after receiving a report from Eliezer that the shepherds were sneaking away from camp to visit Damascus. There was no doubt in his mind what they were doing there. Most of them were impoverishing themselves by giving gifts to Astarte, which meant visiting the prostitutes, or so-called priestesses. Abram had listened to Eliezer's report and said, "We must get away from here."

"I agree—and as quickly as possible."

Now Abram moved along the riverbank, enjoying the silence, his head filled with thoughts of the Eternal One. He began to speak aloud, a habit he had acquired when alone. It was a form of prayer, and he really expected no reply, but somehow it eased him to say his thoughts aloud.

"O Eternal One, you know all things, and you know the thoughts of my heart. Something is wrong about towns and cities. People are different there from those who live in the open. I think I've been blessed not being a city dweller, except for the years I spent in Haran. Something about a town pulls a man down—and a woman too, I suppose. What is that? Why is it when men gather together in crowds they do things and think things they wouldn't dream of when they are alone in the desert?"

For a long time Abram spoke his thoughts aloud, and finally he found himself by a bend in the river that was covered with papyrus reeds that grew so thickly a man could not see through them. He stood watching the reeds as they swayed in the breeze. He was enjoying the blueness of the sky overhead and the smell of the mud and the river itself, which was a pleasant aroma to him.

"If I become a dweller in a town, Eternal One, could I find you there?"

The answer came so sharply that Abram could not tell if the voice were spoken aloud so that anyone could have heard it or whether it was in his own mind.

It would be hard for you to find me there, Abram. It is always hard for people to find God when their lives are so busy. City people lead busy lives. They have no time for silence.

You found me in the silence once, and you will always find me there.

Abram spoke aloud without thinking. "But what about the people who live in those cities?"

But this time there was only a long silence, and Abram pleaded, "Speak to me, O God, the only living God, the Eternal God. I need to know where I'm going. I've left my home, I've buried my parents, and now I need to know what lies ahead."

The voice was so still and faint that Abram was not certain at first that he'd actually heard it, but then he knew—as he had many years earlier—that he was standing in the very presence of the Eternal Creator!

"To your offspring I will give this land. . . ."

Abram stood for a long time listening to the words of the Eternal One, which did not come to him in a strong voice but as a whisper. Nevertheless, he knew he was listening to the voice of the Creator of all things.

An impulse took him then, which he knew had not come from himself. Leaving the river at once, he made his way to the hills. It took him a long time to get there, but when he reached the point where he could see the desert stretching out beyond the river, he began to gather large stones. He piled them high to his waist, then fell on his knees before them. "This altar I build to you, O Eternal One. How I worship you! There is no other God. The rest are nothing but man's vain imaginings, but you are the true God. The One who makes all things. . . ."

Abram did not know how long he stayed on his face before that altar. It was a precious and holy time to him, and when he left, darkness had begun to fall. He walked slowly back toward the camp, knowing that when he reached it, he would need to share all of this with Sarai. She was hungry for God too, a woman of prayer. It was his delight to have such a wife, and he eagerly made his way through the falling darkness.

Abram sat with his arm around Sarai in their tent. He had talked for a long time, and she had remained silent, watching his face constantly as he told her of his experience at the river and of building the altar. She drank in his words, and her heart cried out with joy that God had once again spoken to her husband.

Several times he tried to stop his recitation, but she pulled at him, saying, "No, don't stop. Tell me more about the Eternal One."

Finally Abram shook his head. "I'm hoarse from speaking, Sarai, but my words are weak things. When I repeat what He told me, it doesn't come across the same way."

Sarai took his hand and held it. "Do you think that God speaks to others besides you?"

"I'm sure He must. He made the whole world and all men. He spoke to my grandfather, and he spoke to Noah. He has always spoken to people."

"But we never meet anyone else who knows Him. Why is that, husband?"

Abram had puzzled over this himself more than once. He struggled to answer, then said, "There are more people in this world than we can even dream of, yet the Creator of all things, the Eternal One, made them all. I have to believe He would not leave them without His voice."

"But most men and women never hear it."

"I can't explain it. He is God, and He does as He pleases."

Sarai was silent, and finally she whispered, "Oh, Abram, I wish He would speak to me!"

Abram took her in his arms then and held her. "Perhaps someday He will," he whispered. "Perhaps He will."

Sarai slept little after their conversation. It had been late when Abram had finally stopped speaking and the two of them had lain down together. He had gone to sleep at once, while she had remained awake for hours. Then she had risen before dawn, leaving Abram still sleeping soundly, apparently exhausted by his meeting with the Eternal One.

Now she walked through the camp, met only by a few early risers. Some of the women were building fires to start the morning meal, and she could hear the sheep and cattle moving about, making the sounds they always made early in the morning.

Finally she reached the sheep, spoke to the herdsmen by name, and then moved on by. She came to stand at the edge of the herd and spotted a ewe that was down. She moved closer to it and saw that it was giving birth. Even as she watched, the lamb emerged and struggled feebly in the red light of dawn.

Sarai was moved by the birth, as she always was. She often saw this miracle take place among the goats, sheep, and cattle yet never ceased to be amazed by it. The birth of any child always left her speechless with wonder.

She moved on, finally reaching the river. The waters flowed quietly at her feet as she stood thinking about the birth and then of her own inability to enter into the miracle that God granted so freely to others but had denied to her. Perhaps the greatest blot on Sarai's life was the fact that she had never given Abram a son or even a daughter. Now any childbearing years she might have had were far behind her. Although she still felt herself to be attractive, she had long since given up any hope of having a child. She wondered how many hours she had cried out to God, begging for a baby, but nothing had ever come of it. And now it was too late.

She was startled to hear a sound and turned to see Abram striding quickly toward her. He put his arms around her and said, "You should have awakened me."

"I wanted to let you sleep," she replied, leaning against him and allowing him to stroke her hair. She knew her husband was rare among men. Any other man with a barren wife would have chosen another or would have taken one of the slave girls for a concubine. It was common among the people, even among Abram's own family, and certainly among other nations that surrounded them.

"You could have had a son with another woman." The words tumbled out unintentionally. She had often thought of taking such a step—encouraging her husband to father a child with another woman—but she had never expressed that idea aloud.

"I would not do that, Sarai. You alone are my wife."

The words brought unspeakable joy to Sarai. She nestled closer in his embrace, feeling the strength that was still in his body, though he was by now getting quite old. "Do you think," she whispered, "that the Eternal One will ever speak to me?"

"No one can ever know a thing like that."

"But He speaks to you. Why not to me?"

Abram's arms tightened, and his voice became a mere whisper. "He's spoken to me so few times. You forget, Sarai, the long years that went by when I heard absolutely nothing from Him."

"But you *have* heard from Him! I have heard nothing!" She began to weep gently, her face buried in his chest.

Abram knew the deep longing Sarai had always harbored for a child of her own, and now he saw her equally strong desire to hear the voice of the Lord for herself. He stroked her back gently and said, "The Eternal One has all power. He cannot be forced to do the will of any man or any woman."

The two stood quietly embracing, and finally Sarai drew back, blinking away her tears. "How long shall we stay here?"

"We must move on. I don't want to stay in Damascus. The men—"

"I know. They're causing great trouble."

Abram looked around at the cattle and said, "The drought is getting worse."

"But there's water here."

"Haven't you seen? The rivers here are drying up too. If the rains don't come soon, I don't know what we'll do."

"What will become of us, then?"

"I cannot say, but the Eternal One has brought us this far. He will not let us perish."

CHAPTER

16

Abundant water and fresh-growing green grass were only a dim memory now. The thought of fields covered with the soft emerald vegetation taunted Abram as the days, weeks, and months dragged on. After leaving Damascus they had returned to Canaan, heading south in hopes of finding more life.

But everything spoke of death. The trees reached their bare branches skyward, and the only sound when one threw a stone into a well was the hollow echo of rock striking dry earth. What streams they found had become mere soupy waters, often no more than sludge.

For months Abram and Eliezer and Lot had worked tirelessly, searching out water and forage, but wherever they moved their flocks, they saw that the drought was strangling life out of the land. They passed through abandoned villages, one after the other, where scenes of activity and laughter had once flourished. Somehow they found enough water to survive, but each day they lost an animal, or sometimes a dozen.

Finally Abram could bear it no more. He had mostly kept to himself, but early one morning he called a brief meeting with Lot, Eliezer, and Sarai. As they gathered together he saw how the heat and pressure of their travels had worn them all down. "I've made up my mind," he announced. "We're going to have to find a better place to stay."

Lot was weary to the bone. He had a family now to think about, and fatigue was etched into his features. "Where can we go?" he said. "Back to Haran? We shouldn't have left there in the first place." His tone was bitter, and he stared at Abram with a hard light in his eyes.

"No, we're going farther south—to Egypt."

"To Egypt!" Sarai gasped. "Why, we can't go there!"

"I think we must," Abram said as gently as he could.

Sarai had listened for years to the tales of what was often called "Ham's Country" or sometimes the "Monkey Land of Egypt." Now she protested vigorously. "You know what we've heard of that place, husband. Those people have black souls. They're cursed with the curse of Ham. Why, they wear linen as thin as spider webs, which covers their nakedness without hiding it. And they pride themselves on their nakedness!"

"We don't know that that's all true," Abram said patiently. Actually he was quite certain it *was* true, for like Sarai, he had listened to the tales of the travelers who had visited Egypt, and the claims of the textile vendor in Damascus, who had described the Egyptians' proud displays of nakedness.

Sarai was horrified. "They have no shame, and they stuff the bellies of their dead with spices. And then they put an image of a dung beetle on their dead. They are rich and lustful like the people of Sodom." She was carried away now, feeling an extreme reluctance to go to Egypt. She raised her voice and looked around at the small gathering. "You all know what they say. They exchange wives with one another, and if a woman sees a young man in the street, she lies with him. They are like beasts, husband, and they bow down to the most awful forms of gods!"

Abram listened patiently as Sarai spoke. He was troubled that she would take this stand, but he had made up his mind that there was no other salvation for them. True, he had heard all of these stories about Egyptian life, but it was also common talk that in Egypt there was bread and food and that the Nile offered pasturage for those who herded animals. He waited until Sarai ceased to speak and then gave her a compassionate look. "It's not the thing I would desire most in the world," he said quietly, "but I think we must do it."

———

Eliezer stood beside Lot, watching the men who were digging shallow depressions in the earth. They had reached what appeared to be a swamp, evidenced by seed-topped reeds, which always bespoke water. The herds had scented water and could not be held back. They had stampeded wildly, only to find that the water was too salty to drink. Eliezer instructed the men to dig shallow depressions where the water was sweet. Watching as the animals drank greedily, the two men shouted instructions to the herdsmen to be sure that all got a chance at the water.

Abram came up to stand beside them and said, "They call this marsh the Sea of Reeds. We have to go around it."

"This is the boundary of Egypt, then?" Lot asked, staring into the distance.

"We probably have been in Egypt for several days, but we've got to go farther before we get to the good grass."

Eliezer was not happy. He cast a cautious glance over toward the way they had to travel and shook his head. "I'm not sure what kind of welcome we'll get. There are so many people coming into Egypt because of the drought, they might try to keep us out."

"Or take advantage of us," Abram countered. "We're so worn down, we look like defenseless travelers—easy to rob."

"I thought there was peace in Egypt," Lot said.

"There is . . . of a kind," Abram said slowly. "But Pharaoh is the absolute ruler. He takes what he wants—or I might say, his servants take what they want. That's what I hear."

The next day they moved the herds farther south, and at midday they saw two men, who took one look at them, then dashed away madly.

"What are they running from?" Lot wondered.

"I don't think they're frightened of us. They're just scouts. I expect we'll soon be getting a visit from some official who wants to find out who we are and why we've come."

Abram was correct, for by the time the sun was high in the sky, a party of men appeared mounted on camels, but their appearance did not disturb Abram. He narrowed his eyes and watched as they approached, then said to Eliezer, who stood beside him, "Well, this is good news."

"What is, master?"

"They sent only a small group, enough to show respect. It's more of a political move than a military one. Be careful what you say to them, Eliezer. These are strange people. Sarai was right about their morals. They don't have any that I've ever heard of."

The camels pulled up a short distance away from Abram and Eliezer. The men dismounted, six in all, and one of their number came forward, obviously their leader. He was a man of less than medium height and seemed even shorter because of his rotund body. He was, Abram saw, one of those corpulent men whose fat was at least underlain by muscle. His head was bald, his eyelids were painted green, and his brown body had been rubbed with oil so that Abram smelled him as he came to stand before him.

"Greetings from Pharaoh, the god king. My name is Noestru. We welcome you as visitors to Egypt."

Abram bowed low and noted that Eliezer did the same. "Thank you, sir, for your kind welcome. My name is Abram. This is my steward, Eliezer."

"You have come a long distance?" Noestru asked.

"Yes. Our home originally was in Ur of the Chaldees."

"Ah, Sumerians, you are."

"No, we are called Hebrews."

"Hebrews? I'm not acquainted with that name," Noestru said, his eyes narrowing.

"We are indeed only a small body of people. We have come to Egypt seeking grazing land for our animals. The drought has driven us here, and we ask for your hospitality."

"Pharaoh Mentuhotep is renowned for his hospitality. Perhaps you would show us your people and let us get to know one another."

Both Abram and Eliezer understood this ploy. Noestru was obviously one who weighed the strength of those who came into Pharaoh's domain. Abram knew there was no avoiding this, so he bowed, saying, "It will be our honor to have you, sir. Perhaps you would refresh yourself, you and your men."

"Thank you." Noestru inclined his head slightly and followed Abram, who walked back toward the camp.

Eliezer ran ahead, and by the time the party had reached the camp, he had already started the women preparing food and drink for the Egyptians. He whispered to Sarai, "Don't spare anything, mistress. We must give them the best we have."

Sarai nodded. She quickly organized the women, and as Abram took the leader of the Egyptians through the camp, she saw that the Egyptian was eyeing everything carefully.

"He's an ugly man," she whispered to Beoni.

"Yes. And look at what he's wearing."

"Not enough!" Sarai snapped. She had noted at once that all the Egyptian men in the party were wearing very thin linen skirts, and their upper bodies were bare. "Shameless!" Sarai muttered. "I wish we had never come to this place."

When the meal had been prepared, Abram invited Noestru to sit down and gave orders that his men be fed. They were served roasted kid with fresh bread, plums and raisins in copper cups, and Syrian wine of the finest quality.

Noestru was an astute interrogator and soon asked Abram about his religion. "Which gods do your people worship?"

Abram hesitated. "We serve only one God."

"Only one?" Noestru raised his eyebrows in surprise, or where his eyebrows should have been, for they had been shaved. "I've never heard of such a thing. What is his name?"

"We call Him the Eternal One."

Noestru chewed thoughtfully on a date, daintily taking small bites. His flesh quivered as he turned to study Abram. "I would love to see your idol."

"The Eternal One does not embody himself in stone or wood. He is the one God above all gods."

Noestru grinned suddenly. "That will not sound too pleasant to our pharaoh. He is a god himself, you know, and at times he likes to think he is the most important god of all!" A worried frown swept across Noestru's face, and he whispered, "I'd just as soon you wouldn't repeat that to my pharaoh."

"Certainly not."

"This god, the Eternal One—tell me more about Him. If you can't see Him, how do you know He's there?"

"Because He has spoken to me."

"Oh, so you are a prophet? And do you make sacrifices as well?"

"Yes, I build an altar of stone from time to time."

"So, you are a priest as well as a prophet. Our pharaoh is very interested in this sort of thing. No doubt he will want to speak with you."

"I would be most happy to meet with the pharaoh."

Noestru continued to eat slowly but steadily, wading through the food that was before him, chewing constantly. He had apparently learned to eat, swallow, talk, and watch at the same time. He was, indeed, a clever man, and Abram was uneasy about him.

Finally Noestru said, "The pharaoh is always interested in new wives. Perhaps some of your women will be chosen for that honor."

Abram could not speak for a moment. He did not know how to answer the man. He knew that Pharaoh's word was law, and if his eyes lit upon one of the women in his group, there would be no opposing him.

"That one over there, for example. Who is she?"

Abram glanced in the direction of Noestru's gesture, and his heart sank. "Her name is Sarai. But she is quite old, sir."

"Ah, but beautiful nonetheless! Is she the wife of one of your people?"

There were so many factors at play here! *If I say she is my wife, he will think nothing of poisoning me to get her if Pharaoh commands it.* Abram never knew afterward what prompted him to say the words that flowed off his tongue. He heard himself speak, and it was as if he were listening to someone else.

"That, sir, is my sister."

"Your sister! I have rarely seen a more beautiful complexion, even on a young woman."

"I do not think the pharaoh would be interested in such an old woman."

"Nonsense! The pharaoh has many young women already. If she is your sister, I assume she is also a worshiper of the god you call the Eternal One."

To Abram's horror, Noestru got up and said, "I would like to meet her. She is different from our women."

Noestru walked toward Sarai, and Abram had no choice but to follow. He fervently wished that Sarai had worn a veil. Though she was not young, her complexion reviled those of women half her age, and her eyes were as large and lustrous as ever. Abram saw that Noestru was waiting for an introduction, and he caught Sarai's glance and held it, then said, "Sir, this is my sister. Her name is Sarai." He saw Sarai's startled look but shook his head in warning, then said quickly, "This is Noestru, the servant of Pharaoh. He would speak with you."

Sarai bowed gracefully. "What could a simple woman have to say to the servant of Pharaoh?"

"Many things. Come. Walk around the camp with me. We can talk."

Abram watched as the two moved away, and Eliezer came over to whisper, "What is he doing with my mistress? Why is he talking to her?"

"It's not good news. The pharaohs take many wives, and this one, apparently, is looking for more."

Eliezer's face revealed his shock. "But . . . but she's *your* wife!"

Abram hung his head. "I . . . I told him she was my sister."

"Master, why did you do that?"

"Because they would kill me in a minute if they decided to. These are cruel people, Eliezer. I hated to lie, but it seemed to jump to my lips."

The two men watched as Sarai walked through the camp with Noestru. They finally returned, and Noestru said, "I must take leave of you." He smiled with an oily expression, saying to Sarai, "You are as beautiful as the moon, O woman of the desert."

Sarai did not answer but bowed, and the three watched as Noestru went back and mounted his camel. His men followed him, raising a cloud of dust as they turned and left the camp.

Sarai demanded sharply, "Why did you tell him I was your sister?" She listened to Abram's explanation, then frowned. "I wish you hadn't said that."

"I don't think you recognize how cruel these people are."

Sarai looked at Abram with something like scorn. "Isn't the Eternal One able to deal with them? Are they more powerful than He?"

Abram knew there was no answer for that. Heavily he said, "I think we will have to leave Egypt as soon as the cattle are rested. This place is too dangerous for us." He saw that Sarai was disturbed and followed her as she walked away. She said nothing, and he put his arm around her. "I've always said that there was no woman so fair as you, Sarai. I've never regretted your beauty before, but now it has put us at risk."

"Let's go. Let's leave this place at once."

"As soon as the cattle are rested and fattened, we will go back to Canaan," Abram promised.

———————

Pharaoh Mentuhotep II was unhappy.

This was not good news, for when the king was unhappy, people inevitably suffered. Now as he made his way toward the temple, the priests bowed before him, their foreheads pressed against the earth. He passed through them without a glance and gave no notice to the large sphinxes lining the avenue toward the entrance of the temple. As he entered the courtyard all the priests and workers threw themselves forward on their faces. Pharaoh stopped before a group of the priests, who kept their faces pressed against the flagstones.

"Where is Menhades?"

"O great Pharaoh, he is preparing himself to minister. He is in the pool."

Pharaoh turned and walked across the courtyard, entering a carved doorway into a massive room, the walls of which were covered in paintings of the gods. Because Mentuhotep had built this magnificent temple, he knew every square inch of it. All pharaohs were interested in the gods, but Mentuhotep more than most. He stopped before a figure of Re seated on his throne. The idol had the face of a hawk, with a large crimson ball on his head, representing the sun. Next to Re was a figure of Shu, the son of Re, the god of the air. Shu's daughter appeared next. Her name was Nut, the sky goddess, who was married to her brother Geb, god of the earth.

For one moment the pharaoh stood staring at the images, then whirled and entered another area with a large pool some twenty feet square, surrounded by trees and flowering plants. A priest was washing himself in the pool, and when he looked up and saw the pharaoh, he emerged naked. One of the lesser priests, dressed as a god with the mask of an ibis head perched over his head, stepped forward and handed him a large white linen towel.

"I was preparing to offer sacrifices, O great Pharaoh."

"Get on with your preparations, but we have to talk."

Menhades proceeded to allow his underlings to dry him off. He chewed natron, a kind of salt, to purify his mouth and then inhaled incense from a smoking pot to purify his mind.

The high priest Menhades was in his early thirties and in the prime of life. He was at least a head taller than any other priest, strong, with handsome features. As he allowed his servants to dress him so that he might make his offerings to the gods, he listened carefully to the pharaoh. The pharaoh was the center of all things to the high priest, as he was to the rest of Egypt. Menhades had been born into a priestly family and was gifted with a keenly analytical mind. He had learned the hierarchy of the gods of Egypt while yet a youth, but now he spent more time studying the pharaoh than he did the pantheon of gods that Egypt worshiped.

Finally Menhades was ready and spoke sharply to his assistant. "We will make the offerings now."

"Yes, O great Lord."

"No!" Pharaoh said suddenly. "Come with me. You can make your offerings later."

Menhades did not argue with the pharaoh, since he valued his life. He had discovered other subtler and less dangerous ways of manipulating his king, ensuring that he keep his position *and* his head.

The two men walked quickly out of the temple, Menhades listening to the pharaoh's incessant talk. Menhades saw his ruler was in a foul mood and was surprised to see that they were headed toward the house of women. Keeping Pharaoh supplied with wives and concubines had proven to be an exasperating task. Pharaoh was not an impressive man, being short and chubby for his thirty-odd years. However, despite his appearance, his sexual appetite was voracious, and Menhades had to constantly search for new women to keep the king interested. *I don't know why he's so unhappy with his women,* Menhades thought wryly. *He's got enough of them!*

"Look at them," Pharaoh said, waving his arms before him. Women were everywhere—wives, concubines, slave girls. As they stood watching the harem, Ahut, Pharaoh's harem keeper and one of his chief advisors, came at once and bowed before him.

"You honor us, O God, with your presence."

Ordinarily Pharaoh was pleasant enough, but today he was in one of his moods and didn't return Ahut's greeting. The harem keeper exchanged glances with the high priest, and both men knew there was trouble in the air. They soon found out what it was about.

"Look at them! They all look just alike. They're boring! Boring!"

Having made a long study of the pharaoh's moods, the two men knew where this was leading.

Menhades nodded. "Of course, master. You need a different kind of woman."

"Exactly! A different kind of woman! Ahut, find me one, and don't let her look like these, and don't let her babble like these. Bring her quickly, or you may find yourself out of a job—and maybe without a head."

Pharaoh whirled about and walked away.

"What am I going to do, Menhades?" Ahut moaned.

"You know how he is when he gets an idea in his head." Menhades' lips twisted cynically. "He's a god and must be obeyed. I'd advise you to find a woman immediately—and don't let her look like one of these!"

Ahut was desperate. He had racked his brain trying to think of how to find a woman who would please the pharaoh, but he had come up with nothing. The day was only half gone, yet Ahut was already drunk, having guzzled goblet after goblet of wine. Finally he was joined by Noestru, a close friend of his.

Noestru sat down and asked, "Why are you drunk this early in the day, my friend?"

"This job. It's terrible!"

Noestru grinned. "It's not too bad. You get plenty to eat and drink and anything else you want. You're an important man to the pharaoh."

"I wish I were *more* important. He's going to kill me if I don't find a woman to please him."

"A woman! Why, he's got enough women for a hundred men!"

"But none of them satisfy him."

"What kind does he want, then?"

Ahut drained the goblet and waved to a servant wearing only a small transparent apron, who immediately filled his goblet again. He drank of it, belched mightily, and said, "Something *different*. Now, what does *that* mean? Does he want a woman with two heads?"

Noestru listened as the keeper of the king's women spoke. Finally he said, "I may be able to help you."

"Humph," Ahut sneered. "What can you do?"

"You know that new slave girl that came in from Nubia? You give her to me, and I'll give you a woman whom Pharaoh will at least find interesting."

Ahut was not so drunk that he couldn't recognize a possible way out of his dilemma. "Tell me," he said thickly and leaned forward.

Noestru began to speak. "I recently questioned a band of shepherds entering our country. They call themselves Hebrews. The leader's name is Abram. He's got a sister who, I think, would interest Pharaoh."

"Is she young and beautiful?"

"Not young but very beautiful. But more important than that is her religion. She and her brother worship a god they call the Eternal One. They have no pictures of him, no statues. They say he's everywhere—chief god over all other gods."

Ahut listened and soon began to breathe heavily. "So she's well spoken."

"Very well spoken."

Ahut made up his mind. "You can have the Nubian girl. What's this woman's name?"

"Sarai."

"Well, maybe she can amuse our master. It'll be an honor for a smelly shepherd to share his sister with Pharaoh."

"What if he objects?"

"Then kill him and take the woman."

―――――――

Abram was weary as he returned to camp. He had traveled a long distance looking for grazing ground and was discouraged. It was true that along the banks of the Nile the fields were green, but these all belonged to farmland owned by individuals, much of it by the pharaoh himself. Apart from the narrow band that flanked the river, the grass was scanty. Still, it was better than the dry lands they had left.

As Abram approached the camp, he was aware that something was wrong, especially when Eliezer came running to greet him, his eyes wide and his face tense. Abram asked at once, "What is it?"

"Master, they have taken my mistress."

Abram suddenly understood everything. "The Egyptians?"

"Yes. The one called Noestru. He came with a large guard this time. Many men, all soldiers!"

Abram's heart turned cold as a stone. "What did he say?"

"He only said that Pharaoh had commanded that the lady Sarai be brought before him." Eliezer's mouth twisted. "There was nothing we could do, master. They would have killed us all. I could see it in his eyes."

"It's not your fault," Abram said, thinking quietly for a moment before saying, "I must go at once to the palace. I must see Pharaoh."

"I will go with you."

"No, you stay here. You're in charge, Eliezer. If I don't come back, take the herds out farther. Move away from this place at once!"

"But you will be back soon, will you not?"

Abram only shook his head in answer. He could not know what lay in store for him at the court of Pharaoh. He readied a donkey to take him into the city. It was a huge city in his eyes, bustling with people and animals pushing their way through the noisy streets and avenues. He had to ask several people for directions.

When he finally reached the palace, he found himself barred from entering by armed soldiers. One of them, an officer, stared at him with disdain. "Get away, beggar!"

"I am no beggar. I have come to see after the welfare of my sister, who has been taken into the presence of Pharaoh."

The officer considered this and shrugged. "Stay here. I will find out about your sister."

The officer was gone a long time, and Abram stood, his mind reeling. *I should never have come to this place. O Eternal One, deliver my wife and get us away from here!*

Finally the officer returned, accompanied by a spindly man with sharp features.

"My name is Ahut," the man said. "I am the keeper of the king's women. Your name is Abram?"

"Yes, and my... sister. I must see her."

"That is impossible. Come back in a week or so. I will see what I can do."

"But I must see her right away."

Ahut stared at the tall man before him. To Ahut he was simply a dirty shepherd like many others filing into Egypt from all directions. "Be careful, my friend," he said coldly. "The Pharaoh is law in this land. When he is offended, very bad things happen. Come back in a week or two."

Abram's heart sank, and he turned and walked slowly away. Never in his life had he known such depths of despair.

CHAPTER

17

Sarai tried to appear unimpressed at the size of the house of women. She had been met by a man called Ahut and disliked him immediately. He reminded her of one of the cobras that infested the entire land of Egypt. He was skinny as a snake, and even his pointed features reminded her of a serpent. She half expected a forked tongue to come out of his mouth! He spoke pleasantly to her, though, and now as he brought her into the house, he said, "I hope you will be comfortable here."

"It will do," Sarai said coldly. She knew her safety depended upon hiding her feelings, and what she felt now was fear. She had enjoyed a life of freedom, but now she realized she was a prisoner of the most powerful man on earth. Although she had never met the pharaoh, she assumed that he would be at least as repellent to her as Ahut.

"I have chosen a servant who will take care of your needs," Ahut said. He clapped his hands, and instantly a young woman came out from behind some pillars, where she had obviously been standing.

"Her name is Hagar. If she does not please you, let me know, and I will see that she is . . . reprimanded."

"I'm sure she will be satisfactory."

"I will leave you then, Lady Sarai. When you are rested and washed, the pharaoh will, no doubt, be ready to welcome you."

Sarai bowed slightly to the tall man, and as soon as he left the room, she turned to face the woman before her. "Your name is Hagar?"

"Yes, my mistress."

Hagar was a very attractive young woman, tall and shapely, which was obvious from the thin linen robe she wore. Her eyes were widely spaced and of an odd color, brown with a touch of green in them. They were painted to look even larger. Her hair was a dark brown with tints of red in it. She wore a necklace of colored stones around her neck but otherwise had no jewelry.

"Have you been here long, Hagar?" Sarai said, uncertain as to the woman's standing in this place.

"Seven years."

"You must have been very young when you came here."

"I was nine years old when I was made a slave."

"What happened to your family?"

"They were all killed." Hagar's voice was even, but when she spoke of the death of her family, the greenish tint of her eyes seemed to glow, and her lips drew into a tighter line. She had full lips that men would consider tempting, and she apparently had learned to control herself, for she dropped her head and said no more.

Sarai walked over to the window and looked out on a lush garden. The scent of the blooms was thick in the air, and she lifted her eyes toward the horizon, wishing she could see the camp and especially Abram.

"I hope I will not be a trouble to you, Hagar."

Hagar looked at her, and surprise washed across her features. "A trouble? I am your slave. How could you be a trouble?"

"I imagine the owners of some slaves can be troublesome."

"And cruel."

"Well, I trust I won't be that. But, in any case, I hope I will not be here long."

Hagar suddenly said, "I too hoped that I would not be here long when I was first brought here, but here I still am, as you see."

"I don't know what I'm doing here," Sarai said suddenly. She felt lonely, and the tall woman before her at least provided a listening ear. "I want to be back with my . . . brother," she stammered.

"That may not be."

Sarai was startled. "What do you mean by that?"

"It's common talk already that Pharaoh has brought you here to be a part of the house of women."

"Is that what people are saying?"

"Why, yes! Didn't Ahut tell you that?"

"No one has really told me anything." Sarai began to tremble. She turned away, and tears came to her eyes. She had never felt so lonely in her life. She was startled to feel a touch on her arm and turned to see that Hagar had come close to her. "You have nothing to fear from Pharaoh. He will lose interest in you soon enough, as he loses interest in everything that's not new."

"Why did he summon me here? He has so many women."

"He's fascinated by the gods, and from what I hear, your brother is a prophet and a priest of a different kind of god . . . a god that is above all other gods. And you worship this god also, I understand."

"Yes, that is true. What might I tell Pharaoh about the Eternal One that would interest him?"

Hagar hesitated, not certain how much to trust this woman. "It is not for me to say."

"Please, Hagar, tell me."

"Well . . . all right, if you promise never to let Ahut know what I have told you. Pharaoh would be most interested in anything you have to say about your god. All he thinks about—besides women, of course—are the gods. He spends most of his time talking to Menhades and the other priests, and anyone who comes with word of a different kind of god is sure to have an audience with Pharaoh."

Sarai trembled at the prospect that the pharaoh was going to single her out because of her beliefs. "Oh, I wish we had never come to this place!"

"So do I," Hagar said, "but neither of us came willingly."

"And your family is all gone?"

"My parents are dead. I still have uncles and several brothers who escaped."

"What is your family like?"

Hagar shook her head, and her long, straight hair fell down her back. "They call us a lawless tribe, and it's true enough that our people are not bound by the laws of Pharaoh."

Suddenly Sarai knew exactly what kind of background this woman had. She came from one of the wild tribes that roamed all over Mesopotamia and Syria, and Egypt too, apparently. They were bedouins called Amorites, and Sarai could see in Hagar's face and the attitude of her body that there was a rebellious streak in her that was characteristic of these people. Her defiance may have been caused partly by her captivity and her position as a slave, but Sarai recognized the headstrong quality all the same. She had seen it before in her encounters with other Amorites traveling the trade routes to and from Damascus.

"Come. I will help you with your bath and then put colors on your face."

This ritual proved to be quite an experience for Sarai. The bathing took a long time, and she managed to relax in the warm water, momentarily forgetting some of her fears. Hagar would have washed her all over, but Sarai quickly took over the job herself. She did allow the slave woman to wash her hair, however, and then Hagar took nearly an hour to fix it to her satisfaction.

"Now," Hagar said, "let me help you with the rest of your preparations."

As she worked, the slave woman spoke of the elements of the colors that were used by Egyptian women. She had ground malachite on a palate and mixed it with oil to make the eye paint called *kohl*, which she kept in small, beautifully adorned golden jars. Hagar expertly applied this with a small stick. After this she used henna to paint Sarai's nails and would have painted her palms and the soles of her feet, but Sarai objected. Finally Hagar ground red ochre, mixed it with water, and lightly applied it to Sarai's cheeks and lips.

After the makeup was complete, Hagar brought forth the sheer linen clothing that had been provided, but Sarai protested. "This robe is much too sheer. Why, you can see right through it!"

"Of course you can," Hagar said, puzzled. "What's wrong with that?"

Sarai shook her head. If the woman saw no harm in running about in such a state, she could not explain it to her. She compromised by putting on several of the linen robes, which together provided enough thickness for at least some modesty.

The jewelry Hagar brought forth was so exquisite it took Sarai's breath away. One piece in particular won her admiration—it was a bead collar that came down to her breast and sparkled with gold and precious stones, with the head of a hawk for a clasp. After fastening matching earrings to her ears, Hagar held up a mirror of highly polished metal and said, "There, are you not beautiful?"

Sarai looked at herself and frowned. She did not like all the face paint. She had allowed Hagar to put it on but now had an impulse to wash it all off. She knew, however, that she had to be careful while she was in this place and simply replied, "Your work pleases me. Thank you very much, Hagar."

Hagar raised her eyebrows. "Most people don't bother to thank slaves, mistress."

"I always want to be kind."

Hagar stared at the woman in front of her. She was puzzled by her, partly by her age, for she was much older than the women who were usually brought to the pharaoh. But there was a gentleness about her that fascinated the slave girl. "We will do this every day."

"Do what?"

"Have your bath and fix your face and dress you in beautiful clothes."

"But that would be a waste of water! Water is very precious."

Hagar laughed at Sarai's concern. "Oh, you needn't worry about that. There is plenty of water in the Nile, mistress!"

The lack of activity in the house of women was burdensome to Sarai. For three days she had risen and gone through the ritual bath and allowed Hagar to dress her and adorn her with paint and ornaments. Accustomed as she was to hard work, it was a shocking experience to have absolutely nothing to do all day long.

Hagar kept her new mistress entertained with music and games. She was adept at playing a small handheld harp and had a good singing voice. She knew many of the songs of her people, and Sarai enjoyed listening to her sing them. The slave woman also provided a game called *senet*, which consisted of a board inlaid with ebony, ivory, and gold on which they moved about polished wooden game pieces. Sarai learned the rules quickly, and the two women spent hours playing it.

Much of the time Sarai simply looked out of her window, dreaming of Abram and her people, but she sometimes toured the house, accompanied by Hagar. She did not know how to feel about the wives of Pharaoh, but there was no doubt about *their* feelings. None of them approached her or spoke, and the looks some of them gave her were venomous.

"Why do they hate me, Hagar?"

"They hate any woman who comes to be the wife of Pharaoh, or even a concubine. They're jealous."

"They needn't be jealous of me." Sarai shook her head with despair.

"Pharaoh is all they think about."

Hagar might have said more, but suddenly Ahut appeared. He seemed distracted and wrung his hands as he said, "Quickly prepare yourself. Pharaoh is ready to welcome you."

"I am prepared."

Ahut stared at her in confusion. "No woman is ever prepared."

"Well, *I* am," Sarai said sharply.

"Then come with me," Ahut said. He led her out of the house of women, across a courtyard, and into the palace, a huge building that loomed up several stories. Sarai was overwhelmed by the immensity of the long archway through which they entered. Its walls were covered in paintings of brilliant colors—of gods and pharaohs of old celebrating their triumphs. There were rows of sphinxes, lionlike figures with the faces of men, and everywhere servants were scurrying, moving, whispering. It was like a huge beehive.

"The pharaoh will see you in his private quarters."

Sarai was not at all sure how she felt about this, but she had little choice.

She mounted two flights of stairs to the third story, where the floor was intricately decorated with tile mosaics. She looked down to see men with long spears pictured in a reed boat hunting a hippopotamus. Other mosaics showed scenes of hunters throwing spears to bring down birds. There were many other pictures, but she had no time to look at them, for Ahut led her through a pair of enormous doors. There, at the far end of the room, sat a man, and Sarai felt a pang of disappointment. The regalia of the pharaoh were overwhelming. Riches—gold, silver, and precious stone—were every-where, and the man who sat before her wore a double crown. As she approached, her disappointment increased. She had expected a magnificent figure, but no mere man could live up to the reputation of Pharaoh.

"Ah, the lady Sarai. We are pleased to welcome you to our palace."

Pharaoh Mentuhotep II was a short man, rather chubby, with a boyish-looking face. Sarai knew he was in his early thirties, but he looked no more than twenty. His fingers were fat, and his rings glittered as he lifted his hand in a greeting. He did seem to be a cheerful-looking individual, and Sarai felt a gleam of hope. *Perhaps he will not find me to be interesting. I pray your protection, O Eternal One.*

"I bow before the mighty pharaoh," Sarai said and did bow low before him.

"So this is the sister of my good friend Abram the prophet. Come, lady, and walk with me. I will show you my palace."

"You have met my brother?"

"Not yet, but I assume that I will. My servant tells me that he is a priest and a prophet. Such are always welcome in my kingdom. I want to be on good terms with all of the gods."

The pharaoh's voice was high-pitched, almost feminine, but despite his innocent appearance, there was a light in his eyes that warned Sarai that, childlike as he might appear, there was a carnivore on the inside.

For the next hour Pharaoh showed her about the palace and then finally sat her down at a table. "You will sit with me while we eat," he said. "I know that my cook will find something to please you."

"I am not hard to please, mighty Pharaoh. My people eat very simply."

"Then this will be a treat for you."

The meal was ornate, but Sarai had little appetite for food. She answered the pharaoh's questions, which at first were general, but when the meal was over, he got up and moved over to the couch where she had taken her meal and sat down beside her. "Now," he said smoothly, "this is better." He put his hand out and touched her arm. "What a beautiful complexion." he whispered. Then reaching up, he touched her face. "So clear and so fair. Not like the dusky women of Egypt."

Sarai felt a sense of revulsion as his hand touched her cheek. She knew that this was the first step of intimacy and quickly said, "I understand you are interested in the Eternal One."

"Ah yes." Pharaoh's attention was diverted, and he stared into Sarai's eyes. "I am a god myself, but I like to know about other gods."

For the next half hour Pharaoh interrogated Sarai about her god. He wanted to know everything about the Eternal One, and finally he said, "This is strange indeed. We will speak more of it later." Suddenly he leaned forward and put his arm around her. His fat hand caressed her back, moving slowly up and down, and without thinking, Sarai stood up and said, "I am a little tired. If you would permit me, Lord, I would go back to my quarters."

Pharaoh stood up too, his face darkened. "No woman has ever resisted me."

Sarai did not know what to say to that, and her face showed her confusion.

Suddenly Pharaoh laughed. "No woman can resist a god. You will not be able to either." He laughed again and shook his head. "What woman would refuse a god? Go then. We will speak later."

Sarai nearly burst with relief as she turned and left the room. Ahut was waiting for her, and his face was alive. "Did you enjoy your audience with the god?"

Sarai wanted to shout out, *No, I did not!* Instead she replied calmly, "He's a very interesting man."

"Indeed he is. Did he speak of your god?"

"Yes, he wanted to know all about Him."

"He spends all of his time learning about the different gods." Ahut's mind was working feverishly. After all, this woman could possibly be a wife of Pharaoh one day—she might even rise to become the number one wife. She was different, and that was what Pharaoh valued. Ahut leaned close and whispered, "I can tell that he likes you. It's entirely possible you will become the wife of Pharaoh one day. Then we two will be very close."

Sarai murmured some reply but was glad when she got back to her room. As she entered, Hagar rushed to her and said, "What did you think of the pharaoh?"

Sarai shook her head. "I'm afraid of him, Hagar. I want nothing to do with him."

Hagar stared at her with consternation. "But he is the pharaoh!"

"I will not be his wife, nor his concubine."

"But why not, when you have no husband?"

Sarai almost burst out with the truth, but she did not know Hagar well enough for that, and no word must get to Pharaoh. "If I could only see my brother."

"Are you two very close?"

Sarai smiled wearily and nodded her head. "Very close, Hagar—very close indeed!"

———————

"Master, the Egyptians have brought more beasts."

Abram turned quickly. He had just exited from his tent when he heard Eliezer's voice. He waited until the younger man came and stood before him and saw the troubled expression in his steward's eyes. "So many! Sheep, goats, and cattle, and the officer who brought them said we were to take our cattle to greener pastures where there is better water."

Abram straightened up, his face tense. He had nearly lost his mind over the past six weeks. He had not heard a word from Sarai, and although he had gone regularly to the gate of the palace, all he had received there was a cold warning from Menhades, the chief priest, or Ahut, the harem keeper, that Sarai was still a guest. Every time both men gave a thinly veiled warning that Abram would be better off to simply leave his sister in Pharaoh's hands.

"What does it all mean, master?" Eliezer said. "All these presents! We have more cattle than we've ever had. But what about my mistress?"

"I can't tell you anything, Eliezer. Sarai's fate is in the hands of Pharaoh."

"What kind of a man is he?"

"I've never met him, but he's a man who has always had everything he could ever think of."

"But she's your wife!"

Abram had shared with Eliezer the deceit he had used, and now he said grimly, "I wish I had never made up that lie! Lies are never good. They might have killed me to get her, but I don't think so. I made a mistake, Eliezer."

Eliezer stood irresolutely for a moment, his mind working quickly. He loved Sarai like the mother he had never known. Now he lowered his voice, although no one was there to overhear him. "Master, let's steal her!"

"Steal her! What do you mean?"

"I mean, let's break into the palace, take her, and get away from here."

"Why, that's impossible, Eliezer!"

"No, I think we can do it. We'd have to strike quickly and get away as fast as possible."

Abram put his hand on the young man's shoulder, looking directly into his eyes. "There's a good heart speaking, my son, but it's impossible." He shook his head and said dolefully, "Only the Eternal One can save her now—and us as well."

Sarai sat tensely on a golden chair with purple cushions. Pharaoh had been speaking for some time, as he had many times over the past month and a half. She tried to keep his mind on what he was saying, but her own mind searched frantically for more to tell him about the Eternal One. She had come to realize how little she actually knew about the God she served. And now as she sat there watching his expression, she saw that a slyness had begun to creep into his features. She had learned much about men over her life and could see the lust in his eyes like a sullen flame, but at the same time his eyes seemed mysteriously empty, like windows peering out at nothing.

From far off came the sounds of a priest's incantations, and as a counterpoint to that, a cock crowed, like the clarion call of a trumpet. Pharaoh came over and stood looking down at her. "I'd hoped that my hospitality would make you forget your brother."

Sarai allowed nothing but surprise to show on her face. "You would care little for a woman who could forget her own brother, but I am grateful, mighty Pharaoh, for you have been a gracious host. You have taken good care of your guest."

Pharaoh's eyes narrowed and he whispered, "Perhaps we should think of ourselves more as kin rather than host and guest."

Instantly Sarai rejoined, "Am I to think of Pharaoh as my brother?"

Pharaoh's voice was tinged with irritation. "You're more than a guest, and I would have you to be much more."

"Your kindness is legendary," Sarai said graciously, ignoring the pharaoh's implication.

"Are you pleased with your servant?"

"Hagar? Yes, she's very efficient."

"Then I give her to you."

Sarai knew that Pharaoh was not really giving her anything, but there was no way to refuse. "Your generosity is well-known, my lord."

Pharaoh shook his head. "I have been patient with you, Sarai, but I think the time has come to make my intentions plain, although you have probably already read my desires."

"Indeed not, sir!"

"I think you would fit well within my house of women. I had thought of you at first as merely a concubine, but I see now that you are far above that. So the position of wife is what I'm considering."

Sarai knew that the moment had come, and fear gripped her. She had to make an answer, and she had planned it well. She lifted her eyes and looked at Pharaoh while saying evenly, "Perhaps I have not made it clear. The Eternal One does not look with favor upon his people marrying those who are not Hebrews."

"No, you have not mentioned this," Pharaoh replied, frowning, "but I will make offerings to Him. All will be well."

"I think Pharaoh should consider that great harm may come if he touches one of the Eternal One's servants." She knew then that her life hung in the balance, so she added quickly, "My brother is a favorite of the Eternal One. Think carefully what you do, Pharaoh. The Eternal One is all-powerful and is not to be offended. I do not know what terrible thing might come upon you if you displease Him."

Pharaoh stared at her. He was a man who had known nothing but his own will all of his life. Now he stood up, anger and interest intermingled in his expression. "You are an unusual woman, Sarai, and I must have you. We will speak of this later, but make up your mind that you *will* be one of the wives of Pharaoh."

Sarai then rose and bowed. She was led back to her room by Ahut, who tried to pry the essence of her conversation with Pharaoh out of her, but Sarai put him off.

As soon as she entered her room, she pleaded, "Hagar, you must help me."

Hagar was shocked at the strain on Sarai's face. "What's wrong, mistress?"

"You must take a message to Abram."

"Your brother?"

"Y-yes . . . my brother. Could you do that?"

"No one pays much attention to a slave girl. But if I can find him, I will give him a message."

"When I left he was camped just outside of the city, upriver. Anyone could direct you to Abram the Hebrew."

"What will I say to him?"

"Tell him that he must pray to the Eternal One, that both he and I are in terrible danger. The pharaoh has told me that I must become his wife."

"And you did not say yes?" Hagar was astonished. "You would have everything."

"Hagar, I must tell you something . . . and I put my life in your hands. . . ." Sarai hesitated. "Abram is not my brother."

Hagar stared at Sarai, her eyes flying wide open. "But who is he?"

"He is my husband, Hagar. He knew if he had told Pharaoh this, he would have been killed. Now go and tell him to pray to the Eternal One."

Abram stared at the young slave woman who had come into camp, announcing that she had a message for him from his wife. Fear seized him, for if this girl knew that Sarai was his wife, everyone else must know.

He took her into the privacy of his tent and asked, "How do you know that Sarai is my wife?"

"She has confided in me, master, and you need not fear, for I love Lady Sarai. She has been kind to me."

Relieved, Abram asked, "Is she all right, Hagar?"

"No, Pharaoh is determined to make her his wife. She sent me to tell you that you must pray to the Eternal One. Unless He helps you, all is lost."

Abram spoke with the girl long enough to form a favorable impression of her. "You are a faithful servant, Hagar. I will find some way of making this right with you."

"I did it for my mistress Sarai, but I see that you are a good man. I hope your God can save her from the pharaoh. He is a cruel man in many ways."

"Say nothing to anyone. Tell Sarai that I will pray and she must have faith that the Eternal One will save her."

The two stepped outside the tent then, and Abram said, "Eliezer, escort this young woman back to the palace."

Eliezer had watched Hagar come into the camp. He bowed now and said, "Of course, master." His gaze turned to Hagar. "Lead the way, if you please."

On the return trip, Hagar found the young man handsome and could tell that he was casting secret glances at her. She was used to the admiration of men and wondered what his position was. "Are you a son or a relative of Abram?" she asked.

"No, I'm merely his steward. My mother was a slave girl. He bought her to save her from slavery."

"He is a kind man, then."

"Yes. He's the kindest man I've ever known." He looked at her and asked, "Do you have a husband?"

"No."

Hagar said no more, but when they got within sight of the palace, she said, "You'd better not be seen with me." She bowed before him and smiled, knowing she made a pretty picture for any man. "I will see you again, will I not?"

"I trust that you will, Hagar."

Eliezer watched her as she went into the palace. He turned back, and his mind was full—a mixture of concern for his mistress Sarai, but at the same time he found the young woman Hagar as exciting as any woman he had ever met.

CHAPTER

18

The night sky was sprinkled with more stars than Abram could remember seeing in many years. Looking up in the moonlight, he almost stumbled over the root of a large tree that loomed out to his left. Catching his balance, he stopped and made his way to the trunk. It was a terebinth tree, short trunked, with spreading branches that blotted out part of the heavens above him.

Abram sat down, aware that his legs were weary and that indeed his whole body ached with fatigue. His eyes were heavy and gritty, for he had slept only in fits since the slave girl Hagar had brought Sarai's message. *That was close to two weeks ago!* he thought with alarm. Leaning his head back, he felt the roughness of the bark against his hair and pushed his head against it until the pressure became painful. The night air was so much cooler than the heat of the day, and for a time he sat there struggling against his desire for sleep.

Abram had prayed every way he could think of. He had prayed aloud in a soft voice. At times his voice had risen to a crescendo, but his spirit was in so much agony, he didn't care who heard him. He had prayed sitting, standing, walking, and at times had grown so agitated he'd flung himself full-length on the ground with his lips in the dust, crying out to the Eternal One.

He was met with silence and felt nothing but a deep darkness, like a beast trying to drag him into a silent black hole in the earth. He thought it would be a pleasure to surrender to death, simply to escape the agony that was clawing at his insides.

One day was like every other day to him now, and what little he ate was like eating the dust of Egypt—tasteless and gritty. He even forgot to drink until, from time to time, he would become aware of the fact that his lips were dry as parchment and his tongue cleaved to the roof of his mouth.

The tree had a strong and pungent aroma, and Abram reached back, extending his arms and feeling the rough bark. He pressed his hands against it and curled his fingers, clutching at the bark and breaking off small fragments. He brought them to his nose and smelled their sharp, aromatic fragrance, distinct from other trees. From far off in the distance came the cry of a wild dog. Its plaintive wail emphasized Abram's loneliness, and he was seized with the temptation to emulate the animal and howl his miseries on the Egyptian air.

Abram felt drugged with weariness. He could no longer even speak clearly, so he had avoided the others, spending much of his time by himself out in the pastures rather than returning to camp. But now he knew he desperately needed rest and needed to get back to his tent. He tossed down the pieces of bark and struggled to his feet, so weak he had to grasp ahold of the tree trunk for support. He gained his footing, then leaned back against the bark, trying to gather strength for the walk home.

Leaning there, he glanced up through the leafy branches and saw the stars twinkling. "O Eternal One," he whispered, "you made all these stars. Every one of them. I could not count them in a lifetime. You made this earth and the rivers and the lakes and the streams. It was your hand, O God, that pushed up the mountains and hollowed out the valleys. Every creature in the sea, large and small, was created by your hand. The beasts of the earth, every bird and every four-footed animal and all of the reptiles, these too you created. O Eternal One, you can do all things. I am weary of my own voice, and I am a child crying into the void. Please . . . speak to me, O God, as you have in the past. I ask again that you deliver my wife from the hand of the one who holds her. The whole land of Egypt trembles at his voice, but you are not afraid, for you are the almighty and everlasting one. Let me know that you will not leave Sarai helpless in the hands of that man!"

No sooner had Abram uttered these words than he heard again the blessed voice of the Eternal One!

"Do not be afraid, Abram my son, for I have heard your cry. I am pleased that you have not doubted me but have continued to have strong faith, even though you saw nothing and heard nothing. That is the reason I have loved you and have chosen you out of all human beings that I've created—because you have such a large capacity for faith."

Abram did not open his eyes or move but simply stood listening, no longer conscious of the roughness of the tree against which he leaned. Now he thought only of the voice of his almighty God, who spoke such words of strength and comfort to him.

"Thank you, O Eternal One. I have been so afraid, for I love Sarai."

"Yes, you love Sarai, Abram, but not as much as I do. I am the God of love as I am the God of justice. Now do not be afraid, for I have already put my hand upon the pharaoh and upon his court. Sarai, your wife, will be delivered into your hands, and when that has come to pass, I command you to leave Egypt and go back to Canaan."

"Yes, O Eternal One," Abram whispered, and then he began to thank his God and to joyfully praise Him. The weariness fell away, and with tears running down his face, he lifted his arms. He knew that God was not located upward any more than He was located downward. He was simply the God that was everywhere. Nevertheless, Abram held up his head, and praise poured from his lips as the starlight fell across his face. He gave thanks, as though what the Eternal One had promised had already come to pass.

Ahotep, the court physician, cowered and covered his head with his hands. He whimpered, "Please, O great Pharaoh, please do not beat your poor servant!"

Pharaoh had picked up a reed staff from one of the golden pots. The reeds were there merely for decorative purposes, but now he used one to strike the physician, again and again until it splintered. Pharaoh threw the remains to the floor and screamed, "You are a fraud! I will have you flayed alive!"

Ahotep tried to speak. "Please, O God of Egypt, I promise that all will be well."

"All will be well? I have tried all your remedies, and they are worthless. Get out of my sight!"

Ahotep scrambled to his feet and ran out of the room, his pale face lined with the stripes where the reed had struck him. Panting, he shoved himself through the door, colliding with the high priest Menhades.

"What is going on?" Menhades demanded, looking at the stripes on Ahotep's face. "Did the Pharaoh strike you?"

"Yes, he's lost his mind!"

"Gods do not lose their minds," Menhades said with a cynical smile. "What happened?"

"I went in to treat his affliction, and he just started screaming. He was violent. I know the treatment is painful, but it's necessary."

"You still do not know what this plague is?"

Ahotep was a small, fragile man, and his hands trembled violently. He was wearing a wig that had been knocked askew, and now he pulled it from his head and rubbed his hand over the welt. "I have never seen anything like it, and I have seen every disease in Egypt at one time or another—and most of those in other lands. It . . . it is not a *normal* sickness."

"Have any more men in the court been afflicted?"

"Yes. Frenahoe sent for me this morning." Ahotep wiped his eyes with his hands, for the tears had begun to flow. "It is the same with him. Lesions and sores mostly around the private parts—and impotence. He cannot be with a woman."

"And it is all among the members of the court? Commoners have not been afflicted? You had no reports of such?"

"No. Only Pharaoh and his highest officials." Suddenly Ahotep stared at the high priest. "Sir, forgive me, but have you—?"

"No!" Menhades said sharply. He too had been frightened by the inexplicable plague that had attacked the high court of Egypt. It had begun only three days ago when seven men, including the pharaoh and his highest advisors and closest friends, had sent for Ahotep and the high priest. The rash had been the same in all cases, and Ahotep had treated them as he had treated other rashes. But the raging sickness had spread swiftly, the sores growing worse by the hour, so that now everyone in the capital knew that one of the gods had put his hand on Pharaoh.

Menhades said quickly, "If the pharaoh dies, the country will be lost. There is so much trouble now. Could this be a poison that an enemy has inflicted on us?"

"Not a *physical* enemy, sir."

Menhades stared at the physician. "Are you telling me that it is one of the gods that has done this?"

Ahotep feared the high priest, who had great power. "I think the gods are angry, but I cannot tell why. It is you who must find the answer, O High Priest, not a poor physician."

Menhades stared at Ahotep, speechless. He questioned him long and hard about the remedies and about sicknesses, but Ahotep stuck to his story. The physician finally said in a trembling voice, "It is not a natural sickness. It came too quickly and it struck only a select few, only those in the high court. How could it be anything else, O Menhades?"

Menhades suddenly had a thought. "If I were you, I would keep out of sight for a few days. You know how Pharaoh is. He could have your head chopped off in a moment if the thought struck him."

"I will go to Thebes. Send for me when—"

"I will send for you when he is cured—or when he is dead. Those are the only two ways of safety for any of us."

Menhades turned and walked swiftly toward the house of women. He ignored the servants who greeted him, and as soon as Ahut appeared, he said, "I will speak with the Hebrew woman, Sarai."

"Is the pharaoh worse?"

"Don't ask me questions. Bring the woman to me. I want to speak to her alone. No eavesdroppers."

"Certainly—certainly!" Ahut muttered. He ran quickly, and ten minutes later Menhades turned to see Sarai, who had entered the room. She was wearing a simple linen garment that was not as provocative as the Egyptians wore.

"You sent for me, sir?"

"Yes. I must speak plainly with you."

"Have I offended Pharaoh in some way?"

"I cannot tell." Menhades came to stand before her. He was so tall she had to lift her head to look at him. "You are aware of the pharaoh's sickness?"

"I have heard only a little."

"Have you heard that six of our highest officials have also been afflicted with a similar disease?"

"I have not heard the number, but the rumors are everywhere that there is such a plague."

"Oh, you call it a plague!"

"Pardon me, sir. I do not know what to call it," Sarai said.

Her calmness was not lost on Menhades. He was aware of her strong faith in her God to protect her.

"I will ask you directly, woman. Do you think that your God has sent this sickness to Pharaoh and his court?"

Sarai's heart leaped, knowing that this was the answer from the Eternal One!

"I have told the pharaoh, who asked me to become his wife, that the eternal God whom I serve does not favor the Hebrews mixing with other races. But he would not heed me. I think it is entirely possible, sir, that this sickness is a warning from the Eternal One."

Menhades stared at the woman. Her eyes were clear, and there was such certainty in her voice and attitude that he knew he had to take some action. "I will talk to you later," he said. He whirled, his linen skirt swirling about his knees as he hurried out of the room.

"Thank you, O Eternal One," Sarai said, a joyous light in her eyes. She went back to her room, where she found Hagar waiting for her, as always. "I believe that I will soon be leaving this place, Hagar, and I thank you for your services."

"But you will not leave me!" Hagar said, running over to Sarai and falling on her knees before her. "Please take me with you! The pharaoh himself gave me to you."

"You do not know what you ask, Hagar. Life here is easy. Life on the desert is hard."

"Do you think I do not know that? I came from the desert, and look at this." Hagar turned around and pulled down the top of her dress. Her back was striped with old wounds, and some not so old. "You would not do this to me, would you, mistress?"

Sarai was horrified. She had seen slaves beaten, but this woman had endured torment. "Pull your dress up. You may go with me. You will be my servant."

Hagar did as she was told, her eyes filled with tears. "Thank you, mistress. I will serve you well!"

Menhades went directly to the pharaoh and found him weeping in pain. As Menhades bowed before him, the pharaoh cried out, "Why do the gods torment me so when I honor all of them!"

Menhades knew that his political career, and, indeed, his very life, might be on the line. To suggest that Pharaoh had made a mistake was unthinkable, but there was no other alternative. Taking a deep breath, the high priest said, "I think you have offended the God of the Hebrews."

Pharaoh had been crouched over with pain. Now he forced himself to straighten up. "You mean the woman Sarai?"

"Yes. I have been talking to her, and she says it is their custom that Hebrews marry only within their own people."

"I meant no harm." Pharaoh's face had grown gray with fear. "Quick, Menhades, send for her brother. We must make it right."

"At once, O Pharaoh!"

Abram had come to the gates many times during the past weeks, and always before he had been rebuffed by Noestru, but this time he was met by the high priest himself, who bowed to him in a most unusual gesture. Abram returned the bow and said, "I have come according to your word."

"I thank you for your promptness. The pharaoh wishes to see you."

As the two men walked toward the palace, Menhades studied the tall man beside him. It was his business to know men, and there was strength in the face of the Hebrew that impressed him. "We have a problem, Abram. The pharaoh is sick, as well as several of his high officials."

"I have heard of the sickness."

Menhades had it on the tip of his tongue to inquire more, but he thought better of it and said simply, "I hope you can do something to help our god the pharaoh."

"I am not a physician."

The answer was spare but was delivered clearly and with a glance that warned Menhades that Abram did not come in humility. There was a confidence about him that was almost frightening.

Menhades said no more but brought Abram into the room where the pharaoh languished on his bed. He had been drugged for the pain, but he sat up with the help of his servant as the two men entered.

"Pharaoh, this is Abram, the prophet of the Eternal One."

Pharaoh began to quiver. "Please, Abram, tell me. Have I offended your God?"

"Our women do not marry people outside of our own race," Abram said. He was studying the pharaoh, who was a pitiful sight. He had heard that the sores brought on by the plague were terribly painful. Most of these were hidden by the light garment the pharaoh wore, but he could see the lines of pain in the man's face.

"I was not aware of this," the pharaoh said meekly.

"Did the woman not tell you?" Abram demanded strongly. "And I must tell you this. The woman is my wife."

"Your wife! They told me she was your sister."

Abram saw that his words had horrified Pharaoh. "The men of my people often call their wives 'sister,'" he explained. "It is a term of affection." His explanation had some truth to it, and Abram was relieved that Pharaoh believed him.

"I did not know that," the pharaoh cried. "Your God cannot blame me! I am innocent!" He was shaking frightfully now, and he held out his hand. "Pray for me to your God. Take your wife and go, and I will give you even more cattle."

"The gifts are not necessary," Abram said, knowing that his prayer had been effective. He also knew that this pharaoh would now be aware that the Eternal One was no mere block of stone but a living, paralyzing force. "I will pray for you now, and you will be healed."

"Yes! Yes! Pray for me now! Quickly!"

Abram lifted his voice and prayed for the pharaoh. He had never had such assurance in all of his life, and his prayer was short and direct. When he had finished he said, "You have been healed of the plague, you and your men. I will take my people and leave Egypt."

"You must take the gifts. Menhades, see that he has more cattle. Hundreds of them! See to it!"

"It shall be done, O Pharaoh." Menhades touched Abram's arm, and the two left the room.

Menhades was stunned by what he had just seen, and he whispered to Abram, "Do you really think he was healed?"

"Yes, you will find that he is truly healed—and the others also. Now bring my wife to me at once."

"At once, O Abram, at once!"

Menhades burst into Sarai's room without bothering to knock. Sarai was sitting down, and Hagar was fixing her hair. Sarai saw the excitement and fear on the face of the high priest.

"Quickly, you must go!" Menhades shouted.

"Go?" Sarai said. "Go where?"

"Your husband is here, and you must go with him at once."

Sarai then laughed aloud. She turned to Hagar and said, "Did I not tell you that the Eternal One would set us free? Come, we will leave this place."

Menhades waited impatiently while the two women gathered their belongings. "Is the slave girl going with you?" he asked.

"Yes. The pharaoh himself gave her to me as a gift."

"Then take her and go in the name of all the gods!"

Sarai could not help laughing. "You have been anxious to have me as your guest, but now you are anxious for me to leave."

Menhades found himself afraid, a rare experience for him. But he had seen a miracle, and he whispered, "Please, Lady Sarai, go with your husband and leave Egypt at once."

Sarai hurried outside the house of women, and there, standing in the same robe she had seen him wear the day she disappeared, was Abram. He ran toward her and called her name, and she threw herself into his arms. Neither of them could speak, but finally Abram asked, "Are you all right?"

"Yes. I'm all right. Oh, Abram, the Eternal One saved us! He is God of all things."

"Yes, He is. Now let's leave this place. I don't care if I never see Egypt again!"

The two left, followed by the slave girl. Abram knew that they had been delivered by the power of God, and as he held on to his wife, clutching her as if afraid to let her go, he prayed silently, *O Eternal One, may I never forget this. Put it on my memory so that it never leaves—that you are the God who can do all things!*

PART FIVE

THE BONDWOMAN

[Sarai] said to Abram, "The Lord has kept me from having children. Go, sleep with my maidservant; perhaps I can build a family through her."

Genesis 16:2

CHAPTER

19

Looking up at the sky, Eliezer admired the cloud formation that drifted slowly overhead. He had an active, creative imagination, and for a moment he stood still, picturing in his mind the images that the drifting, fluffy white clouds made. One of them looked like one of the sheep that chomped the grass at his feet. Another reminded him of the head of an old man, with snow-white locks and a beard that rolled down in rangy curls. *You're going to lose your mind if you don't stop letting it wander so much!*

Eliezer laughed under his breath at his own fancies, then threaded his way through the flock of sheep that spread out over the flat pastureland. The grass was adequate for another two days of grazing; then it would be time to move the sheep. The water was good, for they had camped within a short distance of a small stream that fed a larger one ten miles away. His shepherd's mind picked up all of these details without effort, and his glance went from one animal to another. He did not really know the name of every sheep in the fold as Abram had often teased him, but he knew those that had problems. Now his eye picked up a sight that made him turn and hurry quickly ahead.

A ewe had dropped a lamb, and now the tiny animal had struggled to his feet and was staggering around having his first look at the world. "Well, welcome to the world," Eliezer said, smiling. He reached over and picked up the lamb and cuddled it in his arms, wondering at the miracle that had brought a new life into the world.

While he held the lamb, the ewe moved around anxiously and, from time to time, nudged his knee. He began to sing a song that he always sang each time he saw a newborn lamb, a song he had made up himself. He was often teased for his song making and seldom sang in the presence of others, but he frequently serenaded the sheep in his pleasant baritone voice with its smooth, soothing quality.

"Welcome to the world, little lamb!
Welcome to the sweet water!
Welcome to the fresh green grass!
I sing your song and no other,
A song to your beauty and innocence.
Grow strong and fat in your world,
And may your wool make
A gown for a queen
And a robe for a king!"

"That's a nice song. Did you make it up yourself, Eliezer?"

Startled, Eliezer turned with the lamb still in his arms to find that Hagar had approached and now stood a few feet from him. She was wearing a thin garment she had brought with her from Egypt. Her dark eyes were large and lustrous, and unlike Hebrew women, she had painted her eyelids green, making her eyes look even larger. Her hair was carefully tended, and the sun caught the lustrous, dark gleam of it as she stood before him.

"I . . . I just found this one," Eliezer said, stammering a little. He was not a man who was at ease in the presence of women—at least not of attractive young women. In truth, Eliezer had no idea how good-looking he was. He had simply never paid attention to such things. His whole adult life had been spent learning to serve his master, Abram. His friends were always quick to point out the young women who found him attractive, but Eliezer had managed to avoid such encounters. Now he was a mature man, but he had never learned the art of flirting as others his age had. "I always love to watch the newborn lambs," he said to Hagar. "Don't you find them beautiful?"

Hagar glanced at the lamb and smiled. She came closer and put her hand on the lamb's tiny head and stroked it. "They are enticing little creatures," she said. "But then they grow up and lose that quality."

"Not for me, although I guess I just love any kind of animal."

"Even lions and bears and wild dogs that come to take your sheep?" Hagar teased. As she stroked the lamb's head, she allowed her hand to touch his arm, and when he blinked with surprise, she laughed. "You are a funny fellow, Eliezer!"

"I suppose I am."

"You don't chase around after young women like other men your age."

"No, I don't suppose I do."

"Why not?"

"I never learned how."

Hagar's eyebrows arched. "You're not too old to learn."

Any other man would have taken this statement as a direct invitation to press in, but Eliezer let the moment go by. "How do you like this new life?" he asked her. "It's a lot different from being in a palace in Egypt, isn't it?"

"Yes, it is, but I like it."

"Don't you miss all the luxuries you had there?"

"Oh, I suppose I do, but I was a slave there. Slaves don't have many luxuries. They have to steal them if they do."

"Steal them?"

"Of course. Slaves can't own any property. Everything that comes into their hands belongs to their masters. But I learned to make out fairly well."

Eliezer considered this and said, "But out here in the desert with so few conveniences, I'd think you'd miss that life."

"No, not really. You have to remember, Eliezer, I grew up in the desert. My father was a chieftain. We lived very much like you and all of Abram's people do."

Eliezer put the lamb down and said, "I have to walk a little bit to keep an eye on the animals. Would you walk with me?"

"Yes, that would be fine."

As the two walked among the animals, Hagar found herself studying Eliezer carefully. He seemed oblivious to his own good looks, but she found him to be one of the most attractive men she had ever seen. He was tall, as tall as Abram, and the lightweight shepherd's garment he wore left his arms and half of his chest bare. It was a simple garment, supported by one strap over his right shoulder and belted with a leather belt. His skin was a golden olive, even and smooth, and his hair, which he had tied together with a leather thong so that it hung down his back, was black and glistening. He had fine teeth that flashed when he smiled, outlined against his olive complexion. He did not smile often, but when he did, he made a most attractive picture.

"Tell me about yourself, Eliezer."

Looking at her, Eliezer shook his head. "There's really not anything to tell. I've had a very unexciting life."

"People say you're the son of our master, Abram."

Eliezer flushed. Despite his tan, whenever he was embarrassed the blood rushed to his cheeks. "There's nothing to that," he mumbled.

"But everyone says so."

"I don't think it's true."

"But you don't *know* it, do you?" Hagar had picked up the stories of the birth of Eliezer, born of a slave girl who had been redeemed by Abram. It had been perfectly logical to her mind, being reared in an amoral atmosphere, to think that Abram would have had a relationship with an attractive slave girl. She knew all about this from hard experience. She had waited for him to make some sort of approach to her, but he appeared to be impervious to such desires.

Hagar continued to lead the conversation, for it had occurred to her, as it had to others, that since Sarai and Abram had no children, this young man might well be the heir to all the couple's wealth. With this thought in her mind, she stumbled, not accidentally, and grabbed at his arm. "I guess I'm getting clumsy," she said, not releasing her hold. She looked up at him and lowered her eyelids coyly. "Tell me some more about the sheep," she said, and as they moved away, she kept her hand firmly on his arm.

Sarai stretched on her bed, arching her body and pointing her toes, weary after a long day's work at her loom. She loved to weave and spent hours every day at the small loom Abram had made for her. Now her fingers ached, and she locked them together, squeezing, then relaxing them.

"Can't you sleep?" Abram mumbled.

Sarai rolled over and turned to face Abram, who was lying beside her. "I'm not very sleepy, but I am tired."

"You work too hard. With all the servants we have, I don't see why you have to put yourself out so."

"What would I do if I didn't?" Sarai objected. "Lie around and stare at the sky?"

Lying next to her husband in bed had always been the best time of the day for Sarai. She wondered how many nights they had done this over the years. Unlike most men—at least so she supposed from what other women told her—her husband did not throw himself into bed and fall asleep at once. He was always eager to talk with her first, and it was during these moments that Sarai felt the happiest.

She began to speak of how she now realized the Eternal One had come to her when she was a prisoner in Pharaoh's palace. She had told Abram the story before, but she kept remembering new details. It had been an exalted moment for her, and now she whispered, "I am so happy that the Eternal One spoke to me at last, husband. Oh, not like He speaks to you, in a voice that can be heard, but I knew He was with me when I confronted Pharaoh.

I would never have had the courage to do that if I hadn't been sure of His presence."

"Tell me again what it was like."

"It was like . . . well, it was like nothing I had ever felt before. In a way it was as if someone had entered my body. I know that sounds silly, but that's what it was like. I just knew He was in me and all around me, and I knew that whatever I said to the pharaoh would be all right because God would be giving me the words."

Abram listened to Sarai and finally said, "I've thought a lot over the years about how the Eternal One has spoken to me. It's the same way He spoke to my grandfather Nahor, and from what I understand, He spoke in a similar way to Noah, Enoch, and other members of my family. I believe that He speaks to everyone, but He may do it in different ways."

Sarai could hear in Abram's voice the love he had for the Eternal One. She was always conscious of his pleasure in speaking of God. Finally Abram's voice began to trail off, and Sarai, still not sleepy, quickly changed the subject. "Hagar has proved to be a good servant. She's the best maid anyone could have."

"She does a good job of making you lovely, but you don't really need anyone to do that. You're lovely enough as you are!"

Sarai giggled. "You always flatter me, you old man."

"Not flattery at all. You're still the most beautiful woman I've ever seen."

Sarai pulled his head around and kissed him. "From what I hear from other women, you're the only man who says things like that to his wife."

"Then other men are stupid."

"Stupid! Why do you say that?"

"Because I can get anything I want from you when I say nice things."

Sarai doubled her fist and struck his arm. "You beast! You admit to such a thing?"

"Of course! I'm selfish to the bone. Now, if you'll promise to fix me just exactly the meal I want tomorrow, I'll tell you anything you want to hear."

Sarai smiled. She knew he meant what he said, but she also knew that in his teasing he had passed over a great truth. She had long ago learned about herself that she loved hearing words of endearment and appreciation. Fortunately for her, she had married a man who was willing to speak those words for a lifetime. Most men, she knew, would never think of saying sweet things to their wives.

"Have you noticed Eliezer?"

"What do you mean have I noticed him? I see him every day."

"Don't be foolish! I mean have you noticed what's going on between him and Hagar?"

"Going on? No. What's going on?"

"Men are so blind! She likes him."

Abram chuckled. "Hagar likes *most* men!"

Instantly Sarai stiffened. "Has she been making eyes at you too?"

"Of course she has. Are you blind?" Abram laughed. "I think she's just in the habit of attracting men."

"What if Eliezer falls in love with her and they get married?"

"Do you think that might happen?"

"I think it might. He should have married a long time ago. Would you mind if he did?"

"Not if he loves her."

The two talked about this subject, and finally Abram pushed it out of his mind. After a moment of silence, he brushed a kiss across Sarai's lips. "I'm worried about Lot."

"Yes, I am too. Things aren't the same between us. We were always so close—like family—and now he seems almost angry with you at times."

"Yes, you can't miss it."

"Why is he acting that way?" Sarai wondered.

"There's been some difficulty about the grazing land. We both have large herds, and sometimes our servants get into squabbles over it."

"Can't you do something about it?"

"I'm going to have to—it can't go on like this. Go to sleep now. I'll take care of it. Don't worry."

———

"He's cheating you, Lot!"

"No, he's not." Lot was putting on his sandals after rising from bed. He had awakened early, and his wife, Meri, had immediately begun nagging him about the problem he and his men were having over grazing land.

"Yes, he is!" Meri jumped out of bed and stood over Lot as he struggled to fasten his sandals. "You're too easy! You let everybody run over you—especially Abram!"

Lot rose to his feet and slipped into his clothing. He was in a bad mood and wished that Meri would keep her criticism to herself. It was an old argument, and he was weary of it. "Abram has been very fair with us."

"Tell me one thing he ever did that wasn't selfish," Meri demanded.

"All right, I will." Lot glared at her. "The pharaoh gave him more cattle than the eye can see, and Abram gave us half of them. He didn't have to give us any of them!"

"Of course he did. You're just like a son to him, aren't you? What kind of a man would he be if he hadn't given them to you?"

Long ago Lot had given up trying to reason with Meri. She did not have a reasoning mind, but she certainly had a demanding spirit! "We'll work it out," he muttered and started out the door of the tent but stopped when she caught his arm.

"Lot, you need to consider our daughters."

Lot was never able to follow the quick jumps that Meri's mind made. "What are you talking about?" he said. "What do they have to do with grazing land?"

"We've got to move into the city."

"Another old argument!" Lot shook his head. "What would I do in the city? You can't keep herds of sheep and cattle in a town."

"We're rich enough now that you can hire shepherds to keep them outside the town, but I want a house in Sodom."

The argument Meri always made was that their girls had no opportunity to meet suitable young men out in the desert. Lot had heard it a thousand times: *All they ever meet are dirty, smelly shepherds!*" Now she said it again, and Lot replied sharply, "I was a dirty, smelly shepherd, and I did all right!"

This answer did not satisfy Meri, of course. Wearily he listened all through breakfast, and finally he shoved his plate away disgusted. "All right— all right, I'll talk to Abram!"

"You get what belongs to us, and as soon as you do, we'll go into Sodom and see if we can't find a nice house." Her face grew dreamy. "It would be so nice to have a place in town. I could go shopping every day and make life very pleasant for you. You do it, Lot. We've lived out in this awful desert long enough!"

Abram was well aware that Lot had something on his mind. He had been speaking with Eliezer about moving the sheep to better ground when Lot had come in walking stiff-legged and with his jaw set, as he often did when he was troubled. Now Abram walked with him out to the edge of the flock, and Lot explained his problem, which came as no great surprise to the older man.

"Our servants are fighting over the grazing land, uncle," Lot said. "We've got to do something about it."

"I agree."

Lot, who was prepared for a heated argument with his uncle, was taken aback. He stammered for a moment, then said, "You think we should divide the land, then?"

"I don't see any other way, although it would be a loss not to be close to you, nephew. You know how fond I am of you."

A feeling of shame washed through Lot. He knew that Abram had been his best friend in the world, but Meri was making life miserable for him. "How will we divide it?" he asked.

Abram put his arm around Lot's shoulder. "You take the land you want, and I'll take whatever is left over," he said quietly.

Lot was shocked. He knew that by rights Abram should have taken first choice, but here he had freely given it to him. They were standing on a promontory, and the land spread out around them, clear and open to his gaze. He looked first at the desert land, then his eyes went to the watered plains of the Jordan Valley to his left. "Then if you will give me the choice . . ." he said. He hesitated, almost ashamed to choose the best, but Meri was waiting for him at home. "I'll take the plains over here." He added defensively, "Meri wants to live in a town, and I can't put up with her arguments any longer. She's going to drive me crazy, uncle."

Abram had known this, but he tried to put in a warning. "It's dangerous to live in a town like that. You know the reputation of those people."

"Yes, I've heard it all. It's a notorious place. But I don't have to take part in their sinful activities. I can be true to the Eternal One there as well as I can in the desert."

"I think it will be much more difficult," Abram said urgently. He loved this young man as if he were his own son. "It's hard to hear God's voice through all the noise of the city."

Abram did his best to dissuade Lot, but he soon discovered it was useless. Finally he said, "Well, I will pray that you will prosper, Lot, but I will pray even harder that you and your family will stay true to the Eternal One."

Lot felt a sense of despair. He had no desire to live in Sodom. He would much rather stay in the desert. He was that much like his uncle Abram, but he felt he had no choice. "I'll take care of myself and my family," he said stiffly. He knew it sounded churlish and said, "Uncle, I'm well aware of your generosity. You couldn't have treated me better if I were your own son." He turned then and was shocked to find tears forming in his eyes as he walked away from Abram. He knew, somehow, that he was doing a wrong thing, but he could find no way to avoid it.

"Oh, this is a beautiful house!"

Meri was ecstatic over her new home. It was one of the finer homes of Sodom. She walked through the rooms, followed by her two older daughters and Lot. When Meri finally tore herself away from the plans she was making, she turned to her husband and said, "Isn't your father a wonderful man, girls?"

The two girls, Tamar and Camoni, were as happy as their mother. They had been thoroughly indoctrinated by her to desire town life and now were beaming. They came over to kiss their father, one girl on each cheek. "It's going to be wonderful! There'll be so much to do."

Lot was less happy. "I don't care much for the men here in town. I think I'll have to stay out with the flocks a great deal."

"But you've got a good chief herdsman to take care of that," Meri said firmly. "It's time for us to enjoy life a little." She nodded and smiled happily. "We have to make our place here in this wonderful town. You're going to love it, Lot!"

The voice of the Eternal One came without warning: *"Abram!"*

Abram was alone, standing outside the camp. He often rose early in the morning to pray alone. Now he said at once, "Speak, O Eternal God!"

"Abram, lift up your eyes from where you are and look north and south, east and west. All the land that you see, I will give to you and to your offspring forever."

The voice was so strong! Abram had treasured every memory of those times when the Eternal One had spoken to him, and now it seemed to him that the voice was magnified.

"I will make your offspring like the dust of the earth, so that if one could count the dust of the earth, then your offspring could be counted. Go, walk through the length and the breadth of the land, for I am giving it to you."

The voice grew still, but Abram did not move. The promise seized him with its strength and its scope. He stared out at the land and tried to imagine a mighty host of people—*his* descendants. But he could not, and he bowed his head and whispered, "Your will be done, O mighty God!"

CHAPTER

20

After he split the land with Lot, Abram had led his people to Hebron, where he had finally settled around Mamre. Settled, that is, as much as nomadic shepherds are ever settled. The flocks and herds had to be moved from time to time, but Mamre had become more like a home to Abram than anyplace since he had left Ur. The land was not as fruitful there, perhaps, as other places, but he somehow drew comfort from the territory.

One morning, several months after settling near Mamre, Abram wandered among the flocks, stopping to talk to his herdsmen. He knew them all intimately and was involved in their problems. They all knew they could come to their master and he would do whatever he could to help them. Now as he crested the top of a rise, Abram stopped and looked out over the land. His gaze turned to the plain where Sodom and Gomorrah were located. His mind went to Lot and with that thought came a piercing grief. He had been hopeful that Lot would tire of the city life and would return, but he knew there was little chance of that with a wife like Meri!

A flash of something to his right caught Abram's glance, and when he turned, his blood ran cold at the sight of a poisonous serpent rearing up to strike. The snake was no more than two feet away, but Abram's stroke with his staff was quick enough to stop its strike. The staff caught the snake just below the head and sent it flying. The long, lean body flashed for a moment, then stiffened and grew still.

Abram disliked snakes intensely. He harbored a fear of them that he did not often allow to show. For a moment he felt a coldness in his veins, and then his knees felt weak and his hands trembled. He stared at them hard as if willing the shaking to stop, and then, taking a deep breath, he shook his head. "Thank you, Eternal One."

Praying at all times and in all places was a habit Abram had learned over the years. At times he set aside special places for prayer by building altars, but they always had to be left behind, so he had learned to pray as he went. Many times during the day he would turn his thoughts to the Eternal One and breathe a prayer of thanksgiving for whatever circumstance was before him. He would give thanks to God for the safe birth of one of his animals and for deliverance from wild beasts, as from the snake just now. Sometimes out of sheer joy he would pour out his heart, thanking God for his wife and his possessions, and at times he was simply caught up in wonder at the majesty of the great God he served.

As the day approached noon, Abram was conscious of a pressure building up inside of him. He did not know what to call it, but he had experienced it from time to time. It was like the way a stew cooks over a fire. At first the heat stays toward the bottom and the stew shows no sign that it's heating up. But if the fire continues strong, the surface of the stew will eventually begin to swirl and bubble, finally bursting forth like an explosion.

Something like this process had been going on in Abram for weeks. Only Sarai had noticed the change in him, however, and she simply observed that he was quieter and more thoughtful. As the days had passed, the feeling in his spirit had grown stronger, and he would pause many times a day, staring into space and praying silently, *What is it, Eternal One? What is it you would have me do?*

As the pressure intensified, Sarai had become more aware of it, and she asked him repeatedly what was troubling him. "Oh, nothing," Abram would reply, his answer not satisfying his wife one bit.

Abram wandered all day, but by the time he returned home to the tents late that afternoon he knew what he must do, and he announced to Sarai, "I don't know why, but I'm going to have to make a journey."

Sarai looked up from her mending. "A journey to where?"

"I'm not quite sure."

"Is it something God wants you to do?"

"I think it is, but I don't know why. I don't know how long I'll be gone."

Sarai did not show her concern. "Well, you be careful and don't worry about us here. Eliezer will take care of everything."

As Abram made his way south, he felt rested and at peace. He had resisted all efforts of Eliezer and Sarai to take a servant with him. Something deep inside his heart demanded solitude, and he did not want a babbling servant along to disturb his thoughts. He had no specific idea of his destination, but as he moved south, he was aware that this was the journey that had been laid out for him. Now as he moved along the banks of a small stream, sitting easily on his faithful donkey and leading another bearing his small tent, food, and other necessities, he began to wonder what it all meant.

Abram had an innate interest in all things, and Sarai often teased him about it. He would grin sheepishly, knowing that he had more curiosity than any five men, but this was part of what made him Abram.

He stopped beside the stream, dismounted from the donkey, and allowed the animals to drink long and deep. He filled his water bag and then sat down, letting the animals graze on the sparse grass that flanked the stream. As he did so, his mind began to reach out, becoming almost unaware of the donkeys and the scene around him.

I know that the Eternal One wants me to go on this journey. I wonder how long ago it was that He decided this. Is He like a man who makes plans? This must happen and then that must happen, and then I must do something to make another thing happen. That doesn't sound likely. He's not a man. Why should He think like one?

I believe, O Eternal One, that you must have known about this journey I'm on long before it even came into my mind. Why, you might have known about it when I was a child—even before I was born. And if you know that about me, then you must know everything about Sarai and Eliezer and everyone else. All of the Canaanites, the Egyptians, the people across the Great Sea. All the teeming nations—you know every one of them perfectly well. Every thought they've ever had. Every word they've ever spoken. What a God you are to hold all of this in your mind at the same time!

Abram was lost in such thoughts when one of the donkeys brayed, and he came to himself with a start. He grinned at his own foolishness and got to his feet. "All right, I know it's time to go. You've got a foolish old man for a master." Getting on the donkey, he kicked its sides and looked ahead eagerly. Somewhere out there lay a destination that had been chosen by the great Creator of all things, and both anxiety and joy filled him, knowing that he was doing exactly what his God wanted him to do.

Abram looked up at the walls surrounding the city that stood before him. He knew in his spirit that he had reached the end of his journey, and a quiet sense of satisfaction filled him. "Well, we're here, O Eternal One. I don't know why, but you do. So put whatever you have for me in my way."

He followed the road that led to the city, and when he came to the gates, he found himself under careful scrutiny by four guards who eyed him suspiciously.

"What's your business, stranger?" one of the guards demanded.

"Just traveling," Abram said easily. He was aware that these men were competent soldiers and wondered why there was need for such caution. But he also knew that the desert was full of tribes, some of them large enough to be considered dangerous to a small city such as the one before him.

"Traveling where?"

"I'm not sure," Abram admitted. "I would like to stay in here for a few days and rest my animals and buy some supplies."

The leader of the guards approached Abram and stood in front of him. He was a big man, muscular and scarred by his trade as a soldier. "What is your tribe?"

"I'm a wandering shepherd. My name is Abram. My people are the Hebrews."

"Never heard of them!"

"We're just a small group. No danger to you, soldier."

"You're an Amorite, are you?"

"No, we have no loyalties to any of the tribes in Canaan."

The guard continued to pepper Abram with questions and finally seemed satisfied. "All right. You can go in."

Abram hesitated. "I would like to worship while I'm here. What are the gods of your city?"

The guards suddenly grinned. "Worship, is it? Well, you've come to the right place for that."

"You have a great many gods?"

"Not like those of Sodom and Gomorrah. Some people will have their own little idol, but our king is the high priest of the one God."

A feeling like lightning ran through Abram. "The one God?" he managed to say. "What is His name?"

"Our king simply calls him God Most High."

"What is the name of your king?"

"King Melchizedek."

"This Melchizedek... I've heard rumors about him, but I know very little."

"He's our king, but he's also a priest."

"The priest of God Most High." Abram spoke the words softly. "I am eager to meet him."

"The king is always glad to meet seekers after God, but he has no time for idolaters. That's why Salem is different from any city in this land. Go in with you, now. You'll find our king an interesting man, I'm sure."

Abram thanked the soldier and then entered the city. It was not as impressive as the fabulous cities of Egypt he had seen. It was not even as large as Ur or Haran. But there was something about it that pleased Abram. The walls were not as high as other walled cities, but they were well built and strong. The people there seemed much like any other people. The streets were crowded, and Abram rode his donkey through the main thoroughfare, studying the faces of the dwellers of the city.

He stopped in the marketplace and asked a seller of cloth about a place to stay.

"My brother has a good place," the vendor said. "He can quarter your animals and feed them, and he has a room that he lets out from time to time."

Abram followed the vendor's instructions and found that the owner of the house was a pleasant man whose name was Beor. The price was not exorbitant, and after Beor had taken care of the animals and Abram had refreshed himself with clean water, washing his face and hands, he came into the main part of the house. Beor's wife was a cheerful woman. She talked as she fed him an excellent meal of mutton and fresh vegetables.

Abram answered her questions and then finally said, "I would like to meet the king, but I suppose that would be very difficult."

"It depends," Beor said, stuffing his mouth full with a huge chunk of mutton and talking around it. "Why do you want to see him?"

"I understand he is a religious man."

"Yes, he is. If you want to talk religion, you've come to the right place. Men come from all over this part of the world to listen to him. He's the wisest man you'll ever find."

"How would I get an audience?"

"Go to the palace. Tell them what you want. You may have to wait a bit, but he'll see you sooner or later."

After Abram finished his meal, he made his way to the palace, which was simply a house, though somewhat larger and more ornate than the other houses. He was met by a young man who greeted him pleasantly. When Abram stated his business, he said, "The king will probably see you soon. If you will wait here, I will find out his pleasure."

Abram did so eagerly, and he did not have to wait long. The young man soon came out and smiled. "The king would be happy to receive you now, if you'll come this way."

Abram followed the young man down a long corridor and turned into a door leading to a room that was like a patio. It was open on three sides, and green plants and flowers grew abundantly in containers, filling the room with their fragrance. He was admiring his surroundings when the man who turned to greet him caught his eye.

"You are welcome, sir."

The speaker was extremely tall, at least two inches taller than Abram, but much thinner. His face was thin also, somewhat like a knife blade, but his features were delicately carved, and his eyes were warm with welcome.

"Be seated." The king indicated a chair next to his, and the men sat down. "You are a newcomer to our city?"

"Yes. My name is Abram, O King."

"You must tell me about yourself and your people. I know that you are Abram the Hebrew—I have heard of you."

Abram was shocked. "But, sire, how could you have heard of me?"

"You are the Abram who went down to Egypt, are you not, and then came back with large herds of cattle—gifts of the pharaoh?"

Abram could not believe that Melchizedek had heard of his adventures. "Yes, sire, that is true. I can't imagine how you heard of such a thing."

"People come and tell me stories. I try to know what is happening in the land. They tell me also that you are not a worshiper of idols."

"No," Abram said quickly. "I was once, in my younger days when I was growing up in Ur of the Chaldees. Everyone there was an idolater."

"But you no longer believe in praying to a block of stone?"

"No, indeed, O King! I have not believed that for a long time."

"Tell me more about you. The story I heard concerned your wife and Pharaoh."

Abram felt the keen gaze of King Melchizedek. He found himself telling the entire story, not omitting his own fault in claiming that Sarai was his sister. He finished by saying, "It took the hand of the Eternal One to get my wife back. No human power could have done it."

"Tell me about the God you call the Eternal One."

Abram felt comfortable in this man's presence. He had found a kindred spirit in the tall man who sat across from him. "The Eternal One first appeared to me when I was in Ur of the Chaldees. . . ."

He spoke steadily for a long time, then blinked with surprise and laughed with embarrassment. "I have talked like a foolish man. I assure you, O King, I do not usually babble like this."

Melchizedek leaned forward and put his hand on Abram's. "No, you are not a foolish man. You are blessed among men, for the supreme God whom I serve has shown favor toward you."

"What do you call this God?"

"I call Him *El Elyon*, which means, of course, the highest God, for that is what He is."

"Tell me," Abram said eagerly. "Tell me everything about Him, for I love Him as much as I possibly can."

"We shall have many talks together. I will want to hear more from you, and we will share what we know of this great, almighty God we serve."

Abram felt a great peace. "It is good to know my people are not the only ones who believe in the Eternal One," he said, tears filling his eyes. "I have felt so lonely, O King."

"You need not feel alone, for God Most High has people all over the world. They may not be well-known, but He is speaking to men and women everywhere. We shall have many talks. You will stay in the palace with me, and we will learn from each other."

"Yes, O King Melchizedek," Abram said, joy flooding his heart at the knowledge that in some sense he had come home.

Hagar had firmly decided that Eliezer was the man she wanted. Her beauty had drawn other members of Abram's clan seeking her favor, but she had considered them only momentarily. None of them had Eliezer's good looks—an important factor in her decision, for she prized handsomeness in a man. But even more than this, she had become convinced that one day Eliezer would own all of Abram's property. After all, Abram was getting on in years, as was Sarai, and when he died, where would his property go? To his chief steward! Everyone assumed this to be true, and Hagar was very aware of the advantages of material things, having lived much of her life in the pharaoh's palace.

She had given Eliezer many broad hints of her fondness for him, and his reluctance had puzzled her. Her experience with men had been extensive, but they had always been the pursuers. As a slave in Egypt, she had fought off those she could and accepted those she could not reject. Since being with Abram's people, she had not yet been intimate with any man, although she had flirted with several.

The sun was going down as Hagar sat in her tent. She had bathed in the river and then had anointed herself with the spicy fragrances she had brought from Egypt, which were strong and enticing to a man's senses. Now she skillfully applied the eye shadow and lip rouge and stared at herself in her polished bronze hand mirror.

Satisfied with her appearance, she proceeded to put on one of the linen gowns she had brought from Egypt. Its tiny pleats clung to her body, and with this she was also satisfied. Smiling to herself, she went to sit outside the door of her tent. She had plotted her strategy carefully, knowing that it was Eliezer's habit to make a last trip to check with the shepherds who watched over the animals by night. He sometimes stayed late, but Hagar was prepared to wait him out.

The sun went down, and the moon rose, its pale silver gleam dominating the sky. Hagar had long prayed to the moon goddess, and now she looked up and lifted her hand to the moon. "O goddess, give me what I desire, and I will make you an offering that will be magnificent!"

After some time she heard Eliezer's voice. He was a fine singer and often sang softly as he returned from watching the flock. Getting to her feet, Hagar's breath quickened. The moonlight threw its silver beams down over the camp. Most people were already asleep, except for the guards on the outer fringes. She could hear the animals lowing softly, and then Eliezer appeared. He passed close by her tent, and she called out, "Eliezer!"

Startled, he turned and stared at her.

"Would you come here a moment?" she asked sweetly.

Eliezer came toward her, and when he stood before her, she said, "Please stay with me awhile. I'm so lonely and afraid."

"Afraid? What are you afraid of, Hagar?"

"Come and sit with me, and I will tell you. I need to talk with someone."

Hagar took Eliezer's arm and stepped inside the tent. The floor was covered with a fine carpet, and holding his arm, she pulled him down beside her. A small oil lamp threw a golden corona of light over the interior of the tent. Its rays highlighted her figure, and burning incense filled the tent with its aroma. The perfume Hagar wore was rich with a slight musky scent, and still holding Eliezer's arm, Hagar pressed herself against it. "I don't know what I'm so afraid of. Perhaps it's just because I'm a weak woman."

"Why, Hagar, you shouldn't be afraid."

"I know I shouldn't, but women are not like men. You're big and strong and can take care of yourselves, but who can take care of me? What will ever happen to me?"

"Why, you're Sarai's servant! You couldn't find a better mistress in all the world."

"But a woman wants more than a place to sleep and food to eat. She has needs that go far beyond that."

Eliezer was conscious at that moment of his own needs. The richness of her perfume, the softness of her body pressing against him, and the intoxicating incense stirred his passions. He looked into her dark eyes and when she smiled at him, he knew it was an invitation.

"Don't men have needs, Eliezer?" she whispered. She put her left hand on his neck and pulled his head down.

Eliezer found her lying in his arms, and he pulled her close. Her lips were soft and yielding under his, and for that one moment there was nothing in the world for him except the soft form he held within his arms. In the past, he had managed to conquer his needs by setting a stern brake on his natural desires, but he had never before felt anything like this and had never felt so unable to control himself.

As for Hagar, her heart was racing, for she knew that his response was that of a man who wanted her. She held him even closer and ran her hands through his hair, and when he lifted his lips and put them against her neck, she began to whisper endearments to him.

Eliezer suddenly stiffened and abruptly sat up. "Hagar, I can't—" He broke off, his voice thick and husky. Shaking his head, he said, "This is not right."

"But you want me, Eliezer. I know you do."

"But you're not my wife."

Hagar waited, for this was the moment she had planned for. She expected him to ask her to marry him, but instead he suddenly rose to his feet and said, "I'm sorry. This is a thing I must not do. You're a lovely woman, Hagar, but a man must have honor where women are concerned."

Hagar was astonished as Eliezer said these words, turned, and left the tent. Realizing she had been unable to win him, anger flooded through her. She had never been rejected by any man, and the knowledge that she did not have the same power over Eliezer that she had over other men infuriated her. She threw herself facedown on the carpet and beat it with her fists. She cursed him and spat out bitterly, "He'll be sorry! Oh, he'll be sorry that he treated me like this!"

———

Sarai had noticed the change in Hagar as far as Eliezer was concerned. Whereas before she had been all smiles and had gone out of her way to please him by fixing special dishes and had skillfully used all the wiles that a beautiful woman had, now she never spoke to him except when necessary.

Sarai also noticed that Eliezer was stiff and unnatural. She finally stopped him one day when he came into camp. The women were cooking, and Sarai said, "Come and sit down beside me. I never get to talk to you, Eliezer."

Eliezer obeyed but had little to say. Finally Sarai asked, "What's the matter between you and Hagar? Are you having a fight?"

Eliezer did not dare tell Sarai how Hagar had behaved. He merely mumbled something about Hagar's having learned some bad habits in Egypt.

Instantly Sarai knew that Hagar had offered herself to Eliezer and he had refused her. Finally she said, "Well, there are other women. I wouldn't want you to make a mistake in a wife. There's nothing worse than being married to somebody you don't love."

Her words amused Eliezer. "How would you know about that, mistress?"

Sarai stared at him and then covered her mouth as she laughed. "Am I that transparent?"

"Everyone knows you and my master love each other with all your hearts."

"Well, we do, and I want you to have that same kind of relationship with your wife when you get one."

"I think I may never get one." Eliezer put the matter aside with a smile. "I suppose I'm just too choosy."

Eliezer left, but Sarai was worried about him. She missed Abram and wished she could have talked with him about this, but he had been gone for weeks now.

Abram saw sadly that Sodom had not changed. He had come to this city on his way home and now was sorry that he had done so. Lot was very glad to see him, though, and Meri was triumphant. She proudly showed Abram their beautiful house, now packed with belongings she had bought at the bazaars. She spoke of how her marriageable daughters were now invited to all the homes of the city leaders, and waited for Abram to approve of what she and Lot had accomplished.

Abram did his best to compliment them, but it was a feeble attempt. Meri became huffy with him for his obvious lack of enthusiasm.

Afterward Lot and Abram walked through the city at dusk. Abram tried to avoid being critical, but he could not help noting the bands of men that roamed about.

"Who are these gangs of men?"

Lot was embarrassed. "Oh, they're just groups of young men that get together for a good time."

But Abram saw that night what their good times amounted to. He witnessed one gang of men seize a young boy from his own home and carry him off screaming. Abram started to go to the boy's aid, but Lot instantly cried out, "No, uncle, you mustn't! They will kill you!"

"You know what kind of men these are, Lot?"

Lot bowed his head. "Yes, I know. I hate it! I hate every day here!"

"Then come with me. Bring your family and leave this place."

Lot shook his head. "I would love nothing better, but Meri would never hear of it."

Abram did not argue, but neither did he tarry. The city of Sodom had an aura of evil about it, and he left early the next day, anxious to get home.

When Abram returned home, Sarai greeted him with the joy of a young woman, making over him so much that Abram grinned slyly. "I think I'm going to take more trips away from home. You don't appreciate me nearly as much as you should."

Sarai struck his chest with her fist. "You are a vain thing, and you're wrong. I did miss you terribly!"

The two were happy in the days that followed. Sarai told Abram all that had happened with Eliezer and Hagar. He listened and shook his head. "She needs to be married—but not to Eliezer!"

The days and months went by quickly, and Abram settled back. He had received much knowledge from Melchizedek, and he shared it with his family and people. It did them good to hear how the king of a distant city worshiped the same God as they did.

Their happiness was complete until a messenger came one day, disaster written on his face. When he said, "I am the servant of Melchizedek," Abram welcomed him warmly.

"Come in, come in! Let me have the servants wash your feet."

"I am Chalbain, the steward of the king of Salem. My master sent me with urgent news."

Abram stared at Chalbain and knew that the news was grim. "Is the king in trouble?"

"He bids me tell you that a war has broken out." Chalbain sketched the details of the battle and shook his head. "Many have been slain, and many more captured by the enemy."

"Does King Melchizedek wish for me to come and take part in the battle?"

"He bids me to tell you that your kinsman, Lot, and his family have been taken. The city of Sodom was plundered by the enemy. They took your nephew and all his possessions with them."

"Lot taken! I must go at once!"

"The king knew you would be anxious. He bid me to tell you that God Most High has spoken to him about your kinsman."

"What did God tell him?"

"That you would be the instrument of his deliverance. He assures you that you will be victorious and that, if you go in the power of the Most High, your kinsman and all his family will be saved."

Abram said instantly, "We will go and get my nephew back."

Sarai spoke up. "They have an army, Abram. We have only a few men."

Abram said quietly, "King Melchizedek is a priest of God Most High. I believe his word that the Eternal One will fight for us! We will go in the strength of God!"

CHAPTER

21

The war that swept the country had complicated causes. The most powerful of the Amorite kings, Kedorlaomer, was a vicious man—greedy and without pity. He had exacted tribute from weak kingdoms, and when Sodom and Gomorrah and three other small kingdoms refused to pay, he had attacked. He had taken the five kings captive and many citizens along with them, among them Lot, the nephew of Abram.

Abram at once assembled all the men of his clan and began to prepare them for battle. It was Sarai who spoke what most of them were thinking. "Husband, you have only three hundred men. The king of the Amorites has thousands. You can't win against such numbers."

"The Eternal One will be with us. They will be drunk and will take no thought that they will be attacked."

Eliezer was standing beside Abram and Sarai, armed and ready. "What is your plan, master?"

"The Eternal One has spoken to me. We will follow them, not allowing ourselves to be seen. They will break up into small groups when they reach the mountains. The hostages and the captive kings will be close to Kedorlaomer. We will have the victory, for our God is with us!"

There were doubters among Abram's men, but his spirit gave them courage. He led his men into the mountains, and when the enemy settled in for the night, he divided his men into smaller groups. Eliezer was charged with leading the group assigned the task of freeing the prisoners, and Abram warned him, "They will try to kill the prisoners to keep them from being taken alive. You must be quick."

"Yes, master!"

"Then we will fight—come!"

Eliezer led his men forward and discovered that almost all the men guarding the prisoners were drunk. Their numbers were few, so he charged the inebriated sentries, his men cutting them down like cornstalks. The drunken men had stumbled, confused and disoriented, then fled in fear, their screams and flight causing a wholesale panic among the army of Kedorlaomer. Soon the battle became a slaughter.

Eliezer's arm was weary. He had wielded his sword furiously, and now he exulted at seeing the enemy being driven away. He cast a glance to his right, where he saw Abram still unharmed, and felt a gush of relief.

"Press on!" Eliezer shouted. "Don't give them time to recover!"

All of the men of the tiny army that had attacked the invaders were screaming so that they sounded like a mighty host. The air was filled with the clanging of sword against sword, the screams of the wounded, and the fearful shouts of the enemy. As Eliezer pressed on, he saw more of the enemy fleeing and knew the joy of victory.

Suddenly he spotted one of his men with his sword raised over a woman and child on the ground. Eliezer shouted, "Leave those two alone!"

His shout startled the man, and he turned and saw Eliezer coming at him, his eyes blazing.

"Forget them!" Eliezer screamed. "Go find a man, a soldier to fight with."

The man fled as Eliezer ran quickly to the woman and child. He saw that the woman had already been wounded, but he could not tell who had done it. He knelt on one knee by her side, saying, "Are you badly hurt?"

The woman's face was pale, and Eliezer saw then that she had been struck in the side with a sword. Her garment was soaked with blood, as was the ground beneath her.

"Please help my child," she pleaded weakly, the pallor of death on her face.

Quickly he began to try to stanch the flow of blood. "What is your name?" he said. "Where are your people?"

"My name is Ameira. I am the wife of a chief, but he is dead."

"Is this your daughter?"

With great effort, she reached up a hand. "Yes. Please. She has no one now."

Eliezer took the woman's hand and leaned forward. He saw the glaze of death in her eyes, and he spoke impulsively. "Do not be afraid. I will take care of your daughter."

"Will you promise?"

Eliezer nodded. He saw the child watching him, fear etched on her face. She was a thin child, no more than eight years old, and he reached his other hand out and touched her head. She flinched as if he had struck her. "Don't be afraid, child. I won't hurt you. What is your name?"

"Her name is . . . Zara," the mother said. She held to Eliezer's hand with her fragile strength and then cried out, "Vow to your god that you will take care of her as your own. Please!"

"I swear by the Eternal One that I will take care of Zara as if she were my own."

The woman stared at him, and a smile came to her lips. She turned to her daughter and whispered, "This is your father, Zara. He will take care of you."

"Mother, don't leave me! You can't leave me!"

The woman's eyes faded and her body went limp. The child threw herself on her mother's breast, weeping with all her strength.

Eliezer held the dead mother and put his hand out and touched the child's hair. "I will keep you safe, child. Do not be afraid."

"I have no one—no one!"

"Yes. You have me. You heard me vow to God that I will take care of you. I will keep that vow, Zara."

The child looked at him, her face twisted with fear. "Will you promise?" she whispered.

"Yes, I will promise."

———————

Abram looked up to see Melchizedek, the king of Salem, waiting. He was weary after the battle but pleased that he had saved all the kings, and more than that, Lot was safe!

The cheers rose as Melchizedek lifted his hand and cried out, "Blessed be Abram by God Most High, Creator of heaven and earth. And blessed be God Most High, who has delivered your enemies into your hand!"

Abram bowed low, then lifting himself up, said, "I give you tithes of all the spoil, king and priest of God Most High!"

The kings came one by one, all bowing to Abram and promising him great gifts, but Abram shook his head. "I have sworn to the Lord, God Most High, Creator of heaven and earth, and have taken an oath that I will accept nothing belonging to you, not even a thread or the thong of a sandal, so that you will not be able to say, 'I have made Abram rich.'"

Later when Abram was alone with the king, he said, "I knew when I received your message that all would be well."

Melchizedek nodded but was silent for such a long time that Abram asked anxiously, "Is something wrong, master?"

"No, all is well, very well. But God Most High revealed many things to me—about you, Abram."

"About me, sire?" Abram was astonished, but then he asked eagerly, "What did He say about me?"

"Some of the things He told me He bade me keep only in my spirit. But you are to be greatly used, my son! He gave me a vision of what is to come, and you are God's choice to bring many things to pass."

"But I am only a weak man! How can such a thing be?"

"God does not require strength, Abram. He is strong and requires only one thing in any man."

"And what is that, O King?"

Melchizedek put his hands on Abram's shoulders, and his eyes were burning like fire. "No man can please the most high God without faith. And He has shown me that of all the men that He has created, you have more of that than any other of His servants. And I must warn you that in a day in the future, He will ask you to believe a thing that will seem impossible. No matter how impossible the thing seems, Abram, you must believe the word of the Most High! And in believing, you will be the father of all who will believe in times to come!"

Abram felt weak, but he whispered, "Pray for me, master, that I will believe all that God Most High tells me!"

The two men prayed, and when Abram left the king, he felt as if he had been in the very presence of God.

———————

From that day on, the fame of Abram the Hebrew was known throughout the land of Canaan! It was not the victory, however, that Abram remembered most vividly for the rest of his life—the words that God gave him after he left Melchizedek were burned into his mind:

"Do not be afraid, Abram. I am your shield, your very great reward."

"O Sovereign Lord, what can you give me since I remain childless and the one who will inherit my estate is Eliezer? You have given me no children; so a servant in my household will be my heir."

"This man will not be your heir, but a son coming from your own body will be your

heir. Look up at the heavens and count the stars—if indeed you can count them. So shall your offspring be."

Abram thought of his and Sarai's ages, and doubt tried to creep into his mind. But, remembering the words of the king, he shoved the doubts aside and cried out, "Lord God, I believe your promise!"

God said many other things to Abram that day, matters which he never revealed to another soul. But when he left that place, he knew he must go to Sarai and share the promise of a child to come from his loins. As he made his way home, his heart sang with joy that the God of heaven and earth had heard his prayer for a son!

CHAPTER
22

Sarai had taken special care with Abram's midday meal. It began with a bowl of delicious thick porridge, prepared with sesame oil and served with warm cakes of barley flour, radishes, cucumbers, and sprouts of the cabbage palm. Roasted veal followed with loaves of *solet* bread and rich, creamy butter, and then a compote of plums and raisins, all washed down by flagons of fresh milk and sparkling wine.

Abram cut a piece of the tender veal off and tasted it. "This is good, wife," he nodded with satisfaction.

"You say everything I cook is good. I think you might be getting too old to taste the food."

"You're wrong about that." Abram winked. "And I've noticed you're getting a bit plump. Nothing I like better than a plump woman!" He reached over and pinched her hip, and she slapped his hand.

"Keep your hands to yourself," Sarai sniffed. She was actually pleased that he was still teasing her after all these years. Abram was still careful to pay her compliments, and he often took her hand and simply held it, a gesture that Sarai delighted in.

Chewing thoughtfully on a piece of the tender meat, Abram said, "I think we need to go into Sodom and pay Lot and Meri a visit. It's been seven years since we've seen them."

"I don't want to go to Sodom. I thought after you saved him from getting killed in that war, he would have had sense enough to move out of that place."

"I guess he's there for life. It's a shame. That is a wicked, wicked place."

"I don't know why God doesn't simply allow that city to drop into the earth."

"It's no worse than Gomorrah, from what I hear."

"Well, that's not saying a lot."

Sarai picked at her food. A thought had been coming to her for some time now, and she said finally, "Abram, have you ever thought you might have misunderstood what God said to you after you saved Lot?"

"I've never forgotten any of the times that the Eternal One spoke to me. His words were very clear. Why are you asking about that?"

Sarai hesitated. She pushed the meat around with her finger and looked up at him. "It's just that you told me that the Lord said you would have children and grandchildren and one day a whole host of descendants."

"Yes, that's what He said."

"But nothing has happened, and we're old now. Too old for children."

Abram reached over and took Sarai's hand. He held it firmly and said quietly, "He is the Eternal One, the great Creator. He knows all things about everyone, about you and me, Sarai."

"But it's impossible."

"Nothing can be impossible for the one who made the earth and the stars."

Sarai was aware of his strong hand holding hers. He was still a strong man despite his years. "I have a dream over and over again that I'm holding a baby—and it's our baby."

Abram stared at her. "How long have you had this dream?"

"For a long time."

"You've never told me about it."

"I thought it was foolish after I got old, but it's been coming back lately, stronger than ever. It's so real, Abram. I can feel the baby and smell him and look into his eyes."

Abram saw the tears in Sarai's eyes, and he squeezed her hand. "You keep that dream. I think it's from the Lord."

The two sat there for a long time, and finally Abram asked, "Do you think Hagar is going to marry that young man from Benozi's tribe?"

"No, I think she's just playing with him, like she always plays with men."

Abram's face darkened. "I don't like it. She keeps men stirred up. I thought at one time she would marry Eliezer."

"I told you he would never marry her."

"Why not? She's an attractive woman."

"He wants more in a wife than just a pretty face."

"Well, he should have married years ago."

Abram got up and stretched, and then a thought came to him before he left. "What about Zara? How old is she now? Fourteen?"

"No. She's fifteen."

"She's almost a woman, isn't she?"

"Yes, she is. But Eliezer doesn't see that. He still thinks of her as the eight-year-old whose life he saved."

"Well, she's grown up to be a handsome young woman. Eliezer has been like a father to her. I guess he'll keep on feeling that way."

"Yes, but he still thinks of her as an infant. He's going to have to change his ways if he's going to be a father to that girl. The young men are going to come swarming around her."

Eliphaz had come bearing a flower for Zara that he had picked in the desert. Zara liked young Eliphaz. He was a good young man who was constantly bringing her small gifts. He was smitten with her, and this pleased Zara. As she pinned the flower in her hair, she said, "Thank you, Eliphaz, it's beautiful. You're always bringing me such nice gifts."

Eliphaz was no older than Zara herself, thin and intensely bashful around her. He had fallen in love with Zara with the blind passion of an adolescent and spent most of his days and nights dreaming about her. His parents would laugh at him, his father saying, "You're so dizzy over that girl you can't even do your work. Wake up!"

His mother had defended him, saying, "He loves her."

"Love! He's like a calf. He doesn't know what love is!"

But Eliphaz did think he knew what love was, and all morning he had been planning what he would do. He had never touched Zara, but he had talked himself into the notion that she liked him, and now, as she stood before him smiling, he suddenly leaned forward and put his arms around her. He bent his head down to kiss her, but she turned her head so that his lips landed on her cheek.

"Eliphaz," Zara laughed, "what's wrong with you?"

"I love you, Zara."

Zara was amused by this and tried to fend him off. She was not angry, for she liked him a great deal. She was not above a little innocent teasing and was actually enjoying the wrestling match, which was what the embrace had turned out to be. Eliphaz was determined to kiss her on the lips, and she continually turned her head to avoid his caresses, at the same time protesting, "Eliphaz, you are an awful boy! Turn me loose!"

Suddenly Zara did find herself freed from Eliphaz's embrace. She staggered back and saw that Eliezer had appeared and jerked Eliphaz by one arm.

He was a strong, powerful man, and the boy was helpless in his grasp.

"I'm going to thrash you! You behave like a brute," Eliezer said sternly. He started to drag Eliphaz away, looking for a stick, but Zara came after him, taking his arm. She tugged at him and begged, "Please, don't hurt him. He was just teasing."

"Teasing! It didn't look like teasing to me!"

"I didn't mean any harm, Eliezer. Honest I didn't," Eliphaz pleaded. He was terrified at what he had done, and the expression on his face softened Eliezer.

"You deserve a thrashing, and I'm going to give it to you!"

"No, please, don't be cruel, Eliezer. He didn't mean anything."

Eliezer hesitated and looked into Zara's face. She had the most unusual eyes he had ever seen, green like the sea, or like he imagined the sea to be. Her mother's had been the same, he remembered. She had the creamy skin of her mother also. He growled, "Why are you begging for this whelp? You probably brought it on by teasing him."

"I did! So if you want to whip someone, whip me."

Eliezer suddenly released the boy. "Get out of here," he said gruffly, and when the boy scrambled away, he reached out and took Zara by the arm. "Maybe I will thrash you! You deserve it. The poor boy. He didn't have a chance."

"He was silly, wasn't he?" Zara showed absolutely no fear. She reached up and patted Eliezer, saying, "I'm glad you didn't hurt him. Now, go ahead and whip me."

Eliezer knew she was teasing him now. "I ought to," he muttered. Instead he released her but said, "I'm going to stop brats like that from coming around."

Zara's smile faded into a pout. "I'm fifteen years old. Many of my friends younger than I are married. Motina even has a baby."

"Well, you're not getting married, and you're not having a baby, and that's the end of it!"

He saw her face change and then growled, "I liked it better when you were eight years old."

"Well, *master*,"—she stressed the word—"I couldn't stay eight years old all my life, could I?"

"I suppose not, but try to behave yourself."

"I always behave myself. You know that."

Eliezer smiled. He reached out and put his hand on her head. She was growing up, and he could see the traces of young womanhood on her, but he did not want to admit it. "I know you do, Zara. You're a good girl."

He hugged her, then released her quickly, aware that she was no longer a little girl. "I'm going to be away for a few days," he said to cover his confusion.

"Where are you going?"

"Abram's going to pay a visit to Lot. He wants me to go with him. We need some more supplies from the city."

"Take me with you."

"No, I'm not taking you to that awful place. It's no place for a young woman."

"It's no place for a young man either, but you're going."

"I'm old enough to take care of myself."

"You're old enough to take care of me too. Please, Eliezer, take me with you."

"You're not going and that's final! You have to learn that you can't always have your own way, Zara."

Zara was wise beyond her years, especially about anything concerning Eliezer. She had developed a fondness for him that went deeper than Eliezer knew. She had learned she could get almost anything she wanted from him as long as he believed it was his idea.

"All right. If you won't let me go, I suppose I'll just have to stay here."

Zara had also discovered a gift she had. She had found out some time earlier that she could cry at will. She did not know anyone else who could do this, but she had learned to use it to good advantage, for Eliezer could not bear to see her cry. Now she simply allowed the tears to flow into her eyes, making sure that Eliezer could see them.

"Well, wait a minute," Eliezer said. "You don't have to cry about it."

"I'm not crying!"

"Yes, you are."

"I am not!" Zara turned away, or started to, but he caught her by the arm, and she permitted him to turn her around. She dropped her head so he couldn't see her eyes, and then when he put his finger under her chin and lifted it, she allowed the tears to form more quickly. She felt them run down over her cheeks, and she heard him begin to stammer, as he always did. "Wait a minute, Zara, I don't like to see you cry."

"I'm sorry," Zara whispered. "I don't mean to be such a crybaby. You go on, Eliezer. I know it's not right for you to take me."

"Well, wait a minute! I'll make this decision. You always want to make my decisions for me. If I decide you're going, you're going, and that's it!"

"But you said—"

"Never mind what I said. You're going! Now, stop crying." Evidently something happened to Eliezer's powers of reason where this girl was concerned, for he said in some confusion, "Now, let this be a lesson to you, Zara." He made his voice stern and nodded. "You can't always have your own way."

"I know it. I'm just awful."

"No, you're not awful. Well, you can go this time, but no more."

"Yes, master."

"And don't call me master."

"Yes, Eliezer."

"All right. Let this be a lesson to you, now."

Zara hid her smile as she turned away. How easy it was to make this big man do whatever she desired! "I'll remember that," she said softly and then ran away to begin getting ready to go.

Sarai knew that Hagar had something on her mind, for she had been behaving herself extremely well. Finally it came out as Hagar was fixing her hair. "I know you don't like to go to Sodom, mistress, but I'd like to go with the master and Eliezer."

"Why would you want to go to that awful place?"

"I still have some of the money you gave me last year, and I want to buy some nice things. You can't buy anything out here in the desert."

"I'm not sure Abram would let you go."

"Yes, he would. Eliezer's taking Zara, and I'd be company for her."

"Why would you want to go to that place—even to buy things? I shudder to think about it."

"I get bored out here," Hagar admitted, being truthful with her mistress for once. "I always liked Lot, and I'll get to see his daughters. Maybe I'll get to go to some parties with them. Please, let me go."

Sarai sighed, "All right. If that's what you want. But I can't imagine anybody going to Sodom on purpose."

Zara enjoyed the journey to Sodom tremendously, except for having to share a tent with Hagar. When she had been younger she had liked Hagar, for the woman had been kind to her. She had been fun to be with, but during the past year while Zara had been growing to young womanhood, she had somehow found Hagar's ways distasteful. She was as aware as anyone in Abram's company that Hagar flirted with men, not only men from Abram's tribe but with the Canaanite men and the Amorites and the Hittites. It seemed to make little difference to her, as long as a man was young and strong and fairly prosperous. Zara had watched her carefully and knew that Hagar's morals were bad.

Even more irritating was the fact that lately Hagar had been showing a great deal of interest in Eliezer. Zara had learned that at one time Hagar had been very interested indeed in her master, but something had come between them. Now Hagar seemed to once again have decided that Eliezer was a great deal of fun to be with, for she had joined herself to him almost constantly. Eliezer seemed unaware of Hagar's wiles, and at times Zara wanted to shout at him.

One night, on the third day of their journey, Zara was in bed watching Hagar as she prepared to lie down for the night. Hagar had come in late, her eyes glowing with satisfaction.

"Where have you been?" Zara asked. "It's late."

"Oh, Eliezer and I got to talking, and we forgot the time."

"What were you talking about?"

"Things you wouldn't understand."

Hagar's words offended Zara. "I'm fifteen years old. I think I'm old enough to understand anything *you* can say!"

Hagar turned and for a moment anger flared in her dark eyes. Then she came over and patted Zara on the head. "Maybe you will someday."

"What were you talking about? Tell me!"

"Anything he wanted to talk about. That's what you do with a man, Zara. You find out what they like, and you talk about that. Sometimes he bores me to death going on about those smelly old sheep. You'd think they were made out of gold the way he makes over them." She laughed and raised her arms to fix her hair. "Before I'm through with him, he'll love me better than any stinking sheep."

Zara stared at Hagar. She had been impressed for a time by the woman's beauty and liveliness, but now she silently hated her. The thought of having her as a stepmother offended Zara, and besides, Hagar wasn't the right woman for Eliezer.

She'd make him miserable, Zara thought. *She likes men, and she'll never be satisfied with just one. I wish she had stayed in Egypt!*

Eliezer had at first been apprehensive about Hagar. He well remembered the strong seductive message she had sent to him that night in her tent. He had never forgotten it, but she seemed to have changed, at least toward him. He knew as well as anyone that she still liked men, that she had the reputation of being an immoral woman, but he did not believe these rumors. He thought she was simply unhappy with her lot in life and perhaps a little too friendly, but nothing more than that.

He had really enjoyed being with her, for the desert could be a lonely place. His chief occupation was twofold, keeping Abram's flocks and raising Zara, whom he considered to be a daughter or perhaps a younger sister. Hagar had not overwhelmed him with her attentions, and he had slowly begun to enjoy the times they spent together. She mostly came to him when he was out watching the sheep and listened to him talk. He had grown more talkative of late and was happy to find that he had someone to talk to.

More than that, he had discovered that she still was attracted to him. More and more he thought of his single condition, his lack of a family, and the more he thought of it, the more it seemed clear to him that Hagar needed a husband and he needed a wife. He never formulated these ideas into words, but neither did he run from her as he once had.

One evening, on the return trip from Sodom, they were walking together. The moon was full and brilliant, bathing them in silver light.

"It's a beautiful night," Hagar said quietly.

"It is. Look at that moon. You could almost reach up and touch it."

"Let me see you try," she teased him.

"Well, maybe not quite touch it. But it is beautiful."

As they continued to talk, Eliezer had a sense of well-being in her presence. They reached her tent, and he paused for a moment. "It's so quiet tonight."

"The others are asleep, I guess. But I hate to go to sleep. Every night I hate it."

"Why? Are you afraid?"

"Oh no. Just afraid I'll miss something."

Eliezer smiled. "You wouldn't miss much tonight. Nothing much is happening."

"I suppose not."

Hagar made no move toward him, for she had made that mistake before. She simply smiled at him and waited.

Eliezer said, "You know we had a misunderstanding once, but I'm glad we're back together now—friends."

"So am I, Eliezer. I missed you."

"Really?"

"Why, of course I did. You should know that."

"Well, I knew I missed you."

Hagar lifted her eyes to him. "I'm glad to hear that," she said quietly.

She was a bewitchingly attractive woman, and Eliezer slowly reached out for her. He was half apprehensive, but she still made no move toward him. This slight sign of modesty pleased him. He pulled her forward and kissed her lightly on the lips, waiting for her response. Her lips were warm, and she put her hands on his shoulders but that was all.

"You're sweet, Hagar," he said huskily.

Eliezer heard a sound and turned to see Zara standing there, her face in shock. Without a word she whirled and ran away.

"Zara!" Eliezer said, troubled at the girl's expression.

"She'll be all right. She's just jealous," Hagar said.

"Jealous!"

"Why, she'd be jealous of any woman you liked. Didn't you know that?"

"I never thought about it." Now Eliezer was even more worried. "I'd better go talk to her."

"Yes, you had. She's a sweet child. She needs a mother, I suppose—a woman to help her get through this age."

"I've thought of that myself," Eliezer said. He did not see the expression on Hagar's face but added, "I'll see you in the morning. I'd better go talk to her."

"Good night. I enjoyed being with you," Hagar called after him. A smile was on her face as she turned into her tent. "That was just right," she said with satisfaction. "I played the role perfectly."

Eliezer hurried to find Zara. He called out when he saw her standing on the outskirts of the camp. "Zara?"

"What do you want?"

"Can we talk?"

"I suppose so." She was standing with her arms folded, staring at him.

He approached her slowly. "Are you all right?"

"Of course I'm all right. What could be wrong with me?"

Zara's voice was cold, unlike her usual warm tone, and Eliezer saw that she was upset. He felt he had to straighten things out and said gently, "Look, Zara, you're starting to grow up now."

"Oh, really! Fifteen years, and I'm *starting* to grow up."

"Well, you know what I mean. You're not a child anymore."

"Thank you!"

Eliezer was confused. "Nothing I say seems right," he said. "But you know how it is with a man."

"No. Tell me."

"Well, a man and a woman sometimes grow fond of each other."

"Yes, I saw how *fond* you were of Hagar."

"It was just a little kiss. That's all it was."

Tears sprang to Zara's eyes. Not tears that she willed but those that came without her bidding. She was furious at herself and blinked them away. "You're free to kiss anybody you want to, Eliezer! But I'll tell you this. She doesn't love you."

"You just don't understand these things, Zara."

Zara knew she was behaving like a child but could not help it. "I may understand a few more things than you know."

Eliezer knew that Zara was too upset to talk rationally, so he suggested that they return to their tents. He was certain things would be better in the morning. They would be home soon—things could return to normal.

When they reached the tent Zara shared with Hagar, Eliezer stepped forward and put his hands on her shoulders. He leaned over and kissed her cheek. "Good night, Zara. Sleep well and don't worry about . . . anything."

"Good night," Zara muttered, turning away.

As soon as Eliezer disappeared, Zara stormed into the tent and threw herself down on her mattress, ignoring Hagar. As she began to weep, she stuffed her fist against her lips to keep any sound from escaping and whispered bitterly, "She doesn't love him, and he's too blind to see it."

———

Abram made his report as soon as he came back with his party. "It was the worst visit you could imagine. Everybody was miserable. I hated it. Eliezer hated it, and Zara had a terrible time."

"I'll bet Hagar didn't hate it."

"Well, no. As a matter of fact, she didn't. Come to think of it, on the way there and back, she had a fine time. She and Eliezer seemed to be hitting it off again."

"What did Zara say about that?"

"Zara? She didn't say anything. Why should she?"

"Because she's very possessive of Eliezer. He's all she has."

"Well, the way Eliezer was grinning at Hagar, I think she's going to have to share him with her."

"She'll never do that," Sarai said firmly.

"Anyway, I tried to talk Lot into leaving again, but, as usual, it was a total failure. Meri refuses even to discuss it."

"It's so sad. Lot is such a good man, but that awful woman has done nothing but bring him grief."

"You're right, and I'm worried sick about it. Something terrible is going to happen. Lot's stood against the sin of that place for a long time, but he can't go on forever."

CHAPTER
23

From far off came the sound of a dog barking frantically, but Eliezer did not even hear it. He stood straight, his back stiff, and stared at the young man who stood across from him. He knew him well and treasured him as one of his best herdsmen. Eliezer had always had a ready smile for him, but he was not smiling now. Instead his voice was harsh as he asked, "What did you say, Bor?"

The young man with the diminutive name seemed to wilt under Eliezer's glance. He had found Eliezer standing alone, staring out over the fields as he often did, appearing to be counting sheep. Bor had been apprehensive when he first spoke, and now seeing the hard glint in his employer's eyes, he cleared his throat and said, "Well . . . I said, sir, that I would like to—" He broke off and seemed to have run completely out of steam. He straightened up and said as strongly as he could manage, "I would like to have Zara for my wife."

"Zara for your wife?"

"Well, yes, sir, I would. I love her, and I would be very good to her."

"What makes you ask a thing like this of me?"

The question was too much for Bor to handle. He was not a loquacious young man in the first place, and Eliezer's steely glance seemed to have sucked all the words out of him. He looked down at his feet and mumbled, "Yes, sir. Sir, I love her, and I . . . I would be very good to her."

"You said that already. How old are you?"

"I am eighteen."

"Eighteen years old, and you want to get married to Zara?"

"Yes, I do."

"Have you spoken to her about this?"

"Oh no, sir. I knew better than that." Bor was slightly shocked at the idea of going over Eliezer's head. "I wanted to get your permission first. Everyone knows you're like a father to her. The closest thing she has, that is."

Eliezer stared at the young man. He was a good worker. He was steady and could be depended on to tend sheep, but he was not a handsome man, being extremely skinny and having a homely face. "I will speak to you about this later."

"Yes, sir." Bor wheeled and walked away with a mixture of relief and fear on his face.

Eliezer watched him go off and thought, *He's so awkward—and as plain as my ugliest sheep!* This was not exactly true, but Eliezer was disturbed. He turned and went about his business, but all day long he thought about Bor's request, and that night he waited until dark to go to Zara. He found her seated in front of her tent, brushing her long dark hair, and sat down across from her.

"It's been a hot day," Zara said.

"Yes, it has."

Zara waited for him to speak. She knew he was mulling something over, for she had learned to read his moods. She was eighteen years old now and a full-grown woman in every respect. For a time she had been like a young donkey foal, all legs and stumbling over things, but the past two years had wrought a miracle of maturity in her. She had grown taller, and her figure had matured, and despite the modest clothes that she wore, she drew men's eyes. She had also developed a more certain manner, especially where Eliezer was concerned. For years she had known exactly how to handle him, and now she said gently, "What is it, Eliezer? I can tell you're troubled."

"Well, I wouldn't say that."

"Why don't you just tell me what's bothering you? You can't hide it from me. You never could."

Eliezer grinned ruefully. "No, I never could. I think you can see right through to my head."

"And your heart too."

Eliezer stared at her, wondering what that meant. He knew that for some time she had been apprehensive that he might marry Hagar. In truth he was still attracted to the woman, but something held him back. Hagar had grown impatient with him, but not harsh, so he still kept going back to her, wondering if she was the right woman for him.

"How do you know what I'm thinking?"

"Your face is easy to read, and you never could conceal anything."

"Well, that's good, isn't it?"

"I think it is, but most men have a lot to conceal. You don't."

"How do you know? I may be stealing sheep from Abram. I might be running with those wild bedouin girls over in the next camp. You don't know what I do."

Zara simply smiled and continued brushing her hair. "Yes I do," she said. "Now, what's bothering you?"

Eliezer threw up his hands. "I give up," he said. "Well, Bor came to me today, and you'll never guess what he wanted."

"He wanted me for his wife."

Eliezer stared at the young woman. She had spoken with complete ease and was not at all excited or troubled. There was a serenity about her that pleased Eliezer. But sometimes he wondered if she didn't need more spirit. "Well, aren't you ashamed of yourself?"

"What for? Why should I be ashamed?"

"Because you've obviously been encouraging him."

"No, I haven't. I've tried to tell him many times I would never marry him."

Eliezer's face changed so completely that Zara put her hand over her mouth and giggled. "You're happy now. I can see it in your face."

"Blast it, Zara. Stop reading my mind!"

"Well, you are glad, aren't you?"

"Of course I'm glad. I wouldn't want you to marry a puppy like that."

Zara was amused at Eliezer. He often thought he was being so profound, yet she could read him easily. "Do you want me to tell you the names of the other puppies that have been asking me to marry them?"

"You mean they come to you behind my back?"

"Yes. They're afraid of you."

"Afraid of me? My men aren't afraid of me."

"That's what you think!"

"Well, I've never harmed a one of them."

"They're afraid of displeasing you. And, besides, they know you'd never agree to let me marry any of them."

Eliezer stared at Zara. "What makes you say a thing like that?"

"Well, you don't want me to marry any of them, do you?"

Eliezer blinked with surprise and began to think. Zara could read his thoughts as clearly as if they were printed on his forehead, but she waited for him to work it out. Finally he said, "Well, obviously, Zara, you must marry . . . someday. Maybe not very soon."

"You never said that before. And you've never married."

"That's different."

"I don't see why. Why haven't you married?"

Zara sat there while Eliezer lumbered along, trying to put his thoughts and feelings into words. He tried to explain love and marriage to her, but she felt pity for him. *He's so smart in every way except about women and love,* she thought. *And he's just a baby. That woman's got her claws into him, and he doesn't even know it.* She forced Hagar out of her mind and smiled as Eliezer continued to explain the intricacies of courtship and marriage. From time to time she would say, "Really! Is that right? I would never have thought of that," with a straight face while inwardly laughing.

Finally Eliezer ran out of words, and Zara asked, "Do you think you'll ever marry, Eliezer?"

"Why, I don't know. I suppose I will."

Zara waited for him to go on, but Eliezer felt strangely uncomfortable. "Well, I'm glad we got this straightened out about Bor. He's a good herdsman, but he is no husband for you."

"Thank you, Eliezer, for helping me with my decision."

After Eliezer left, Zara went to Sarai's tent. She found Sarai softening a lambskin, carefully scraping it with a sharp blade. "Mistress, let me do that."

"No, I like to do it. What have you been up to?"

Sarai listened as Zara related the scene she had just had with Eliezer. "He's so transparent, mistress," Zara said with some exasperation. "He's so simple in some ways—just like a child."

"Where women are concerned he *is* a child."

Zara reached out and took Sarai's free hand. "I think, mistress, you can read my heart as easily as I can read Eliezer's."

"Of course I can. If he weren't blind, he could read it for himself. You love him, don't you?"

"I've loved him since I was eight years old. First like a child—but not any longer."

"No, like a woman now."

The two women talked quietly, and finally Zara said bitterly, "It's that Hagar! He can't get her out of his mind. Why can't he see her for what she is?"

"Women have a power to cloud men's minds."

Zara was fascinated by this statement. "What does that mean?"

"I don't know how to explain it, but I've seen men who were perfectly sensible in every way except where a woman was concerned. One of the best friends I ever had back in Ur was a man called Mapor. He was so intelligent and gifted, but he was in love with the worst woman in the world. Everyone knew it except him. She slept with half the men in the camp, and many more, but he never had the least idea of it. He was like a man born blind."

"And you think Eliezer is that way about Hagar?"

"Yes, he is. I've wanted to shake him, and I've tried to tell him about Hagar. But he can't see it."

"If Hagar would get married, that would take her out of his mind."

Sarai suddenly looked across at her young friend. Her voice was strangely tight when she spoke, and Zara saw a strange expression in her eyes. "Something like that may happen," she said. "And you're right. That would take her off of Eliezer's mind. He's too good a young man to go to another man's wife."

Zara did not understand what she had seen in Sarai's face. When she left, Sarai held the knife in her hand and felt the soft texture of the lambskin, but her mind was elsewhere. She had a preoccupied look, and finally she said, "Yes, it's what I must do."

———————

Sarai watched as Abram read the scrolls that were so important to him. Some of them came from his grandfather Nahor, who had written down some of the history of his people. *Abram must have them memorized by now,* Sarai thought as she watched him peering at the parchments, *but he never tires of them.* She waited until he wrapped them up carefully and put them away, then said to him, "I need to talk to you, husband."

Abram looked over at Sarai and studied her face. He saw something there that kept him silent for a moment, and then he came over and sat down beside her. "What is it? Is it trouble?"

"You're eighty-six years old, and I'm seventy-six."

"I know that. But you don't look like a seventy-six-year-old."

"I feel like one," Sarai said quietly. She did not speak for a time, and Abram waited patiently. It hurt him to see that she was troubled. Finally she said, "You don't have a son, Abram."

The stark statement shocked Abram. They did not talk about this problem often, had not, as a matter of fact, for years. Both of them always had in the back of their mind the promise of the Eternal One that Abram's seed would one day become many. But years had gone by, and there had been no child. Sarai had ceased being of childbearing age many years ago, and neither of them had the bright hope they had once shared of an heir for Abram.

After thinking carefully, Abram said, "Eliezer is my son in all but blood. He will be my heir."

Sarai reached out her hand, and Abram took it. He held it firmly, waiting for her to speak.

"I have never asked you this, Abram, but I am asking you now. Please do not be angry with me."

"You know I won't."

Sarai took a deep breath, then asked the question that had lain dormant in her heart for many years. "Is Eliezer your blood son? Are you his father?"

Abram tightened his grip and studied Sarai's face. He saw the anxiety there and said quietly, "I should have told you years ago. But then, you should have asked me years ago."

"I was afraid to. I was afraid you'd say yes."

"We torment ourselves foolishly so many times." He reached out and put his hand on her cheek. She felt the roughness of it and waited for him to go on. "No, I am not his father."

"Do you know who is?"

"Yes."

"Can you tell me?"

Abram left his hand on Sarai's cheek, and his voice grew whisper soft. "I vowed I would never tell anyone, and I will keep my promise. But I can promise you it was not me."

Sarai turned from Abram and pondered what was in her heart. She waited so long that Abram said, "What are you thinking?"

Sarai turned to him with a strange expression. "I've been thinking about the custom among the Canaanites and among some of our people too."

"What custom?"

"Those women who cannot bear a child give their maid to their husbands. The bondwoman bears the child, but in all except blood, the child belongs to the mistress."

Abram listened, shock and amazement on his face. "Sarai, you can't mean that!"

"How do we know that it's not what the Eternal One intends?"

"It can't be!"

"Yes it can!" Sarai insisted. "All that God said was that your seed would have many descendants, and the promise was to *you*, not to me. If I had died, you would have had another wife. I don't understand why I haven't been able to bear you a son, but I want you to have one. And if you do have a child through Hagar, the child will be mine as much as yours." Sarai did not believe this deep in her heart, even though according to the unwritten laws, the child of the bondwoman became legally and in every respect the child of the mistress.

Abram shook his head stubbornly, and Sarai began to speak softly. She talked for a long time and finally said, "I know this comes as a surprise to you, but your blood must not die out, husband. God has said that you must have many descendants, and this way you provide the son through which those descendants will come."

Abram was silent for a while, then sighed heavily. "I will think about it, wife."

"Think of it as a way to fulfill the promise of the Eternal One."

After a long, difficult discussion, with grief in her heart, Sarai left Abram, who had just given his consent to her proposal. Despite his agreement, she felt no triumph. As she went to find Hagar, she felt a growing depression. Her heart was heavy, and she prayed, "O Eternal One, I am only a weak woman. I want my husband to have a son, a real son of his own blood. I would love to look into a child's eyes and see there the kindness and goodness of my husband. That is why I do this thing."

Hagar was washing her clothes at the riverbank when Sarai approached. She turned and smiled, saying cheerfully, "Good morning, mistress. You are up early."

"Yes, I am," Sarai said. "Hagar, listen to me." She waited until Hagar, with a look of surprise, laid the garment down, then stood to face her. "I have made a decision that may surprise you."

"What is it?"

"It is obvious that I will never have a child, and I want a son of my own. The only way I can have one is through you. You know the custom. Would you do this thing for me and for Abram?"

"Why, of course I will."

Sarai had seldom been as surprised as she was at Hagar's ready agreement.

"After all, I am your maidservant," Hagar went on. "I'm bound to serve you in this way as in every other way."

"This is a little different. No—it's quite different!"

Hagar was smiling. "It will be a good thing, mistress."

"You realize that the child will be mine in all but blood."

"Oh yes, I understand."

"And you realize you cannot marry. It will put you in a terrible position, Hagar. You're still a young woman."

"I am your servant, mistress. We will do this thing. Does the master agree?"

Sarai nodded slowly. "Yes, he agrees."

"Then it will come to pass. You will have a fine son, and the seed of Abram will continue." Hagar's eyes sparkled. She had thought of marriage many times, but this would be better. Her son would be Abram's heir! That was all that mattered. Sarai could not live long. That would not be a problem. She watched as Sarai walked away, and when she was out of hearing distance, Hagar threw up her hands and laughed. "Of course I'll have a son! That old man and I will produce a glorious boy!"

Hagar had thought over Sarai's plan, and although she had agreed readily, a second thought had come to her. As always, she was a crafty woman, and when she worked it out in her mind, she went to Eliezer. When they were alone she told him without ornamentation what Sarai had asked of her.

Eliezer was dumbfounded. "I've heard of such a thing, but surely not Abram. . . ."

"It's very common," Hagar said.

"Are you going to do it, then?"

"That depends on you, Eliezer."

"On me! No, not at all. It depends on *you*."

"If you and I were to marry, we would have a son. Many people think you're Abram's son anyway."

"But you've already agreed with the mistress to have the child."

"I can change my mind, and she loves you. You can talk her out of this idea. We can tell her that our son would be hers and Abram's in all except blood. They're old. We can convince them."

Eliezer did not even have to consider this. "No," he said. "I will not do it, and you should be ashamed to mention it."

Once before, Eliezer's refusal had sent Hagar into a furious rage. This time she felt not a raging fire but coldness like ice. She smiled cruelly. "I will be mistress of all this someday—Abram will die and Sarai will die, and my son and I will own it all. You will regret it. My son will be Abram's heir. Not you."

Eliezer was shocked at what he saw in this woman. Whatever feelings he had for her died an instant death, and he felt a sudden sense of relief. *I might have married her*, he thought, and the horror of being married to such a creature shook him.

CHAPTER
24

"Nobody cares how sick I am—especially you, Sarai!"

Hagar lay on her back, staring up at the tent over her head. Her body was swollen, and her eyes glinted with a hard light as she turned to look at Sarai, who was bending over her, mopping her brow and wringing out a cloth in cool water. She waited until Sarai put it on her face and then knocked her hand away. "You're strangling me with all that! What are you trying to do, kill me?"

Sarai glanced over at Zara, who was on the other side of the prone woman. She saw the disgust in Zara's eyes and spoke quickly before Hagar could notice. "I'm sorry," she said, "I'm just clumsy."

"I've got to have something to drink. My tongue's dry as dust. Zara, go get me something."

"I'll get you some water."

"Not water. I want something else. Some wine."

"I'm not sure it's good for you to have wine," Sarai said.

"Don't argue with me, Sarai. I said I wanted *wine*! If I want it, the baby must need it! When a pregnant woman craves something, it's because the baby wants it. I'd think you would know that."

Sarai had never heard such foolishness, but she kept her face from revealing her thoughts. "You may be right. Here, would you like to sit up awhile?"

"That's what you'd like, isn't it? You know how tired I am after that walk you made me take. I'm exhausted, and now you're demanding things of me I can't do. You just don't understand what it's like to have a baby!"

The words penetrated Sarai like a knife, but still she said nothing. "Go get her some wine, Zara," Sarai said meekly.

"Yes, mistress."

"Find something to fan me with," Hagar said irritably. "I'm burning up!"

Sarai produced a sheet of parchment and began to fan Hagar with it. As she did so, she thought about much how things had changed. She remembered with pain how she had separated herself from Abram after they had decided that Hagar should have his child. It was as if he had died, for Sarai would not sleep in the same tent with them. When it became clear that Hagar was pregnant, Abram returned to his place beside her. All this time Hagar smiled and seemed happy.

As her pregnancy progressed, however, things changed. Hagar began to behave in a more insolent fashion than Sarai would have dreamed possible—but never in the presence of Abram. She was careful to keep a sweet manner, mild and meek, while he was there, but when she was alone with Zara and Sarai she was unbearable.

As Sarai fanned the still air, creating a breeze, hot though it might be, she wondered, not for the first time, if she had done the right thing. Abram had been opposed to the idea at first, but now that a child was on the way, she could see that he was happy. She was careful to keep from him how badly Hagar behaved, what insolence she showed toward her when they were alone. She took her joy in the fact that the child would soon come and then she could deal with Hagar's behavior. In the meantime Abram was happier than she had seen him for years. A faint resentment stirred in her as she thought of what had happened, of his intimacy with Hagar. But she knew that his love for her had not changed, and, therefore, she held her peace.

Zara stayed angry most of the time. She was a witness to Hagar's harsh behavior toward Sarai, and she herself was often the object of Hagar's anger. Now as she went to get the wine, she saw Eliezer coming in from the fields.

"Eliezer, you're early."

"Yes, there's nothing much to do. How is Hagar?"

"Fine." Zara's voice dripped with bitterness, and she shook her head. "Abram would never believe how awful she is to Sarai. She acts like *she's* the true wife, not a mere bondwoman."

"Why doesn't Sarai tell him?"

"You just don't understand women, do you, Eliezer?"

"Well, I never claimed to be an expert."

"Expert!" Zara managed a smile. "No, you're far from that. But she'll never tell Abram, because she sees he's happy, and she'll do anything to keep him that way."

"Oh!"

"Yes, oh. Now you understand it all. Here, take this wine back to her."

"You know I can't stand to be around her."

"Well, *that's* changed. At least one good thing came out of all this. You were as blind as a bat, Eliezer. Why, you might have married that woman."

"No, I never would have," he said feebly.

Zara came over and put her hand on his forearm. She felt the strong, corded muscle and took a pride in his strength, as though it belonged to her. "Yes, you would."

Eliezer managed a smile. "I suppose a man has to be a fool sometime."

"Well, you've had your turn," Zara said. "Now, take her the wine."

"She shouts at me and screams at me every time I get close to her."

"Good! If she's screaming at you, she can't be screaming at Sarai. Go on, now."

Eliezer straightened up, took the wine, and with a bitter face, trudged toward the tent. When he stepped inside, Hagar turned and glared at him. "What do you want?"

"Zara gave me the wine you asked for."

"Why didn't she bring it?"

"Oh, I think she had something else to do."

"That's the most selfish girl I've ever seen in my life! She never thinks of anything but her own comfort! Here I am suffering, and she's out flirting with some shepherd, no doubt."

Eliezer glanced covertly at Sarai, who was fanning industriously, her face turned away.

"Well, here's the wine."

"I don't want it now. I want some water. Some cool water."

Eliezer said, "All right. I'll get it."

"Well, hurry up! I'm dying of thirst!"

Eliezer stepped outside the tent. He stared at the wine, drank it, then nodded with satisfaction. "There," he grunted, "you won't get that." He scurried off to find the water, knowing that another tongue-lashing would be waiting for him when he brought it.

Abram found Hagar sitting down fanning herself, her face puffy with the heat. "How do you feel today, Hagar?"

"Terrible! Just terrible!"

"I'm sorry to hear that. Let me get you something. Some cool water, perhaps, or some milk."

"No, I was sick again this morning. I thought I'd throw my insides up.

Nobody who hasn't had a baby understands what that's like. Sarai doesn't understand. Abram, she's so mean to me!"

"Sarai mean?" Abram stared at Hagar with astonishment. "I can't believe that. Sarai's never mean to anyone."

"Oh, she doesn't strike me or anything like that, but she doesn't care for me properly. I lay here for two hours this morning dying for a drink, and do you think she'd bring me one? And Zara's no better," she said quickly.

"Perhaps you need a servant of your own."

"Oh no, that's all right. I wouldn't want to be any trouble." She reached out her hand and Abram took it. "I never saw a man so pleased that a baby was on the way."

"I am indeed pleased, Hagar."

"It's going to be a beautiful child."

"It's going to be a beautiful boy."

"Maybe not," Hagar said. "It may be a girl."

"No," Abram said firmly, "it will be a boy."

Hagar laughed. "I hope you're right. He'll be a handsome child. You and I are both so fine looking."

"Well, you are anyway."

"Nonsense. You've always been a good-looking man. I'd like to have seen you when you were eighteen years old."

Abram laughed. "You flatter me. I wasn't nearly so fine looking as Eliezer."

"Oh, him!" Hagar waved the idea of the comparison aside. "He's nothing. What will we name the baby?"

Abram failed to notice that Hagar had slipped into a possessive manner with her speech, when actually she had no right at all to name the baby anything. The child would legally be Sarai's, but Hagar appeared to have forgotten that. Others noticed it but not Abram. "I'll speak to Sarai and Zara and see that they're more attentive to your needs."

"That would be nice." Hagar smiled contentedly.

———————

"Sarai, I wish you and Zara would pay a little more attention to Hagar."

"More attention?" Sarai looked up and her lips drew into a tight line. She had been struggling with Hagar's demands for weeks now, and they were getting more difficult all the time. "What do you mean more attention? How do you know we're not paying enough attention to her?"

"Why, she happened to mention that she didn't get a drink of water for nearly two hours."

Sarai was so angry she was afraid she would lose control. She bit her lip to keep from speaking foolish words, then said in a tense voice, "I'll try to see to it that she gets all the water she needs."

Abram was surprised at Sarai's tone. "I know you're doing the best you can."

"Thank you," Sarai said dryly. "It's always good to hear one's work commended."

"You might speak to Zara too. She could be a bit more thoughtful."

"I'll speak to her."

"Good. That settles that."

It did not settle that, however, for this was the last straw for Sarai. She could put up with Hagar's demands and her attitude, but to be lectured by her own husband about not caring for a bondwoman was more than she could bear. She went to Zara and told her what had happened, and Zara grew red in the face. It was all Sarai could do to keep her from going to Abram and shouting the truth at him.

"No, he must see for himself. Here's what I want you to do. . . ."

———————

Sarai glanced over at Hagar, who was complaining as usual. She was aware that Zara had gone to Abram and that the two of them were standing outside the tent. Zara had careful instructions not to let Abram appear to Hagar but just to listen.

"Bring me something to eat," Hagar demanded. "I'm starving to death!"

"I don't think it's good for you—" Sarai began.

"Shut up! What do you know about a pregnant woman? You're as barren as a brick!"

"I was going to say," Sarai said softly, "that it might not be good for you to eat so much in this heat."

Hagar glared at her. "I'm not going to put up with this any longer! I'm carrying Abram's child, and that means I'm the most important one in his life."

Hagar continued to scream at Sarai, insulting her in every way possible, but she broke off when Abram suddenly stepped through the door of the tent. Hagar at once turned pale, for there was no smile on Abram's face now.

He came and stood over Hagar but did not speak to her. "Sarai, would you leave us alone please."

"Yes, husband."

Hagar was trembling, for Abram's face was as stern as she had ever seen it. She smiled and said meekly, "I'm a little out of sorts this morning, I'm afraid." She waited for Abram to acknowledge her statement and went on. "I sometimes lose my temper. I'll have to watch myself more carefully."

"You don't have to watch yourself, Hagar. *I'll* be watching you closely, and I'll have others watching you too. I'm going to turn you over to Sarai to do with you as she sees fit."

"What do you mean?" Hagar whispered, frightened by the severe look on Abram's face.

"I mean if I hear one complaint from anyone about your lack of respect toward my *true* wife, you will find yourself abandoned in the desert. Don't make me have to say this again." He turned and walked away, and Hagar got up, trembling. She was heavy with child now, and the thought of being abandoned frightened her worse than she had ever been frightened in her life. She stood there unable to move, and finally Sarai came back into the tent. Instantly Hagar said, "I've been wrong—"

"Shut up, Hagar! Close your mouth. Sit down." Sarai's voice was cold, and her eyes glittered. "You give me one excuse, and you'll leave this camp forever."

On the day that Abram's son was born, he was happier than anyone had seen him for years. His face would not lose its smile, and Sarai tasted the bittersweet fruit of her own decision. She was happy to see Abram holding his son in his arms and saw the pride in his eyes. But she fought her bitterness toward Hagar, who now looked at her triumphantly. True enough, she had handed the child to Sarai and made the formal declaration that Ishmael, as the child was named, belonged to Sarai and not to her. But nonetheless there was triumph in her eyes, and Sarai could read her intentions.

She thinks I'll die soon and that Abram will then have her for his true wife.

Sarai looked at Abram and saw the joy on his face, now seamed with age and weathered by a thousand suns. *He's happy now*, she thought. *He has a son, and he will be our son.* She struggled with the thought, not able to keep her eyes away from Hagar, who was watching Abram slyly with triumph blazing from her eyes.

PART SIX

THE PROMISED SEED

Sarah became pregnant and bore a son to Abraham in his old age, at the very time God had promised him.

Genesis 21:2

CHAPTER
25

Abram never forgot any of the times that God had spoken to him, but the one that always was clearest in his mind was the occasion just before Ishmael's thirteenth birthday. Abram had been praying for a long time, alone in the desert. He had built an altar and offered a sacrifice, and as the smoke rose, the presence of God fell on the place, and the voice of the Eternal One came to the old man clearly.

"I am God Almighty; walk before me and be blameless. I will confirm my covenant between me and you and will greatly increase your numbers. As for me, this is my covenant with you: You will be the father of many nations. No longer will you be called Abram; your name will be Abraham, for I have made you a father of many nations. I will make you very fruitful; I will make nations of you, and kings will come from you. I will establish my covenant as an everlasting covenant between me and you and your descendants after you for the generations to come, to be your God and the God of your descendants after you. The whole land of Canaan, where you are now an alien, I will give as an everlasting possession to you and your descendants after you; and I will be their God.

"As for you, you must keep my covenant, you and your descendants after you for the generations to come. This is my covenant with you and your descendants after you, the covenant you are to keep: Every male among you shall be circumcised. You are to undergo circumcision, and it will be the sign of the covenant between me and you. For the generations to come every male among you who is eight days old must be circumcised, including those born in your household or bought with money from a foreigner—those who are not your offspring. Whether born in your household or bought with your money, they must be circumcised. My covenant in your flesh is to be an everlasting covenant. Any uncircumcised male, who has not been circumcised in the flesh, will be cut off from his people; he has broken my covenant.

"As for Sarai your wife, you are no longer to call her Sarai; her name will be Sarah. I will bless her and will surely give you a son by her. I will bless her so that she will be the

mother of nations; kings of peoples will come from her."

Abraham began to tremble violently. He fell on his face, his fists clenched and his mind reeling, his thoughts tossed like a wind caught in a storm. He lost all sense of time, never knowing how long he bowed there. He straightened and looked upward, his face contorted. For so long he had considered Ishmael God's answer to Sarai's childlessness, and now he could not bring himself to think that he had been so wrong. In the back of his mind, he was crying out, *Will a son be born to a man a hundred years old? Will Sarah bear a child at the age of ninety?* Doubt assailed him like an armed man, and he knew the agony of losing his fondest dream. Loudly he cried out, "If only Ishmael might live under your blessing!"

But God's voice came firmly: *"Yes, but your wife Sarah will bear you a son, and you will call him Isaac. I will establish my covenant with him as an everlasting covenant for his descendants after him. And as for Ishmael, I have heard you: I will surely bless him; I will make him fruitful and will greatly increase his numbers. He will be the father of twelve rulers, and I will make him into a great nation. But my covenant I will establish with Isaac, whom Sarah will bear to you by this time next year."*

Abraham's mind was filled with pain and confusion, but at that moment he remembered the words of King Melchizedek, which he had spoken after the battle of the four kings. *"No matter how impossible the thing seems, Abram, you must believe the word of the Most High!"*

And Abraham knew at that moment exactly what he had to do. Putting away all his hopes for Ishmael, he rose and turned his face toward his home. As he went, he made plans to obey God, but the thought of Sarah having a child filled him with wonder.

He thought of the names that he and his wife would bear. His given name, Abram, meant "high father," but the new name, Abraham, meant "father of nations." It was a name he would not have chosen for himself, and he knew it would bring mocking among many when he announced it as his new name.

The name of Sarai had always seemed wrong to Abraham, for it meant "she who argues." It may have had some truth when she was very young, before they married, but since then, his wife had grown into a woman of great patience. The new name, Sarah, meant "princess," and Abraham the Hebrew smiled as he thought of it. She had always been a princess to him, so her new name fit her exactly! Then the significance of his own new name sobered him, and he shook his head in wonder, whispering, "You know best, O God Most High!"

———

A fierce glow of pride rose in Abraham as he watched Ishmael move stealthily across the broken ground. Abraham had paused underneath the shade of a terebinth tree, out of breath after climbing the steep hill. Now as he leaned against the tree watching his son, he suddenly thought, *Ninety-nine years I've been on this earth, and I'm still stronger than many men half my age.* He thought of how difficult it had been for him to adjust to a new name—and how it had been even more difficult for his wife. He remembered her look of stunned amazement when he had told her, "Your name is now Sarah—and mine is Abraham." It had taken some time for his family and tribe to adjust to the new ways, and even now occasionally Sarah would forget and call him Abram.

Abraham saw that Ishmael was not even breathing hard as he paused and turned to face his father, a smile on his bronzed face. He pantomimed a gesture, then drew an arrow from the quiver on his back.

The picture of Ishmael standing straight, half-turned, and drawing a bow that many grown men could not pull brought a warm glow to Abraham's heart. Ishmael was only thirteen, but he had become the most proficient hunter in the tribe. He had been going out alone now for three years and almost never failed to bring back some game for the pot. Now as the youth drew his bow, Abraham admired the muscles of his son's back and arms and thought quickly over the years that had passed.

His desire for a son had been fiercer than he had realized, and ever since the birth of Ishmael, he had thrown himself into making the boy into a strong, fine man. Physically this had not been difficult, for from the first, Ishmael had been strong and agile. He had walked long before most infants and had been extremely active through his early years. Abraham and Sarah had had some tense moments when the boy had wandered off. He once took a small bow with him that Abraham had made and stayed away all day. As the sun was setting he had returned triumphant, holding a bloody rabbit, his eyes alight with joy.

Abraham still remembered that day, and now as he watched Ishmael loose the arrow and then let out a cry of triumph, he moved forward. He was recovering his breath now, and when he reached Ishmael, the boy was removing an arrow from a large male antelope.

"That was a fine shot, my son."

"Oh, it was easy." Ishmael laughed, his white teeth flashing against his bronze face. He had his mother's glossy black hair and for one so young was well muscled. He was tall and moved with an easy manner that Abraham could not help admiring.

"This will make a good meal for you, Father."

"For all of us," Abraham said, nodding.

"You carry my bow, and I'll take the animal, Father."

"Very well." Abraham received the bow and the quiver and watched as the boy picked up the deer with ease and slung it over his shoulder. "The next time we go hunting, I'll bring a donkey along to carry your kill back."

"Or maybe two."

"You're proud of yourself, aren't you?"

"I like to hunt."

"You've become the best shot of any man in the clan," Abraham said. "I'm proud of you, son."

Ishmael smiled and started walking jauntily back toward camp. Abraham kept pace with him, but when they were halfway there his old legs gave out. "You need to take a rest."

"Oh, I'm not tired, Father."

Abraham laughed. "Well, I am." He sat down in the shade of one of the scrub trees, and Ishmael tossed the animal down and sat on it, using the beast for a cushion. Abraham took the water bottle fastened over his shoulder by a thong, drank deeply, and handed the bottle to Ishmael, who drank his fill. He was smiling faintly. Abraham tried to read his thoughts but could not. Finally he said, "When we get back to camp we'll build an altar and give thanks to God for your success."

"All right, Father, if that's what you'd like."

"Wouldn't you like it too?"

"Oh, I suppose so."

Abraham shifted uneasily at Ishmael's obvious indifference toward the Eternal One. He had spent many hours since the boy was barely able to walk telling him the stories of his people and how the Eternal One, the immortal Lord of heaven and earth, had spoken to them. These stories had thrilled Abraham when he had heard them from his grandfather, but they seemed to have little attraction for Ishmael. Neither did he seem to show an interest in the tremendous promises that Abraham had been given by the Eternal One. He listened, but Abraham could always tell that his mind was elsewhere. "You must learn, my son, that the almighty Creator is everywhere and knows everything. For years I've struggled to understand how the Eternal One could know what everyone on this earth is thinking at the same time. I can't even know what *one* other person is thinking unless I look at his face, and even then I may be wrong. But the Eternal One knows all of the thoughts of our hearts.

I think He knows we went hunting and that you killed this antelope. Isn't that amazing?"

"Oh yes, it is," Ishmael said absently. He took out his knife made of fine Damascus steel, which Abraham had purchased for him—an expensive item for a young man—and he ran his hand along the smooth blade, admiring the strength of the weapon.

Abraham sat silently, knowing that if he started to speak of hunting or the physical world, Ishmael would be all attention. *Well, he's young. He'll change as he grows older. I suppose I didn't think much about God myself when I was his age.* He knew this was not true, but the rationalization gave him some comfort, and he finally said, "Well, let's go home. It's growing dark."

―――――――

As Eliezer passed by Hagar's tent, he saw that she was talking to Jameel, one of the herdsmen. Jameel was a tall, strongly built man of thirty, who had two wives but was always interested in any other woman who put herself in his way. Eliezer had often been forced to speak to him about his attention to the wives of his fellows in the clan, so, for the most part, Jameel confined his attentions to women outside of the family of Abraham.

The two were engaged in conversation so deeply that they did not hear Eliezer approach. He saw Jameel reach out and run his hand down Hagar's bare arm. She had never learned to dress modestly. Perhaps her days in Egypt had spoiled her forever, he thought. She was looking up into Jameel's face, a provocative smile on her lips.

"Jameel, I think you'd better get back to the herd."

Jameel, caught off guard, turned, and his face showed his shock as he saw Eliezer. He scowled then and said, "I've finished my work."

"Then I'll find some more for you to do. Go out and gather that herd we left over by the twin mounds. Bring them to the main herd."

Jameel said resentfully, "It's late and I'm tired."

"You heard what I said. Now go!"

Hagar's eyes flashed with anger as Eliezer turned to face her. "Why do you always have to interfere with me? What I do is none of your business."

"Yes, it is," Eliezer said.

Hagar laughed scornfully. "You had your chance with me. Now you're jealous."

"Don't be ridiculous," Eliezer said stiffly.

"Your face is easy to read. You still think about me." Hagar moved closer, her eyes half closed. "I know you do. You watch me when you don't think I know it."

This was a bit too close to the truth for Eliezer. For years he had turned his back on Hagar after she became the mother of Ishmael, for she was, in a sense, Abraham's second wife. He knew that Abraham had never touched her in all the years Ishmael was growing up, but he had seen Hagar try to tempt the father of her child into intimacies.

Hagar moved closer, so close that Eliezer could smell the strong perfume she always wore and was aware of the smoothness of her skin. "I know why you haven't married all these years," Hagar whispered. "You can't get me out of your mind."

"Don't be ridiculous. All that was a long time ago. I'd forgotten it."

"No, you think about me at night when you're alone in the dark and your bed is empty. Well, you had your chance. Now, don't try to tell me who I can talk to."

Eliezer whirled and left. This was not the first time Hagar had taunted him. She was a strange woman. At times she ordered him about like a slave, and he tried to accommodate her whenever possible. When she became too demanding, he simply ignored her. At other times she would try her wiles on him, and this was more difficult to bear. As he hurried away from her, he thought, *I wish that woman would behave herself, but she never will.*

Eliezer was an introspective fellow. In fact, his inner life was much more active and varied than his outer life. His days were occupied with work, and as the years had passed, he had become so proficient that Abraham entrusted him with most of the decision making. While Abraham was preoccupied with raising his son, Eliezer was the one all the men looked to for decisions, such as when to change camps and where the wandering tribe would go next.

Inwardly, Eliezer lived an imaginative life. He loved to read the scrolls Abraham treasured so much. He studied them faithfully, and he and Abraham had long discussions about them. He loved the God that Abraham had introduced him to and had become a man of strong principle, second, perhaps, only to Abraham. He also wrote songs, for he had always loved to sing. He didn't share them with anyone, for it seemed a frivolous occupation for a man of his station. He spent much time with the travelers they encountered, pumping them for stories of distant lands and the customs of other people. As a result he had an accurate concept of the geography of the region.

Despite this richness, Eliezer's life was empty in other ways. He had never married, and he missed not having a family, for he loved children. He always paid the babies and youngsters in the camp much attention, so that he was a great favorite. He supposed his lack of a wife was due to his many years serving Abraham, then caring for Zara. But Zara was a grown woman now, yet still he had not married.

A week after his conversation with Hagar, he kept remembering her accusation that he had not married because he still loved her. He had been disturbed by her words, and all week long a new thought had been growing within him. He got up after a fitful night and made his decision. *A man must marry. Abraham and Sarah have been after me for a long time. Now I'm going to please them.*

Zara was sitting beside a small stream, absently watching the flocks as they grazed in the distance. She had come out to fill a water pot but had sat down and listened to the pleasant music the stream made as it flowed over the rocks. She heard footsteps and turned to see Eliezer coming. When he got close enough, she said, "Good morning, Eliezer. Fine day."

"Yes, it is." Eliezer squatted beside her, picked up a stone, and flipped it into the small stream. "This is good water," he said. "Not enough for all of our flocks, but it's better than some places we've been."

Zara studied Eliezer carefully. *He looks even better now than he did when he was younger.* She took in the strong form, the tanned face, and the thick, lustrous hair without a trace of gray. He had lines around the corners of his eyes from years of being out under the blazing sun, and his hands were strong, although the fingers were longer and more tapered than most men of his race.

Zara had loved Eliezer for most of her life. She could barely remember her life before he had saved her and promised her mother he would keep her. He had kept that promise, and a warmth came over her as she thought of how careful he had been with her. He could be exasperating, though, and at times thickheaded. Now she knew that something important was on his mind and waited quietly until he found the courage to tell her.

"I've been thinking a lot, Zara," Eliezer said slowly. He met her eyes, then seemed to find that difficult and stared off into space. "I'm getting along in years now, you know."

"Yes, you're tripping over your long white beard."

"Well, I don't have a long white beard, but I've decided I shouldn't live alone anymore."

Instantly Zara grew still. Her heart began to beat wildly, and she found it difficult to breathe. *He's going to ask me to marry him*, she thought, and she turned to face him, her lips parted with expectation and joy.

"Most men my age already have families. I'm just slow at some things. And, of course, I wanted to talk to you."

Zara clasped her hands together and waited. *He thinks I'll refuse him,* she thought. *Will he be surprised! I would have married him when I was fifteen years old if he had asked me.*

"I should have married when you were a child and that would have given you a mother, but it's too late to go back to that. Anyway," he said, "I've decided to marry Orma."

Zara sat stunned. *Orma! Why, he doesn't love her!*

She jumped to her feet, furious, tears of humiliation and anger stinging her eyes. *He's so blind! He's never seen me as a woman!* Orma was a plain woman—good in her way, but not the imaginative woman he should have.

Eliezer rose quickly and caught a glimpse of her face. As always, he could not bear that Zara would be hurt, and he said quickly, "Maybe you think I shouldn't do this."

"You do what you please, Eliezer, but you don't love that woman!"

"Well, she's a good woman, and I think she would be a good companion for you. Part of my decision is for your sake."

Zara's frustration became so strong she could not bear it. She bowed her head and to her horror heard herself beginning to sob audibly. She turned to run away, but he caught her, turning her with his strong hands and said, "Why, Zara, if you hate it that much, then, of course, I won't do it." She was weeping uncontrollably now, and he put his arms around her and held her tightly. He could remember doing this many times when she was smaller, but he had not embraced her like this for years. "Please don't cry," he whispered. He kissed her cheek, and then . . . suddenly he was aware this was no longer the child he had found beside a dying mother. She was a woman in the fullness of maturity, and a consciousness of her femininity swept through him. He was tremendously embarrassed by his reaction and released her quickly, saying, "You know you're like a daughter to me, Zara, and—"

Zara reached out and struck Eliezer in the chest. "You're an idiot!" she cried, and turning, she ran blindly away toward her tent.

Eliezer stood in shock and amazement. He was ashamed of himself, for passion had risen in him as he had held her soft form close to his chest, and he was puzzled by her anger. He watched her until she disappeared and then muttered, "Well, it's plain she doesn't want me to marry . . . so I guess I won't."

CHAPTER

26

Soon after Eliezer's attempt to explain to Zara that he would marry, he found that Zara was behaving in a manner completely alien to everything he had known about her. For one thing, she was ignoring him, speaking to him only when she had to. This hurt Eliezer greatly, for it had been Zara alone he had talked to about what he read in the scrolls, and it had been with her he had shared his songs. She had been the one who had gone with him to listen to the visitors from foreign lands, and afterward when he spoke excitedly of these things, she had been his audience.

Now all that had changed, and Eliezer knew that his words to her concerning marriage had changed her. He had asked himself many times what he had said that could have so offended her and finally decided she would feel left out if he married—that a wife would take him away from her.

She'd be wrong about that, he concluded. *Even if I married, we could still be like we've always been.*

But although the distance between himself and Zara troubled Eliezer, another change was even more obvious. She had long been sought after by the young men of Abraham's tribe and other tribes. She was a beautiful woman, and men would often come to visit. In the past, he had said something once or twice about trying to find out if she liked any one of these more than another, but she had merely laughed, saying, "They're all clumsy oafs." Her words had relieved him, and when he saw the trouble that some men's daughters gave them, he had rejoiced that she had been such an easy child to raise.

But soon after their talk he noticed that she had begun showing a different side. She began to wear clothes that were not as plain; in fact, some of them were luxurious. Eliezer had, from time to time, bought fine cloth from traveling merchants, and he had urged her to make nice clothes, but up until now she had continued wearing plain working clothes.

More than this he noticed that she was spending more time with several of the young men, obviously playing them against one another. She laughed, and her smile and enchanting eyes drew them, and finally Eliezer grew disgusted and decided to put a stop to it.

One evening when the activities of the camp had ceased, he sat in front of his tent watching as Yamar, a tall, strapping young fellow, was visiting Zara. He had noticed that Zara had fixed a special dish for this young man, who came from a good family and was much sought after among the young women. The time dragged on, and Eliezer glowered as he watched the two of them walk away and come back very late. It was night now, but the silver moon overhead cast its light down. He heard their voices and observed them carefully as they came to her tent. He could not make out their words, but suddenly he saw Yamar reach out and take Zara in his arms. Eliezer's anger rose, but he clamped his lips tight. Finally he heard Zara laugh, and the young man turned and disappeared into the night.

Eliezer got up and walked toward Zara's tent. She had already gone inside, so he called her name. "Zara, I need to talk to you."

She stepped outside, wearing a startlingly blue dress. He remembered how much she had loved the color from the first time he had brought her the soft material. At his encouragement, she had made an attractive dress in the Egyptian style, with small pleats that clung to her figure.

"What is it?" she said.

"I want to know why you've been acting so peculiar."

"I haven't been acting peculiar at all. You'll have to be more specific."

"I mean dressing yourself up every day like a ... like a ..."

"Like a what?" Zara demanded.

"Well, you know what I mean."

"No, I don't. Tell me."

"Well, you don't dress like you used to."

"You want me to put on sackcloth and ashes? Would that make you happy?"

This was not the Zara Eliezer knew. She was normally a sweet-tempered woman, but anger glinted in her eyes now, reflecting a rebelliousness he had seldom seen in her. "What about this Yamar?"

"What about him?"

"I saw him kissing you."

"You saw me kissing him too, didn't you?"

Her question shocked Eliezer. "I won't have you acting like this. Running around like a . . ."

He could not finish his sentence and fell silent.

"Well, you're my master, so tell me what to do. Give me your commands, master."

"Don't talk like that, Zara. You know it's not like that with us."

"Oh, I know! You're my old father, and I'm your young child. If I weren't your slave, I would run away and go to the city!" She had no intention of such a thing, but she saw her words shocked him.

"You're not my slave! Don't be so foolish. You know I promised your mother I'd take care of you."

Zara suddenly realized how badly she was behaving. She had indeed loved Eliezer like a father or an elder brother. As a child she had been aware that he had molded his life to fit hers, to make things easy for her. When she had grown into womanhood her childhood impressions that he was a good man had been confirmed. Men had come after her, but Zara had never been serious about any of them, for she loved this tall man who now stood before her with pain in his eyes—pain she knew she had caused.

"I'm sorry to be so awful."

"You're not awful," Eliezer said consolingly, taking her hand and holding it. "You're a fine young woman. It's just that I worry about you."

Zara was totally conscious of her hand in his. *How much would I give if he'd just put his arms around me and hold me and tell me he loves me as a woman and not as a child?* She stood there silently, and when he finally dropped her hand, she said, "I'll try to behave better."

"I know you're upset with me, but you don't have to be worried."

"Worried about what?"

"I know it bothered you when I talked about getting married. I could tell you didn't want me to and it disturbed you." He reached out and squeezed her upper arm. "Don't worry. We'll go on just as we are."

"Good night, Eliezer." Zara turned and moved inside the tent. She stood for one moment irresolutely, then whispered, "He's so wonderful in so many ways, but he is absolutely thickheaded where women are concerned!"

Visitors came often to Abraham's camp, and there was an unwritten law of hospitality among people such as Abraham—it was the responsibility of the host to make strangers welcome. Abraham had experienced this generosity himself when he had gone on journeys and had arrived hungry and exhausted at a camp. Except among the warlike Hittites or the wild Amorites, he could be sure of a warm welcome.

The code was well established. Once a stranger was accepted as a guest, he was privileged in unusual ways. If an enemy came to him, his host would fight for his guest's life as much as if he were his own family. No matter how little the host had, he would feed his guest generously, even though he and his family had to go on short rations. Abraham, being a wealthy man, had never had to suffer for the kindness he showed visitors, but he liked the customs. One afternoon he looked up to see three men moving out of the west with the sun at their backs, and he immediately stood up. "Sarah," he said, "here come three strangers. We will offer them the hospitality of our home."

The two watched as the three men approached, and Sarah whispered, "I'll start preparing the meal."

"Be as quick as you can. They're probably hungry."

Other members of the tribe were watching the three strangers approach, but none of them came forward. It was up to Abraham to welcome them, and he did so at once.

"You are welcome, sirs. Please come and rest yourselves. You must be weary. I am Abraham the Hebrew." He waited for the three to identify themselves, but the leader, the tallest of them, said only, "That would be most appreciated." He did not give his name, and it would have been bad manners to inquire. Abraham felt that they would reveal themselves sooner or later. "Come, we will have water, and my servants will see to it that you are refreshed. My wife is preparing a meal."

Abraham watched as the three men nodded. As he bowed low, he had a strange feeling he could not define. Two of the men seemed quite ordinary, but the leader, a tall man with piercing dark eyes, had a presence one did not often encounter. As the men refreshed themselves, Abraham waited, and finally when they came out, he said, "Let us sit here. There's a breeze, and my wife will soon have our meal prepared."

He saw to it that his guests were seated under the shade of a tree and had his servants bring wine.

Finally Sarah said, "The meal is prepared, husband."

"Please serve us, then."

Sarah put the meal out and stood back. She did not join them, as was the custom, but returned to her tent.

Abraham urged his guests to eat, and as the meal progressed, he found himself doing most of the talking. But suddenly the leader of the three abruptly asked, "Where is Sarah, your wife?"

"She is in the tent."

"I will surely return to you about this time next year, and Sarah your wife will have a son."

Sarah had been listening to the conversation, and the words at first struck her dumb. Then she laughed to herself and thought, *Me, have a child? That cannot be.*

The tall visitor stared at Abraham, saying, "Why did Sarah laugh? Is anything too hard for the Lord? I will return to you at the appointed time next year and Sarah will have a son." He rose abruptly, and Abraham stood up in a panic. He was numbed by the words that the leader of the three visitors had spoken. He found it difficult to respond, and finally the leader drew near to him and said, "I am not going to hide from you the thing that is going to happen."

A sudden chill came to Abraham. "What's wrong?" he whispered.

The face of the tall man grew stern, and his voice was short and clipped. "Sodom has become a stench in the nostrils of the Eternal One. He is going to destroy that entire city."

"Oh no, not everyone!"

"The whole city, and Gomorrah as well, will be totally destroyed. Those who live in it have given themselves over to evil so completely that judgment is going to come. You must prepare yourself, Abraham."

Abraham was suddenly filled with a terror he could not contain. "A whole city! No—two cities, with everyone in them. Men, women, children, old people, all slain!" It never occurred to him to doubt the man's words, for the look in his eyes was terrible and grim.

"We must leave now," the stranger said.

"I will escort you out of the camp."

Abraham followed the three guests as they headed back in the direction from which they had come. This seemed strange to Abraham, but his mind was working on what he had heard. He tried desperately to believe that all that had occurred was just a dream or that the man did not mean what he had said. Maybe the Lord was going to kill just the leaders in those evil cities. That hope grew in him, and he began to formulate a plea in his mind.

He had no chance to utter it, however, for when they were out of sight of the camp, the leader turned and said, "Go back to your people, Abraham."

"But—"

"Sodom and Gomorrah will be destroyed."

The finality in the man's face, and in his tone and words, was like a cold stone door closing. Abraham knew that protest was useless with this man, and he stood speechless while the three walked away. He watched them disappear over a rise, and then tears sprang to his eyes, and he began to sob. His first thought, of course, was for his nephew Lot and his family. He felt as if he might lose consciousness, the stress was so great. He had never fainted in his life, but now he sat down hard, his legs no longer able to support him. He pulled up his knees, put his face against them, and began to shake.

"I must do something," he cried. "But what?" He struggled to his feet and stood there helplessly, and even as he watched out of the gloom of darkness that had already fallen, a light began to glow, and he felt the presence of God. Eagerly he cried out, "O Eternal One, please don't let this thing be true!"

"You have heard the truth, Abraham. Sodom and Gomorrah will be destroyed."

"But, Lord, will you destroy the righteous along with the wicked? What if there were fifty righteous men, would you not spare it for them?"

"If I find fifty righteous in Sodom, then I will spare the place for their sake."

"What if there were only forty-five, O Most High?"

"I would spare it for their sakes."

"Oh, be not angry with your servant, but what if only forty were found?"

Abraham continued to plead for Sodom, amazed at his own boldness, and finally when God said, *"I would spare it for ten righteous men,"* Abraham bowed and gave thanks. *Surely*, he thought, *there are at least ten righteous people in that place!*

CHAPTER
27

"Master, the animals have not done well. We've lost many to sickness, and last week a bear took six of them. Actually, I think it was more than one bear."

Lot listened as Mal, his chief herdsman, recited the litany of disasters that had befallen the herds and the flocks. The short, stocky herdsman was usually a happy enough fellow, but now his face was frowning, and he shook his head as he continued to report the losses.

Lot had left Sodom early that morning, and for a time his trip to visit his herdsmen and take a count of his animals had been pleasant. Now as he stood listening to Mal give a lengthy, meandering account of his flocks and herds, Lot suddenly realized that, despite the bad news, the only time he had any peace of mind was when he was outside of Sodom. He had not reasoned this out before, but he took every available moment he could to get away from Meri and the girls, out walking the hills and the plains and drinking in the world of skies and hills and fields and valleys. He had recognized years ago that he was not made for town life. He envied Abraham and deeply regretted his decision to move to Sodom.

For years now his existence in Sodom had been miserable. He had never been accepted by the city's leaders, for he had steadfastly refused to participate in their immoral activities. At first they had tried to entice him to join in the orgies that took place almost continually, and it had been the consensus that sooner or later he would change his mind. But as the years had passed, and he kept himself aloof from their sexual perversions, he had become an object of suspicion in the city. This did not disturb Lot greatly, for he had no desire to become a part of that life. More than once Lot had desperately tried to convince his family that life would be better if they returned to living in tents.

"Living in tents! Have you lost your mind?" Meri had almost screamed at him the last time he had mentioned it. "We have a place in this city. I visit all of the most important women here, the wives of the council and the chief. And my girls are enjoying civilized lives."

"Civilized!" Lot had protested. "I wouldn't call the men in this town *civilized!*"

"Those are all just rumors. There may be a few of the men who are— well, not what they should be, but that would be true anywhere. It's true out in the desert."

Lot had given up protesting. Over the years his wife had developed the habit of listening only to her own voice. When she got an idea in her mind, nothing could change it, and she was firmly and unalterably convinced that the key to their happiness lay in Sodom. She had learned to close her eyes to the sins that went on all around her. It was a source of constant amazement to Lot that a human being could live in a world of her own and ignore the real world on the outside.

And his daughters were no better. His two older daughters had married years ago, but their husbands had not pleased Lot. They came from prominent families but had been part of the gangs that roamed the streets of Sodom almost every night, looking for young male victims. Lot had pleaded with his daughters not to marry them, but Meri had overruled him. Lot still had some hope for his two younger daughters. They were women now, but they were still young enough to change, and as Lot stood before his herdsman Mal, he tried to scrape up some hope that they could be redeemed.

Finally Mal ended his list and shook his head. "I'm sorry, master, I have not done a good job."

"You've done a fine job, Mal," Lot said quickly. He trusted the herdsman completely, for he was faithful and honest, a rare enough thing these days!

"Will you stay long? We could go hunting tomorrow if you'd like."

"I'd love to," Lot said quickly, "but I promised my wife I would be back. There's some kind of a celebration tonight I must attend."

Lot stayed out with the flocks for only another hour and then mounted his donkey and rode slowly back to the city. Not anxious to return home, he made no effort to urge the animal forward. Whenever he approached Sodom, it felt as though he were entering under a huge dark cloud. Looking overhead, he saw the skies were clear, and yet in his own mind and heart there was an oppressive darkness over the land, which always intensified as he approached the city.

He entered the city gates, greeted the guards, then wound his way through the labyrinthine streets until he came to his own house. A servant emerged, spoke to him, and took his animal away. Lot went inside, aware that he would have to put on a better face than this. Meri had reproved him often enough for wearing a long, sad face at festive events.

"About time you got back!" Meri appeared in a belligerent mood and shook his arm. "You've got to hurry and get cleaned up."

"All right," he muttered like a man defeated. He waited for her to ask about the state of the flocks and herds, but she had no interest in such things. She saw Lot's work merely as a means of bringing in more money for clothes, jewelry, and perfumes.

"Hurry up, now," she snapped, irritation in her tone. She was wearing a dress that had cost enough to pay a herdsman for six months, and he had to admit that she looked good. She carefully watched her figure, spent a fortune on perfumes, oils, and ointments, and kept three maidservants in the house to work on her appearance and that of her daughters.

Lot hurried along to his room, and as one of the female servants furnished water and towels, he cleansed himself from the dust of the desert. Meri had often insisted that he hire a man to take care of him, but he had steadfastly refused. "I'm able to take care of myself!" he had asserted, firmly standing on this principle, despite her displeasure.

When he was ready, he stepped out of his room and stood listening to his two younger daughters chatter and giggle about the party that evening. Shaking his head, Lot moved outside, murmuring, "It'll be just like all the rest of the festivals." Outside the house he saw that the streets were already beginning to fill up. His house was away from the center of town, as far away as he could get, almost next to the city wall. He had built it with a large open area filled with plants and gardens in the back, which was where he spent most of his free time.

Now, however, he sat outside and fought off the depression that almost overwhelmed him. He thought suddenly of Abraham, and his mind went back to the early days with his uncle when they had hunted together, tended the animals, moved to new territory. It had been hard work and there had been difficulties, but those were the happiest days of Lot's life.

As Lot looked down the street, he was startled to see two men suddenly appear who were strangers to him. His eyes narrowed, and when he saw that they were headed toward his own house, he stood up. They were both unusually tall men. One of them had a face that would have commanded attention and respect anywhere. The other had a dignity about him also, but secondary to the one who was obviously the leader.

Lot came forward and bowed. "Good day, sirs."

"Lot, we have come to speak with you."

Lot was instantly wary. Were these new members of the council coming to try his virtue? "I'm glad to see you," he said quickly.

"You will not be when you find out why we have come."

Lot stared with astonishment at the speaker. There was a depth to the man's steady gray eyes that seemed to have no bottom, as though they could see right into his heart, and a cold fear touched him. Who were these men and what did they want?

"I don't understand you, sir."

The two men stood silently, both of them examining Lot. He felt like a prisoner in front of a judge who had the power to condemn or to free him. "What is it you've come to speak with me about?"

"You are a good man, Lot—weak in many ways, yet you have found favor in the eyes of God Most High."

The weakness Lot was feeling grew even more acute. His knees had turned to water, and something about these two frightened him terribly. "I thank you for your words, but what is it you have to tell me?"

"We are the messengers of God Most High," the taller of the two men said. "The stench of this place has gone up to the nostrils of the Eternal One. This city is going to be destroyed. We have come to warn you."

"Destroyed," Lot whispered. "What do you mean?"

"Exactly what we say."

Then the other messenger spoke. His eyes were so dark they seemed to have no pupils. His beard was short and clipped, and he exuded a strength that was more than bodily. "Get your family and leave this place at once or you will all die."

Lot's hands were trembling. He clasped them together in a futile attempt to conceal the shaking. "Surely the Eternal One will have mercy! He would not destroy everyone here."

"He is a just God, and this city has turned itself over completely to evil."

Lot pleaded with the two. They listened, but there was firmness in their countenance, dreadful judgment in their eyes, and Lot knew that all was lost. Nonetheless he appealed to them again. "Let me fix you something to eat, and perhaps you can pray to the Lord, and He will spare the city."

But even as he spoke these words, he saw a crowd coming down the street. It was one of the gangs of perverts that roamed the city, and he saw the chief magistrate in front of them—he who should have protected the people was leading this group of evil men!

"Come inside," Lot said hurriedly, practically dragging the two men inside. He shut the door and shoved the bolt into place, but it was too late. He heard the shouts outside, men calling his name.

"Lot! Lot, open the door! We've seen these men!" The voice was that of the chief magistrate.

Lot's fear increased until he was filled with terror. "These are my guests," he shouted through the door.

"Open the door or we'll break it down! Bring them out that we may know them!"

In a panic Lot put his hands on the door as if to hold it in place. He could feel the vibrations as fists struck it, and the words grew vile and more demanding.

"Run out the back way, quickly!" he urged the messengers. "You can get over the city wall there."

"They cannot harm us."

"But you don't know how awful these men are and the vile things they do."

"We do know," the leader said calmly. "Let us go out and talk to them."

"No," Lot cried out, "you must not!" He called out through the door to the angry crowd. "Listen, you must not harm these men. It would bring terrible things on our city. I have two young daughters here. I will give them to you to do with as you will." He could not believe that he had said such a thing; he was horrified to think of the depths he had reached living in this city.

Outside, the voices grew more shrill. "Come out here, Lot! You came here as a stranger among us, and you would tell us how to live! Now we'll treat you worse than we were going to treat them."

Suddenly one of the visitors stepped forward and pushed Lot aside. The other unbolted the door and swung it open. Both men went outside, and Lot stood watching them in astonishment.

"You mustn't!" he cried, and he dashed outside with them. He found himself surrounded by a swirling crowd, faces burning with lust and rage. He knew these men loved to torture people and that their sexual appetites knew no bounds. He shouted, trying to get their attention, but one of the crowd leaned forward and struck him in the face, and Lot felt blood running down beside his mouth.

What happened next Lot could never explain. He saw the chief magistrate reach out for one of the guests—but then he stopped and shook his head. He put out his arms, his hands outstretched, and cried out, "What's happening to the light?"

Lot stared at him with astonishment as the magistrate rubbed his eyes and looked around. "I'm blind!" he screamed. "I can't see anything!"

All the others were shouting the same thing.

"Quickly, come inside." Lot's arm was seized by a steely hand, and he was drawn back inside the house. He could not understand what was happening, and then one of the visitors ordered, "Go get your family—your daughters and their husbands, your wife and younger daughters—and get them out of this place, or you will all die."

Lot straightened up. "Yes," he whispered huskily, "yes, I will."

"Do not tarry. You do not have much time."

When Lot delivered this message to his wife, she just stared at him. "Are you crazy?" she shouted.

"Didn't you hear that wild mob out there?" Lot pleaded.

Meri was allowing one of the maids to fix her hair. "They do that a lot. They don't mean any harm by it."

"They were going to kill those two men who came to warn us."

"What two men? I didn't see anyone. What do you mean warn us? Of what?"

"The city's going to be destroyed," Lot said. "Quickly! Come. We've got to get away. You get the girls. I'll go get Tamar and Camoni and their husbands."

Lot wheeled and left the room. He heard Meri protesting, screaming after him that she had no intention of doing any such thing.

"I've got to get them all out of here," he whispered to himself. "We've got to leave this place or we'll all die."

When Lot reentered his house completely defeated, he shook his head. "They wouldn't come. None of them would come. They say I'm crazy."

"I think you've lost your mind!" Meri screamed.

Lot began desperately pleading, telling her what he had seen, then saying, "Everyone in this city is going to die. I'm leaving, and you're going with me."

For the next hour Lot acted in a way Meri and their daughters had never seen. He actually slapped Meri and shouted at her, "You're leaving, and that's all I want to hear about it! You girls get what you can carry. We're getting out of here!"

It was a frantic scene, and Meri finally gave in but started ordering the servants to pack their things.

"There's no time to pack!" Lot shouted. "Did you hear me? The city's going to be burned up!"

"But I can't leave all of our things here."

"You can bring only what you can carry. Now come on!"

Meri protested, weeping, but Lot was adamant. They left the house, the girls frightened and crying but nothing like their mother, who was hysterical. "I can't leave all of my beautiful things!"

"We're going out to the desert, and that's where we're going to stay!" Lot shouted. "Now come on!"

Lot hurried his family out, and when they were outside the gates after amazing the guards with their distraught words, Lot said, "Come on. We don't even have time to get our animals."

The darkness was profound, but Lot moved ahead, leading the way. They had gone only a short distance when, short of breath, he turned and saw only two figures in the gloom. He hurried back, "Where's your mother?" he demanded.

The older of the girls was weeping. "She went back to get her jewelry. She forgot it."

"She went back! No!" He took two steps and then suddenly looked overhead. The air was filled with an ominous roar. "That's not thunder," he whispered as he stared up into the heavens. An eerie light began to sweep across the sky, growing brighter and brighter. He cast one agonizing look toward the city and knew it was too late. "Come on," he said to his daughters. "We'll have to run."

The three ran awkwardly away as the sky grew brighter and a terrible roar filled the earth.

———

Meri reached the house out of breath. She started to run inside, but the light above stopped her. She looked up and saw that the darkness of the sky was turning to an eerie white. "It's night," she whispered. "That can't be the sun!"

And then she heard the sound. It was a keening wail, as of a woman moaning and screaming in pain. She had never heard anything like it, and she turned in terror, knowing she had made a terrible mistake. "Lot!" she cried, starting toward the gate. "Lot, I'm coming!"

But it was too late. A flashing brilliance struck the earth and exploded. Meri saw a fountain of white-hot sparks fly upward and she threw up her hands. Other missiles were striking the earth all around, and the intense heat engulfed her.

"Lot," she gasped, "don't leave me!"

But as the fire from heaven fell upon the city, Meri, the wife of Lot, knew she was doomed.

———————

Morning came, and Sarah crept out of the tent to stand beside Abraham. All night long they had watched in terror as the night sky glowed intensely in the east. Abraham had told her of the visitors' prophecies, and all night long they had prayed. But both knew their prayers were useless now.

Abraham stood absolutely still, then, his voice choked with emotion, said, "He's gone, Sarah. Lot is gone."

"And those cities are both gone," Sarah uttered in disbelief.

The two stood silently, letting the truth sink in, truth they found almost impossible to accept. Finally Abraham whispered, "I did not know that God was so hard. But we do know that He is just and will judge evil when He must, and He is strong and must be obeyed."

———————

Sarah and Abraham could no longer stay in the place where they had witnessed the terrible wrath of God poured out on the cities of Sodom and Gomorrah. The smoke continued to rise from the remains of the cities for days, and every time they looked toward the horizon, they saw the haze hanging over the hills—a painful, daily reminder of the tragedy. They prayed fervently that Lot and his family had managed to escape, but when days passed and they heard nothing, they grievously assumed that Lot's family had not been spared.

"I cannot bear it any longer," Abraham said to Sarah one morning after returning from a solitary time of prayer. He had stood on a high hill looking out over the Jordan Valley—now scarred and blackened where the city of Sodom had once teemed with life, weeping for the thousands of lost souls who had met such sudden judgment there. "We must move on to a place where we can find some peace," he told her.

Abraham gave orders to the herdsmen to move the flocks and herds as far south as they could still find water, and the tribe packed up their tents and moved on. The scouts returned each evening to tell Abraham of what lay ahead, and he pushed them ever onward, until they reached the desert region of the Negev. They located a town named Gerar, near a large oasis, and settled on the outskirts, near enough so that they could water their animals.

The king of Gerar went out to greet the newcomers, and when he saw Sarah, he was greatly impressed by her beauty, even though she was by this time very old. The look in the king's eyes brought an icy fear to Abraham, and without thinking, he found himself telling the king that Sarah was his sister.

Sarah shot him a glance of disbelief, but she quickly recovered her composure and went along with the ruse.

When two of the king's guards rode out to their camp early one morning, Abraham watched their arrival with trepidation. "Sarah," he said, his voice trembling, "get to Zara and Eliezer's tent as fast as you can and don't come out. I am terribly afraid that the king is sending for you!"

"Don't worry, husband," Sarah said. "Didn't God protect us in Egypt when Pharaoh tried to make me his wife? You have told the king a foolish thing, but I have no reason to believe that He wants harm to come to us now." Then she obeyed Abraham and quickly made her way to Zara's tent.

It was as Abraham had feared. The guards of King Abimelech demanded that Abraham bring out his sister. "The king wishes her for a wife," they said.

The guards were armed with heavy swords, and Abraham knew he had no choice but to obey. With heavy heart, he fetched Sarah, whispering to her desperately, "We will find a way to rescue you."

"Don't worry, my husband. I am trusting God himself to rescue me."

And with that Sarah walked calmly to the waiting guards.

———

Abraham stayed on his knees all night, praying out to the Eternal One to have mercy on Sarah and begging God's forgiveness for his own sin in not being truthful with the king.

When the light of dawn touched the horizon, he lifted his head and could not believe his eyes. Approaching the camp was Sarah riding on a donkey, flanked by two guards on either side of her. Behind the riders walked a half dozen servant girls, and following them were several dozen head of cattle and sheep, being kept together by herdsmen on either side.

Abraham ran to meet them as fast as his old legs would carry him. When the entourage reached the edge of the camp, the guards helped Sarah dismount and she fell into her husband's waiting arms.

"I have so much to tell you, husband!" she said. "The Eternal One answered our prayers again. He spoke to the king in a dream, warning him to let me return to my people. He was so frightened by the vision, he did not wait for the light of day to fetch me and send me on my way! He has sent along these servant girls to us as a gift"—she made a sweeping gesture with her arm—"and all these cattle and sheep."

Abraham could not believe what he was hearing. "But surely the king wants something of us in return."

"No, my husband," Sarah said. "He knows now that the hand of a mighty and powerful God is upon you, and he has told us we can live here in peace!"

———————

Sarah and Abraham never forgot the tragedy they had witnessed of the destruction of Sodom and Gomorrah, and they grieved the deaths of Lot and his family, but with each passing month the memory became a little less painful as they enjoyed a peaceful life near the oasis of Gerar.

One morning they arose and sat outside their tent, contentedly watching the camp come to life and the flocks and herds grazing on the nearby hillside.

"God has been so good to us, Sarah," Abraham murmured.

"Yes . . . His blessings are more than we can count." Then she put a trembling hand on his arm. "Husband," she whispered, "I have something to tell you."

Abraham turned to look into her eyes, which sparkled in the morning light. "What is it, wife?"

"Do you remember that the visitor said I would have a child, and I laughed? Well, I . . . I was wrong."

Abraham did not understand. "What do you mean you were wrong?"

"I *am* going to have a child, Abraham."

He looked at her, incredulous, and a smile crept over his lips. Her expression shone with the joy and pride of any new mother, and her eyes revealed the staggering truth. For so many years he had struggled to keep believing in God's promise, for they were both old. Now he began to tremble as he asked, "Is it true? Are you sure?"

"It is true," Sarah said simply. "I waited to tell you until I could be sure." She fell against him, and he held her tight as she cried out in joy, "The Most High has visited us! I know it's impossible in the flesh, but I am with child. We will have the son of promise, husband!"

CHAPTER

28

Standing at the door of her tent, Sarah gazed out and watched gauzy clouds drift across the sky. The pale sun burned against the blueness of the horizon. A tremor went through her, and she put her hand on her rounded abdomen. A jubilance like nothing she had ever known filled her as she stood holding herself. The child within her had stirred!

He's alive! My son is alive! O Eternal One, how merciful you are and how faithful! Forgive me for doubting you. Bring this miracle son into the world, and put your hand on him every day of his life!

The smell of cooked meat wafted to her on the breeze, bringing a wave of nausea. During the first months of her pregnancy she had suffered wretched morning sickness. She had become so weak she had been unable to do more than simply lie flat on her back and wait for the nausea to pass. Abraham had prevailed upon Zara to help Sarah through her pregnancy. The young woman had become like a right hand to her, and Sarah had grown to love her like a daughter.

A dog suddenly appeared to her right, an ungainly yellow creature, raw-boned, with an abnormally long, thin face. He was in pursuit of a smaller dog, and Sarah watched as they dashed through the center of the camp and then disappeared. As she listened to the sounds of the camp, to the murmur of voices and the crying of a child somewhere, memories drifted across her mind, like ghosts floating across a stage. She remembered how Abraham had first come into her life, and a smile turned the corners of her lips upward as she relived their courtship. How awkward he had been! And what a beast she had been to treat him so badly! She thought tenderly of their early days of marriage, remembering how thoughtful and kind Abraham had been. For all his strength he had been as gentle as a woman. He had awakened love in her that had grown over the years, though the early love she had felt for him had matured from a blazing fire to a warm bed of hot coals. She knew she would love him until the day she died.

Her back began to hurt, and she moved over to the chair that Abraham had asked his herdsman Dulog to make. Dulog was skillful with his hands and had built a lightweight chair out of wood, with a leather seat stretched across a frame. It was deep and comfortable, and Dulog had fashioned a cushioned back, so now Sarah settled back with a sigh, still watching the scenes of the camp.

Across from her tent she saw Dulog's wife, Mara, carrying a load of clothes down to the river to be washed. Mara smiled and waved at her, and Sarah waved back. She remembered that Mara, who had a three-month-old child of her own, had come to say, "If you do not have enough milk, I have plenty enough for your baby."

Everyone's been so kind, Sarah thought, *and it's unlikely that I'll be able to furnish enough nourishment for a baby, but there are half a dozen nursing mothers in the camp, and any one of them would be honored to nourish the child of Abraham.*

She thought of the child as Abraham's child. She was the bearer of the life, and the child would be hers as well as his, but God's promises were all tied to the seed of Abraham. Still, a fierce pride burned in her as she realized she was bringing a son into the world whose descendants would be more abundant than the stars of the sky.

Sarah sat quietly for a time but soon became uncomfortable even sitting in the soft seat. She rose and arched her back to ease the pain and began to walk around her tent. She knew her body did not have the resiliency of that of a young woman, and she wondered if she would have the strength to survive the birth.

"Good morning, mistress." Zara had fallen into step beside Sarah. "Did you sleep well last night?"

"Well enough. You look refreshed this morning."

"It's a beautiful day. I'm going to make your breakfast now. What would you like?"

"Nothing sounds good."

"Well, I'll make it good." Zara smiled. "I'll get some fresh milk and make you some of that lentil porridge you like so much."

Sarah allowed Zara to cajole her into smiling, and a short time later she was sitting down in her chair, eating a bowl of porridge. She ate a few bites of it, then shook her head. "I don't think I can get any more of it down."

"You must eat, mistress," Zara said firmly. "I know you're not hungry, but you're eating for two now."

Sarah suddenly smiled. " 'Eating for two.' You don't know how wonderful that sounds to me. To think that I'm carrying a life, a son for Abraham."

"Everyone is so happy for you. No one's talked about anything else since you found out you were pregnant. And not only here," Zara said, "but all through the land the word has gone out. Everyone's saying what a miracle it is."

"You're right about that," Sarah said. She took another bite and forced it down, then said, "I didn't tell you what I did when the three men visited us."

"Who were those three men?"

"I'm not really sure, but I can't help thinking they were heavenly messengers. When their leader told Abraham that I was going to have a child, the strangest thing happened."

"A strange thing? What was it?"

"I didn't actually laugh out loud, but inside I was laughing. You know how that is?"

"Yes, of course."

"Well, it was as if that man knew exactly what was going on, for he told Abraham that I had laughed, even though I hadn't made a sound."

"How strange."

"I think they were messengers of the Eternal One," Sarah said quietly. "After I knew that I was going to have a baby, I thought back on that day, and I remembered that I'd laughed at them. I felt so terrible about my unbelief." She shook her head, and her lips formed a firm line. "I'll never laugh at anything God tells me again."

The two women sat talking quietly, and finally Zara said, "Are you afraid, mistress?"

"You mean afraid to have the baby?"

"Yes. It's a hard thing even for a young woman."

"I'm concerned but not afraid. That's one thing I've learned. When the God of all the earth sets out to do something, it will be done." She reached over and took Zara's hand, and a light was in her eyes. "I know it will be hard at my age, but I don't mind, for I know the hand of God is on me."

Night had fallen upon the camp, and Sarah lay panting in the heat. Abraham lay beside her, but he had fallen asleep long ago. As for Sarah, she could not get comfortable in any position, and she had tried them all. Laboriously she pulled herself over to lie on her side, then put her arms around the bulge in her stomach and tried desperately to drift off to sleep.

Her pregnancy had gotten harder, until she had become almost as help-less as a child. She could have borne the discomfort of the pregnancy, but a problem had come to plague her that simply would not go away. And that problem was Hagar and Ishmael.

I wish I had never thought of allowing Hagar to have a child by Abraham. I should have believed the Eternal One, but it was so hard, and I just couldn't. It's been many years, and Ishmael and Hagar have all this time been secure in their position. If not for my son, Ishmael would be the true heir of Abraham, the real son.

The child within her would be the child of the true wife, and Abraham would, by custom and tradition, make him the heir. Hagar was not even a concubine and really had no position at all. But Abraham had always been kind to her, and as for Ishmael, Abraham had doted on him all of his life.

At the cry of a hunting night bird, she clutched at a sudden drawing pain in her stomach. Instantly she felt a tinge of fear. She had told Zara she was not afraid of giving birth, but now that it was upon her, she did feel great apprehension. Slowly she rolled over on her back, her hands on her stomach, and waited to see if the time had come. Her mind went back to Hagar, and she reviewed her relationship with the bondwoman. She remembered how Abraham had stepped in and defended her from Hagar's attacks against her and how Hagar had run away for a time. It had seemed impossible that the two women could ever be friends again, but Hagar had returned to camp more subdued. They were no longer friends, but Sarah had tried to be civil toward her. She felt she owed her a debt for bearing her husband a son, but she could never bring herself to love the woman who had become her rival.

Her mind worked nervously as she went over the things that were trou-bling her about what the future might hold. She was old now and would not, in all probability, live to see her son grow up to manhood. And what if Abraham died? Ishmael would be a strong man, and their son, why, he would be only eight years old when Ishmael was in his twenties! Sarah tried not to think of it, but she knew that Ishmael had some wild blood in his veins. It came, of course, from his mother, who had come from a wild and violent tribe.

The possibility that her son would be at the mercy of a much stronger Ishmael, backed by an ambitious mother, terrified her. She was trying desper-ately not to think any more about it when she was hit with a pain much stronger than any she had felt yet, and she quickly forgot everything else.

"Abraham!"

"Yes?" Abraham awoke at once.

"I . . . I think it's time. The baby is coming."

"I'll get the women." Abraham scrambled to his feet, threw on a robe, and disappeared. Sarah lay quietly and waited, and before he returned, another pain swept over her. "O Eternal One, have mercy on me and this child," she prayed.

———————

The birth was difficult beyond belief. Sarah was willing, but her body was weak. She did not have the strength to push the child. Her bones were too brittle and her joints too frail to sustain the sitting position, and the midwives could do little to ease her pain. She lay hour after hour waiting for the child in agony.

Finally, after her mind was almost paralyzed by the terrible pain, she was surprised to feel some relief. In the dimness of half-consciousness, she was aware of a sensation of release. At first she thought she was dying, but then she heard cries of joy. She could not understand it at first, but then she felt a hand on her head, and she came back to the world. She saw Abraham's face, but her vision was blurred, and she could see him only unclearly.

"We have a son, Sarah! A beautiful baby boy!"

And then the joy came. She felt Abraham's hand on her, patting and stroking her. She heard the cries of the midwives, and she managed to say, "Let me hold him."

Almost at once the bundle was placed in her arms, and her vision cleared. She looked down at the tiny bit of humanity, and her heart knew great joy. "Our son, Abraham. Our own son!"

"Yes. You have done well."

"The Eternal One has given us this child. We must never forget it, husband."

At that moment the child uttered a feeble cry, which grew stronger. Sarah felt herself slipping away again, but she also, strangely enough, laughed aloud. "There," she said. "I laughed once in disbelief, but now I laugh because God has given me great joy."

Abraham's eyes were filled with tears, but he managed a smile. "We will laugh together over this son of ours. His name shall be called Isaac, for this is the name given to him by the Lord of all the earth!"

———————

Zara lifted the infant high in the air and rocked him back and forth.

"What a fine, handsome boy you are, Isaac," she crooned. She pulled him back into her arms and saw that he was drooling. She wiped his mouth, then sat down beside Sarah, who was watching her fondly. "This is the most beautiful baby in the world, mistress."

"Well, I think so. But, of course, I'm prejudiced."

"You're not in the least prejudiced. He's our miracle baby, and the great God above is going to do wondrous things with him."

Sarah was feeling very good indeed. She had recovered slowly from the ordeal of birth, but now that terrible night was three months past, and she remembered it only faintly. What was real to her now was Isaac. Her days were filled with him, and Zara had become a second mother. Sarah had not produced enough milk for the child, but several of the women with infants had clamored over the honor of nursing the child of Abraham and Sarah.

Sarah studied Zara, pleased with her appearance, as always. She watched the young woman's lips purse together as she made cooing noises to Isaac. There was a glow in the younger woman's eyes that made her beautiful, and Sarah felt a great love for her—almost like that of a mother to a daughter. A thought came to her, and she spoke it aloud.

"You should be holding a child of your own, Zara."

Zara quickly turned, and a strange expression crossed her face. It was fleeting and Sarah could not read it completely. Silently Zara rose and put Isaac into Sarah's arms. Sarah took the baby and asked, "What's wrong? Have I offended you?"

"No, of course not, mistress. But I am not sure that I will ever marry."

"Why, you must!"

"Some women don't marry."

"Only those who can't find a husband. But there must be at least a dozen men who would gladly marry you. I watch their eyes as they follow you."

Zara shrugged her shoulders. "Perhaps someday," she said, turning away. "I must go fix Eliezer's meal."

After Zara left, Sarah shook her head. "She needs to marry. She was made to be a wife and a mother." Isaac grunted then, and Sarah pulled him up to a sitting position. She poked his fat cheek with her finger and said, "You beautiful baby, you! Your mother loves you, and your father loves you. You're going to be the most wonderful man who ever lived!"

CHAPTER
29

A thin moon lay low in the southern sky, faintly lighting the river's surface. Upstream a rain had fallen, turning what was usually a quiet stream into a frothy turbulence. Abraham and Sarah walked hand in hand along the bank, speaking quietly and watching the youngster who ran ahead of them, stopping from time to time to throw a stone or dabble his feet in the water. Abraham's senses were alive to the life all around them—beetles and owls, animals small and large. He fancied he could even hear the trees growing, so much did he feel a part of the pulsing life of the earth all around him.

"Don't fall in the river, son," Abraham called out.

Isaac stopped and straightened up, and by the faint silvery light the pair could see his smile. "I won't," he cried out, "but I just saw a turtle, I think."

"Don't let him bite your toes," Abraham called and watched as the boy splashed the water upward and then ran farther downstream, his feet making a sucking noise in the rich mud of the bank. Overhead the wind was ruffling up the leaves of the small trees in the thicket to their left, and he savored the smell of the land that rose with the earth's dissipating heat. Overhead the clouds made streaky currents across the ebony sky, swiftly moving ghostly shadows.

Suddenly a star fell, scratching the velvety blackness of the heavens. The two stopped to watch it in wonder, and Sarah said, "I don't know why, but that always scares me a little."

Abraham squeezed her hand. "Why should it scare you?"

"I don't know. If one star falls, another one might. What keeps them from all falling?"

"I don't know, but I believe that God would never let that happen. I like to think that a falling star is another way God speaks to us, to get our attention and make us think about the wonder and mystery of His creation."

Sarah contemplated this and then pulled at him. "Come along. Isaac's getting way ahead of us."

"He's growing like a weed, isn't he?"

"Yes, he is," Sarah agreed. "I can't imagine what I did without him. It seemed like my life started the day he was born."

"Mine too, in a way." He looked up and saw the stars making their pattern across the sky. "Look at them all, Sarah."

"I know. They're beautiful, aren't they?"

"And so many. And yet the Eternal One said that our descendants would be even more numerous. It is too wonderful for me to take it all in. From that one little boy will come multitudes."

The two walked along the stream bank, staying close to Isaac, and the shadows of the night lay in velvet pools along the pathway. From far away a wolf howled, adding an indescribable note of wildness to the night. The diluted silver moonlight, the sounds and smells of the night, lent an air of ancient mystery to the scene. It seemed as though the night's blackness was squeezing down on the earth with its weight and its loneliness.

Suddenly Sarah turned to Abraham and asked, "Have you noticed how quickly Ishmael has become almost a man?"

"Yes. He was always a good hunter, and now he far surpasses any man in the tribe."

Sarah did not answer for a moment. She called out once for Isaac to slow down, and then she turned and said quietly, "The Eternal One told you He'd make a great nation of Ishmael too, didn't He?"

"Yes, He did. I don't understand that, but the Eternal One is never wrong."

Sarah was troubled but could not voice her fears to Abraham. His whole life was now tied up in Isaac, yet she knew he still had a fondness for Ishmael. She did not trust Hagar. Although the woman had not caused any trouble for a long time, Sarah could not help feeling there was something about Hagar and Ishmael that was not right. She shook off the thought and called out, "Come along, Isaac. Time to go back home."

———

"Is there any more mutton?"

Hagar glanced up and saw that Ishmael had completely consumed the meal she had put out for him. "Yes, it's cold but there's plenty more."

"I don't care. Let me have it."

Getting up quickly, Hagar crossed to the meat that hung from a pole. She sliced off a large chunk of it with a sharp knife, brought it back, and put it down before Ishmael.

Ishmael picked it up in both hands and began gnawing at it as if he were starving, and Hagar shook her head. "You eat too fast."

"Well, I'm hungry."

"You always are, but you're growing so fast I suppose that's only right." Sitting down, Hagar poured some wine out of a goatskin bag and sipped it slowly. It was bitter, but she liked it that way, and as she drank, she studied Ishmael. He did not look so much like Abraham as he did her own father. Abraham had always been relatively thin, but Ishmael was thick and heavily muscled. He was, in fact, a mirror image of Hagar's own father, and Hagar took pleasure in this. *There's more of me and my family in him than there is of Abraham,* she thought with delight.

Hagar had become an unhappy woman since the birth of Isaac. In her mind, the newcomer had burst from the womb and shoved his way into first place in the affections of Abraham and Sarah. It did not surprise her, for Hagar was a woman who understood the call of blood ties and the meaning of family. She was well acquainted with the fact that Abraham claimed God had promised him a son by his true wife, and there was no denying it was a miracle for Sarah to have had a child at her age.

Sipping the wine, Hagar was teeming with frustration. She studied her son, who was now as strong as any man in the camp, very fleet despite his size, and the best hunter anyone had ever seen. Still, her spirit was as sour as the wine she drank, for her hopes of Ishmael being the heir had vanished like a mist with the appearance of Isaac.

"What's the matter, Mother?"

Hagar looked up quickly to see Ishmael, who was chewing his meat and watching her steadily. "I'm just wondering what's going to become of us."

"What do you mean by that?"

"We can't stay here forever—not like this." Dissatisfaction swept across Hagar's face, and with a frown she put down the wine and folded her hands. Staring at him with her large dark eyes, she said, "We have no place, son."

"Why, we've got a tent. I can bring in all the food we need."

"That's not enough."

Ishmael swallowed the last of the meat and belched loudly. He then drained the wine from his wooden cup and set it down hard. "I don't know what you mean."

"You were born because Abraham wanted an heir, and for a time you were his heir. But then Isaac came along, and now where are we?"

Hagar spoke steadily, expressing her displeasure, and saw her words sinking into Ishmael. A heavy frown darkened his face, and when she fell silent, he said, "It's not fair! My father never pays any attention to me."

"No, not anymore. He did once."

"But no more. Now all he wants to do is play with that Isaac."

Hagar listened as Ishmael complained. She had sown this seed of dissatisfaction in him, and it had found fruitful soil. Now she reached over and took his powerful hand in both of hers. The strength of it gave her assurance, and she said, "Well, there may be one hope."

"I don't see any."

"It may be well yet. After all, Isaac is only six." She hesitated and then dropped her eyes, murmuring, "Lots of young children die."

When she lifted her eyes, Hagar saw that the thought had come forcefully to Ishmael. He held her glance for a moment and then a smile twisted his lips. "That's right, isn't it? If something happened to him, I would be the heir."

"Yes, you would."

Ishmael said no more, but he got up, and Hagar watched him leave the tent. She did not tell him that she had been praying steadily to the Canaanite gods for Isaac to die. She had no faith at all in the God of Abraham, and even now she was thinking, *I'll make a larger offering than ever for that brat to die!*

"Eliezer, let's go into the village tonight."

Eliezer had been carving a cup out of a piece of extremely hard wood he had bought from a traveler. It was almost black and hard as stone. He enjoyed working with his hands, but now he looked up and studied Zara. He liked to watch her face, the slight changes of her expression. Her hair rose back from her temples, made a mass on her head, and then was caught into a fall behind.

"Why do you want to go into the village?"

She smiled and said, "They're having a festival of some kind there."

"Probably to some god you don't even need to hear about."

"We don't have to pay any attention to that."

"We do if it's a festival celebrating an idol."

"Please, let's go." Behind her composed expression, an eagerness like that of a little girl stirred and displayed itself.

"What if I say no?"

"Well, then we won't go."

"Yes, we would. You'd find some way. I don't know how you do it, Zara, but I always find myself giving in to you."

"That's because I'm so sweet."

Eliezer laughed. "I've seen you a few times when you didn't seem all that sweet. All right. Get ready and we'll go."

The evening was a pleasure for both Zara and Eliezer. The village was crowded with people from all over the countryside. Eliezer had discovered that it was a harvest festival, and true enough, there was talk of a god of the harvest, but people, after paying token attention to whatever god it was, had thrown themselves into the spirit of the celebration.

Eliezer watched as Zara enjoyed herself. This was the greatest pleasure of the evening for him. He also liked the music and singing and found it refreshing to be in a place of merriment instead of out in the lonely stretches of the desert. There were times Zara was like a little girl, he decided, in spirit at least. Eliezer never ceased to marvel at her almost childlike enthusiasm and the range of her spirit. She could be quiet at times, so quiet that he would worry about her, but tonight she was laughing, her eyes dancing bright in her face.

"Are you having a good time, Eliezer?"

Zara had reached up and taken his arm to draw his attention. When he turned around and looked at her, he saw that her face was flushed and her lips slightly parted. She had unusually beautiful teeth, and the texture of her skin was smooth and clear, almost like a baby's. "I suppose it's more fun than tending sick sheep."

"Oh, you old grouch!"

"Yes, I'm having fun." His eyes went over to one of the booths, where he caught the glint of yellow metal. "Let's see what that fellow has," he said.

The two went to the table the vendor had set up. He was a small man with bright eyes and used his hands incessantly as he talked. "Buy a present for the lady. Beautiful earrings. And look at this...."

Eliezer watched as Zara examined the jewelry. She hardly ever asked for anything, yet it was a pleasure to buy her gifts because she was always very grateful. Now she was taken with a pair of golden earrings that flashed in the light of the torches.

"How much are these?" Zara asked.

The trader said, "Almost nothing. I'm practically giving them away." He named an exorbitant price, and Zara at once handed them back. "No, that's too much."

Eliezer studied her, and as he expected, the man immediately lowered the price. He reached out and took the earrings. "Put them on. Let's see what they look like."

"They cost too much, Eliezer."

"I didn't say we'd buy them. Just put them on. Here, let me do it." He touched her cheek with his hand as he slipped on one earring, then got the other one fastened and stood back to examine her face. He twisted his head to one side, rubbed his chin thoughtfully, and said nothing.

"Well, do you like them?"

"Yes, I do."

"But they cost too much," she said with a sigh.

Eliezer laughed and made an offer for the earrings. He went through the customary process of bargaining, finally paid for them, and the two turned away.

"You shouldn't have paid so much, Eliezer."

"But they look so nice. As a matter of fact, you look very nice tonight, and I like the earrings."

Zara did not speak for a moment, and when she turned to face him, he noticed her lips had gone soft and a change had come over her face. There was an expression in her eyes that stirred some old memory he could not identify, and he reached out and put his hand on her cheek. "You should always have nice things. Beautiful things. A beautiful woman should have beautiful earrings."

He saw tears come to her eyes and said in amazement, "What's wrong?"

"Oh, nothing. I just like them so much. Thank you, Eliezer. I'll keep them always."

As they walked Eliezer noticed Zara touching the earrings from time to time. They came upon a group of musicians playing stringed instruments and drums, and many were dancing to their lively tunes. Zara took his arm and said, "Come on. Let's join them."

"But I'm not much of a dancer."

"I'll teach you."

"I don't think that's possible."

But it was possible, and besides, Zara was a good enough dancer for the two of them. Eliezer saw how light on her feet she was—like the wind—and he marveled that he had never noticed this before. She even made him feel as if he were doing better than he really was.

As they danced Zara noticed a man watching them. She had seen him watching them throughout the evening, and after they left the dancers and stopped to buy water from a vendor, she saw him approach.

"You two dance very well together," the man said.

Eliezer turned to face the man. He was a small, wiry fellow, with gray hair and a face like a ferret. "Thank you," Eliezer replied.

"My name is Agag."

The man waited for their names, and Eliezer reluctantly gave his. "I am Eliezer, steward of Abraham the Hebrew."

Recognition gleamed in Agag's small but brilliant eyes. "I have heard much about him. You're camped near this village?"

"Not too far away."

Agag turned and studied Zara. "You seem very familiar, lady. Is it possible we have met?"

"No, I don't think so."

Agag had forgotten Eliezer. He stood watching Zara now, his gaze devouring her. "I have a wonderful memory," he said quietly. "I know we have met. It may have been a long time ago."

Zara was troubled by his examination. "I don't think so," she said shortly. She reached out and took Eliezer's arm, and he sensed that she was ready to go.

"I doubt if you've ever met this woman," Eliezer said, nodding to Agag and leading Zara away.

"I don't like that man," Zara said quietly.

"You don't? Why not?" Eliezer asked.

"I don't know—just a feeling. He made me uncomfortable looking at me like that."

"Well, you won't have to see him again. We won't be coming back to this village, and I think it's about time to move the herds again."

The two walked on out of the village into the darkness, and when they arrived at the encampment, he stopped beside her tent. "I had a very good time tonight, Zara."

"So did I," she said softly, reaching up and touching the earrings. "Thank you so much for the earrings. They're beautiful."

"You never ask for anything."

"But you give me things, and it's better when you think of it yourself."

A silence enveloped them, and they stood speaking quietly. Finally he said, "You'd better get to sleep. It's late."

She hesitated, as though waiting for something. He saw an expression rise in her eyes, and she reached out and put her hand flat on his chest. "You're so good to me, Eliezer. I don't know what would have ever happened to me if you hadn't taken me in when my mother died."

Eliezer put his hand over hers and said, "You've been a brightness in my life." His words stirred her, he saw, and then she quickly turned, pulled her hand away, and disappeared without another word.

"What did I say wrong now? It seems I'm always putting my foot in my mouth with that woman." He turned, shaking his head, and went to his own tent.

CHAPTER

30

Zara was walking in the midst of the flock, a pastime that gave her pleasure. The fluffy sheep were like a lake of undulating white waves. They swarmed around her as she made her way through, and the sheep dog, with its lolling tongue, lifted his head and barked sharply at her. Raising her hand, Zara laughed and said, "I'm not going to hurt your sheep. Now, mind your own business."

Peor, a shy boy of sixteen, stole a glance at the woman as she made her way through the flock. He fancied himself in love with her and made up songs to her beauty, which he never allowed anyone else to hear. Peor was a romantic lad and had been in love, or fancied himself so, with other women too, but something about Zara spoke to his heart.

He studied her with a surreptitious look, noting how pleasing she looked in her loose-fitting garment, a yellow smock with a red border patterned with black moons. The smock hung free and comfortably from throat to hem, showing her small feet and her sandals, but the gown was fitted around the shoulders, displaying their appealing fineness and slenderness, and the sleeves reached only halfway down her upper arm, exposing the smooth flesh. Her black hair tumbled rather than curled, and two braids curling at the ends hung across her cheeks and down on her shoulders. And her face . . . Peor let his glance linger on the charm of her smooth cheeks, but most of all he was intrigued by her oddly colored eyes. They were green or gray, sometimes one, sometimes the other, depending on the color of the garment she wore.

"Good morning, Peor," she said, smiling at him.

"Good morning, mistress," Peor whispered, feeling his knees go weak. "Fine day."

"Yes, it is." A humorous light danced in Zara's eyes. "How are you getting along with Meori?"

"Meori? Why, not at all. Why should I be interested in her?"

Zara laughed, exposing her lustrous white teeth. "You were so much in love with her a month ago you were running into trees and falling into holes."

Peor blushed darkly. "I was not!"

Zara smiled and shook her head. "You are a romantic fellow, Peor."

Peor watched Zara continue on her way through the flock, hopelessly admiring her figure. Then he heard the sharp bark of his dog and turned away, going about his business but all the while composing a song in his mind to Zara's eyes.

When Zara reached the camp, she knelt down by the hollowed-out grinding stone and placed a few handfuls of barley grain in it. Then she lifted a rounded stone and began to pound it. As she worked to make flour, she sang a song under her breath. She was strangely happy this morning. From her ears dangled the earrings Eliezer had bought her, and once she put down the stone, dusted off her hands, and gently caressed them. She grew warm as she thought of their evening together in the village and made up her mind to ask Eliezer to take her back to another festival soon.

She went back to her grinding, working steadily until she had filled the clay jar beside her with flour. As she finished she looked up to see a cloud of dust in the distance and wondered who could be coming into camp this early. *Probably traders. Maybe they'll have something I can use.* She rose, carried the jar of barley flour inside the tent, wiped off her hands, and then went back outside.

The men were closer now, and her eyes narrowed as she recognized one of them. It was the small man with the shifty eyes who called himself Agag. It had been only two days since the festival, and Zara remembered her dislike of him. Curiosity got the best of her, and she moved closer to where the four men were dismounting from their donkeys. One of them was obviously the leader, a large, strong-looking man with a face darkened by the fierce desert sun. Zara noted that the others fell slightly back, allowing him to step forward. Abraham was not in camp, and Eliezer had disappeared for the moment, so Eli stepped out to greet them. Eli was an older man in his sixties, not strong in body, but a man in whom Abraham put his trust. Zara was close enough to hear him greet the visitors.

"Good morning, sirs. You are traveling early."

"My name is Zoltar," the big man said. He studied Eli only for a second, and then his eyes began to scan the camp. They rested for a moment on Sarah, who had also drawn closer to see who the strangers were. His glance took her in, then moved on, resting on Zara. He had strange-colored eyes, flat, as if there was nothing behind them. His mouth was sensuous and cruel, and he moved quickly. He came to stand before Zara and said, "What is your name, woman?"

Zara was startled by the quickness of the man's action and put off by his arrogance. "That is none of your business, sir."

Zoltar laughed. "Yes, it's my business. I know you."

"I think not."

Sarah and Eli had come to stand beside Zara. "This woman is part of our clan," Sarah said coldly. "What is your business?"

"She is my business." Zoltar lifted his arm and pointed at Zara. "Your name is Zara, isn't it?"

Zara was shocked that he knew her name, and then her eyes fell on Agag. But old memories had already begun to stir in her, and fear came over her. She had put away memories of her mother's death, trying never to think of them.

Zoltar laughed. "Well, I found you again."

"What are you talking about?" Sarah demanded.

"This girl belongs to me."

And then Zara remembered. She was so frightened she could not speak. It had been a long time ago, but she remembered well that during the war this man had killed her father. She had tried to bury that memory, but she could see him now, a huge man with his eyes flashing fire, who came with a sword and cut her father down. She and her mother had not even had time to weep, for he had grabbed them, tied them up, and marched them out of the camp.

"I took this girl and her mother captive in the war against Kedorlaomer," Zoltar said.

"You have no claim on her," Sarah said loudly. She looked around desperately for Abraham or Eliezer and then was startled when Zoltar stepped forward and seized Zara by the arm. "I remember you well enough. How could I forget those eyes? You belong to me now."

Eli stepped forward in protest. "You can't take this woman. She belongs to—" He did not finish his sentence, for Zoltar reached out with his free hand and struck him with the flat of his palm, driving the old man backward to the ground.

Sarah screamed out, "Eliezer! Eliezer!"

"Shut your mouth, woman! You'd better hope nobody comes. I'm taking this woman with me. She's my property."

Zara felt herself being pulled toward the waiting donkeys. She cried out and struggled, but his strength was frightening.

As for Zoltar, he merely laughed at her efforts and said, "I like a woman with some spirit in her. It's entertaining! Now, are you going to ride this beast or do I have to tie you on?"

Terrorized, Zara was twisting, trying to get away, when she saw Eliezer appear from behind a row of tents. He had his staff in his hand, and he dashed across the ground, pulling up only a few feet from where Zoltar held her.

"Let her go!"

"Leave or I'll kill you!" Zoltar yanked a sword from his belt and slashed the air with it, taunting, "Come on. I'll remove your head from your shoulders."

The two men who had come with Zoltar had not said a word, but now Agag bellowed, "Come on. We'll kill this fellow for his insolence."

Eliezer saw the three men form a semicircle. Agag was grinning and said, "You remember me? You were insolent at the festival, but where's your insolence now?"

Eliezer moved so swiftly that Zara had difficulty catching the movement. He swung his staff and struck one of the men on the shoulder. The man cried out but did not drop his weapon.

"Kill him!" Zoltar said coldly.

"It'll be a pleasure," Agag laughed. He stepped forward, holding his knife, and the other man approached from the other side. "We'll leave you for the wild dogs," Agag sneered. Lifting his knife in a practiced fashion, he moved forward.

Suddenly there was a hissing sound, and the man Eliezer had struck grabbed at an arrow piercing his chest. It had gone completely through his body on his left side, and he fell to the ground, kicking and crying in a muted voice. But his cries did not last long, and the blood stained the ground underneath him.

Zoltar whirled and saw the young man who had launched the arrow. He was tall and dark-haired, with wild eyes that now blazed with fury. He nocked another arrow and drew his bow. Zoltar saw that the arrow was aimed right at him, and he immediately loosed his hold on Zara. "Don't shoot!" he shouted.

"Hold your fire, Ishmael," Eliezer ordered; then to the men, he yelled, "Take that carrion and get out of here!"

Zoltar was a man of rash anger, but he was not a fool. He knew the arrow had gone exactly where the young warrior had aimed it and that his own life lay in the fingers that still held the string back. "We're leaving," he grumbled, letting Zara go. "Help me get the body on the donkey, Agag."

Eliezer held out his hand, and Zara fled to him. He put his arm around her shoulders and gave her a quick, reassuring smile. She was trembling, and he whispered, "Don't worry."

Zoltar and Agag loaded the body on the donkey and tied it down. Zoltar wheeled his donkey around. When they were beyond arrow range, he turned back and yelled, "We'll be back, and we'll bring plenty of help with us!"

Eliezer watched the men leave, then turned to the frightened woman. "You're all right, Zara. They're gone."

"I remember him, Eliezer. He's the man who killed my father."

"Well, you're safe now."

Eliezer dropped his arm and walked over to Ishmael. He was closely followed by Zara. "You saved us, Ishmael."

"Yes," Zara said quickly. "Thank you so much, Ishmael."

Hagar had joined the group. She had come out only in time to catch the last act, but her face was warm. "I'm so proud of you, my son. Abraham will know that you are his best warrior." She gave Eliezer a triumphant glance, and he knew she was thinking that this would put him in a bad light before Abraham.

Abraham listened to the story. Everyone had gathered around him when he had come back, explaining what had happened. He was concerned for Zara when she told him that this man was the leader of a wild tribe. "He's a cruel man, sir, and he said he would come back."

"We'll be ready for him. Don't worry, Zara." Abraham turned to Ishmael, and a warm light came into his eyes. He walked over to him and threw his arm around the young man's shoulders. Ishmael was as tall as Abraham now, solid and strong, and a look of satisfaction was on his face. "You're a brave boy. No, a brave man, and you deserve a reward. I'm going to buy you the best bow money can possibly buy."

"Why, that would be wonderful, Father."

Hagar was standing close to her son, soaking up the scene. When her eyes fell on Sarah and Isaac, she smiled at them almost cruelly. It was as if she were saying, *Now we see whose son is the best!*

People in the camp were talking of nothing but Zoltar's attack. Zara said little, for the thought of the huge man dragging her away had frightened her speechless.

The night had come, and she had tried to sleep, but she tossed and was troubled by evil memories of when she was a girl. She could not get the sight of her father being cut down by the huge chieftain out of her mind, and finally she rose, put on her robe, and went outside to sit before her tent.

A chilly air made her shiver, making the night seem cold and menacing. She heard a stirring and turned to see Eliezer. "Not asleep yet?" He sat down beside her, saying nothing for a while, then said, "I know it troubled you, that man coming as he did."

"Yes. I can't forget how he killed my father."

Eliezer was close enough he could smell the faint perfume she always wore. He leaned over until his shoulder touched hers. "You're safe, Zara."

"I don't think any of us are safe. So many things can happen."

Eliezer was shocked at the depth of her fear. She was not a fearful woman, and now he reached out and took her hand. He held it in both of his and felt it trembling. "You'll be all right." He patted her hand and then squeezed it. "I can't afford to lose my little sister."

Zara stiffened. "Eliezer, I'm not your sister! Why do you persist in calling me that?"

"Well, I called you daughter once, and you got upset about that."

"Of course I did. You're not my father, and you're not my brother!"

"I feel like both of them sometimes. What am I to you, then, Zara?"

Zara felt the warmth and the strength of his hand. "You're my friend," she whispered. She turned to him, and he saw tears in her eyes. "You're the best friend I ever had, Eliezer."

"I'm glad you know that." Eliezer sat quietly and waited until Zara felt more at peace. He could sense it as it came to her, for he had learned to read at least some of her moods. Finally he said, "Do you think you can sleep now, or do you want me to sit and talk with you?"

"You don't have to talk, but stay with me for a while."

"Of course."

The two sat there listening to the sounds of the night, and it came to Eliezer that the most peaceful moments he had in his life were times like this when he sat beside this woman. It gave him a warm feeling, and although they said nothing, he felt the goodness, faithfulness, and beauty of this woman next to him.

CHAPTER

31

A faint, wild-scented wind crossed the desert as Zoltar stared up into the bitter black depth of the sky, glaring at the glittering stars. An orange-silver moonlight vaguely diluted the darkness, and the mountains, which lay far away to the east, were solidly black, lending an air of danger and mystery to the scene. The night was cool, but that only affected the outer world. Inside of Zoltar's breast smoldered a heated anger, and only by a force of will did he keep from bursting out and expressing it. Memory of his humiliation at the hands of the Hebrews burned like a white-hot coal, and he seethed with the certainty that only the spilling of blood could wipe out his disgrace. A wild dog lifted a mournful cry far in the distance. Zoltar's ears focused on the sound, listening to it until it faded into the silence. He then picked up a stick and began poking at the fire, sending a shower of dancing sparks swirling upward until they appeared to mingle with the glittering stars overhead. The action brought no relief, and with a vile oath he threw the stick far from him. He watched it cartwheel into the air, throwing off sparks, then fall to the earth, its last glow swallowed by the darkness.

"I'll gather every able man"—Zoltar spoke into the silence, his voice harsh—"and we'll kill every man, old woman, and child in their camp. I'll keep Zara for myself, and we'll make slaves of the rest of the younger women."

Zoltar's flat lips stirred, and from across the fire a small man with sharp eyes and a heavy black beard studied his leader. Zephir was the craftiest of Zoltar's men. He was not the strongest, and in battle he had been known to hang back when the odds were too great. But for planning, Zoltar needed him.

Zephir spoke, his voice as soft as a summer's wind. "Perhaps there should be another way."

"Another way? I've told you how it's going to be."

Knowing his master well, Zephir fell silent for a time. He knew that trying to stop the big man's fury was like trying to stop a raging wind. One had to wait it out. Wait for the proper moment and then plant an idea into Zoltar's head.

Agag had been quiet ever since the fight. He had helped bury their fallen companion, and he had angry thoughts about the death of the man who had been his cousin. He could still hear the hissing sound of the arrow as it sliced the air and heard the deadly clunk as it drove itself through the chest. Agag tried to force the memory away, but cursed with a vivid imagination, he could only relive it in his mind's eye—the frantic grasping at the arrow, the futile attempts to pull it out, and then his cousin's feet drumming a tattoo on the hard earth before he slipped away into that mystery called death.

Agag put the heels of his hands against his eyeballs and pressed, hoping to shut out that vision. Finally he removed his hands and stared at Zoltar. "I think Zephir may have a thought worth considering, master."

Zoltar stared across the flames, his lips growing even more stubborn. "I told you what we're going to do!"

"No doubt we could defeat them," Zephir said quietly.

"Of course we can! And I'll have that one called Eliezer staked out on the ground and let the ants eat him. It could take a long time, and I would enjoy watching that."

Neither man spoke for a time, and then Agag exchanged a fleeting glance with Zephir and nodded slightly. Encouraged, Zephir said, "As I say, we will probably win, but it might be costly."

"Don't be a fool! They're nothing but a bunch of herders!"

"I think that may not be altogether so," Zephir warned cautiously. "You should remember back in the war against Kedorlaomer."

Impatiently Zoltar shouted, "Of course I remember! That's where I got the girl and her mother in the first place. You think I've lost my memory?"

"I know you remember it well, sire," Agag put in. "You remember Abraham, the master of the Hebrews, took a few hundred men and defeated whole armies. They're shepherds all right, but when faced with battle they go into a frenzy."

Zoltar fell silent, and both men waited. Zoltar was an impulsive man, ready to jump into the fire if the mood struck him. It took patience and a willingness to endure humiliation to guide the big man's thoughts along safer paths.

Seeing Zoltar pause, Agag argued persuasively, "It would be a lot safer if we just stole the woman."

"Stole her! You mean right out of the camp?" Zoltar demanded.

"Look, Zephir can follow the camp for a few days. They haven't seen him. We can go back and get more weapons and food supplies and a few more men if we need them."

Zoltar's first impulse was revealed by his gesture. He threw out his hands in an angry fashion, but then memories began coming back. *Those Hebrews were devils with sword or spear or even their bare hands.* He remembered well how the Hebrews had overcome experienced fighters. He also remembered that he had lost a considerable number of men on his last raid and did not need to lose any more. "Do you think it could be done?" he finally demanded.

"Easily! Zephir will go into camp and pretend to be sick. I assure you it will work," Agag said quickly. "Those Hebrews slavishly follow the law of hospitality. When he goes into camp, he will be welcomed and treated well and will have the freedom to learn the ways of the woman, sire."

The two men combined their persuasive powers, and finally Zephir said, "It won't be any trouble. The woman has to be alone part of the time. As soon as I learn of her habits, I'll get word to you."

Zoltar was as changeable as the wind. Only a few moments before he'd been willing to risk the lives of half of his men in a pitched battle against the Hebrews, but now he tossed that idea aside and nodded. "All right, Zephir, you do it."

Zoltar abruptly rose and walked off into the darkness. The other two men put their heads together and arranged for a time and place to meet, where Zephir could give his report.

Finally it was Zephir who said with a sigh of relief, "We would lose too many men in a direct attack. But that's all he thinks about."

"I hope this works. You've got to do your job right," Agag said.

"Don't worry. I'll take care of it."

"You're not eating much, husband."

Abraham looked at Sarah, who had sat down beside him. Smiling, he replied, "I guess I'm not very hungry."

Sarah knew this man better than anyone in the world. He was clearly troubled—it showed in the way his eyelids crept over his eyes and in the tension of his mouth. Another sure sign was his hands, for in moments of stress, he would clasp them together, squeezing them tightly as if that would bring some answers to his mind.

"What's the matter, husband?"

"Nothing really. I feel all right. It's just that sometimes I get discouraged."

"We all do that."

"I've been thinking about all the years I've wandered with my flocks— some of them seem pretty useless. Sometimes I think it's only the little things that matter, Sarah."

"What little things?"

"Oh, I don't know... a little sunlight, a little laughter. I think of the flashing anger in the eyes of a man who hated me. I think of all those years at Ur, seeking after God. Sometimes my life seems like just a series of unrelated scenes that fade out behind me."

"Your life is much more than that." Sarah reached over, and when she touched his hands, he separated them and folded her small hand in his large ones. They were still strong hands, and she leaned against him, joining with his solidness.

"There are good things in the world too," she said. "Songs ... good times ... friends."

"I know." His hands squeezed hers, and he turned to smile at her. "And you are always there for me, never far out of my thoughts." She returned his smile, and the strong touch of his hands as they enfolded hers gave her pleasure. She remembered how all through the long years, he had always been there for her. She well understood what it was like to think at times that life was impossible and very fragile. But she knew this one thing about Abraham of the Hebrews—he might have his moments of quiet despair, but they would not last. She had seen that in him over the years. He had a resiliency like no other man. No matter how difficult things got, his faith would lift him up and enable him to reach out to those he loved, drawing them to him. It was this quality in him she loved as much as anything else.

"I know what's wrong with you," she said.

Abraham's eyes glinted, his mouth turned upward in a wry smile. "You always think you know what I'm thinking. What is it that's worrying me, then?"

"You're worried about Ishmael," she replied simply. She saw his face change and knew that she had touched on the source of his unhappiness. "I know you too well."

The muscles of Abraham's face twitched, and he nodded. "You're right. Did you notice how he changed after he killed that man?"

"Yes. He's only a boy in years, but it wasn't a boy's face . . . it wasn't the eyes of a boy I saw that day—I saw a murderous pleasure in his face. He watched that man squirming on the ground dying, and he actually took pleasure in it."

Abraham sighed. "There's something wrong with him."

Sarah did not argue. She had seen the innate hardness grow in Ishmael. He could be cruel, although at other times he did not show it. "He's not going to be a gentle man, husband."

"Life is difficult, and sometimes a man must be hard," Abraham said, struggling to find a justification for the change in Ishmael.

Sarah just squeezed his hand and said, "Try to eat more. I'll get you some more milk."

Zephir felt a sense of satisfaction as he disappeared behind one of the rolling hills. He was pleased with himself. He had found it almost ridiculously easy to walk into Abraham's camp and pretend to be a sick traveler. As he and Agag had anticipated, the Hebrews stuck to the code of hospitality fervently. Abraham had greeted him and, when Zephir had put on an excellent act of being weak and starving, had commanded that food be brought.

Now as Zephir followed the track of an ancient bone-dry waterway, he smirked, thinking, *No one could have done a better job. I've fooled them all!*

He had made himself at home in the camp for the best part of a week, during which time he had kept Zara under close surveillance. He knew her ways now and had left the camp for his rendezvous with Zoltar. A movement ahead caught his eye, and he lifted his hand and called out. At his cry, Zoltar and Agag appeared along with four other men. *Reinforcements*, Zephir thought.

Zephir greeted Zoltar. "Well, master, good news!"

Zoltar had chosen four of his best warriors, who now gathered around Zephir while Zoltar asked, "You're sure they didn't smoke you out?"

"They're fools. Or perhaps I'm just a good actor." Zephir smirked.

"What about the woman?" Zoltar demanded.

"It'll be easy. She leaves camp every morning and goes to a water hole to get water."

"And guards?" Zoltar said.

"Another woman and just one man go with her."

"Only one man?" Agag grinned. "It should be easy."

"He's nothing but a pup," Zephir said with a shrug.

"All right," Zoltar said. "What time does she go?"

"Early in the morning, just after dawn."

"We'll do it in the morning, then. You follow her. We'll be waiting."

A sickly pleasure touched the flat surfaces of Zoltar's eyes. "We'll see, Zara, who's your master now."

———————

As Zara exited from her tent, she looked up and saw that, although there was a milky breaking of light in the east, the stars were cold and brilliant in the sky. She watched the faint pulses of light diluting the cold blackness of the earth. She loved the stars. They were like glittering gems against the blackness, and she often wondered at the mystery and magnitude of the heavens above her.

"Good morning, Zara."

"Good morning, Miriam." She turned to meet the woman who approached from the east tents. Miriam had become a close friend over the past year, and now Zara said, "You look tired. You stayed up late last night."

Miriam shrugged. "I did at that. You went to bed early."

"Yes. The days have been so hot. It's good to get to enjoy the coolness of the night."

The two women spoke together softly, each of them lifting a large clay pot as they headed out of the camp. They were met by a figure stepping out of the shadows. "Who are these beautiful young women?"

Miriam laughed. "Don't you come making up to me, Benjamin."

The young man walked beside Miriam and, reaching over, took her jar. "Why shouldn't I make up to you? You're the prettiest woman around—" He suddenly remembered Zara and said, "Except for you, Zara."

"So Zara's prettier than I am," Miriam said. "That's not what you told me last night."

The women were amused at Benjamin, who was barely into early manhood. It seemed he was smitten with a different woman each week, and this past week it had been Miriam's turn. "I'm disappointed in you, Benjamin," Zara teased. "You told me not a month ago you would never look at another woman besides me."

"But—"

"And you told me the same thing last night," Miriam jibed. "You're not a man to be trusted."

Benjamin argued vehemently that he was indeed reliable as the three ambled out of the camp, following an old streambed. Zara enjoyed the warmth of the earth under her feet as the sun began to heat the ground. The morning hours were the best for her, and she threw her head back and savored the touch of the air on her face.

"The water is low," Zara said as they came to the edge of the water hole in the middle of the streambed. "I hope it doesn't dry up completely."

"So do I," Miriam said. "I like this spot. I'd hate to have to move."

Zara leaned over and allowed the pot she carried to sink. The gurgling of the water made a pleasant sound, and her mind was on the task when she heard the pounding of running feet. Surprised, she turned, expecting to see someone from the camp, but by the milky light that illuminated the plain, she saw a group of men coming. She could not see their faces at first, but fear shot through her as she recognized one of them. "It's Zoltar!" she screamed. "Run, Miriam!"

Both young women dropped their pots and made a dash at right angles to the riverbed. Benjamin uttered a cry of surprise and drew his sword. He was immediately surrounded, and Zara risked one glance to see one of the men drive his sword all the way through Benjamin's chest. Terror flooded her then, and she put every ounce of her strength into making an escape.

The pursuers had cut them off, however, and Zara felt a hand grab at her. She twisted away only to fall into the hands of another. "Run, Miriam!" she screamed.

Miriam ducked under the outreached arms of one of the attackers. She smelled the sweat and stench of his body as she brushed against him. Then she dashed away back toward the camp. Two men started after her, but Zara saw they were hopelessly left behind.

"Let her go," Zoltar called out. "We'll get away from here." He reached out and grabbed Zara by the hair. "Now you see I've come back for you."

Zara did not speak. She knew the cruelty of this man, and as he dragged her toward the waiting donkeys that two of the other men were holding, she said good-bye to her life. She well knew what Zoltar had planned for her and wished that she had been killed instead of captured.

Eliezer heard the first scream and turned quickly. He had just prepared himself to go out and check the herds when he saw Miriam running frantically. A coldness seized him, and he dashed toward her.

"Miriam, what is it?"

"It's Zara! They killed Benjamin, and they took Zara prisoner!"

"Was it the men who were in camp last week?"

Miriam's face was stretched taut, and she had lost all her color. "Yes, the one called Zoltar. Oh, Eliezer—they killed Benjamin!" she sobbed, dropping to her knees with her head in her hands.

Eliezer straightened up and shouted, "Every man to his animal!"

He turned back and ran to his tent to get his weapons, and when he came out, Abraham was approaching. "What is it, Eliezer?"

"It's Zoltar. He's taken Zara and killed Benjamin."

Abraham's knees buckled and Eliezer ran to hold him.

"I must go now," Eliezer said, "before he kills Zara as well."

Abraham looked up into the face of this man he loved like his own son and saw the hardness in his eyes. "Yes, you must go now. May God be with you. I'll pray that you bring Zara back."

"Thank you, sir." Eliezer nodded and then ran off, shouting, "Get the swiftest beasts we've got! Every man arm himself."

Abraham stood watching as Eliezer gathered his men and rode out furiously, raising a cloud of dust. "O Eternal One, be with Eliezer. Give his heart wisdom and his arms strength that he may prevail."

CHAPTER

32

A brilliant flash of sunlight caused Eliezer to narrow his eyes. He stared eastward, toward a high line of hills that stood like an armed fortress. He studied the peaks and valleys, considering how best to ferret out the enemy lurking in the inhospitable terrain. Sunlight caught brittle flashes of mica particles in the dry, scratchy soil, and heat dropped down from the sky, pressing on Eliezer like a giant weight as he stood pondering his next move. Sweat streamed from his forehead, rolling over his cheeks, and he deliberately threw a brake on his spirit. What he desired more than anything else was to drive his animal straight ahead until he dropped, but caution ruled him as he weighed his options. With his brow drawn taut, fugitive shadows chased themselves in and out of the corners of his mouth, his lips twitching with the strain of what he faced.

The picture of Zara was never out of his mind for long. It lingered there like a fragrance coming from afar, and as he stood there in the full heat of the sun he remembered the last time he had seen her. It had been evening, and they had talked for a long time, walking under the stars. Finally she had given him a smile and touched his chest with the flat of her palm and then whispered good night. The memory came sharply into focus, piercing him with its clarity.

A slight movement to his right caught Eliezer's attention, and he turned his head to see Ishmael, who had come to stand beside him. Excitement glittered in the young man's eyes, and he opened and closed his fists, revealing the tension that was building up in him. "We're never going to catch them like this, Eliezer."

"We'll catch them."

Ishmael shook his head stubbornly. Bright points of light danced in his eyes, and strangely he smiled. A deep wrinkle broke out at the corner of each eye. The glance he gave Eliezer was bright and wise and old, despite his youth. "We're tied down to the slowest animals."

Eliezer moved his head impatiently. He knew this fact as well as Ishmael, but now his voice was harsh as he said, "We don't know how many there are."

"Of course we do," Ishmael said. "By their tracks. There are only half a dozen of them at most."

"You want to move ahead, then, and leave the slow ones behind?"

"Yes, it's what we should have done at first, don't you think?"

As a matter of fact, Eliezer had been thinking along those lines. And now that Ishmael had come to lend credence to his idea, he said, "All right. You and I will go ahead, but it'll be dangerous."

"We'll get them. Come on. Let's go!"

Eliezer gave orders to the others to proceed as quickly as they could. "Ishmael and I are going ahead," he said, grim determination in every line of his body and a steely glint in his eyes.

"I'm going with you too." The speaker was a thin man, not tall, but with hardness in his voice and eyes. "They killed my brother. My beast is as fast as yours, so I'll go with you."

Eliezer nodded. "All right, Eben. That is only right. Let's go. The rest of you follow our tracks and come as fast as you can."

Eliezer glanced ahead where the land heaved away in an irregular monotony. Rocky hills rolled on and on under the strengthening sun. They had just crossed areas of strewn rock, and a powdery dust rose behind them in dotted clouds. Eliezer studied the land before him, moving more slowly now, for the signs were much fresher. His eyes darted from point to point, and he was aware that Ishmael and Eben were doing the same. He knew this country well. It was an area of extremes—bone-searing dryness, interspersed by sudden cloudbursts that would send violent torrents rushing down the narrow canyons. It was a raw, primitive place that scoured the softness out of a man.

Eben pulled his animal up and broke the silence. "They're very close. Perhaps behind that next set of hills."

"I think you're right, Eben." He studied the ground ahead of him and said, "One of us will have to go ahead and locate them, then come back and tell us where they are."

"Let me do that," Ishmael said at once. His eyes glowed, making him look like a fast young animal.

"All right. But don't let yourself be seen."

"I'll be back," Ishmael said, grinning. Then sliding off his animal, he unfastened the water bottle and looped it around his shoulders by a thong and set off toward the nearby hills. He moved swiftly, almost like a running deer, and as he left, Eben shook his head. "He's young, but I never saw a man quicker or crueler when the time for fighting comes."

"We'll wait here for Ishmael to return, Eben. But I don't think we can wait until the other men catch up to us."

"There's no need. The three of us can do it!"

The waiting was hard. Eliezer spoke little, lost in his thoughts, keeping his eyes on the hills ahead. He and Eben had taken shelter under a skinny scrub tree. It did not offer much shade, but it did provide some relief from the heat. Though the sun was approaching the horizon, the air was still fiercely hot. From time to time Eliezer stood up and walked. The anxiety and eagerness in him to come to grips with the raiders was more than he could stand.

Eben watched him pace back and forth and said, "We'll get her back, Eliezer."

"Yes, we will."

"But I can never get my brother back. He was such a fine young man. He had great promise."

Compassion flooded Eliezer at the realization of his friend's loss. He had loved the young man himself, and now he said quietly, "It's hard to lose those we love."

A depression had fallen on Eben, and he said, "We lose everything we love sooner or later."

"But all the more reason to treasure everything that's dear to us every day, every moment."

"That's true. I think now of so many good things I might have done for Benjamin."

"No point thinking thoughts like that. You were good to your brother. Everyone saw it."

"I wish I had been better. I wish I had spent more time with him. I wish it had been me who died instead of him. He was so young and full of life."

The two fell silent then, enduring the desert heat and conserving their strength for the battle ahead. Finally a slight movement caught Eliezer's eyes. "I think he's coming."

The two men stood up, and Eben put a hand over his eyes to shade them. "Yes. That's good. He wouldn't have come back unless he knew something."

Moments later Ishmael came to a halt in front of them. Sweat made a sheen on his tanned face, and excitement stirred his features. He smiled, his teeth making a white slash against the darkness of his skin. "I found them."

"Did they see you?"

Ishmael cast a disdainful glance at Eben for asking such a foolish question. "Of course not." He pointed back toward the close range of hills. "They're down in a gully. There's some water there, a little pool in the riverbed."

"Do they have any guards out?"

"Just one. We'll have to get him first." He spoke quickly, and both of his companions saw the pleasure that the idea of a fight gave him. "We take him out silently and that will leave five more. We sneak in until we're close, and then we take them all."

Eliezer nodded. "It should be dark enough soon."

"Yes," Ishmael agreed, nodding. "The darkness will make it easier for us to sneak up on the guard. Or they may have more out by now."

"All right. Let's move out. They'll be having a meal soon and will be off guard. Prepare to attack!"

The cords cut into Zara's hands. They were tied in front of her so tightly that her hands were white. The other end of the cord was fastened firmly to a stake driven into the ground. She had been out in the blistering sun since midday, with only a small portion of water given to her late in the afternoon. Now as darkness was falling, her lips were dry, and she sat on the hard ground, her eyes turned downward.

Zoltar, who had gone out to check on the guard, now returned. Standing over her, he began to taunt her. "You're a good-looking woman, Zara. I'll sell you, but first I'll enjoy your favors."

Zephir said, "Now is a good time, master."

Always a creature subject to his own desires, Zoltar looked down at the woman. She was wearing only a thin dress, and the sight of her suddenly inflamed his desires. "You're right, Zephir. Come along, my pet."

Zara's heart went cold as she watched Zoltar loose the rope from the stake. He pulled her to her feet and jerked the cord, bringing pain to her wrists. His eyes were bright, and his mouth was twisted in a gesture of lust.

Reaching out, he caressed her, put his hand under her chin, and forced her face up. "Have you ever had a man?" he demanded.

Zara did not answer. Hope was gone. She had been praying that the rescue would come in time, but now she knew what awaited her inside that tent toward which Zoltar was dragging her. She held back, and he jerked at the rope, bringing a cry of pain from her.

"Come along, my little dove. I'll show you what a real man is—" Zoltar did not finish his words. He heard Agag cry out and wheeled quickly to see the small man clawing at an arrow that had gone right through his stomach. Zoltar bellowed to his men, "Kill them! There! They're coming!" He drew his sword and saw two of his men grab up their weapons and engage a figure that had emerged from the gathering darkness. But then he heard the hissing of an arrow, and another of his men fell to the ground, kicking and clawing at the arrow in his throat.

At that same instant a dark shadow appeared before him. He struck out with his sword as he recognized his enemy—Eliezer. With a roar Zoltar began raining blow after blow. He had never encountered anyone who could stand up to him with a sword, and he drove his opponent backward. He was aware of shouting and screams and half expected an arrow to catch him, but he would kill this one before he died!

Zara's hands were still tied, but her heart was crying out with relief. She saw the fight between Zoltar and Eliezer and was sickened to see that Eliezer was getting the worst of it. His chest was bloody, and his left arm was dangling helplessly, the blood running off in crimson streams.

Eliezer knew he was no match for this man. He felt a shock, and his sword was driven from his hand. He heard Zoltar yell in triumph and saw the big man lunge at him.

At that moment everything but the huge figure of his adversary seemed to be blotted out. Eliezer saw the sword rising and knew he had only one chance. His hand dipped to his side, and he came up with the dagger he always carried there. The sword was coming down, but Eliezer threw himself forward, catching Zoltar off guard. The big man had expected him to go backward, but he had stepped inside the swing. The sword hissed through the air and at the same time Eliezer pushed up against the trunklike body of Zoltar. The smaller man shoved his dagger forward, felt it hit bone and grind on it, then forced the blade in clear to the hilt.

Zoltar gave one short cry, then coughed and straightened up. Eliezer was faint from the loss of blood and knew he had no strength left to defend himself. He had seen Ishmael and Eben take down their adversaries, but

Zoltar was still alive. As Eben approached the pair, his weapon drawn, the big man groped for the dagger and tried to pull it loose, but he too had lost his strength. He opened his mouth to speak, and blood burst from his lips, spattering on Eben and Eliezer.

Zoltar straightened, his eyes rolling upward. He turned and took two steps, then his legs lost their strength, and he fell. His fingers grasped at the ground as he struggled to hold on to his life, but it poured itself out on the dry sand, soaking it with crimson blood.

Zara saw Eliezer sinking, and by the time he fell, she was at his side, as was Ishmael. The blood was terrible! "Eben, Ishmael, cut me loose and help me bind these wounds."

Ishmael sliced her ropes, and Eben ripped off his tunic and tore it into strips to bind Eliezer's wounds.

"He's too badly wounded," Ishmael whispered.

"No, he's not! He won't die!" Zara cried.

And there beneath the desert moon, Zara bound the wounds tightly and then took Eliezer in her arms, cradling him like a child. She began to cry out, "O Eternal One, save him. Do not let him die!"

PART SEVEN

THE SACRIFICE

"Take your son, your only son, Isaac, whom you love, and go to the region of Moriah. Sacrifice him there as a burnt offering on one of the mountains I will tell you about."

Genesis 22:2

CHAPTER

33

"Zara, you must rest. You're going to make yourself sick if you're not careful." Sarah had come to bend over Zara, who was sitting beside the still form of Eliezer. She studied the young woman's pale face and saw the lines of strain. "I'll sit beside him. You go lie down."

Zara did not move. It was as if she were asleep, but her eyes were open, fixed on the still form before her. "No, I'm not that tired."

Shaking her head, Sarah paused for a moment, and her mind went back over the three days that had passed since Eliezer had been brought back to the camp, near death. The sword wounds had been deep, and he had lost a great deal of blood. A man named Aaron had sewn up the wounds. He was old, but his hands were still strong and certain. Sarah had watched him sew the torn flesh back together, and when he had finished, the two of them had simply stared at each other. Doubt had flared in Aaron's eyes, and he had shaken his head and left without saying a word.

The noises from outside the tent seemed distant—dogs barking, children shouting, the muffled sound of a man and woman arguing over something—but inside the tent was silence. Sarah gave a compassionate look and then laid her hand on Zara. "I'll be back in a little while and then you *must* rest."

Zara only responded by nodding as Sarah left the tent. She went directly to Abraham, who was standing a short distance away, his eyes lifted toward the east. He turned quickly to meet her and asked at once, "Is there any change?"

"No, I don't think so."

"He can't die." Abraham made the statement with his teeth clenched, as if by his will he could repel death. "I didn't realize how much I loved Eliezer."

"It's when we are in danger of losing people that we realize how very dear they are to us."

"Is there any change at all?"

"Not that I can see. Well . . . perhaps a little. I thought I saw some color in his face. It's hard to tell. He looks so pale—as though there is no blood left in him."

The two stood speaking quietly, exhausted and worn by their long vigil. The thought of losing Eliezer was almost intolerable. As they had watched him lying helpless after Aaron had sewn up his wounds, all strength gone, his chest barely stirring, their hearts had been drained of strength.

"She loves him so much, Abraham."

"We've known for a long time that she is in love with him."

"Yes. She wouldn't let it show before, but it shows now. I don't know what will happen to her if he dies."

"He mustn't die!" Abraham straightened up and whispered, "I'm going out to pray. The Eternal One will help. I know He will."

Sarah watched as Abraham strode purposefully away. She waited until he was out of sight and then went to their tent. She knelt down in the faint darkness and began to cry out within her heart, although her lips were still, *O Eternal One, give us the life of this one we love so dearly. . . .*

───────────

Eliezer found himself suspended in a place with no sound or motion— nothing but an immense impression of space above him, around him, beneath him. He swept through it as though he were on the end of a rope and felt a hot wind brushing his face. Sometimes he was drawn upward into space, rising above the sun, past the stars—then he would fall, fall, fall, until he sank into a place devoid of all light. Once he seemed caught in a storm that tossed him end over end, but then he was floating, as if in the outer darkness, a place without any sense of life.

There were brief moments when, as he drifted in this sea of unconsciousness, he heard voices, felt the touch of hands on his face. The touch was cool and soft and gentle. He strained toward it, wondering whose hand could give such comfort. The coolness only emphasized the heat in his body, the sensations of fire that tried to suffocate him. He yearned for the touch of the hand and for the comfort of the sweet voice that was so soft and gentle. Then he would drift away again into nothingness. Each brief moment of awareness was swallowed all too quickly by the void, and before slipping away again he would despair that he would never know the difference between what was real and what was only in his mind.

Time had ceased to have any meaning. He tried to imagine how long he had been in this place of darkness and burning, but a moment or a year were all the same to him. In one of his more lucid moments, he thought, *I am dead.* The thought neither frightened him nor gave him relief. It was simply there, and he gave himself up to being a shadow. *That's all I am*, he thought. *A shadow among shadows.*

Then, to his surprise, time suddenly began to have meaning again. He did not know how it happened, but he gradually became aware of things other than darkness and the sound of a storm. He realized he was lying on something solid, and he was hearing real sounds. He even began to notice smells, such as the distinct odor of a burning lamp. The oil was smoky and acrid, and he sensed that he was coming out of the dark and lonely place where he had wandered for . . . for as many years as it took to build a huge temple, he thought.

As he stepped out of one world into another, Eliezer realized that his lips and his tongue were dry—so dry he had nothing in his tissues to moisten them with. He tried to lick his lips, but there was no wetness there.

And then the pain came in his chest and along his side. It was a dull throbbing, and when he moved he felt as if someone had struck him with the point of a dagger, slicing through the flesh down to the nerves.

He heard the voice that had come to him many times when he was unconscious. Opening his eyes, he saw nothing at first. The place was dark, except for a small light. Something had come between him and the light. As he blinked his eyes, a face came into focus, and he heard the voice he knew he had heard many times in the void.

"Eliezer, can you hear me?"

"Yes." The word was hard to pronounce through his cracked lips, and he tried to smile, but his lips would not respond. "Zara," he whispered in a voice not his own.

"Here. Take this."

An arm slipped under his head. He felt himself lifted, and the pain slashed at him. But then there was a wondrous coolness, and moisture came to his lips, soaking his dried-up tissues. He guzzled the water avidly, swallowing some while part of it ran down his face, his chin, and onto his chest. Even that felt marvelous. He felt he could never get enough, even if there were a lake or a river of it.

"That's enough. I'll give you some more in a moment."

Eliezer blinked his eyes several times and licked his lips. "Zara?" he said, this time his voice a little stronger. "Is that you?"

"Yes. It's me." He saw her lean forward and put her hand on his forehead and then on his cheek. It was the same hand he had felt before. "Your fever is gone."

Memory came rushing back, and Eliezer recalled the fight amid the rocky hills. "How long . . . have I been here?"

"Four days. You were injured very badly."

He stared at her. There was something important he wanted to say, but he could not think what it was. Instead he asked, "Can I have another drink?"

"Yes. Sip it slowly."

Eliezer sipped very slowly, following her command. When she pulled the cup away she lowered his head again but kept her hand under it. Setting the cup down, she turned and laid her other hand on his cheek. He studied her. His mind worked so slowly it troubled him. He saw tears on her cheeks and tried to think why she was crying. Finally he reached up and touched the tears. "Don't cry," he whispered.

"I can't help it."

Her voice was the same, and her face was the same. Another memory came—this one was of the moment he and the others had burst into the camp. He kept his hand on her cheek, and his voice was almost inaudible. "Did he . . . hurt you, Zara?"

"No. You came in time." He knew she was leaning forward, and he felt the touch of her lips on his. It was the lightest caress possible, and then she laid her head down very softly on his shoulder. He smelled the fragrance of her hair and felt it, but then weakness overtook him, and he sank into sleep. He knew this time he was not descending back to that featureless void, but he could sleep peacefully now, knowing that he had returned to the world of men and women.

———————

His chest itched, but when he came awake enough to scratch it, he found something holding his hand back. It irritated him, and he turned from side to side. The motion caused the pain to stab at him, and when he opened his eyes, he found Zara standing over him holding his arm. "My chest itches," he told her.

"I know, but you mustn't scratch it."

Eliezer felt exhausted, and his lips were rough. He touched them with his tongue, and as he did, he noted that Zara's face was drawn and there were lines he had never seen before. Concerned, he whispered, "Are you sick?"

"No. Just tired. Here, let me get you some more water."

"Let me sit up."

"You're too weak."

"No. I want to."

Zara hesitated, then helped him into a sitting position, his back against a stack of cushions placed against the central pole of the tent. "That feels better," he said. He watched as she poured water from a clay jar into a wooden cup and took the cup when she offered it to him.

"Drink it slowly. Let it soak in," she said.

He obeyed, taking a sip at a time, then paused to say, "There's nothing better in this world than water."

Zara poured more water in the cup. "Keep taking very small sips. We've had a hard time getting you to drink."

He was fully conscious now, and for a time he sipped the water and asked her questions, wondering how long he had been there.

Finally she said, "I need to change your bandages."

"All right."

As she removed the bandages from around his chest and left arm, the sight of his flesh sewn up like a piece of cloth sobered him. "He nearly killed me."

"Yes."

She bathed the wounds carefully and then dabbed on some soothing ointment. She had to reach around him to put on fresh bandages, and as she did so, he touched her hair as it fell down her back. "I've always loved your hair," he whispered.

Zara laughed. "You must be getting well if you can pay compliments to a woman."

He let his hand run down her silky hair, her face very close to his, and a faint memory brushed against his mind. He waited until it grew clear. She was very still as his hand rested on her cheek, and he said, "I remember when you were just a child. No more than ten or twelve. I looked at you and thought how clear and smooth your skin was. It's still the same. You never change, Zara."

Zara knelt beside him, perfectly still. She had suffered through agonies when it seemed as though he would die before her very eyes, but now she could see that the color was back in his cheeks and his eyes were clear. Then he removed his hand, and the moment passed. She asked briskly, "Are you hungry?"

"Starving."

"I'll get you something to eat." She rose and left the tent, and as soon as she was outside, a weakness overtook her. She was blinded by her tears, and her knees felt as though they would not support her. *He's all right*, she thought. *He's going to live!* And she knew that, since he was alive, she too could go on living.

———

"What do you think you're doing?"

"I'm sick of that bed. I've got to do something or I'll take root in there."

Zara glared at Eliezer, who had gotten up and left the tent. She watched as he stood blinking in the strong sunlight. He swayed and put his hand out, and she stepped over and took his arm. "I told you you're not ready to be outside yet."

"Yes I am. I'll go crazy if I stay in there anymore. Help me to walk."

"You must be getting better," Zara said as he put his hand over her shoulder. "You're cranky." She put her hand around his waist, and he leaned on her as they moved in short steps into the camp. As they made their way, everyone came with smiles to wish Eliezer good health. He waved at them, saying to her, "It's good to be alive, Zara."

"Everyone was so worried about you. Especially Abraham and Sarah."

At that moment Isaac came rushing forward, his eyes bright. "Eliezer," he said, "you're well!"

"No, he's not well. He's stubborn, like all men," Zara said crossly.

"Are you mad at him?" Isaac asked, his eyes growing wider.

"She's just being a woman. They like to fuss. You'll find that out."

Zara laughed aloud. "You talk mighty big now that you're able to walk a little."

He smiled at her and said to Isaac, "I had a good nurse."

"When will you be able to take me fishing again?" the boy asked.

"It won't be long."

Isaac continued to pepper Eliezer with questions, so Zara shooed him off, saying, "Go away, Isaac. Eliezer can't go fishing with you for a few days yet."

"He's a fine boy, isn't he?" Eliezer said, conscious of the firmness of her shoulder and of her arm around his waist. A light danced in his eyes as he went on. "I like walking like this. I think I'll always do it this way."

Zara stared up at him in astonishment, and then she saw that he was laughing at her. "You'd like that, wouldn't you?"

"I can't think of anything better. You can keep on feeding me my meals in bed too. That isn't bad."

"You are impossible!" Zara could not keep from laughing.

The two continued their walk until he grew tired. "I guess I'm not as strong as I thought."

"You were badly hurt." She looked up at him, and when his eyes met hers, she said, "I can't tell you how afraid I was, Eliezer. I couldn't bear it if I lost you."

The slight breeze ruffled the edges of her hair, and a tremulous smile tried to form itself at the corners of her lips. He watched the changes of her face, the quickening and the loosening, the small expressions coming and going. She had always had the most expressive face he had ever seen, but then she ceased to smile. Her spirit seemed to brush against him, and a change went over her face he could not understand.

"Is something wrong, Zara?"

A stiff, desperate look changed her mouth, and he watched her tears make bright points in her eyes. "No," she whispered. "I'm fine."

Despite her words, he knew something was troubling her, and when she left him in his tent, he sat there wondering what it was. It had not been an unhappy look, but he felt troubled over it nonetheless. For a long time he sat, until finally he lay back, thinking of her as he fell asleep.

———

The stillness of the night fell over the camp, and Eliezer awoke, aware of the small stirrings and noises that went on even when the camp was asleep. A sudden feeling of joy gripped him. *I'm glad just to be here, to be alive.*

He went to the edge of his tent and saw the moon hanging low on the horizon. It made shadows on the earth and bright patches of light among the trees. The night was a time he loved more than any other. The darkness seemed like a cape thrown loosely over the world, and he felt contentment as he watched the rising moon, a quarter moon painted a dull silver. For nearly an hour he sat there going over old memories in his mind. He went through his past, bringing out memories as a man would bring precious things out of a chest. He held them up and lived them over again. Some of them were so bright and clear, it was almost like going back to the past.

Many of the memories were fleeting, but he discovered the clearest, most vivid, and most pleasing of all were those that involved Zara. As he sat there quietly with the stars beginning to dot the ebony dome overhead, he went back to the time he had first met her, a frightened child—frightened of him as well as every other man. But he remembered how she had lost her fear of him quickly and how she had clung to him as her only solid portion of the world. She had been such a sweet girl, anxious to please, and his heart had gone out to her from the first. He recalled how many times during her growing-up years she had come to him with one of the fears young girls have and how he had been able to comfort her. He continued to review those times, thinking how she had seemingly overnight become a beautiful young woman instead of the leggy girl, awkward and unsure of herself.

His thoughts were interrupted as she appeared unexpectedly to his right, from where her tent was located.

"You're still awake?" she whispered.

"Yes. Can't sleep. Sit beside me."

Zara at once sat down beside him, and he could smell her fragrance. He did not know what she used to make herself smell so fresh and pleasant in this hot climate.

For a long time the two sat there, neither saying anything. Finally he turned and studied her face, which was three-quarters turned toward him as she regarded the camp. He was gripped by the ivory shading of her skin and the gentle turn of her lips. Her black hair was free and cascaded down her back. The silver moonlight spilled over the full, soft lines of her body, and then she turned to him and smiled. A small dimple appeared at the left of her mouth. He admired the will and the pride that showed itself in her eyes, her lips, and her carriage.

As he sat there admiring her, Eliezer felt something begin to grow within him. Part of it was a recognition of how much of his life was tied up in this woman who sat beside him. He knew there was a fire in her that made her lovely, and within her was a rich quality often hidden behind the cool reserve. The feeling grew, and he knew now that he had thought of her as a child for a long time but that this was wrong. Now he saw her as a woman, and he suddenly felt the strange things a man feels when he looks upon beauty and desires it for himself.

Zara turned and looked him full in the face, a provocative look in her eyes. Something had touched her. Her breath came quicker, and color ran freshly across her cheeks. And then, without intending to do such a thing, his mind broke through a barrier that had been there for a long time. It came as a shock to him, and he thought, *Why, I've been waiting for this all my life!* He reached over and took her hand, and then when she turned more fully toward him, he put his hand on her shoulder, turning her to face him. "I nearly died, Zara. I would have if it hadn't been for you."

Zara saw something in Eliezer that brought a stillness to her. She found it difficult to breathe. She had loved this man for so long, yet he had never returned her love in the same way. Now something in his eyes held her, and she knew that what she saw there was not created by her wishful thinking. "What is it, Eliezer?"

Eliezer was basically a lonely man, and as he studied Zara's face, he saw a quiet waiting, as if in anticipation. He stood poised and balanced. The step that he considered could change his life forever, and yet he knew what he had to do. A recklessness came over him, and he reached forward and slowly pulled her to him, waiting for her to resist. If she had, he would have been forever silent about the thing that he felt in his heart. But she did not pull away. He lowered his head and kissed her. Her lips were soft beneath his own, and it was with a shock that he realized, *This is right!*

As for Zara, she sensed Eliezer's desires. She reveled in the strength of his arms and the demand of his lips. She put herself against him, and her arms went around his neck, pulling him ever closer. She had loved him for so long, and now she knew she would never again be to him a small girl or a leggy adolescent but a woman, full of the things a mature woman brings to the man she loves.

Lifting his head, Eliezer whispered, "I love you, Zara, and I want you to be my wife."

The words fell on Zara's ears, and a joy she had never known seized her. She put her hands on his cheeks, holding his face, and said, "Of course, Eliezer. I've always loved you."

And then Eliezer gave a glad cry and pulled her to him. It hurt the wound in his chest, but he did not care. For a long time he simply held her, inhaling the fragrance of her hair. And then he whispered, "I feel like a man who's just come in from a long, tiring journey. You're all I ever want, Zara!"

And then Zara knew that she too had come home. She felt the tears in her eyes and could not speak. She clung to him, knowing this man was hers, and he was all she would ever need.

CHAPTER

34

Eliezer's recovery seemed tied to his joy in his newfound love for Zara. Of course, he quickly realized his love for her was not all that new—rather he had finally released the love he had denied for many years. As the days passed and he grew stronger physically, things began to come together in his mind, and one day he spoke to Zara of the things on his heart.

The two of them were walking along the edges of the small stream that fed the flocks. They both breathed in the spongy odors of spring. The season of renewal had come almost with a single bound, and the two were pleased with the birds, their morning twitter and clatter, their shrill cries and whistle notes. Zara ran ahead and pulled up a tiny yellow flower and came back smiling to share it with him. "It's beautiful, isn't it?"

"Not as beautiful as another thing or two I might mention."

Zara laughed. "I've never seen a man change so much."

"Have I really changed?"

"Yes, and for the better."

Eliezer put his hands on her shoulders and gazed into her eyes. The brook whispered as it fell over rocks, and the sun played a game of hide-and-seek from behind clouds that drifted in from the north. "It doesn't seem to me that I've changed a great deal."

"Oh, you're still the same man—the kindest man I've ever known."

"But you haven't known many men," he said, smiling.

She reached up and pulled his hair. He winced and shook his head. "You've got a cruel streak in you," he said, laughing. "Here I am being romantic and tender, and you pull my hair."

Zara flashed him a brilliant smile. "You'll have to take me just as I am."

"I suppose I will. No other man would have you the way I've raised you. Spoiled to the bone!"

As they walked on, talking foolishly and laughing at nothing, Eliezer said, "We need to marry right away."

Pleased at his eagerness, Zara said, "No, I'm going to make you wait awhile."

"Wait awhile! What for?"

"Well, you've made me wait for years. It won't hurt you to wait a few weeks." She saw the expression in his face and smiled. "Maybe not so long, but we'll have a big celebration. Sarah and Abraham both want to show how much they love us. Especially you."

"All right, but let's not wait too long. I don't think I could stand it!"

Growing up in a land of little water, Isaac loved any kind of it, so he had been excited when Ishmael allowed him to come with him to the river. The two had spent the earliest part of the morning fishing and had caught several small fish. Isaac was often reserved around Ishmael because he did not know his older brother very well, but today he was joyful and talkative.

As the sun rose in the sky, Ishmael jumped up and called out, "Come on. Let's go swimming!"

"Oh no, you go—I don't want to."

"Oh, don't be so quarrelsome, Isaac. Every time I suggest anything, you say no."

"No, I don't. I came fishing with you, didn't I?"

"Well, swim with me now. It'll feel good."

Isaac liked to be near the water but not in it. Ishmael, he knew, was an expert swimmer, but he himself had gone under once six months earlier, and the water rushing into his nose and mouth had terrified him. He still had bad dreams about it.

"You don't have to get out far," Ishmael assured him. "Just enough to cool off."

Isaac continued to resist, and finally Ishmael shouted, "Well, if you're going to be that kind of a baby, you'll not go fishing with me again!"

Taken aback by the young man's threat, Isaac acquiesced. "All right . . . but I don't want to get out very deep."

With a yell, Ishmael plunged into the water, and Isaac stepped in with trepidation. He waded out as far as his knees and then sat down. He had to admit the water did feel good. It was cool, and he splashed and watched as Ishmael swam energetically back and forth in the river.

Ishmael headed toward Isaac and said, "You need to learn how to swim."

"No, I don't want to," Isaac said, shaking his head vigorously.

"Come on," Ishmael said, a gleam in his eye. "You can't swim in knee-deep water." He grabbed Isaac and started dragging him out toward the center of the river. It was not a particularly fast river, but there were deep holes in it. Isaac began to cry and begged Ishmael, "Please let me go! I'm afraid of the water."

"You'll never get over your fear if you don't throw yourself into it. Come on. You'll be all right. I'm right here."

Isaac protested vigorously, but Ishmael dragged him into the deeper water until the older boy himself was chest deep. "Now just lie on your back and float. I'll hold you up."

Isaac was petrified that he couldn't touch bottom. The water flowed around his face, spilling into his mouth as Ishmael held him up. "Please, Ishmael, take me back to the shore."

"No, you have to learn to swim. Here—" Ishmael reached down and caught Isaac under the knees and brought him up. The water splashed into Isaac's face and went into his nose, and he gasped. "Please take me back!" he cried.

"Don't be such a baby. See? You float." He laughed, and there was a triumphant note in the sound. "Now I'm going to let you go."

"No, don't—" Isaac panicked as he felt Ishmael's hands disappear. He sank at once and struggled to get his footing, but the water was over his head, and he held his breath until he splashed to the surface and then gurgled, "Ishmael, help me!"

Ishmael, however, paddled away from Isaac, letting him flounder. "You're all right," he shouted. "Just paddle your arms and kick your feet."

By now Isaac had lost all sense of reason. His head dipped again, and as he sucked water into his lungs, black terror filled him. He tried to scream, but the water choked him, and he could only flounder.

"Ishmael!"

Ishmael turned to see Zara and Eliezer, who had come to the edge of the river. He saw the fury on both of their faces and then Zara plunged into the river, calling Isaac's name. Ishmael's face turned pale, and at once he made a wild grab for the younger boy. He caught Isaac's arm, pulled him up, and struggled to get the boy's head above water. He backstroked toward shore, pulling Isaac by his head and shoulders. By the time they neared the shore, Zara was there grabbing for Isaac.

"He's all right," Ishmael cried out quickly.

"All right? He was drowning, you fool! Were you trying to kill him?"

Ishmael protested. "We were just swimming."

Zara paid him no heed, and when he tried to help her lift Isaac, she shoved him back. She turned to Eliezer, who was beside her now, and the two of them pulled the choking, gagging boy toward shore. They pulled him onto the bank, and Zara made him lie on his stomach. Her eyes were filled with anxiety as she pushed at the back of his shoulders.

After spitting up water, Isaac gasped and shuddered, then lay panting and quietly crying.

"Are you all right, Isaac?" Zara asked quietly into his ear.

Isaac started to speak, and then he saw Ishmael, who had come to stand close. He turned and grabbed at Zara. "Don't let him put me in the river again, Zara!"

"I won't. Ishmael, get out of here!" Zara demanded.

"You can't tell me what to do," Ishmael said sullenly.

Eliezer stepped forward and grabbed Ishmael by the arm. He was still weak from his recent injuries, but even so, his hands were strong. "You heard what Zara said—and you can be sure that I'm going to tell your father about this. I hope he beats you until you bleed! Now, get out of here!"

Ishmael flushed. "You can't talk to me like that!"

"Oh yes I can." Eliezer shoved the young man away, and Ishmael stumbled back, sprawling on the ground. He staggered up, his eyes flaring with anger, his face suffused with blood. He did not speak, but a murderous fury was clearly delineated on his face. He whirled and ran away without another word.

"He's gone now, Isaac. You don't have to be afraid," Zara said, holding the boy and smoothing his hair. "It's all right."

"I don't want to be around him anymore. I'm afraid of him," Isaac cried, clinging to Zara.

"You don't have to be afraid, Isaac," Eliezer said. "Just stay away from him. I'll have a word with your father. That'll put a stop to it."

―――――

Abraham stared at Zara, noting the anger in her face. He had listened as she and Eliezer told him what had happened.

"I can't believe Ishmael meant any harm," Abraham said quietly.

"I think Isaac would have drowned if we hadn't come upon them," Eliezer said. He wanted to say more, but the stricken look on Abraham's face gave him pause. This was a man he loved more than any other man on earth. He knew also of Abraham's great love for both his sons.

"Ishmael is just rough," Abraham said. "He doesn't realize how strong he is."

"No, it's more than that," Zara protested. Ordinarily she would never have dreamed of confronting Abraham, whom she revered greatly. "If you had been there, sir, you would feel as I do. You need to keep those two separated."

Abraham sighed. "How can I do that?"

"You must find a way," Zara said and then fell silent, knowing she could say no more.

"My advice is that you give Ishmael a good caning," Eliezer said.

"But—"

"I know you love him, but he's got a wild streak in him, and he needs to be brought up short. And I agree with Zara. Don't let the two of them go out alone together."

Unconvinced, Abraham finally said, "I'll have a word with Ishmael. I'm sure it was just one of those accidents that happen when boys play together."

Zara cast an incredulous look at Abraham. She could not believe Abraham would ignore such a plain, blunt warning! Without a word she turned and left the tent.

Sarah, who had been listening to all of this, waited until the two had left and then said, "They're right, husband."

Abraham turned toward her, deep pain in his eyes. "I just can't believe Ishmael would deliberately try to harm Isaac."

Sarah then said firmly, "He *is* too rough, husband. I have worried about it many times. I want you to forbid him to take Isaac anywhere alone."

Abraham bowed his head and said heavily, "All right, Sarah. I will do that much." He turned away, shoulders bowed, but Sarah was not happy. She knew Hagar's disposition well, and it was clear to Sarah that she had passed on what was in her character to Ishmael. He was Abraham's son, but it was Hagar's blood that controlled this wild boy.

CHAPTER

35

Sarah was delighted when the two told her and Abraham of their desire to marry and Eliezer boldly declared his love for Zara. Sarah embraced them both, laughing with pleasure.

Abraham was equally pleased, chuckling as he teased Eliezer. "She's been bossing you around since she was a child, so she ought to make a good wife." Then he gave them his blessing and said, "You will probably be wanting to go into business for yourself now."

Abraham smiled at Eliezer's reply. "No, master, I will always serve you."

Tears dimmed Abraham's eyes, and he hugged the young man fervently. "You are another son to me, Eliezer, indeed you are!"

Everyone noticed a change in Eliezer after he and Zara had agreed to marry. He had always been a fair man, but he had also tended to be silent much of the time. Most attributed it to his being a deep thinker. "There's no telling what goes on in that head of his," people would say.

But now there was a lightness, almost a frivolity, about the steward of the house of Abraham. He made jokes and laughed and played games with the children in a way he never had before.

As for Zara, she felt she had found a new life. When she awoke in the morning, her first thought was of Eliezer, as was her last thought at night. Many times she would steal away from camp, find a quiet place, and kneel down to thank the Eternal One for bringing Eliezer into her life. She had developed a deep love for the God of Abraham—as had Eliezer—although neither she nor Eliezer had ever heard His voice or seen Him in a vision. Still, their faith was strong, for they had witnessed miracles and heard the stories Abraham told of his ancestors who had served the Eternal One.

Often, when the two were alone together, Eliezer would tease Zara in a way she pretended to dislike but actually enjoyed. She was sitting alone one morning outside of her tent, having finished her cooking, thinking with pleasure of her coming wedding day. He came by and asked, "What are you doing?"

"Just thinking."

"I always hate to see a woman think."

"Why would you say a thing like that?"

"Oh, it gives a woman notions when she starts thinking. And those can be dangerous!"

"I've got a right to think the same as you have!"

He continued to tease her and finally picked up a mirror she had brought out from the tent to polish. It was made out of highly polished brass, and he held it up and stared at his face. He was quiet for so long that she finally said, "What are you staring at?"

"At myself," Eliezer said. His face was solemn, and he shook his head in wonder. "I just don't understand it."

"You don't understand what?"

"I don't understand how you ever persuaded a handsome fellow like me to marry you. My heavens"—he shook his head and stared at his reflection with admiration—"I *am* a handsome man!"

Zara shrieked, jumped up, and began beating on his shoulder. "Why, you awful man!"

"Wait a minute, now. You're always telling me how handsome I am. I'm just agreeing with you."

They both burst out laughing. Still holding the mirror, he reached around her and pulled her close. She willingly rested her face against his chest. "Yes, you *are* handsome," she murmured.

She lay still in his arms, and Eliezer savored the moment, brushing his hand over her hair. "You know I love the simple things in life. I love just standing here with you. Nothing to do. No problems. Just standing here, holding you in my arms. That's what I'm going to do for the rest of my life."

Zara loved to hear him talk like this. He had a poetic fancy that he had kept bottled up all his life, but now that he was in love, he could no longer contain it.

"We'll starve," she said. "You have to work."

"We'll just live on love," he said, stroking her cheek.

To Eliezer's surprise Zara laughed and grabbed his hair, shaking his head gently. "No, you have to work hard and buy me lots of beautiful clothes and rings and copper bracelets. I'm going to be a very demanding wife."

"And I'm going to be a very demanding husband," he said. He pulled her forward, held her body against his, and kissed her thoroughly. "Very demanding," he whispered.

————————

Planning the wedding celebration was a joy for Sarah. She insisted that it last for several days, and on the first days she drove all the servants so hard they protested. They made dozens of loaves of solet bread. Olive oil was freshly pressed, wine was strained, and wild game, a sheep, and two cows were slain to provide the meat for the wedding feast.

A large tent, used only for special occasions, was erected and hung with colorful awnings, then lit inside and out by dozens of earthenware lamps on tripods. Thick porridge prepared with sesame oil and lentils was set to boiling in huge pots, and large platters were filled with sprouts of cabbage palm, radishes, and cool cucumbers. Goat's milk and wine hung in great earthenware jars. Old family treasures were brought out for serving the feast—copper basins, milk vessels, goblets—and as the meal went on, the prospective bride and groom sat on a low stool especially made for two. When the porridge was served, Eliezer dipped out a large spoonful for Zara. "There," he said, holding the cow's-horn spoon to her mouth. "I always wanted a fat wife. Eat all you can hold."

Zara's laughter at his antics and her sparkling eyes made her even more radiant in her new dress she had been saving for a special occasion. Made of a shiny blue-green material, it caught the reflection of the lamps as she moved. Her eyes followed Eliezer wherever he went, and she was hardly aware of the celebrations going on around her.

Throughout the days of celebration there was feasting, and those who were gifted in song entertained those who had no such gift. Some of the wives and daughters and servant girls joined together in a hymn of praise for a great harvest. It was actually a song to an idol, which Abraham frowned upon, but he could not deny that their singing was beautiful. They created a web of sound with their voices, as if they were weaving together a garment with all the colors of the rainbow.

After they had finished, the men applauded and shouted their approval, and more singing and storytelling followed. As the week's festivities grew to a close, Eliezer's eyes met Zara's. "You're beautiful," he said simply. "And you'll always be beautiful to me."

"Even when I'm fat?" she teased.

"Even then."

"Even when I'm old and wrinkled?"

"Your beauty comes from the inside, Zara," he murmured. "And that will never change."

She reached forward and touched his face, tears brimming in her eyes, then spilling over. She could say nothing, but joy filled her as fine wine fills a cup.

———————

Hagar had long ago learned how to put on a face to hide what was in her heart. The wedding celebration was as bitter an experience as she had ever known, for although she would have died before admitting it, she had always felt a desire for Eliezer. Now as the days of feasting came to a close and she stood and watched the simple ceremony that made the two husband and wife, the bitterness and rage in her boiled over. She waited until the ceremony was over and then forced herself to stand before the pair, who were surrounded by well-wishers. She met Eliezer's eyes and smiled. "I hope you will be very happy." Then turning to Zara, she said, "May you have many children."

"Thank you, Hagar," Zara said. She tried to feel some warmth toward the woman, but she was still convinced that there was cruelty in her.

Eliezer watched as Hagar turned to leave and then shook his head. "She's a sad woman," he whispered.

Zara answered, "Yes, she is. She really has nothing to love."

"Except Ishmael."

Zara nodded. "Yes, she has Ishmael."

———————

For a week after the wedding, Zara and Eliezer learned what it meant to be a husband and wife. Hearing other women talk about the marriage night had made Zara a bit apprehensive, but Eliezer, for all his strength, was a gentle man, and by the time the week was over, she met him with a full passion of her own.

As for Eliezer, he was happy in a way he had never dreamed possible. Each day they awoke and found a new joy in simply being together. Abraham had insisted that he turn all of his duties over to the chief herdsman for a few days so they could get away by themselves, and Eliezer had not argued.

When they arose the morning after their return to camp, Zara fixed a special meal for him. He loved roasted kid seasoned with fresh herbs, and Zara had taken care to prepare it just as he liked. She sat down with him as he ate heartily, especially enjoying the plums and raisins soaked in wine.

"I think *I'm* going to be the one who'll get fat," Eliezer said, laughing. "You're a wonderful cook, wife."

Zara loved it when he called her "wife," as he often did. She knew some husbands never showed affection to their wives, at least not in public, but it had pleased her to learn that, like Abraham, he did things quite naturally that other men would have considered a weakness. For instance, as they were walking, he would take her hand and hold it, pressing it from time to time. It was a small thing, but it made her love him more strongly than ever.

"What shall we do today?" Eliezer asked.

"I need to go out and gather some more herbs. If you're going to eat like this, we're going to need a good supply."

"All right. We'll go now."

As the two were leaving the camp, Eliezer whispered, "They're making fun of us," nodding toward two of the shepherds who were laughing openly at them.

"Why are they laughing?"

"I suspect they know what we've been doing."

Zara flushed, and her chin went up. "Let them mind their own business."

"Exactly what I say. Come along. I'll race you to that big rock over there."

They raced to the rock, laughing and holding hands, then slowed down and wandered over the countryside, searching out the watered spots where they might find the herbs they were looking for. They stopped to take a drink from a stream, and Zara said, "Look, my bag's almost filled."

"Better go home, I guess."

The two turned and started homeward. He took her on a roundabout way, wanting to show her the new cattle he had traded for recently. They were cresting a low hill when Eliezer stopped, uttered a cry of shock, and raced forward.

"What is it?" Zara cried, and then she saw.

Just ahead, down in a natural basin, she saw Isaac and Ishmael and wondered what they were doing together out near the herd. A large bull of a dull red color lifted his sweeping horns toward the boys as they approached the animals. He lowered his head in warning and started toward them.

Then Zara witnessed a scene she knew she would never forget as long as she lived. Ishmael grabbed the six-year-old boy by the arms and held him in the bull's path. Isaac kicked and screamed, trying to escape as the bull picked up speed.

Eliezer dashed madly across the open space to intercept the huge animal. He still had not completely recovered from his wounds, but he forgot all that.

Even while straining every nerve, he could see that Ishmael was holding the boy facing the bull, and Isaac was crying and struggling to free himself.

Finally Ishmael shoved the boy forward and, wheeling, dashed away, leaving Isaac in the bull's path.

The bull was charging full speed now, running directly at the boy, who was struggling to get up. Putting forth every ounce of strength he had, Eliezer began to yell. His only hope was to catch the bull's attention. He knew that bulls like this had a habit of charging straight on and not turning aside, but he yelled anyway and saw the bull turn his head. He continued to run and scream, and the bull wheeled around and started straight for him.

Eliezer cut at a right angle from the bull's path, leading the animal away from Isaac. He caught a glimpse of Zara, who was headed toward the boy.

He circled, leading the bull back, dodging in a zigzag pattern to confuse the animal. He finally picked up a fist-sized rock and stood still. In its confusion the bull swung its massive head around, looking in all directions, then spotted Eliezer and charged him. When the bull was close enough, Eliezer yelled and threw the rock, striking the bull on the nose. Blood gushed forth, and the bull stopped and shook his head. Picking up another rock, Eliezer threw and struck again. This time it landed on the beast's cheekbone. Snorting, the bull turned and trotted back toward the herd.

Assured that they were now safe, Eliezer ran to Isaac and Zara. Ishmael was nowhere to be seen.

"Well, that was a close one, wasn't it, son?" He knelt down by Isaac, who was cradled in Zara's arms, and wiped the tears from his cheek. The boy's face was pale, and he was shaking so badly he could not answer. "Here," Eliezer said, picking the boy up. "Let's go back." Isaac threw his arms around Eliezer's neck and clung to him fiercely.

They returned to the camp in silence, the grim set to their faces speaking of their firm resolve not to let Ishmael get off so lightly this time.

"I'm sorry that I have to tell you these things, master, but it happened exactly as I described. Ishmael deliberately put Isaac into the path of that bull."

"Eliezer's right, and it's not the first time he has placed him in harm's way," Zara said. "We tried to tell you before how he almost drowned him."

Sarah had been listening to all this silently. She saw her husband's face contort and knew that this time there could be no mistake. Sitting beside Abraham, she grasped his garment until he turned to face her. "Do we have to lose our son, the child of promise, in order for you to learn what's in Ishmael's heart?"

Abraham began to tremble. He was a strong man, but his hands were unsteady. He looked down at them, unable to speak.

"If you let Ishmael stay here, he'll kill Isaac." Then in a high-pitched wail, Sarah cried, "Cast out the bondwoman and her son!"

The strength in her voice and the fire in her eyes shocked Abraham, and he looked at her for a long time without speaking. Finally he nodded, his mouth pinched into a white line. "Yes," he whispered. When he arose, his shoulders were drooping, and his feet stumbled as he left the tent.

Sarah began to weep. "He loves Ishmael."

"I know he does," Eliezer said, "but Ishmael and Hagar must go."

"It was my idea for her to have a son by Abraham," Sarah whispered. "It was the worst mistake I ever made in my life."

Hagar stared at Abraham when he came to her tent. She took one look at his eyes and knew that all was lost. Fearfully Ishmael had told her what had happened, knowing that she would find out soon enough, and now he stood behind her, unable to say a word.

"I would have kept you here forever," Abraham said, "but I must protect my younger son. The two of you must leave."

Hagar did not argue. She had known for some time that it might come to this, so she asked simply, "Where will we go?"

Abraham said, "I cannot decide that. I will give you money. Now come and get provisions."

"You mean we have to leave now, Father?" Ishmael said. And then he stood up straighter, his eyes hard. "You're casting us off?"

"You've cast yourself off, Ishmael," Abraham said, glaring. He waited for the young man to speak, but Ishmael said no more. "Come. I will see that you have food and water."

After they had gathered the necessary provisions, Abraham accompanied Hagar and Ishmael out of sight of the camp. Now he stood silently, looking at the pair.

Hagar turned to him and whispered, "You never loved me."

Still Abraham remained silent. He held her eyes for a moment, then turned to meet Ishmael's gaze. "This is not my choice. It is yours, Ishmael."

In a flash of anger Hagar whirled and shouted, "You'll regret this! My son will become a great man. We will have our revenge on you and all your people! Come, my son."

Abraham stood his ground and watched as the two walked steadfastly away, tears streaming down his cheeks at the pain his choices had brought to so many. Not once did either Hagar or Ishmael look back, and when they had disappeared over a rise, Abraham heard again the voice of the One he loved more than life itself.

"Abraham, do not be so distressed about the boy and your maidservant. Listen to whatever Sarah tells you, because it is through Isaac that your offspring will be reckoned."

Abraham stood long and listened to the voice that spoke to him. It was a voice filled with comfort, and Abraham, who had thought that nothing could comfort him, found that the Eternal One was indeed able to do all things. He knew he had brought this on himself, but even so, the voice carried no tone of censure, no condemnation. Abraham heard nothing but love, and he fell on his face and cried out, "O Eternal One, you are the strong God, but you are also the God of goodness and mercy."

CHAPTER
36

Two oil lamps cast an amber corona of light over the interior of the tent. They twisted the shadows into tortured shapes, shedding yellow, flickering beams on the carpet and walls of the tent. Abraham's face looked worn, for the lamplight deepened the shadows of his eyes and the hollowness of his cheeks and made the lines of his face more apparent.

The boy who sat across from him had none of these, for at the age of fourteen, Isaac's face was smooth, his eyes clear, his features showing traces of his mother's beauty. He studied the game board in front of him carefully, then reached out and moved one of the pieces. He looked up and laughed. He had a good laugh, in keeping with his name, which meant "laughter." His skin was olive but fairer than most boys of the tribe, more like his mother's in her youth. His voice was high and clear. "I've beaten you again, Father!"

Abraham looked down at the board and shook his head as if he had just awakened from sleep. He searched for a way to extricate himself, then had to concede that he was indeed trapped. His lips turned upward in a smile, and he shook his head. "You ought to be ashamed of yourself, Isaac. Beating your old father like that!"

Isaac's face softened and he said gently, "Well, you're not thinking about the game, Father. You're thinking about Zara."

Sarah, who sat holding Zara's one-year-old infant, smiled at this. Isaac had all the qualities that she most admired in a man—gentleness, goodness, compassion. *He can't even stand to beat his father in a silly game,* she thought. Suddenly a sigh caught her attention, and she looked down to see Zara's sleeping three-year-old daughter curled up on the floor. Looking at the little girl's lovely face highlighted by the glow of the oil lamp, Sarah spoke her thought. "These girls are the very image of their mother."

Abraham turned away from the board and studied the two children. "You're right," he said. A glow of humor touched his eyes, and he said, "And it's a good thing they take after their mother. She's a lot better looking than Eliezer."

Isaac spoke up. "I don't think Eliezer's ugly, Father."

"No, of course not. But these girls here, they're going to be beauties just like Zara."

Isaac turned his head at the sound of a woman's cries of agony coming from a nearby tent. "Are you worried about Zara?" he asked Abraham, and then his eyes went to Sarah, as they always did. She and Isaac were very close, and she understood what he was asking.

"Giving birth is always a dangerous matter, son. Many women die bringing new life into the world."

Isaac grew thoughtful as the two adults watched him. He had a way of thinking things over. One could almost hear his mind working. He was not quick to speak, as a rule, but he often asked very difficult questions.

"Why does having a baby have to be so hard on a woman, Mother?"

Sarah blinked with surprise. She glanced at Abraham, who was waiting for her answer, his hand covering his mouth. She knew that he was smiling at her, but this didn't trouble her. "I don't know, son."

This answer did not satisfy Isaac. "I don't see why everything can't be different."

"What do you mean by different?" Abraham asked.

Isaac struggled to put into words what was troubling him. He looked up and met his father's eyes. "Why are some things in this world so beautiful and some so terrible?"

Abraham shook his head in wonder. "Men have been asking that question for thousands of years, son."

"And women too," Sarah added, rocking the sleeping child back and forth. "The world is not what God intended it to be, son. He made it good, but people sinned and brought pain and suffering into the world, spoiling His perfect creation."

"Well then, why doesn't God just destroy everything bad and make everything good again?"

Abraham folded his hands and leaned forward. He began to speak earnestly, as to an adult. His son was young in years, but he had been asking questions since he had learned to talk. At first they had been simple ones, but as the boy grew they became more and more difficult, framing problems that the seers of all nations in all generations had struggled with.

"You've heard me tell the stories as they came down to me from my grandfather. He got them from his father, stories that had been passed down through generations."

"Yes, Father, but don't those stories tell of how God destroyed the world with a flood because it was so evil?"

"Yes, they do."

"Then everyone in the world goes back to Noah."

"That's right. You've learned your lesson well, Isaac."

"But then if God destroyed all the evil, why is it still here?"

Abraham sighed and struggled for an answer. "I think because when our first father sinned, something in him changed, and he somehow passed that on to his sons."

"Yes—I remember the stories. Cain killed Abel, and then Adam and Eve had another son, Seth."

"That's right. And all of our line comes down through Seth, the more righteous of the sons of Adam. Nevertheless, the descendants of Adam all had evil in them, and they spread it again throughout the earth, even after the flood."

Isaac sat listening as Abraham talked, but when his father fell silent, Isaac said, "When the first man sinned, I wonder why the Eternal One didn't just destroy him and start all over with another good man."

"No one can answer that question, son. The Eternal One does what He chooses, and we mustn't question it." He leaned forward and took the medallion he had worn all his life from beneath his robe. He rubbed it with his thumb and studied the lion with the uplifted paw and the fierce, noble face, wondering what it all meant. For a long time he remained silent, then said, "I think that someday one is coming who will be what the first man, Adam, should have been. And he will set all things right again. There'll be no more ugliness in the world or injustice or sin."

Sarah watched as Abraham continued to speak. Her eyes fell on the medallion, and she wondered if Isaac would be the next to wear it.

A cry came from outside, and Isaac rose and flew to the door of the tent. "It's Eliezer!" he cried. He stepped back in as the tall form of Eliezer entered.

Sarah saw the relief on his face and cried out, "Is the child here?"

"Yes." Eliezer had to keep himself from shouting. He had such joy on his face, they did not need to ask if all was well.

"Come and see our son," Eliezer said, his face beaming. He reached over, picked up his sleeping daughter, and left the tent.

Sarah tried to get up, but the child she was holding was heavy.

Isaac reached out to take the baby. "Let me carry her, Mother."

As Sarah surrendered the child, a warmth grew in her heart over Isaac's concern. It pleased her that her son loved all children—especially the daughters of Eliezer and Zara.

Sarah stepped out of the tent, and Abraham took her by the arm, making their way as quickly as their old legs would carry them to Zara and Eliezer's tent. Eliezer had arrived ahead of them and was now kneeling by his wife and baby. Sarah moved closer and saw that Zara was exhausted, her face pale and wan. Yet she had a beautiful smile.

"Let me hold my son," Eliezer whispered. He took the child, and the three visitors moved forward, gathering around to stare down into the red face of the infant.

"Why, he looks like you, Eliezer," Isaac said.

"That's right," Abraham said. "I can see he's going to be a fine, strong man just like his father."

While Isaac and the men admired the infant, Sarah went to Zara and kissed her, whispering, "You've done so well. What will you call him?"

Zara smiled as her eyes went to the baby. "His name is Zani."

Abraham had taken his turn holding the infant. " 'Gift from God,' " he said, smiling. "What a wonderful name!"

Eliezer had gone over to kneel again beside Zara. He put his arm around her and kissed her on the cheek. "You did so well. Thank you for giving me such a fine son."

Zara touched Eliezer's cheek and said fervently, "I hope he's as good a man as his father!"

The sun had already gone down when the moon made its appearance, a pale globe in the sky. It was five months after Zani's birth. Sarah looked up at the moon and turned to Abraham, who was sitting beside her outside their tent. "Last night I was holding Zani," she said, "and he saw the moon."

Abraham turned to her with interest on his face. "That's an observant young fellow. He's growing so fast."

"Yes," Sarah said. "He's a beautiful boy. I was looking at the moon, and suddenly I saw his eyes focus. And you know what he did?"

"What?"

"He reached for the moon, just as if he could reach out and grab it in his hand."

Abraham chuckled. "I guess I've been doing that myself for a long time."

Sarah smiled. "I think you've been reaching for something as long as I've known you. Probably even before."

Abraham took her hand. "Well, I don't have to reach anymore. I have you, and I have the son God promised."

He would have said more, but suddenly there was a sound of an animal approaching. There was still enough daylight left to see a traveler come to the edge of the camp and dismount. He was immediately challenged by the guard and stopped. Abraham and Sarah could hear the voices, then could see the guard wave the traveler on into the camp. They watched as the tall man strode purposefully toward them.

"Who could that be coming this late?" Sarah asked quietly.

"I have no idea."

They could not make out the man's face, but finally he came to stand before them, and a shock ran through them both.

"Ishmael!" Sarah uttered.

Abraham was so surprised he found it difficult to speak. Ishmael was robed in a thin black garment with a black turban wrapped around his head. His eyes had always been deep set and sharp, but now they were like the eyes of an eagle. Strength was in every line of his body, and for just an instant both Abraham and Sarah felt a touch of something close to fear. This son of Abraham's was so vital and strong he could be dangerous.

Abraham rose, as did Sarah. "Welcome, my son. Come in. You must be hungry and tired after your journey."

Ishmael bowed low and said, "Father, it's good to see you." He turned to Sarah and studied her briefly and smiled. "It's good to see you also, mistress."

Sarah raised her voice, and a servant appeared. She commanded that food and drink be brought, and Abraham invited Ishmael into the tent. Sarah helped with the meal while the two men talked. When the food was ready, she set it before Ishmael. Abraham was not hungry, so the couple simply sat down across from him as he ate. At Ishmael's request, Abraham told him about various members of the tribe. When Ishmael had finished his meal, a servant carried away the plates. Ishmael took the cup of barley beer, drank it down, then nodded, saying, "The food was good. I was hungry."

Abraham hesitated, then said, "I have heard, my son, that you have done well—that you have a family now and that many are joining your clan."

"Yes, Father, that is true." Ishmael looked at Abraham with a question in his eyes. "Are you well, Father?"

"Yes. Sarah and I are very well."

"And Isaac. Is he well too?"

An instant's hesitation revealed Abraham's agitation over the circumstances leading to Ishmael and Hagar's dismissal from the camp. He could not read anything in Ishmael's eyes, so he finally said, "Yes, very well."

Ishmael nodded. "That is good. I am glad."

Sarah raised her voice and asked the question that was on her mind as well as on Abraham's. "How is your mother, Ishmael?"

"She is dead."

The blunt announcement brought a pang of grief to Sarah. During the last years Hagar had been with them, there had been much trouble, and Sarah had grown to hate her. But she remembered how kind Hagar had been to her in Egypt, and she whispered, "I am so sorry. When did she die?"

"Only a month ago. She caught a fever and could not get rid of it."

Abraham was silent. "She was a strong woman," he said. Then he cleared his throat and spoke the question that was most on his mind. "Son, did your mother ever forgive me?"

Ishmael dropped his head, unable to meet his father's eyes. "She was not a forgiving woman, Father."

"I'm sorry to hear it." Abraham knew he had one more question that he must ask. "And you, my son, have you forgiven me?"

A silence fell over the tent, and both Abraham and Sarah waited tensely for Ishmael's answer. They were both relieved when he looked up and managed to smile. "I hated you for sending us away. I couldn't help that. But I've gained a little wisdom in the years since."

His comment took away the weight that had been on Sarah's heart for years. Ever since Ishmael had left, she had been afraid that he might return to seek vengeance. Now she saw that the big man had changed.

"I had bitterness in my heart over being cast off, but it was right to make us go. If I had stayed, I might have done something terrible."

"It was one of the most difficult things I ever had to do," Abraham said, "and I know it hurt you."

Ishmael was silent for a time and then turned his head to one side. "A woman of my tribe was holding a block of wood while another was splitting it with a sharp ax. The ax missed and cut off her finger. She picked it up and held it to the stub and quickly they bound it together." He smiled and said, "It grew back. It was not as flexible as the others, and there was always a white ring where the finger grew together. So she never quite forgot it, but at least she had her finger. I suppose," he said, "I will always remember our disagreements. But it has become bearable. It was the right thing to do."

Relief washed through Sarah, and she rose, saying, "I will go prepare a place for you, Ishmael."

"No, don't do that." Ishmael rose, his large frame filling the tent. "I came only to do what I have done." He knelt before his father and said, "Please give me your blessing, Father."

Abraham's hands trembled as he touched Ishmael's head, but he was happy to pray for him and bless him.

When Ishmael rose, he said, "Isaac is the son of promise. You did the right thing in sending me away. Good-bye, Father." Ishmael turned to Sarah and said, "Good-bye, mistress." Then he left the tent and walked purposefully away, disappearing into the gathering darkness.

Sarah found herself relieved but trembling. It had been a tense moment. "He's such a strange man!"

"Yes, and a violent man too. Some of that is still in him."

"I'm glad Isaac is not like him. He has a natural gentle spirit."

"Like you," Abraham said, putting his arm around her.

She leaned against him and whispered, "God Most High has given us a precious gift in our son."

"Yes, wife, and as long as I have Isaac, I will never doubt the Lord God!"

During the months after Ishmael's visit, Abraham and Sarah talked often of it. Their lives were filled with other things, though, and the memory of his return gradually faded. Their fear that Ishmael might come back for vengeance was now gone, and Abraham and Sarah turned their lives fully toward Isaac. Abraham spent all of his free time with him, pouring the lore and history of his people into him. Isaac in turn listened and asked questions, some of which Abraham could answer and others that he could not.

It was on a bright, sunny morning, when Abraham was walking toward a flock of sheep guarded by a single herder, that he became aware of a familiar sensation. He stopped abruptly on top of a small rise. The bleating of the sheep faded, and he knew he was in the presence of God. He waited, standing still, and after a time the voice spoke.

"Abraham!"

"Here I am," Abraham replied, trembling. The voice no longer sounded warm and comforting as it almost always had in the past. Now it sounded harsh and demanding:

"Take your son, your only son, Isaac, whom you love, and go to the region of Moriah. Sacrifice him there as a burnt offering on one of the mountains I will tell you about."

It was as if a bolt of lightning had burst upon him, striking him and sending burning pain throughout his entire body. Abraham cried out loudly, "O Lord God, not Isaac! You cannot ask me to give up Isaac!"

Abraham fell on his knees and began to cry out... but there was no answer. The only sound was the bleating of the sheep and in the distance the howling of a wild dog, but the voice Abraham longed for was not to be heard. His heart shattered, he wept before God, praying that he had heard wrong. "God, he is the son of promise. He is the one you sent us in our old age. Please, Lord, tell me that I need not do this terrible thing!"

The silence became profound, and Abraham, with tears streaming down his face, lay full-length on the dusty earth and begged the God whom he loved to speak to him again. But there was no answer, and finally Abraham the Hebrew rose to his feet. A longing for death overtook him, but he knew that would not happen. He turned and stumbled back to the camp like a blind man, knowing that God had asked him to sacrifice the most precious gift in all the world.

CHAPTER

37

As four donkeys bearing riders crawled upward over a long, steep ridge, the wind ruffled up the dead grass and leaves that lay in a thicket to the east. The smell of the land rose with the earth's dissipating heat, whirling in streaky currents as the sky grew darker. The smoky haze that marked the end of a long hot summer made a blue-gray ceiling over the desert. There was the smell of cooler weather in the air, and behind them three rising lines of smoke, marking three camps or villages, reached upward into the air. The earth was thirsty for the rains that had not yet come, and the donkeys' hooves stirred up the powdery dust, which rose behind them as they crested the hills.

The four had traveled hard for two days, and now weariness made the third beast in the row stumble, and the young man astride called out, "Master, the beasts are exhausted! We've got to rest."

Uzziel, who rode immediately behind the speaker, whispered, "Good, Rayel! He's going to walk the legs off these animals, and I'm starving."

Abraham, who sat on the lead donkey, jumped at hearing the servants' voices behind him. He had spent much of the journey in lonely silence, focused on what lay ahead and barely aware of Uzziel's and Rayel's chatter. Only twice had he talked to them—once when they had stopped for a brief meal at noon, and another time when they had found water and allowed the thirsty animals to drink. Now he turned to them to address their concerns. His dark preoccupation lifted momentarily and he told them, "All right. We'll make camp over by that thicket."

"Good," Rayel grunted. "About time." He slid off his donkey and led the animal forward until Abraham called a halt, saying, "This will do for the night. Gather wood for the fire."

Rayel and Uzziel tied their animals up and began to move over the ground. Fortunately they found a fallen tree that would provide them with firewood, and as they began breaking off the dead branches, Uzziel said, in a voice tinged with discontent, "Why do we have to go so far just to make a sacrifice?"

"Because the master said so. That's why. You know his crazy ideas about God."

Uzziel was unsatisfied. "Why couldn't we go a short walk from the camp and sacrifice at the usual spot? How far are we going?"

"I don't know. The master hasn't told me," Rayel snapped. "Why don't you go tell him that it's time to stop fooling around and get down to business?"

Uzziel grinned, his teeth showing white against his dark face. "I'll let you do that." He put another stick on top of the pile he held in his right arm and shook his head. "How long do you think we will travel before we return home?"

"He wouldn't even tell his own wife where he was going or when he would be back. You think he's going to tell us?"

"How do you know that?"

"Because I heard them talking. When we left she asked him right out, 'Will you be back tomorrow?' "

"What did he say?"

"Nothing. He just kissed her and got on his donkey and rode out."

"He's been walking around in a daze, hasn't he? Everybody's noticed it."

"Yes, and did you see his wife's face? She's worried sick about him."

"Well, I've got problems of my own. I hope we get back soon."

"I know what's the matter with you," Rayel said, grinning. "You're afraid Dekaz will run off with your girl."

"That clod couldn't run off with anybody!"

"Come on. Let's get back."

The two hurried back and busied themselves making a fire and cooking the meat they had brought with them. It was tough and stringy, but the men ate it as if it were a feast. When the servants had filled their bellies, they both lay down and were soon fast asleep.

Isaac was sitting in front of the fire, feeding it small sticks. He picked up a long splinter, stuck it into the fire, then pulled it out, watching the tiny orange flame on the end consume the bit of wood. Then when it reached his fingers, he tossed it back into the fire. He looked across at his father, who was sitting slumped with his back against a tree, staring at nothing, it seemed. "Are you all right, Father?" Isaac asked softly.

Abraham stared, then nodded. "Yes, I'm all right."

"You haven't said much since we left. I thought maybe you didn't feel well." Isaac, always sensitive to the moods of his parents, had been one of the first to notice three days earlier that Abraham had fallen silent—had become almost mute. Isaac had questioned his mother, but she could not answer him, other than to say that she was worried about him.

When Isaac and his father had said good-bye to Sarah, she had put her hand on her son's head. He was almost as tall as she was now, though he was lean. She had kissed him and turned to Abraham, saying, "Be careful of Isaac. He's not a hardy boy."

Isaac thought about the drawn expression that had crossed his father's face when she had said these words. In a husky voice he had simply replied, "I'll do my best, Sarah." Isaac had noticed that the lines of his face had seemed more marked, and his eyes appeared almost empty, not bright as usual. Now Isaac studied him in the quietness and by the light of their camp-fire. The only sounds were the popping of the burning wood and the scur-rying of dry leaves across the hard surface of the earth.

"Are we going far?" Isaac finally asked.

Abraham seemed not to hear him for a moment, and then he shook his shoulders and cleared his throat. "About another day. We're going to Mount Moriah."

"And we're going to make an offering to God there?"

Again the long silence was punctuated by a deep sigh from Abraham. "Yes," he whispered. "We're going there to make an offering to God Most High."

Isaac considered this and focused his attention on his father. His father was much older than his friends' fathers, but that had never bothered the lad. Even though Abraham was now more than a century old, he was still a strong man and could do more work than any of the older men in the tribe without growing weary. But in the last few days he seemed to Isaac to have aged suddenly, in a way the boy could not understand. Whereas a few days ago he was still standing erect, now his shoulders were slumped, his back bent, his lips drawn together in an expression of pain or sadness.

Abraham became aware of the boy's gaze fixed on him and passed a hand across his face. He got to his feet stiffly, went over to the water bag and took a drink of water, then replaced the bag onto the branch of a stunted tree. He stood for a moment, gazing off in the direction they were to take in the morning, almost gasping for breath—as if he could feel the mass of Mount Moriah pressing down on him. Then suddenly he turned and came and sat down beside Isaac. He put his arm around the boy and hugged him hard.

Surprised, Isaac faced his father. The hug was not an unusual gesture, for Abraham was given to such things. Isaac was well accustomed to having both of his parents touch him on the head or squeeze his arm or hug him with an arm around the shoulder. He leaned against his father, still wondering about the silence that had enveloped him, then asked, "Will we build an altar out of stone when we get to Mount Moriah?"

"Yes, son, we will."

"How did you know to do that? Did your father build altars?"

"No, he never did. But my grandfather did."

"Tell me some more about Grandfather Nahor."

Abraham began to speak of his grandfather, which he did often, telling Isaac as many things as he could remember that the old man had poured into him. He spoke for a long time about Nahor's search for the Eternal One and how glad he had been to find out that he had a grandfather who, like himself, was eager to know God.

Isaac listened until Abraham paused; then he reached out and put two more sticks on the fire. The flames jumped up with the added fuel, and the sharp, acrid smell of smoke began to arise afresh. "Is the Eternal One kind, Father?"

Abraham recoiled at the question, and Isaac felt it. He turned to look at his father and waited for a reply. It came slowly, after some thought.

"The Eternal One is different from men," Abraham began. "He's not a man as we are. He has no body. He is everywhere. And He created all things, Isaac."

"Everything?"

"Yes, every grain of sand on the desert. Every animal that walks or flies or swims. And, of course, every human being on the face of the earth."

Isaac pondered this briefly, then said, "I wish I could hear Him speak to me as He spoke to you and to Grandfather Nahor. Do you think He ever will?"

"Yes, I think He will someday. You must wait and pray and seek His face."

"Tell me again about the first time He ever spoke to you."

Abraham told the story again to his son, as he had done many times in the past. He had thought about it for so many years that it was indelibly fixed in his mind, yet somehow it was still fresh at each new telling. Finally he stopped and looked at Isaac. The boy sat staring into the fire but was listening with rapt attention. *He loves to hear about God,* Abraham thought, and a searing pain tore anew at his heart. *How can I do what you have commanded, O God?*

Abraham waited, listening with every fiber of his being. But there was no answer . . . and in truth he believed there would never be one. He simply had to obey.

Isaac continued listening and asking questions, and finally Abraham spoke of the promise God had given concerning the boy himself. "I was an old man, and Sarah was too old to bear children," he said. "Yet He came to me, and He told me that Sarah would have a baby."

Isaac understood well the penalties of age. Even in his brief lifetime, he had seen older people wither up and die, and he knew that animals did the same. He also knew that old women simply did not have babies. He turned again to face his father and asked, "How could you believe that would happen when you knew it was impossible?"

Abraham remained silent for a time, then put a trembling hand on Isaac's head, stroking the boy's long hair. "Sometimes, my son, things have to be believed in order to be seen. I believed that God had made all things, and I believed that He could do all things. So when God told me Sarah would have a son, I questioned it at first, but then I ignored what I saw—that your mother was too old to have a child. That had never happened before, but I ignored the facts and put all my faith on God himself—on what He *is*. If He could make the world, He could make an old woman have a child. So I threw myself on Him. I ignored everything that looked impossible, and I simply believed God. Oh, I knew that men would say I was a fool, but I didn't care."

A log on the fire burned through, collapsing with a hissing sound and sending sparks upward. Isaac watched them go, and then he turned and said with a sweet smile, "That's what I want to do, Father. Just like you did."

"And that's what I want you to do too, Isaac. Do you think you can love the Lord—even when things look bad and wrong? Can you put your faith in God Most High?"

"I . . . I hope so. But I might be afraid," he added.

"It's all right to be afraid, but what is wrong is not believing in God's promises." He sat there with his arm around the shoulders of his son, the son he loved more than life itself. He had prayed for God to take him in Isaac's place, if someone had to die, but God had remained silent. The heavens had been cold and empty, and the silence had frightened him. Now, as he had done before when God had asked of him to believe the impossible, he whispered, "God Most High can be trusted, son. Others in this life may fail you, but He never will!"

———————

Mount Moriah had been looming ahead of them all the previous day. It was not a high mountain at all, but rising out of the flatness of the desert land, it seemed to crouch there like some ungainly beast. They had camped on the third night, and now the morning had come. Abraham had commanded the young men to strip one of the donkeys of the supplies and load him down with wood.

He had not slept at all, and now he felt weak as he took the bridle of the donkey loaded with branches and turned to the servants. "You wait here, and my son and I will go up the mountain to worship."

The two young men assented with nods, and Abraham turned, his face bleak. Isaac followed and, from time to time, picked up pieces of wood and carried them in his arms. They had eaten only a few bites of dried meat for breakfast and had washed it down with a little water, and he was hungry. Still he did not complain. Plodding along behind his father, he saw the sun rising behind the mountains, making a white line that grew brighter as they moved forward.

Finally the tip of the sun cleared the mountains, and looking back, Isaac could no longer see Rayel and Uzziel. "Will we go far to make the sacrifice?"

"Not much farther." Abraham's voice cracked and sounded strange. It troubled Isaac, and he pulled up even with his father and looked up into his face. Abraham kept his eyes fixed on the distance. Isaac knew his father was deeply troubled and this caused him to be sad, for he loved his father with all his heart. He kept silent then, and while the sun slowly climbed above the mountain, they forged steadily ahead.

By midmorning they reached a broken place that had suffered some catastrophe, for stones were strewn all around, some of them no bigger than Isaac's fist, others too large to move.

Abraham stared at the rocky area and said, "We will build the altar here, Isaac."

"Yes, sir." Isaac put down the wood he had carried while Abraham tied the donkey to a tree. Abraham began to gather stones into a big pile. Isaac wondered at his silence, but he began to do the same thing. As the sun rose directly overhead, the heat radiating from the rocky ground and their labor made both of them perspire.

Isaac had seen altars before. He knew that an altar was simply a pile of stones on which the sacrifice could be placed. A thought that had been lingering with him came to his lips. "Father, we have the wood and the fire, but where is the lamb for a burnt offering?"

Abraham stiffened as though something had struck him. He did not turn to look at Isaac, and his voice was so muffled Isaac had difficulty hearing his father's answer, but he made the words out. "My son, God himself will provide a lamb for a burnt offering."

The answer puzzled Isaac, but he asked no more questions. He worked diligently, and finally Abraham paused and stood over the pile of stones they had raised. It was not a large altar, no more than two feet high, and the top of it was level. They put the wood on the altar; then Abraham stood absolutely still.

Isaac waited quietly, seeing that his father was staring at the altar fixedly. The silence ran on, and Isaac, seeing no movement in his father, thought he was praying. Then his father turned around, and Isaac saw that tears were streaming down his face. "My son," Abraham said in a husky voice, "we have talked much about trusting God. You have heard how I had to trust God when things were very bad."

"Yes, I know, Father."

Abraham struggled for words. There seemed to be a great emptiness in him that was filled with the sound of a howling wind. His own voice sounded strange to him, and he said, "Isaac, my son, you asked about the lamb for the sacrifice, and I told you that God would provide it."

Isaac stared at his father. "Yes, Father. When will He do that?"

Abraham licked his lips. "He's already done that. Isaac, do you love your father?"

"Oh yes!"

"Do you trust me?"

"Yes." Isaac felt strange, for something in his father's eyes made him fearful. "What's wrong, Father?"

"Isaac, the Eternal One has spoken to me. He has commanded me . . ." Here Abraham could not contain himself. Tears ran freely down his face and he sobbed, "He has commanded me to offer my only son on the altar as a sacrifice."

Isaac stood stunned. He stared at his father silently, and his lips began to tremble. "You mean *me*, Father?"

"Yes, my son."

Abraham's vision suddenly narrowed until he could see only his son's face. He saw there the fear that anyone would feel at such a time. Isaac was a tender young man, not rough like others his age. He had never liked the butchering of animals for food, refusing to take part in it, and now Abraham saw in the boy's eyes the impulse to run away. And for that moment he wished fervently that Isaac would do exactly that. That would take the matter out of his hands. He could not sacrifice Isaac if he could not catch him. He knew with one side of his mind that this was a futile thought, but it grew in him until he forced it away. Finally he said, "God is good. Everything He does is for our good, my son. I know you are afraid... and so am I. You cannot know how... how hard this is for me. It would be easy if He had asked for my own life, but He's asked for the life of the one that I love most in this world. But it must be your choice too."

Isaac listened as his father spoke. His limbs were trembling; fear was growing in him like a monster. He wanted to cry out, to scream, to run— but then something inexplicable happened. Suddenly, the terror that was piercing his heart like a sharp knife and sending his mind into a frenzy gently began to fade. He felt his limbs grow strong. Something he could only describe as a warmth filled him from the top of his head and flowed down through his body. All the fear, the agony, the terror drained away, and he knew that the Eternal One, God Most High, was with him.

"Yes, Father, it shall be as you say... and as the Most High says."

Abraham could not believe what he was hearing. He had seen his son's eyes grow clear and the trembling stop, and for a long moment he stared at Isaac, knowing that his son had been touched by God Most High. There was no other answer.

Isaac moved forward and allowed his father to bind his hands and lay him down on top of the wood on the altar. Abraham, with knees and hands trembling, leaned forward and kissed the boy, stroking his hair and letting his tears fall freely. Isaac was looking up at him with a calmness in his eyes that Abraham could not bear. He pulled the knife from beneath his garment and lifted it high in the air with both hands on the hilt. Beneath him Isaac lay perfectly still, and his eyes did not flicker. Abraham gave a great cry as he prepared to lower the knife.

"Abraham!"

The voice was loud and sharp and unmistakable. Abraham could see nothing, for the tears blurred his vision. But he knew the voice. "Here I am," he uttered.

A bright light—brighter than the noonday sun—surrounded the father and son, and the voice was strong and warm and filled with love. *"Do not lay a hand on the boy. Do not do anything to him. Now I know that you fear God, because you have not withheld from me your son, your only son."*

Abraham dropped the knife and fell across the body of his son. He was weeping as he had never wept before. Then he raised himself and helped Isaac sit up, frantically cutting away the cords and saying, "Did you hear the voice, my son?"

"Yes, Father, I heard it."

"Then you have heard the voice of Him who made all things."

While the two were clinging to each other, Abraham looked up and saw a ram caught in a nearby thicket. With a shout of joy, he said, "My son, did I not tell you that God would provide a sacrifice for a burnt offering?"

Together they ran to the thicket, freed the ram, and brought him to the altar. Abraham slew the beast and Isaac lit the wood. As the flames rose and consumed the offering, Abraham put his arm around Isaac's shoulders and said, "We will call this place *Jehovah-jireh*, my son, for we have seen God Most High provide!"

While they bowed before the altar, with joy in their hearts at the mercy of God, the voice spoke again. *"Because you have done this and have not withheld your son, your only son, I will surely bless you and make your descendants as numerous as the stars in the sky and as the sand on the seashore. Your descendants will take possession of the cities of their enemies, and through your offspring all nations on earth will be blessed, because you have obeyed me."*

Father and son wept as the transcendent light slowly receded, and they began to make their way down the mountain. With each step Abraham remembered his words to Isaac two nights before: *"God Most High can be trusted, son. Others in this life may fail you, but He never will!"*

Before returning to the servants, Abraham stopped and hugged Isaac close, then looked into his son's face and whispered, "Never forget this moment, my son!"

Isaac returned his father's gaze with joy in his own eyes. "I never will, Father!"

Sarah had slept little since the departure of Abraham and Isaac. She had tossed fitfully on her bed, and now she hated to count the days. But on this day she was certain they would return soon.

She helped Zara with the baby, and the two looked up when Eliezer came running in, his face alight. "The master and Isaac are back."

Sarah felt faint, as if the world had suddenly rocked. She knew then how deep her fear had been, for Abraham had behaved so strangely. She forced herself to remain still until the faintness passed, and then she went out to greet them. As the four came into the camp, Isaac broke away, running straight for Sarah. She put out her arms, and he caught her and held on to her so tightly she cried out, "Don't break me in two, Isaac!"

"Mother, listen. The Eternal One—He is also the Merciful One!"

Others had gathered around, and as Abraham joined them, Sarah saw a wide smile on his face. His eyes were alight, and he was standing tall.

"What happened?" she said as he put his arms around her.

"I will have to tell you tonight when we are alone."

"All right." Sarah hugged him tightly and then went to Isaac, who was more excited than she had ever seen him.

"I must tell you everything, Mother."

"You will, and now come in and wash yourself and eat."

Sarah sat beside Abraham. Isaac had been too excited to sleep. The three of them had talked until the boy's eyes had drooped and Sarah insisted that he go to bed. He had kissed her then, embraced his father, and stumbled away.

Now Sarah took Abraham's hand and said, "Tell it all again. Isaac was so excited he wouldn't let you talk."

Abraham squeezed her hand. He was weary to the bone yet not sleepy. "I don't know if I'll ever sleep again," he said. "I suppose I will, but it's like nothing that ever happened before." He began to speak of how God had commanded him to sacrifice Isaac. He went through the whole story and finally ended by saying, "I had the knife ready to slay our son when God stopped me."

"I don't think I could have done that."

Abraham was silent. "You know what was in my mind as I raised that knife?"

"I can't imagine. Fear?"

"Yes. Despair. Anger at God for asking such a thing. I was almost a crazy man. But one thought had been with me ever since God gave me the command."

When Abraham paused, Sarah urged him on. "What was that?"

"I thought if God forces me to sacrifice the child of promise, then He'll bring him back to life again."

Sarah was startled. "Such a thing has never happened!"

"But the Eternal One—God Most High—can do anything!"

Sarah held his hand in both of hers. "You love God with all your heart—better than anything else in the world. I think that's what the Most High wants from all of us, but most of us can never give it to Him. That's why He chose you, Abraham, way back in Ur of the Chaldees. He saw something in you that He doesn't see in other men."

"What did He see?" Abraham whispered.

"He saw a faith that was stronger than death, stronger than love, stronger than natural affection. I wish," she whispered, "that I could love God like that and believe Him like that. I wish everyone everywhere could."

The two sat silently, and from time to time they looked up at the stars. Abraham suddenly squeezed her, holding her close. "We've come a long way since I shoved you into the mud, haven't we?"

"A long way," Sarah agreed, her voice quiet. She leaned against him and said, "Look at all those stars."

The stars spangled the blackness of the heavens. It was a clear night, and they sparkled and twinkled like diamonds across the sky. "And our son, Isaac, will have children, and they will have children, until your descendants will be more than all the stars we see."

Abraham was quiet for a time, but he pulled the medallion out from under his tunic and held it in his hand.

"Will you give the medallion to Isaac?"

Abraham ran his thumb over the face of the lion and whispered, "I will give it to the person God tells me to. I don't know what the lion means or this lamb on the other side, but you know, Sarah ... someday another man who is better than I will look at this very medal, at this lion and lamb, and will understand its meaning. And he will also know that he is in the line through which the great redeemer will come."

Tears came to Sarah's eyes, and he leaned over and kissed her on the cheek. Again they looked up at the stars, which seemed to be making a mighty chorus of music overhead. The two bowed their heads as they sat beneath the blinking, sparkling orbs, and Abraham the Hebrew, with Sarah, his wife, began to praise the Maker of all things.

Discover the Faith
That Will See You Through Anything

Tracie Peterson's YUKON QUEST series links the lives of three women during the Alaskan Gold Rush. Each woman's story is an example of courage in the face of daunting circumstances and passionate faith that refuses to be overwhelmed.

Treasure of the North – Grace Hawkins struggles to begin a new life, but her past will not let her rest.

Ashes and Ice – When Karen Pierce's carefully ordered world is shaken by tragedy, she discovers God's deep faithfulness.

Rivers of Gold – Though faced with the most dire of situations, Miranda Colton trusts in God's unflagging provision.

Delight Your Heart!

Available at your bookstore.

◆ BETHANYHOUSE

11400 Hampshire Ave. S., Minneapolis, MN 55438
www.bethanyhouse.com